A gratifying tale of grit and gumption, *By the Sweet Gum* is a true inspirational read set in the Depression era of the South. You'll cheer for the heroes and hiss at the scoundrels ... but who are the true villains? Author Ane Mulligan keeps you guessing until the very end.

~**Michelle Griep**
Christy Award-winning author of *Once Upon a Dickens Christmas*

Hope and heartbreak, love and loss are woven seamlessly throughout this unforgettable tale. Readers will laugh, cheer, and weep with Tommy and Genessee, two characters sure to enthrall readers from the first page to the last.

~ **Elizabeth Ludwig**
Author of *A Christmas Prayer* and *It Really IS a Wonderful Life*

Battling tragedy, duty, and the nefarious dealings of an evil mill owner, *By the Sweet Gum* tugs on the heartstrings and shows us what sacrificial love truly means. Genessee and Tommy's story carried me through a rollercoaster of joy, weeping, and hope. An excellent tale woven around the power of family, community, and love.

~ **Tara Johnson**
Author of *Engraved on the Heart, Where Dandelions Bloom,* and
All Through the Night

Ane Mulligan writes with depth and sensitivity on an important issue in American history. I'm better for having read this book. Realistic characters, skillful plotting, and overall excellent storytelling make *By the Sweet Gum* a rewarding venture into a bygone era.

~ **Janalyn Voigt**
Author of the Montana Gold western historical romance series

Other Books by Ane Mulligan

The Georgia Magnolias Series
In High Cotton
On Sugar Hill

Chapel Springs Series
Chapel Springs Revival
Chapel Springs Survival
Home To Chapel Springs
Life in Chapel Springs

A Southern Season: Four Stories from a Front Porch Swing

Coming Home: A Tiny House Collection (Penwrights Press)

When the Bough Breaks (independently published)

BY THE
Sweet Gum

ANE MULLIGAN

IRON
STREAM
FICTION
An Imprint of Iron Stream Media
Birmingham, Alabama

By the Sweet Gum

Iron Stream Fiction
An imprint of Iron Stream Media
100 Missionary Ridge
Birmingham, AL 35242
IronStreamMedia.com

Copyright © 2022 by Ane Mulligan

Library of Congress Control Number: 2021947787

Scripture quotations are from The Authorized (King James) Version. Rights in the Authorized Version in the United Kingdom are vested in the Crown. Reproduced by permission of the Crown's patentee, Cambridge University Press.

ISBN: 978-1-64526-332-6 (paperback)
ISBN: 978-1-64526-333-3 (ebook)

1 2 3 4 5—25 24 23 22
MANUFACTURED IN THE UNITED STATES OF AMERICA

DEDICATION

This book is dedicated to my sister Pam Squires.
You are my hero.

ACKNOWLEDGMENTS

A VERY SPECIAL THANK YOU TO Billie Cook for writing *Central Georgia Textile Mills*. Your book gave me so much wonderful information, but the time you spent answering my questions and giving me websites and cities to visit for those all-important research trips was invaluable to me. I hope I represented a mill town accurately.

Thank you to Peggy Copeland Roberts and the members of the private Facebook group, I Was Raised on Bibb Mill Village #1. Thank you for allowing me into the group and answering my questions. Your help was invaluable.

Once again, Sugar Hill Councilman Brandon Hembree sat with me and answered a gazillion questions. His love of history and being on the board of the Sugar Hill Historical Preservation Society has made him a go-to research resource. Thanks, Brandon, for always being willing to have your ear bent.

More of my sweet city's officials helped me find elusive facts and names. Jane Wittington, Sugar Hill's city clerk, is one of those. The phone number she gave me for the Archival Records for Georgia resulted in a personal phone call and not only how to find the information but the info itself. Jane, you saved me hours of research time. Thank you!

A huge thank you to Shant'e Ragin of Porterdale History Tours and Kay Piper of Magnolia Realty Group. Shant'e gave me an amazing private tour of several of the buildings at the historical Porterdale Mill and village, as well as sharing her extensive knowledge of Porterdale's history. Shant'e introduced me to Kay Piper, who is the daughter of a former Bibb Mill superintendent. Kay graciously opened her home to me—the superintendent's home she grew up in—and shared her memories with me. You two ladies have helped lend authenticity to my book.

As always, my heart's gratitude to my fabulous critique partners, Michelle Griep, Elizabeth Ludwig, and Tara Johnson. Your brainstorming and critiques make my writing so much better. You hold my feet to the fire, and you pray for me. You're my village.

How am I so blessed to have Denise Weimer as my editor? Denise, after our first book together, I no longer kick cabinets but happily make any changes you suggest. Your editing has made my writing better. That you have become a friend is the icing on this cake.

The longer I write, the more stories I have brewing in my mind. And that is because of my Creator and Savior, Jesus Christ. He whispers to my heart and makes my heart whisper back in stories. Thank You for this wonderful gift.

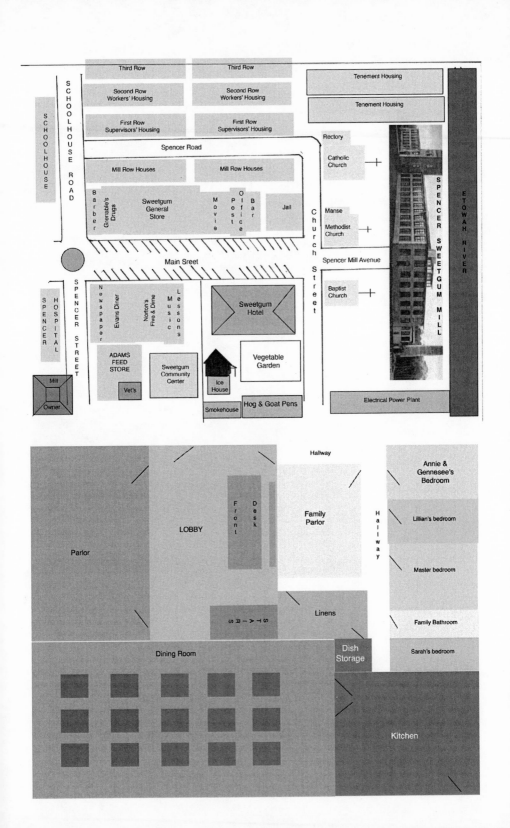

"It falls to every generation to leave their world a better place for the next. If you aren't doing something to improve conditions, you are missing the purpose for which you are placed upon this earth." – Frank Taylor, Sweetgum Baptist Church, February 1928

Chapter 1

Late spring, 1930

AN EAR-SHATTERING GONG OF A huge brass bell splits the quiet morning. My sister Annie screams, Sarah, our cook, shrieks, and the bowl of cold, baked potatoes in my hands falls to the floor with a crash. Mama cries, "Dear, God, no! Please don't let it be another child."

I freeze, unable to move. Tremors quiver through me as my heart cries, *Not Tommy! Please, Lord!*

There's an accident at the cotton mill.

The horror I feel reflects on Mama's face. "Go, Genessee." She shoos me out. "Find out who it is."

She's already picking up the potatoes and whispering prayers as I race out the door. The mill lies no more than one-hundred-fifty-yards from the hotel entrance. I run up the road as fast as my legs can move. Slamming through the front door, I follow the sound of the screams coming through the stairwell from the floor above. I fly up the steps. Normally, noise from the machinery obliterates every other sound, but when that bell clangs during work hours, most of the machines stop.

When I reach the second floor, I skid to a stop outside the spinning room, bend, and put my hands on my knees, trying to catch my breath. I'm not sure I want to see what's on the other side of this door.

"Out of the way!"

I jump aside as two medics carrying a stretcher run past me. Slipping through the door behind them, I stand with my back against the wall. The air is thick with cotton fibers, making a deep breath difficult. How do people work in this?

A crowd parts around one of the machines for the medics. A small girl lies in a bloody heap on the floor. Oh, dear Lord, it's Ruthie Ralston. She's barely six years old. A belt is cinched around the upper part of her arm.

There is no lower part.

I turn and flee down the stairs, and pushing through the outer doors, I gulp deep draughts of fresh air. Somehow, I manage not to spew my breakfast. I wipe the tears from my face with a balled fist and turn my feet toward home.

There is nothing I can do.

Coattails flapping as he runs, my father rushes toward the mill. When he spies me, he pauses, hugs and then releases me, and hurries on his way. Someone called him since Daddy is the Ralstons' pastor, and poor Mrs. Ralston most likely saw the accident happen since Ruthie works beside her.

Heading home, I walk backward for a few steps, looking at the block-long, two-story mill, the color of weathered cement. How can a place give hope and destroy it at the same time?

I turn around and settle my gaze on home—the Sweetgum Hotel. Its white front porch beckons me. Red brick rises three floors—four if you count the attic. My sisters and I spent hours in that attic playing dolls when we were little. Poor Ruthie. Will she play dolls again?

When I reach the hotel, Mama meets me at the door. I shake my head and lean into her arms. She holds me, rubbing my back. The circular motions soothe.

"Who is it and how bad?"

"Ruthie Ralston lost her arm."

With a sharp intake of breath, Mama nods, then puts her hands on my shoulders and peers at me. "Are you all right?"

Am I? I twirl a strand of my hair, golden brown like Mama's. I'm a carbon copy of her, so everyone says. "Yes, ma'am. It shook me up a little at first, but I've seen so many—"

"Don't let yourself become hardened, Genessee, not if you want to continue helping people. Keep your generous heart tender." She pulls off her apron and hands it to me. "Go see what Sarah needs. I'll tend to Mrs. Ralston with your daddy." She plops her hat on her head and hurries toward the mill.

In the kitchen, I retrieve the bowl of potatoes needing peeled. I pick up a knife and get to work. The mill workers who make their home here at the hotel will expect their dinner to arrive at noon. No matter what, life goes on in Sweetgum.

Used to be, we'd take the dinners to the mill in individual baskets, but as the number of lodgers swelled along with a few short-term residents, we didn't have enough basket girls. Now we tie up each dinner in a napkin and load those in baskets. That way, each of us can deliver a half-dozen dinners in a single basket.

Sarah keeps one eye on me, so I smile—or try to. Our cook since I can remember, the widowed Irishwoman has always been a wise confidant for me. She lives with us in our family quarters and knows all of us inside out.

"Methinks your daddy will be off to Rome to speak with the legislators this week, aye?"

My knife gouges out a potato eye. "How many children have been maimed or killed already this year? And it's only May. Ruthie *should* be looking forward to school letting out at the end of the month. Instead, she's now facing life with one arm—if she survives."

With a few precious minutes to spare before we take dinner bundles to the mill, I go out front to collect the newspapers from the front porch. As I turn, I catch a glimpse of our town's namesake, the sweet gum tree. Just seeing it makes me feel better. Tommy and I fell in love beneath that hundred-and-fifty-year-old tree. It sits smack dab in the middle of the town circle.

I know. Most villages have a town *square*. New Orleans has Jackson

Square. Savannah has Johnson Square—and several others. Not us. In Sweetgum, Georgia, it's a town circle. Tommy and I meet there nearly every evening. We talk about our future and spoon a little if no one's out and about.

"Get him!" Annie, our family's budding thespian, screeches from inside. We never know whether her dramatics are real or if she's acting.

"I can't reach him. He's gone under the bed." My big sister Lillian's voice floats out the window. What *him* are they referring to?

I sigh and hurry inside, the *thwack* of the screen door adding to the chaos. Yep. Life goes on.

"There he goes!" Annie races across the hotel lobby, just missing me. At seventeen, she's the most athletic of us three girls. Her wavy, dark hair ends at her jawline, framing her pixie face.

Lillian follows hot on her heels, strands of her long hair escaping her jellyroll. She's always so put together. What is the cause of this commotion? She hollers over her shoulder. "We've gotta stop him before he scares anyone."

My heart slams against my ribs. Could *he* be a hobo? There have been a lot down by the river recently. It's not out of the question that one could have slipped in the door, looking for a meal. I drop the newspapers on the front desk and hurry into the dining room.

Lillian peers beneath a table still littered with the remains of breakfast, while Annie races to the kitchen.

I catch my breath. "Who are we looking for? And when are you bussing the tables?"

Annie stomps back into the dining room. "He's not in the kitchen. How can he move so fast with a cast on his leg?"

That can only mean one thing. She left the cage open, and the ferret escaped our family quarters. I ball my fists on my hips. "He's got three *other* legs."

A flash of fur streaks out through the dining room doorway.

"Get him!" Annie spins.

We dash after my wounded rescue, across the lobby, and skid to a halt outside the parlor, where he slipped inside. Lillian puts her ear to the door, then turns to me in wide-eyed horror. Annie snickers at the dramatic turn of events.

I frown at the little troublemaker. "Who's in there—"

A loud scream answers. I cringe.

Annie's snickers grow into giggles. "Old lady Grundy. See ya later, sis." She swivels away.

Catching her collar, I stop her. "Oh, no, you don't. You're the reason he's loose. You're coming in with me."

I grab her wrist as I push open the door and yank her inside. Before the ferret can escape, I quickly close the portal. Mrs. Grundy, a hotel resident, teeters atop an ottoman. For a woman in her fifties, she's remarkably spry. Why is she here and not at work? Cowering in a corner beneath a side table, the young ferret looks as frightened as her.

"I'm so sorry, Mrs. Grundy. He won't hurt you." On my hands and knees, I stick my head under the table and scoop my furry patient into my arms. He immediately starts shivering and snuggles against my chest. "He's just a baby."

She clambers down, her face pinching in a glare. "Humph. Last month it was a raccoon." She sniffs. "And you still haven't found my wedding ring that critter stole. It's all I have left of my William." She holds a hankie beneath her nose, then turns an evil eye on me. "You'd better find it. And soon."

Behind her, Annie rolls her eyes. I have to agree. Mrs. Grundy is as dramatic as my sister.

"It won't happen again." I raise an eyebrow at the culprit. "Annie has promised not to open any more cages without me there."

Mrs. Grundy harrumphs. "You said that last time." Now Annie is the recipient of her evil eye. "I ought to report you to Mr. Spencer."

No! My stomach roils and my hands grow clammy. "Please, Mrs. Grundy. Don't do that."

Mr. Spencer owns the mill and a good portion of the town, including this hotel. We only manage it. And live here. If she reports us, we could be out, without a home or jobs. Daddy's salary from the church isn't enough to keep body and soul together. And if Mr. Spencer tosses us out, he would fire my father from the general store he also manages.

Mrs. Grundy peers at me through squinty eyes. Her finger wags with each word. "You keep that thing and any others outside in the barn. They don't belong in the hotel."

I briefly close my eyes. "Yes, ma'am. He won't bother you again."

Annie, the ferret, and I make a hasty retreat. After I return the now-snoozing baby to his cage, I go in search of my sisters. Annie is sorting the mail behind the lobby desk. She stuffs an envelope in Room 203's slot.

"Where's Lillian?" I want to jerk her tail.

Annie snaps her thumb over her shoulder. "Left for the Five an' Dime."

"Well, she should have stopped you." At nearly twenty-four, Lillian's the eldest and is supposed to know better. "And please do not open the cage again without me there."

Annie hangs her head. "I'm sorry, but he looked so sad, I just wanted to pet him."

I soften. It's hard to stay mad at Annie. "I can't find fault with your intentions, Little Sis. But we'll get into big trouble if Mr. Spencer hears of this."

My gaze shifts to the still-dirty tables in the dining room. Well, it can't be helped. Even though this morning's accident at the mill has left us at odds with our emotions, work goes on. Lillian's work at Norton's dime store often forces her to leave this task undone, and she depends on Annie and me to pick it up. She does do my laundry if I have to bus tables for her. It's not too bad of a trade-off. Most importantly, she adds some cash money to the family with her job.

I let out a sigh. "Come on. Let's get the tables bussed."

She wrinkles her nose. "I swear, Lillie always skips out on her work."

"One, ladies don't swear. Two, don't let her hear you call her Lillie." She hates the nickname—says it isn't dignified. Our Lillian is all about keeping up appearances—not an easy task in a mill town where everybody knows everyone and their business. "And three, remember she shares her paycheck with all of us."

In the dining room, we remove the dirty dishes, loading them on trays, pushing through the swinging kitchen door, and leaving them by the sink for the kitchen girls to wash. Mama, Sarah, and the staff of four young kitchen girls—Grace, Glory, Beulah, and Delilah—keep busy with all our lodgers and short-term guests. I swanney, the hotel stays full because of Sarah and Mama's cooking.

Mama stands at the marble baking counter, kneading dough. Someone is always mixing up another batch of bread. The sunlight streaming in the kitchen window shines on her curly, golden-brown hair. Though she's forty-five, my mother doesn't have any gray. Not like Sarah, who's been the cook for as long as I've been alive. Plump as a proper cook should be, her hair is mousy-brown and silver. She always wears it pulled back into a serviceable bun, but there are forever shorter frizzles that escape the hairpins and fly around her face.

I return to the dining room with a bucket of warm water and two dishrags.

Little Sis grabs one. She dips it in the water, wrings it out, and attacks the first table. "If'n I ran out without doing my chores, Mama'd take a switch to me."

Annie always makes me laugh with silly fabrications. "You've never been switched in your life, little girl." She's a coddled baby. Well, not a baby anymore. Though the youngest, at seventeen, she's become a lovely young woman. A frown ends my laughter. I only wish she'd get the flicks, as she calls them, out of her mind. She talks movie stars day in and day out. She itches to be in the movies.

Moving to the next table, she flashes a sassy grin. "I'd love to see Lillian switched."

"You wouldn't really. You'd cry." I rinse my dishrag in the bucket and scrub another table. "Your heart's far more tender than you pretend."

Fifteen minutes later, clean tables gleam in mid-morning sunlight. "Here." I extend a stack of napkins. "Put these on the tables, then go help in the kitchen. I'll finish this."

Annie blows a kiss. "Thanks." She tosses a stack of four napkins on each table and runs into the kitchen.

Not quite what I asked. I sigh. Setting tables is her least favorite chore, and I don't mind, but it takes a good bit of time. I carry the tub of flatware to the first table. We have twenty-nine lodgers right now. We're not at full capacity yet, but we will be soon. The tub gets lighter after each table until it's finally empty, and I lay down the last setting. Fourteen-year-old Grace and her sister, Glory, carry in a container of newly washed flatware and put it below the serving station.

Back in the kitchen, Sarah stands at one of the two large stoves, stirring a pot. Mama lays a towel over another bowl of dough, placing it on the other stove's warming shelf to rise. Those will be rolls for supper and loaves for tomorrow morning. Annie helps Mama measure out flour for another batch of bread.

I snatch an apron from the rack and check the staging table to see if the kitchen girls have all the napkins laid out for the dinner bundles. I count twenty-nine. Good. Delilah lays an apple on each napkin while Beulah wraps cookies in wax paper. Good thing the ferret didn't get into those. Oh, before I forget, I'd better tell Mama about him and Mrs. Grundy.

"I'm going to take a cot and sleep in the barn tonight." The little ferret still needs a feeding during the night.

Mama pulls a bowl of pastry dough from the icebox and hands it to me to start rolling out for meat pasties. "Now why would you want to sleep in the barn?"

At the baking counter, I pick up the rolling pin. "The ferret got into the parlor while Mrs. Grundy was in there." I sprinkle a little flour on the marble surface. The dough drops onto it with a thump.

"Oh, Genessee. You know you need to keep your animals in cages." She tilts her head and studies me. "Ahh, I think I see. Annie let it out, didn't she?"

I don't know how my mother figures these things out. Then again, maybe I do. Little Sis has always run headlong into trouble. I nod and roll out the dough into a large square. "In her defense, she didn't mean to let him go, just love on him a little."

Using the back of her wrist, Mama pushes an errant curl away from her eye. "The weather is lovely, so I don't mind. How's the little fellow's leg coming along? Will you let him go soon?"

"His leg isn't as well as I'd hoped. It was badly mangled by that trap, and Dr. Adams says he'll remain lame. I can't let him go. He won't survive in the wild on his own." I shiver, thinking what could happen to him. With the dough rolled out, I search the drawer for the six-inch circle cutter amid a tangled mess of utensils. I need to reorganize this drawer.

Mama washes and dries her hands. She always thinks things through first, so once her decision is made, she won't change her mind. "You'll have to keep him away from the lodgers. Not everyone has your love of animals, sugar. But I don't think he needs to be banished to the barn."

"I'll put a strong padlock on the cage and wear the key on a string around my neck." I cut the dough into rounds, pondering what to name the little ferret. Annie's good at names. I'll ask her later.

Sarah lifts her head from her work and chuckles. "A padlock won't be stopping our Miss Annie if she gets it in her mind to play with the wee critter." She hands me a bowl of filling for the pasties. I portion out the contents—which appear to have a little leftover pot roast and a lot of carrots, peas, and potatoes—onto the pastry rounds. When the bowl is empty, Sarah and I fold the dough over the filling, pinch the edges, and brush them with a little egg wash. She slides the pans into the ovens of both stoves.

I'm wiping down the baking counter when she leans her head toward me and whispers, "Did I tell you Annie brought the ferret in here the other day? I gave him a wee piece of mincemeat. After he ate it, he investigated me apron pocket, curled up in it, and napped." She glances to make sure Mama isn't listening. "He's a peach, he is. Me brother had one as a pet when we were *bairns*. He hunted rabbits with his." She winks at me. "I do love a good rabbit pie."

I toss her a thankful grin. Maybe I could teach this little guy to hunt rabbits. Daddy'd like that.

By the time the meat pasties have baked, the kitchen girls have the napkins loaded into the baskets with an apple and a wax paper-wrapped sugar cookie. Our lodgers eat better than most of the mill workers, who take sandwiches like mashed potato and hotdog or peanut butter and mayonnaise. One little boy eats a peanut butter-stuffed onion twice a week. My nose wrinkles as I glance at the kitchen clock. Ten minutes till noon.

"Come along, girls." Sarah and Mama slip a pasty onto each napkin. The kitchen girls tie the bundles and place six in each basket. We all pick up a basket and begin the less-than-five-minute stroll to the mill.

The moment we open the door to the mill's entrance, the noon whistle blows. "Right on time." We disperse, each going to where we will find our lodgers to give them their meal. They empty the bundle, handing back the napkin. The girls have instructions not to leave until they get the napkin back. We can't afford to replace them all the time.

On my way to distribute the dinner bundles, I search the cavernous space but don't see Tommy. My heart flutters. How did I get so lucky to have him fall in love with me? After this morning, I yearn for a glimpse of him now, but I guess I'll have to hold my horses until he comes by the sweet gum tree tonight. I pray nothing happens to stop us meeting.

Chapter 2

ANNIE AND I HURRY BACK together from the mill for dinner. Daddy will be home shortly, one of the privileges of managing the general store. In the kitchen, Mama hands me the plates to set on our family table, which is situated in the corner by the back door and a window, so we can get a breeze in the hot months. I make sure Daddy's newspaper is beside his plate.

The back door opens. "How are all my girls?"

How can he always be so joyful? So energetic? This morning, his pastor job wasn't an easy one. I set the plates down and hug him.

Mama greets him with a kiss. "You're missing two of your girls. Lillian is working her shift at Norton's, and Annie is ... well, I don't know where Little Sis is." With a raised eyebrow, Mama turns her question to me.

"She dropped her basket by the back door and left. I suspect she's at Fannie Spencer's." Those two girls are thick as fleas on a hound's back.

Daddy frowns. "I'm not sure I like her at the Spencers' house so much." He glances sidelong at me. "Annie tends to talk before she thinks. If she slips and Benjamin Spencer learns of our involvement in the labor—"

I shake my head. "She'll be good." I'm positive she will, but Daddy doesn't look so sure. "She knows how important it is to keep that private."

Mama takes his hat and sets it on the coat rack by the back door. "Sit down now, so we can eat."

Daddy asks the blessing, and after the *amens*, the five of us dive into chicken-fried steak with sawmill gravy and sweet peas. The "steak" is a tough cut of beef that Sarah tenderized with a new mallet that makes little cube designs in the meat. Our usual staples are chicken and pork since we raise our own to help with the cost of feeding all our lodgers. This is a rare treat.

Daddy swallows a bite. "Delicious. A welcome change, Emma. Sarah, it's as tender as can be. Good job."

Mama turns rosy pink, as she always does at Daddy's compliments. "Thank you, darling. I thought you'd enjoy it."

Sarah only nods and smiles since her mouth is full.

A faint breeze stirs the curtains over the kitchen sink and wafts through the back door. Daddy mops his neck with his handkerchief as he taps the newspaper with his finger. He always encourages us to be up on world events, and talk turns to the paper's headlines, failing banks, and then the accident involving Ruthie.

Daddy's mouth dips downward. "She's in a bad way. We need to hold a prayer meeting for her."

Mama winces. "Frank, please. Let's not discuss it during dinner, darling."

Daddy closes the newspaper, laying it beside his plate. "I'm sorry, sweetheart. Forgive me." He puffs out a sigh. "But I wish Spencer would stop hiring five-year-olds. They belong in school."

I offer the perfect conversation changer. "Since we're keeping the ferret, I need a name for him. Anyone have a good idea? By the way, Sarah tells me we can train him to hunt for rabbits."

"Well, now ..." Daddy wipes his mouth with his napkin and returns it to his lap. "I'll think on—"

The back door flies open, hitting the counter with a *thunk*. Our drama queen leans against the doorjamb, the back of one hand on her forehead. "Gimme a whiskey, ginger ale on the side, and don't be stingy, baby." She glances to see if we're watching her as she mimics Greta Garbo from *Anna Christie*. "For I have just lost my heart." She grins and jumps into her chair.

Rolling her eyes, Mama pulls Annie's plate from the stove's warming shelf and sets it before her.

Daddy closes one eye, staring at Little Sis. "And who did you lose it to? Not Charlie Spencer, I hope?"

She giggles through a mouthful of peas. "Ew, no, Daddy." She swallows. "It's from *Grand Hotel*. But you believed me." Her grin is infectious. "That's the important part. I *neeeed* to be in flicks."

We laugh at her dramatics, but I can tell Daddy still worries Annie might be too trusting with the Spencers. If she shares stories of the ferret, or worse, mentions our efforts for new labor laws, it could bring disaster down on our heads.

Tommy takes my hand as we leave the front porch, entwining his fingers with mine. His little sister, Vera, clutches my left hand, chattering about her day. The evening is balmy, leaving a gentle sheen on our skin as we stroll along Main Street. Everything in Sweetgum is within walking distance except some of the outlying houses belonging to business owners. Hardly anyone here owns a car.

Instead of crossing the street to the movie house, Tommy heads toward the town circle. I glance at him and sigh. He's tall with sandy brown hair and eyes the color of nutmeg. His jawline is almost chiseled, and when he smiles, all is well with my world. He's quieter than usual tonight. I'm not surprised, with the accident on everyone's minds. I'd rather talk with him and Vera than go to a movie, anyway.

As we pass Evans Diner, Josie Evans peers out the window and waves. I nudge Vera, and we both wave back.

I swing the little girl's hand and smile down at her. "I have a story to tell you about the ferret."

Vera pulls her fingers from mine and claps her hands. As I relay today's escapade, she's agog with delight.

"Mrs. Grundy's funny." Her nose wrinkles. Tommy chuckles but doesn't say anything. Something else is weighing heavy on him. Mill business?

I keep my tone light. "How was work today?"

Vera yanks on my arm. "My friend Billy lost his big toe in a spinning machine."

Another accident? I snap my gaze to Tommy. "Hank's little brother?" Some accidents aren't bad enough to ring the bell for the medics. If it isn't rung, the rest of us don't know.

He nods and warns Vera with his fingers to his lips. The sweet girl nods solemnly. It angers me that a six-year-old understands the need for whispering in this town.

My heart squeezes. "First Ruthie and now Billy. Two in one day?"

Tommy's fingers tighten on mine. With his free hand, he holds his thumb and index finger an inch apart. "He came this close to losing his whole foot."

"How did it happen?"

Vera pokes out her bottom lip. "He slipped."

Tommy nods. "Cotton fibers are all over the floors." His jaw clenches. "Spencer never has enough people sweeping." He bends down and whispers to Vera, who grins and skips ahead of us to the town circle, where she investigates the flowers.

Tommy's gaze remains on her. "Thank the good Lord there was a man close by. He grabbed Billy at the last second, just before the rest of his foot was sucked into the gears. He's small enough his whole leg could have—"

Thankfully, he stops, and I let my breath out in a whoosh. "The poor baby. We've *got* to get a law passed, and soon. What if someone hadn't been there? Look what happened to Ruthie."

Tommy nods once but doesn't say anything for a minute. He thinks things through, like Mama. "I'll talk to your dad tomorrow. I have an idea I'm fixing to try." He squeezes my fingers. "Are you set on seeing this flick?"

I tip my head to his shoulder for a brief moment. The earthly, manly scent of his Aqua Velva floats around me, making me feel secure. "Not tonight." I smile at him. "I'd rather sit and talk about our future."

The town circle is in the middle of the intersection. When the mill owners built the town after the War of Northern Aggression, I'm sure they didn't realize that a circle would save a few lives in the future. Perhaps young men back then raced their horses and wagons, and that's why they made it this way.

Vera joins us, bringing me a posy. We sit on one of the wooden benches by the old tree. Tommy's arm slides around me and draws me close. I lay my head against his shoulder, the muscles there made thick from his pitching. Vera giggles, reminding us of her presence. Tommy pulls a small rubber ball from his pocket and gives it to her. She promptly starts a game of bouncy ball against the sweet gum's huge trunk.

The moon is full tonight—God's light to illuminate hidden dangers. I long to ease the heaviness in Tommy's spirit. "Who are the Weavers playing this weekend?"

A slight smile lifts one side of his mouth. "Super Twisters from Atco Mills."

A great team. "Do you think you'll win?"

He makes a muscle with his other arm. "I'll do my best to make that happen. Scouts are starting to pay attention to the league." Hope wraps a swath of determination around his words. He gazes at me and smiles. "When I get signed by a team scout, we'll get married, and I'll take you with me, wherever that may be."

My pulse beats fast. Tommy's dream to play on a major league baseball team might actually come true. He's good enough. And if that happens, we'll escape Sweetgum and Mr. Spencer.

But deep inside, soft voices cry, *What about us?*

I run my fingers along Tommy's arm. "If we leave Sweetgum, who will help the children?" I nod toward Vera. Her ball misses the trunk, and she disappears behind the tree in pursuit.

He squeezes my hand, but his gaze fixes on something far away that I can't see. "Your daddy will. Your mama and sisters can help him."

"I guess so." I *hope* so.

It's hard to convince people not to let their children work. They need the money, and when they're new to textile mills, they don't realize the dangers. Children just want to be with their parents and beg to go. I sometimes feel like we're the only ones in town who care.

Tommy's jaw may be chiseled, but his eyes are soft. He glances at

Vera, whose back is to us, then dips his head. His lips find mine and leave me breathless.

"I see you kissing," Vera's sing-song accusation breaks us apart. We laugh, and Tommy rests his forehead against mine. "I love you, Gen."

My heart flips over. "I love you too." That hasn't changed since I was sixteen. It's only gotten stronger. At twenty-two, I'm ready to be married. Most girls are by now. Lillian will end up an old maid if she isn't careful. She says I got the best man in Sweetgum. Hank Barnett is sweet on her, but she won't give him the time of day. Says she won't marry a man who works at the mill.

Chapter 3

My alarm clock rings, jarring me from a dream of walking down the aisle to marry Tommy. I'm wearing Mama's wedding dress, and Tommy looks so handsome in a tuxedo—like one of Annie's movie stars. I don't want to get up, but it's four o'clock, and Little Sis and I have to collect the eggs. The chore needs to be done before sunrise. There's much to do before breakfast at five-thirty. Gathering eggs has been easier since Daddy hung lanterns in the hen house. Now, the hens lay when *we* want them to. For some reason, left on their own, chickens will lay after sunrise, some even six hours later. Crazy birds. Don't they know eggs are for breakfast?

I throw off the sheet and hurry to the bathroom to bathe. Ten minutes later, I'm back in our room and toss a slipper at Annie, who's still buried deep in her bed.

"Hey, grumpy, wake up. Time to collect the eggs."

A groan emits from beneath the pillow. Silly girl sleeps with it over her head instead of under it.

A quick yank uncovers her. "Get up now, or I'll use all the hot water, and all you'll get is a cold bath."

That works. She leaps to her feet and races to the bathroom, laughing all the way. I won't tell her she didn't really snooker me. I don one of my four work dresses, a green-and-white checkered frock I made from a Gingham Girl feed sack.

Back in the bedroom, Annie reaches into the closet and pulls out a dress with a floral pattern in yellow, green, and shades of pink. It's appropriately made from a chicken feed sack.

In the henhouse, we each take a side.

Annie reaches beneath one of "the girls" and collects her egg. "Bet

I get more than you today."

"You're on!" I hurry but not too fast. If I rush, I'll get pecked. Annie's the best at it. She never upsets the girls, whereas I often do—usually because I let my mind wander. We don't allow Lillian in here anymore. She agitates the chickens by shoving and grabbing. Not only does she get pecked, but she's also bloody when she's done, and the next day, the girls refuse to lay.

After all the lodgers have eaten—Mrs. Grundy still giving Annie and me the evil eye—they hurry off to the mill. If anyone is even one second late, Mr. Spencer docks an hour from their wages.

The rest of the morning is spent getting dinner cooked and bundles filled. Finally, it's time to relax for a while. Annie either practices being dramatic in front of her mirror or goes to a flick with Fannie. Normally, I like to read, but today, I'm on a mission.

I slip on my beret. I don't bother with gloves. I've relaxed my stand on those, at least here in Sweetgum on weekdays. After all, we're modern women now. Sundays are another matter, however.

Sarah catches me before I leave. "You're going over to talk with your daddy, aren't you?"

I nod and wait.

"Be careful, lass. Don't let your mouth overload ya' tail."

"I will." Or should that be, *I won't*? I never know how to answer her little homilies. I kiss her cheek and scoot out the door. It fascinates me how Sarah's Irish accent has mellowed over the years and now has bits of Southern twang in it. It's rather comical, really. Her *r*'s roll if they're in the beginning or middle of a word but flatten to a Southern "uh" if they're at the end.

Sweetgum General Store is diagonally across Main Street from the hotel. It takes all of a minute to slip over. I find my father stocking cans of Campbell's soup on the shelves.

I glance around but don't see anyone other than the Pattersons' cook. I wave and lower my voice. "Did Tommy tell you Ruthie's wasn't the only accident yesterday?"

Daddy's head snaps up. His eyes meet mine with a clear warning in them. A sharp lift of his chin indicates someone in the next aisle. He mouths, "Duckworth."

The Spencer's housekeeper. I nod and help Daddy stock shelves until she moves farther away. Then I keep my voice low. "I'm guessing you heard?"

He nods. The fewer words we use, the better. He taps his watch. "Tonight." Then he shoos me out.

I leave, but frustration at having to wait gnaws at me. Patience isn't one of my virtues. With time on my hands, I head toward Adams Feed Store, where Dr. Adams houses his veterinary clinic in a back corner. He'll want an update on the ferret.

I wave at Leroy Allman. He's one of the hotel lodgers, but he doesn't work in the mill. He works here, at the feed store. It's my guess he'll move out of the hotel and into one of the tenements when he finds some other men to help with the rent. I scoot past the chicken feed and open the door to the clinic.

Dr. Adams' wife, Katie, sits at the front desk. A smile brightens her face when she sees me. "Good morning, Genessee. How's the ferret?"

"He's coming along as well as can be expected, but I'm afraid he'll always be lame. I'll have to keep him."

The phone rings. She picks it up and waves me on into the back of the clinic. I push through the door, closing it behind me. The central hall, off which are two examination rooms, serves as Dr. Adams' laboratory. At a counter on one side, he peers into a microscope. Upon hearing me enter, he lifts his head. In his late-thirties, his hair is dark blond with no signs of gray or any middle-age spread.

"Genessee, come see this." He steps back, allowing me access to the microscope.

I lower my head and put the scope against my eye. Fascinating little squiggly things wiggle on the slide. "What is it?"

"Ear mites."

"Then it's not bacteria."

"Correct. They're parasites, common in dogs." He takes the slide out and puts it away. "How's the ferret?"

"Getting around quite fast, cast and all. Not quick enough to be let out in the wild, but I'm going to keep him." The two exam rooms are empty, and his medical bag is packed. "Are you going out on a farm call?" Not a lot of people in Sweetgum have pets. It's hard enough to feed their families, let alone pets. A few do, but it's farm animals that provide the vet's bread and butter.

"Yes, a horse is ready to foal. It's her first, and we want to be sure all goes well. Want to come along?"

"I'd love to, but it's too close to supper, and I'm needed in the kitchen." I reluctantly turn to leave, then remember Billy's toe. "I've got a quick question. What's the best plant for infection?"

"Human?"

"Yes. Billy Barnett lost a big toe yesterday. I want to take something by for his mother to keep on it. They can't afford store-bought medicine."

"I heard about Billy, and that Ruthie Ralston lost her arm. A sad day for the mill." He thinks for a moment. "Calendula. Make a salve, mixing a half cup of calendula oil with about a half ounce of rendered pork fat." Dr. Adams removes his glasses and wipes them with a handkerchief. "You might be well served to add some bloodroot to draw out any infection. The two together will be a good remedy."

"Thank you, Doc. I know Mrs. Barnett will be appreciative." I wave and open the door to leave.

"Be sure you try a small amount on another area. Sometimes, there are allergic reactions."

"I'll remember."

Walking home, I thank God for Dr. Adams and his willingness to share his knowledge with me. I'd be lost without him. So would Sweetgum. The thought doesn't lift my spirits as it should. Deep down, I worry that Sweetgum is already lost. And nothing I can do will save it.

As I enter the kitchen door, it's time to deliver dinner bundles. I lift two of the baskets while the others pick up theirs.

"Miss Genessee?" Twelve-year-old Beulah bounces on her toes, waiting for my attention. It must be important. Oh, I hope she isn't quitting. We need more help, not less, since Lillian started working full-time at Norton's Five & Dime.

"What is it, Beulah?" The dinner basket digs into my fingers. I move it in front of me and use both hands to carry it.

"My sister, Charity, finishes fourth grade next week. She'll be ready to bus tables, sweep, an' help make beds, if'n y'all are fixin' to hire anyone."

Thank heaven! "That's the berries, Beulah. Have her come in on Saturday, and I'll train her."

Beulah's grin is wide, showing off her white teeth. "Yes, ma'am. Thank you, Miss Genessee." She skips on ahead.

There's more spring in my step, too, after that news. We finish the dinner deliveries and hurry home.

Sarah and Mama bustle about getting our dinner served. A large tureen sits in the middle of the table, and by the aroma, it's Sarah's chicken and dumplings. I love how hers are in a thick broth, almost like a soup.

I raise the lid and sniff appreciatively. "Our lodgers will be so happy at supper tonight." Because we have to make easy-to-eat dinners for the workers, they usually get a pasty—with or without meat, depending on the supply—or a sandwich, and what we have for dinner, they'll have for supper.

Annie is already in her place at the table when Daddy arrives. Mama sets a bowl of sweet peas in the middle and sits. After the blessing, we're all quiet for a few minutes and simply enjoy Sarah and Mama's delectable dumplings.

I cut another dumpling with my spoon. "Has anyone thought up a name for the ferret? I've wracked my brain but come up blank on anything that fits him."

Daddy butters a roll, but his eyes are on me. "How about naming him after a gangster? After all, ferrets *are* notorious thieves."

I wrinkle my nose. "Not unless it's a cute name. Al Capone isn't cute. Bugsy or Baby Face might work, but those are too obvious. Pass me the peas, please, Sarah."

She hands me the bowl. As I dish up a spoonful, the name of one of my favorite comedians pings around in my head. I laugh out loud. Everyone stops eating and stares at me.

"Oh, sorry. I think I have the perfect name." I grin at Annie. She'll appreciate it, I'm sure. "Buster. After Buster—"

"Keaton!" The word flies out of Annie's mouth, along with a pea that lands on the table. She slaps a cupped hand over the pea. "Sorry. Buster's a corker, Gen. Wait till I tell Fannie."

I gasp. Lillian drops her fork. Daddy inhales sharply and starts to cough. Mama jumps up and pounds him on the back.

After a few whacks, he holds up his hand and takes a drink of water. "Annie, you don't need to tell Fannie anything about the ferret."

Her eyes grow large. Her mouth opens, but she doesn't say anything.

Oh, please, no. I lower my fork, staring at her. "Did you already say something?"

"I may or may not have." She lifts her spoon and scoops up a bite of chicken.

While Daddy delivers a lecture on the dangers of letting any of the Spencers know about our private business, I try to think of a good hiding place for Buster.

Mama fixes her gaze on me. She is so in tune with me, she knows what I'm thinking. She grins at Daddy. "I've got an idea."

The love in Daddy's eyes when he looks at Mama is moving. "Tell me your idea."

"How about you and Gen build a pen for him beneath the back porch? That way, he's safe, out of sight, and easy to get to."

It's perfect. "And I don't have to go all the way to the barn." Using my little sister's acting methods, I raise my eyebrows, place a plea in my eyes, and turn to Daddy. "Would you help me, please?"

He folds his napkin and lays it over his empty bowl. "That could work." He makes a stern face at Annie. "And no more family business told to the Spencers." His scowl deepens. "I can't understand why you did it."

Annie drops her gaze. "It sort of slipped out." She lifts her chin, and her words come out faster. "Fannie's always talking about her wonderful Percy." She scrunches her face and crosses her eyes.

I love to watch her try to explain herself. She almost doesn't need verbalization—her face is so expressive.

Daddy scratches his temple. "Who is Percy, and what does he have to do with the ferret?"

"He's her fat, bad-tempered pug that snorts all the time." She shudders. "I wanted her to know what a really fun pet is."

Mama and I suck in our lips to keep from chuckling. Daddy's hand covers Annie's. "Your heart is tender, sugar, but you need to learn to think first, then speak."

"Yes, sir." Little Sis looks at me. "I'm sorry, Gen."

"You're forgiven. There's no real harm done."

Except it's another black mark against the Taylor name.

Chapter 4

SARAH POINTS A WOODEN SPOON to a jar sitting in her Dutch oven on one of the stoves' warming shelves. "What in the name of St. Patrick is that?"

"It's calendula oil I made yesterday." I open the icebox door and pull out the tin of pork fat. "I'm making a salve for Billy Barnett's foot."

"Ah, that's a good thing to do. His parents can't afford any extra expense."

Sarah removes the jar of oil from the Dutch oven and sets it on the table for me. "I remember me sainted mother making medicinal oils in the same manner."

After straining the liquid and discarding the petals, I melt a half ounce of rendered pork fat. When it cools, I'll mix it with four ounces of calendula oil and a little bloodroot, put it in a small jar, then take it to Billy's mama.

At the counter next to the sink, Mama turns the meat grinder's handle, mincing pork to put in shepherd's pie for tomorrow. While Billy's salve cools, I chop cabbage, carrots, and onions to add to the pie. Charity scoops the vegetables into a bowl.

"Thank you, Charity." She's a fast learner and a good kitchen girl.

After I finish the vegetables, I wash my hands, set the bowl in the icebox, and twist the lid on the salve jar. "If you don't need me for anything, I'm fixing to take this on over to Mrs. Barnett."

Mama pauses the grinder handle. "Tell her how sorry I am about Billy." Her forehead puckers. "It's hard to know what to say. Part of me wants to ask what she was thinking, letting her five-year-old work there. Another part understands the financial need. But the cost ..." She bites her lip, saying no more.

She's grieving for Ruthie. We all are. We got word early this morning that she slipped off to Jesus during the night. Too much blood loss and trauma.

"Is Daddy over at the Ralstons'?" I set the jar of salve in a small basket, along with a few of Sarah's cookies for Billy.

"Yes, he's helping them plan her funeral." Mama glances at the clock. "He's working so hard, I worry. Did you see the newspaper today? They say unemployment has reached twenty-four percent." Staring out the window, she wrings her hands. "People all over the country are living in their cars, if they own one, or else in tent shantytowns by rivers."

I set down the basket and squeeze Mama's shoulder. "It's going to be all right. I'm sure it is. Remember the sparrows."

Her smile reaches her eyes, and the tension drains out of her. "You're right, sugar. As always. I sometimes think your faith is the strongest of any of us. Go now."

My heart is a little lighter as I head toward the Ralstons' house. For late spring, it's hot outside, and the air is thick with humidity. My feet kick up little dust clouds as I walk down Church Street toward the mill housing. First Row is where my best friend, Mary Patterson, lives. Her daddy is a supervisor at the mill, so they get to rent one of the larger houses. In First and Second Row, the houses are all painted white. Identical, they look like the cookies Sarah stamps out from a cutter.

Behind the white houses are the rows of workers' shanties. These are much smaller and unpainted inside, with only a thin whitewashing on the outside. The rest of the mill families live here or in the tenements. I turn onto Fourth Row. It's nothing more than a dirt alleyway between the rows with small patches of scruffy grass. At number eleven, I step onto the porch and knock.

Inside, a dog barks. Mrs. Barnett's soft voice silences it. The door opens.

"Genessee, I had a feeling you'd be around to see Billy." She steps back. "Come in."

Billy's dog jumps up for a petting. I stoop to oblige. "Hey, there, Rover." I give his ears a good scratch. Tongue lolling in a doggy grin,

Rover goes back to his corner rug.

The Ralstons' bare wood walls have a photograph on one and a framed botanical print on another. The botanical looks like it's been torn from a magazine. It must be one Mrs. Barnett likes. I'll have to ask Lillian to press some flowers for her to make a real one. We can find some old glass to put the flowers between, and Daddy could frame it.

"I brought some salve for Billy's foot. It will help prevent infection or draw out any that's already there." I hand her the basket. "There's some cookies for him too."

She sets the basket on the table, moving aside a small vase holding two daisies. "Thank you, dear. I'd hoped you'd have something for us. The doctor wrote a script, but it's expensive."

The window in the main room is open, but no air is moving. "How's Billy feeling?"

Mrs. Barnett pushes a funeral fan toward me and glances at one of two closed bedroom doors, her shoulders bent. "He's sleeping right now. He was in a lot of pain last night. I gave him some chicory root juice. That finally helped." She straightens. "But children heal so quickly. I'm grateful he's alive." A shadow falls over her eyes. "I heard about Ruthie."

I fan myself to get a little relief from the stale air while she opens the bedroom door and peeks inside. The layout here is the same in all the workers' houses—one large room with the kitchen stove, sink and pump, and a cupboard in one corner. A plain wooden dining table and chairs occupy the middle of the room, with a settee and chair at the other end. Two bedrooms are off that main room. The privy is in the yard.

Mrs. Barnett quietly closes the door behind her. "He's still sleeping, or I'd have you go in to see him. He loves you so."

"That's all right. I have to get back to the hotel." I lay the fan on the table and rise. "Oh, I almost forgot. Try a small bit of the salve on his wrist first, to make sure he isn't allergic to it. Wait a few minutes. If he itches or turns red, don't put it on his foot. Let me know, and we'll try something else."

Walking home, I pray for the salve to work. Otherwise, poor Billy could lose his entire foot. When I pass the mill, I pray again. This time, it's for protection for all inside.

Sunday is my favorite day of the week. We work harder on Saturday to prepare food that only needs reheating the next day. We only serve breakfast and supper for the hotel lodgers on the sabbath. Dinner is on the lawn behind the Methodist church. All three churches share that area. Everyone brings something to contribute to the community-wide picnic. Our lodgers provide drinks or jars of pickles, packages of store-bought cookies, or pickled pig's feet—things they can pick up at the general store.

After the final notes of the last hymn and Daddy's benediction, everyone hurries out to the picnic tables. The atmosphere turns from contemplative to festive. I pull our plates from the picnic basket and lay them on one end of a table. Since Tommy has a baseball game and he never eats before he plays ball, I won't save him a place.

"Gen!"

I answer without turning. "Hey, Mary." We've been best friends since we were old enough to crawl across the church nursery. I spin around and take her arm.

Beneath a sassy red beret, her light brown hair sweeps back from her face into a jellyroll. Poor Mary. She curls her poker-straight hair every night in rags, but by ten o'clock in the morning, it's straight again. We keep reading in magazines about permanent waves, but even though her daddy is a mill supervisor, they can't afford frivolous things like that. She'd brave those scary-looking machines for curly hair though, so she keeps asking.

She looks around the grounds. "Is Tommy getting ready for the game?"

"Yes, but I can't go." My mouth pulls downward, though I try to stop it. I busy myself setting the flatware by the napkins.

"Why not? You've never missed one of his games."

I relay what happened with Buster and Mrs. Grundy. Mary claps her hand over her mouth, giggling.

"I can see her on that ottoman."

"Daddy and I are building a pen for him after dinner."

"Hey, if I come help you and Pastor Frank, maybe we can finish before the game is over." She helps pull the wax paper off the bowls of food.

"That will be swell."

Daddy calls for the blessing. We all hold hands and bow our heads. At his "amen," Mary finds her parents and brings them over to eat with us. Vera spies me and runs over for a quick hug.

"Tommy said to give you that, but I want to give you my own." She hugs me a second time. I hug her back, then send her to her mama for her dinner.

Mr. Patterson tugs at his tie, loosening it as he takes a seat on the bench. He and Daddy immediately start talking baseball. Mrs. Patterson sits next to Mama, and they chat about how to help the Barnetts and Ralstons.

Mrs. Patterson slaps her hand on the tablecloth as a sudden breeze lifts the edge. "I imagine Joe Ralston won't be playing today, will he?"

Daddy shakes his head. "No, Ruthie's funeral is tomorrow."

The discussion ends there. It's a dance, speaking of those things with a mill supervisor. While he and Daddy have been friends for years, this is one subject that everyone holds close to the vest. I glance sidelong at Mary, whose potato salad has her rapt attention.

Mr. Patterson lifts a pickle from his plate. "How about I help you with that ferret pen?"

"That would be great. Thanks, Irving." Daddy's voice booms.

Mr. Patterson winks at Mary. "We'll teach these girls some new tricks. We'll be done in no time and all make the ball game." He pops the pickle in his mouth.

Daddy stands some long boards against an empty stall in the barn. Mr.

Patterson sets two sawhorses a few feet apart and lays one of the long boards on top, then hands Mary a saw.

"Cut that board in half."

I giggle when she looks at the saw like it's a snake. I take it from her. "Get the tape measure for me." I point to Daddy's tool belt. She pulls it out and hands it to me. "Now make a mark at four feet."

With a smirky grin, she takes it and makes the mark, then draws a line across the board. I cut it and set the saw by the stall. "See how easy that was?"

Mary picks up the saw. "I want to try it." She looks around for another board to cut. Daddy and Mr. Patterson move the sawhorses six feet apart, then lay several boards across them.

"Cut four inches off each of those ten boards." Daddy points to the lumber against the wall.

Once they're all cut, we begin to assemble the pen for Buster. When we're done, it has a floor, so he can't dig his way out. It's eight feet long, four feet wide, and a little over a foot high. The framed top is hinged and has heavy wire mesh to keep Buster inside.

I'm tickled pink with it. "Buster will be safe in there. Plus, he'll stay cool underneath the porch. I'll get some bedding for him—and a litter box."

While our daddies get the pen situated on a tarp under the back porch and layer the bottom with wood shavings, Mary and I go to my room to clean up. Ten minutes later, we're all walking over to the field. The crowd roars and I grab Mary's hand.

"Come on." We break into a run.

The baseball field is behind the schoolhouse. We run down Main Street, around the town circle, and across Schoolhouse Road. When we round the corner of the building, someone's bat connects with the ball. The crowd cheers again. My heartbeat picks up. I sure hope that's one of our boys.

We jump up onto the bleachers. I don't bother to see where our fathers park themselves. My eyes are on the field. Tommy is on second base. The scoreboard reads, *Weavers 4. Super Twisters 3.*

I slide my gaze over the crowd. Vera jumps up and down on the bleachers, waving to me until Mrs. Mack makes her sit again. I know everyone in the village, although I spot one man I've never seen before. He could be somebody's visiting relative. Or the Tigers scout?

Mary nudges me with her elbow, pulling my attention back to the field. "I hope we can keep the lead." Her eyes roam over the players.

I take the opportunity to tease her a little about her new crush. "Looking for Leroy?" He lives at the hotel, and she met him a couple months ago.

Her cheeks turn rosy, and she nods shyly. My attention goes back to the field and sticks on Tommy.

"Hey, batter, batter, batter." The Atco Mills crowd baits Hank Barnett, who waits at home plate for the next pitch. He's got a terrific batting average, so I'm hoping he hits a homer.

The pitcher winds up … lets the ball fly. Hank connects but it's a foul. The umpire holds up one finger of his right hand, and his left makes a fist. The count is one strike and no balls.

Tommy steps off the base and inches toward third. I hold my breath. The pitcher checks over his shoulder. He spins and throws the ball to second, but Tommy dives and slides for the base. He's safe! I let out the breath as he stands up and brushes himself off.

The air is humid but filled with excitement. The sun beats down on us, and I'm glad I wore a large sunhat. I wave a funeral fan, but it creates an anemic breeze. The pitcher winds up and lets the ball go. Hank's bat connects again. This time, the ball flies into left field, past the fielder, and it's a home run. We jump to our feet, cheering. Tommy rounds third and heads for home. I hear little Vera's excited shouting for her brother to slide. Hank lopes around the bases, and the scoreboard changes to *Weavers 6*.

I spot Lillian and Annie farther down the bleachers. Annie waves. Lillian's eyes are on Hank. When did he become an object of interest for her? She's never acted like she cared for any of the boys in town. I'll have to ask her tonight.

Two more Weavers strike out, and the side retires. Tommy takes the pitcher's mound as the rest of the team gets into position.

Mary's elbow pokes my ribs. "Do you see anyone who looks like a scout?"

"How would I know what one looks like?"

"Hey, batter, batter, batter." She taunts the Twisters player. "I thought maybe Tommy told you."

"No, but"—I nod toward a section of bleachers to our right—"I did notice a man I've never seen before."

"Where?"

I point but he's not there anymore. "I guess he left, whoever he was."

Tommy strikes out three Super Twister batters in quick succession. We cheer and whistle. The Weavers have a great record of wins and only two losses. It's looking like we'll win this one too.

When the game is over, we triumph by three points. I wait for Tommy to find me before heading home. When he trots off the field toward me, I go meet him.

"I was so proud of you." I squeeze his hand. "Did you happen to see that man sitting over there?" I point to where I'd seen him.

Tommy grins. "Yeah, I sure did. He's a scout for the Detroit Tigers."

My heart quickens. "Did you talk with him?"

"No. He just watched this time. But I think he'll be back. We had a great game." Tommy glances around, but nobody is paying any attention to us. He lowers his head to give me a quick but sweet kiss. "I'll see you tomorrow evening. Meet me by the sweet gum at seven?"

"Always."

With my heart full of love, I watch him lope toward the team bench, then I head home. We have to get supper on the tables for the hotel lodgers. A new thought hits me. Did that scout leave Sweetgum, or will he be coming to the hotel?

Chapter 5

THIS EVENING IS BALMY AND perfect to relocate Buster. He'll be happy in his new home, I hope. I got a large animal baby bottle from Dr. Adams secured with wire on the side of the pen for Buster to get water. Now if he just won't chew on the nipple. He'll get a bath if he does.

As I leave my bedroom with the ferret, Annie stops me in the hallway. "Where are you going with Buster?"

I stroke the little fellow's head. "He's got a new home. And please, Annie, don't ever let him out without me."

She reaches over and pets him. "I won't, I promise. I want to see him stay here. He's so cute." He licks Annie's fingers, making her giggle.

I settle Buster in the pen, along with a collection of toys, his bedding, and litter box. His food box is attached to the side next to the water. He's a smart little thing and takes a drink from the bowl. He checks out the bottle above it but loses interest quickly, which is good. I leave him exploring every corner of the new pen.

Back inside, Daddy has the radio tuned to the news in our family parlor. I sit with a magazine, half listening.

"In the world today, Walt Disney has named a new character after the recently discovered planet, Pluto. Disney states, 'With people's interest in space, we thought it was a good idea to give Mickey Mouse a canine companion.' Movie-goers seem to agree, sending scores of letters to Disney. We should see Pluto in the cartoons soon, Disney says."

"Genessee?" Daddy's voice pulls my attention away from the radio.

"Yes, sir?"

"How would you like to go with me to see Representative Davis?"

I've never gone with Daddy when he lobbies. I lower the magazine and sit upright in the chair. "Yes! But why now?"

He shrugs. "It's time. You're a grown woman, and women are taking their rightful places in politics."

The front desk bell rings in our hallway. Horsefeathers. I hop up. "I'll get it." We aren't expecting any new lodgers from the mill. Could it be the baseball scout?

The man awaiting service in the lobby is definitely not the scout who was at the baseball game. This gentleman is taller, and his suit and waistcoat appear new, displaying none of the tell-tale shine of worn-out material. He wears the suit comfortably, as though he's never spent one day of his life when he hasn't shoved his arms into those well-tailored sleeves. Not like fellows I know, who strut when they have a new pair of dungarees.

My cheeks warm when I suddenly realize I've been dissecting him like a June bug pinned to a board. I clear my throat and lift my chin. "May I help you, sir?"

"Yes, thank you." His brows dip slightly as he stares at me. "Surely, you're not the manager?"

Why do strangers think I can't deliver what they need? "No, I'm his daughter. Do you need a room, sir?" I smile, hoping he will allow me to help him. Daddy needs to relax.

"I'd prefer to speak with the manager, if you'll be so kind as to get him. I'm here to inspect the hotel. Then, I'll need that room."

Inspect the hotel? Only decorum stops me from asking why. I gesture toward a floral settee. "If you'll have a seat, I'll go get him." I turn and go through the door to our private apartments. Daddy has his head buried in a newspaper.

"Daddy, there's a man out front who says he's here to inspect the hotel." Trying not to wring my hands, I end up cracking my knuckles.

The newspaper lowers. "Did you ask him why?"

"No, sir. Should I have? He asked to see you."

Daddy rises, lays the paper on his chair. "No, you did the right thing. Shall we go together?"

The man is standing in the archway leading to the dining room. He turns at our footsteps. Daddy offers his hand.

"Frank Taylor. May I help you?"

"Darrell Forsythe." His manner is pleasant as he shakes Daddy's hand. "I'm a partner in the Sweetgum Mill and here to inspect the hotel."

Daddy cocks his head. "I've never had an inspection before. Has there been a complaint?"

Mr. Forsythe slides his hand into his breast pocket and withdraws a handkerchief, which he pats to his glistening brow. "I try to see all living facilities at the mills where I have investments."

He's adroit at avoiding Daddy's question. I'll bet my Sunday gloves Mrs. Grundy made good on her threat to tell Mr. Spencer.

Mr. Forsythe gestures toward the dining room. "May we?"

I lead the way, and my eyes do a fast perusal. Thank goodness Lillian and Annie finished bussing the tables. Everything gleams, from the silverware to the glasses. Mr. Forsythe wipes a finger over one tabletop, then rubs it against his thumb and nods. He repeats his actions at a few more random tables. He then turns his attention to the side counter, where we keep the serving pieces.

When he's satisfied, he asks to see the guest parlor, where we find a few lodgers reading and playing cards. They glance up and smile. Mr. Forsythe dips his chin pleasantly in acknowledgment. He walks to the window and looks out. As he does, his hand casually rubs the windowsill. He looks at his finger and an eyebrow rises.

It's Sunday! We don't allow our staff to work beyond putting the food out for the lodgers. I glance at Daddy. This isn't fair. We follow Mr. Forsythe out of the parlor.

"I'd like to see the grounds, please."

Daddy and I share a glance. *Buster.* I'm right. I'm sure of it. It's Grundy. We lead Mr. Forsythe out the front door and around the hotel to the back. He inspects the pig pen, testing the strength of the posts. Right now, there are four sows and thirty-seven piglets. He looks in the barn and checks our two goats and three milk cows. What is he looking for?

He glances in the chicken coop, then raises an inquisitive eyebrow at Daddy. "Why is there a light in here?"

I'm proud of my father's modernity as he explains how the light makes the chickens lay when we need them to.

Mr. Forsythe looks closely at the kerosene lantern. "And you don't worry about one of the chickens knocking this off the hook?"

Daddy's lips twitch ever so slightly. "A chicken's flight is short-lived. Up to their roost is about all they can manage, Mr. Forsythe, and as you see, the lantern is higher than that. It's safe."

"Well, I'll be. I don't think I ever put much thought into a chicken's flight." He chuckles. "So you always have fresh eggs for the workers?"

"We do." Daddy is confident in his answer.

We head back toward the hotel. Then Mr. Forsythe stops and points to the porch. "What is that beneath the veranda?"

"That is the ferret's pen. My daughter has a gift with injured animals. The local veterinarian often brings her some, and others, she rescues. Then she nurses them back to health."

"And they are kept here? Not inside the hotel?"

Daddy pauses. Then he sighs. "On occasion, one will be taken into our private apartments for an hour or two. This ferret—my daughter's named him Buster—is lame and will never be able to be returned to the wild. Buster's become a pet."

"Thank you for your honesty, Mr. Taylor. May I see it?"

Daddy nods to me, and I unlatch the pen. Buster immediately comes to me. He nuzzles my neck when I lift him out. Then I hand him to Mr. Forsythe.

The inspector takes him gently and cradles him. The ferret must sense he's not in danger because he immediately tries to search Mr. Forsythe's vest pocket. He laughs at Buster's antics. "As a boy, I had a ferret myself. This little fellow is very clean. Do you bathe him often?" He addresses his question to me.

"Yes, sir. He loves the water."

With a smile that reaches his eyes, he hands Buster back to me. Then his business demeanor returns. "I'd like a room, please."

I open my mouth, but Daddy puts his hand on my arm. "Of course."

We return to the lobby, where Daddy opens the registry and slides the book toward Mr. Forsythe. "If you'll fill this out, I'll get you your key. Do you have any bags, sir?"

"Yes, I have an overnighter in my car. I'll get it a little later." He writes his information in the book, and Daddy hands him the key to room two-ten.

"If you'd like, my daughter can retrieve your bag while I show you the room."

Mr. Forsythe looks at me and nods. He reaches into his pocket and withdraws his keys. He selects one and holds it up to me. "This fits the padlock on the trunk. That's where you'll find my bag."

I take the key and go out front. Parked at the curb is a beautiful 1929 Cadillac Touring car. Wow, this guy has some money, all right. I retrieve his overnight bag from the trunk, careful to close the lid properly and secure the padlock.

I hurry up the stairs and find Daddy and Mr. Forsythe in two-ten. The inspector turns at my entrance.

"Ah, there we go. Thank you, young lady." He takes his bag and sets it on the bed. "The room is fine. What time is breakfast? I'll eat with the workers."

Daddy gently pushes me toward the door. "Five-thirty."

"I'll be there. And thank you." He closes the door.

Daddy raises a warning finger to his lips and ushers me down the stairs. I wait until we're in our quarters.

"What did he say while I was getting his bag? Did he tell you if we passed his inspection?"

"He didn't say, but he couldn't have found anything that would put us in a bad light. However, I'm glad we got Buster's pen done yesterday. Mrs. Grundy must have told Spencer about him."

I start fuming. "I wish she'd get married and move into a house. Maybe I should work on introducing her to a widower. Except, I can't imagine who'd want an old sourpuss like her for a wife."

"Genessee …"

Daddy's warning stops me. "Okay, but she's certainly our 'Paul's thorn.'"

He laughs and hugs me. "Go on to bed. It's late … and four o'clock comes around mighty quick."

This morning, I get a rare win when Annie and I gather the eggs. Back in the kitchen, I transfer the baskets to the dairy icebox. We need three large iceboxes to manage the food. I sure wish we had electricity in Sweetgum. Then we could get one of those electric cold rooms. Mr. Spencer had a hydroelectric plant built for the mill equipment, but even though we're close, nothing outside the actual mill connects to it. That man's tighter than a tick on a hound.

Sarah and Mama make today's breakfast—biscuits and gravy, scrambled eggs with the last of the country ham diced in them, and cheese grits. Mama makes goat cheese with Nanny and Belle's milk. At the stroke of five-thirty, we have the food on the tables. Annie rings the bell, and footsteps thunder down the stairs.

When Mr. Forsythe takes a seat at Mrs. Grundy's favorite table, I have to bite my lip to keep from laughing. Annie snickers softly through her nose. We carry coffeepots around to fill cups so we can watch the fireworks when Mrs. Grundy arrives.

Mr. Forsythe is enjoying his breakfast as the object of our mirth walks up behind him. She clears her throat loudly. Intent on his breakfast, he pays no attention. She reaches out and flicks his ear.

"Ow!" He twists his head to look at her. Being a gentleman, he rises. "May I ask what that was for, madam?"

She crosses her arms and lifts her chin. "You're sitting at my table."

I elbow Annie and whisper, "Watch this."

Mr. Forsythe glances at the table, and his brow dips in puzzlement. "I don't see a placard indicating it's private." He's had enough of her rudeness and sits to finish his breakfast.

She huffs and plants one hand on her skinny hip. Her other hand holds her plate. "Well, I never. Do you know who I am?"

He peers up at her sternly. "No, madam, I do not. Do you know who I am?"

Now she looks unsure, but never one to surrender, her expression turns frosty. "I do not, nor do I care." She crosses to another table where two young men eat. As soon as she makes her intentions known, they grab their plates and retreat to empty seats across the dining room.

Mr. Forsythe sets his gaze on me while one eyebrow rises in question. I smile an acknowledgment. He lifts his coffee cup, and I scurry over to refill it.

His voice stays low. "I'm guessing that is Mrs. Grundy? The one who complained about your Buster?"

Suddenly, I get a check in my conscience. "It is, but I feel a little sorry for her. She was widowed four years ago. She came to live here after that. I'm sure it has something to do with her attitude." I fill his coffee cup.

Mr. Forsythe smiles warmly. "You're a nice young woman, Miss Taylor. My report will say there was nothing found but perfect cleanliness and excellent service at the Sweetgum Hotel."

Relief loosens the band around my chest. "Thank you, sir. I'll tell my father."

I hand him a morning newspaper and go into the kitchen to release a whoop fighting to get out. Sarah and Mama look up when I holler.

Mama winks at Sarah. "Something has our girl very happy."

"Mr. Forsythe's report is wonderful. Nothing here to complain about." I laugh out loud. "He met Mrs. Grundy. She found him seated at her table."

Mama claps a hand over her mouth and chuckles.

Guffaws tumble out of Sarah's mouth as she slaps her knee. "I wish I'd seen that."

They both go back to baking with gleeful smiles.

I go about my work, but inside my head, a warning twinges. Mrs. Grundy has a reputation for retaliation. I can only hope it's Mr. Forsythe, and not my daddy or Buster, who is her target.

Chapter 6

With Beulah's sister Charity now on staff, I have her take my place delivering dinner bundles to the mill. As soon as the girls depart, Daddy and I will head out to Rome. Mr. Davis, our state representative, is in the county seat office today, and Daddy made an appointment with him since he's leading the battle for better child labor laws.

Daddy cranks the engine handle on the old general store truck. When it catches, he climbs in the driver's seat, and we leave Sweetgum, a smoky plume billowing behind us. I've left my suit jacket off since it's hot in the truck even with the windows open. Fortunately, I remembered to secure my hat with bobby pins. The breeze through the window ruffles my hair, providing a little relief from the sticky heat. The road winds next to and then away from the Etowah River and back again, but the scenery is lost on me. The reason for our trip weighs heavy on my heart.

"What's on your mind, daughter?"

A sigh escapes me. "I feel like a rat at times. If we help the children, we hurt their parents." I turn and lean against the door so I'm facing Daddy. "I wish there was another way."

His long fingers drum the steering wheel. "I'm in the same position, sweetheart. I'll take wages from them on the one hand but give them healthier and better-educated children on the other. Unfortunately, most only see today. They have nothing to really give them hope for a better future."

I glance out the window as I chew on that. Farmland has given way to houses as we get closer to Rome. An old, abandoned farmhouse sits back from the road. A hundred yards away, a dilapidated barn lists to one side. Did the owners leave their land and go to a mill? Many folks did for the reason Daddy said, but when they arrived in Sweetgum, they ended up not gaining much at all. "Why is Bibb Mill preferable to Sweetgum?"

"They're the largest in the South—perhaps in the country. They make more products." Daddy glances at me. "They do a lot more for their workers than Spencer can or is willing to do. Ah, here we are."

We pull into a parking spot. The imposing municipal building before us is two stories of red brick with tall, white columns. The truck's engine shudders to a stop.

"Daddy, what does Bibb do for its workers that we don't?"

He looks at his wristwatch, then glances up at the brick clock tower in the distance. "For one, they have a social worker at each village who arranges for clubs and athletic programs beyond baseball and coordinates medical care." He pulls the stem out on his watch and moves the hands. "The mill pays for all that. They also pay higher wages."

I slip on my suit jacket as we get out of the truck. "Our Weavers had to pay for their own uniforms."

Daddy glances at the clock tower again.

"What are you doing?"

"I always set my watch with the tower when I'm here. It's never wrong." He takes my hand. "Let's go. We don't want to be late."

Inside, a man who appears to be in his early thirties meets us and ushers us into a conference room. Well-dressed and groomed, he introduces himself as an aide.

"Representative Davis will be with you shortly. May I get you some coffee, sweet tea, or water?" His words reverberate off the high walls and marble floors.

"Thank you. Water would be nice." Daddy turns the question to me. "Genessee?"

I nod, finding myself tongue-tied in the echoing room. Devoid of furniture except for the conference table and chairs, the room's lower half is paneled in dark wood and painted a soft, creamy white above that. Portraits of men hang on the walls, but I only recognize two—

President Hoover and Governor Hardman.

The aide returns with a tray containing three glasses and a pitcher of water. He's followed by a tall man with gray at his temples and in his mustache. Oddly, there isn't any gray in his eyebrows. Does he pluck them out?

He holds out his hand to Daddy. "Good to see you, Mr. Taylor." He turns to me. "And this can't be Genessee. You've grown up."

Heat rises to my cheeks. I don't remember meeting him. I glance at Daddy, hoping he'll swoop to my rescue.

He winks at me. "Kids don't remember adults when they're at a county fair. Had you been a goat or a chicken, she'd remember."

I groan inwardly. I hope Mr. Davis didn't see my eyes roll.

He merely chuckles. "Let's have a seat." When we settle, he pours water for us, then leans back in his chair. "Tell me what's been happening in Sweetgum."

Daddy rests his forearms on the table. "It's not good, I'm afraid. One boy lost part of his foot and his big toe, and a little girl lost her life after her arm was ripped off."

The representative flinches and momentarily closes his eyes.

Daddy waits until the man makes eye contact again. "These kids were way too young to be working. They should be in school. How many more have to be maimed or lose their lives before we get stronger legislation passed?"

Mr. Davis pulls out a small notebook and pen. "The mill owners have persuasive lobbyists." He jots a note in his book. "I must say, Sweetgum seems to have more than its share of accidents, though—the highest in the state." He rises. "I have the hotel's phone number, Mr. Taylor. I have an idea I want to run by a few of my colleagues. I'll get back with you when I have more to tell you."

That's it? In less than five minutes, the meeting's over?

Daddy stands and shakes hands with him. I wait until we leave, then ask, "Are all your meetings with him like that? We could have telephoned that in."

"He's a busy man, sugar." Daddy cranks the truck's engine while I climb inside.

I shake my head. "It seems like a long way to come for a five-minute meeting."

Daddy puts the truck in gear. "And that's why I usually combine the trip with an errand like purchasing for the general store or the hotel. But this meeting had worth on its own. It's always good to keep our faces fresh in his mind. Only one in a thousand people will write a letter to their legislators. Therefore, that one letter equals the voice of a thousand people. When you think of how few actually go to see them, our faces mean many more thousands of like-minded people. And each of those people equals a vote."

The evening is beautiful. An afternoon thunderstorm lowered the temperature a good ten degrees. As soon as I get to the sweet gum tree, Tommy takes my hand.

"Let's walk." He leads me toward the river. The sun won't set for another hour or more, so there's plenty of time before the path becomes too dark to see.

"Where's Vera tonight?"

"Mama kept her home. She knows we need time for ourselves." He chuckles. "That little scamp adores you. She tried to sneak out and follow me, but Ma caught her."

We leave the road and cross the meadow. It's filled with wildflowers—Bowman's Root, Yellow Colic Root, Red-wing Milkweed, and more. Tommy bends and picks a Coral Honeysuckle and hands it to me.

"Thank you, good sir."

He laughs as I tuck the blossoms in my hair. When we come to a secluded spot where we can dangle our feet in the water, we stop. I unbuckle my sandals and slip them off while Tommy tucks his socks into his shoes.

Cold water runs over my feet. I wiggle my toes. "Ooh, that feels so good."

Tommy takes my hand again. "I want our children to grow up near a river, but not in a mill town." His brows knit together. "I never want one of ours to work in a mill. It's dangerous enough for a grown man."

Tommy is a bit of a dreamer, for which I'm thankful. "What do you want them to be?"

He plucks a blade of sweet grass and sticks it in his mouth. "A pastor like your daddy. Or maybe a doctor." He leans back on his elbows. "If I get a ball contract, we might be able to save enough to send one of them to college." His voice has an intensity to it that I haven't heard before. "I want our kids to have choices, Gen. That takes education."

"Me too. I want our daughters, as well as our sons, to be able to choose to be … well, a veterinarian, if she wants to. And before we have any children, I'll work too. We can save all my wages for those college degrees."

His eyes crinkle with amusement. "How many children are we looking at here?"

I can't resist teasing him. "Oh, I don't know. How about a half dozen?"

Tommy's sharp inhale nearly draws in the blade of grass he's chewing. He sputters and spits it out. "You're kidding, right?"

"Of course, I am. Sort of." I lift my feet, watching the water trickle off before I lower them back into the river. "I've always pictured myself with at least three."

He settles back onto his elbows. "That's a good number."

"Or we could have four—two boys and two girls." I sigh, picturing boys who look like Tommy. The girls will look like Annie—adorable.

"Or if we had nine, we could have our own baseball team."

I laugh. "You'll have to catch me first." I jump up, grabbing my sandals as I do, and run. It isn't more than a minute before Tommy grabs my arm and spins me around in the meadow. As our spinning slows, Tommy draws me to his chest. His eyes close, and his mouth lowers to claim mine. My heart pounds hard in my ears, and for one blessed moment, I forget all about mills and danger.

∞

At my dressing table, I pick up my brush and run it through the length of my hair. I need a trim again to keep it just below my shoulder blades. Any longer is too hard to manage.

Lillian sits on the floor by my bed while Annie perches on the mattress above her, braiding her hair. Our Lillian is a contradiction, claiming to be a modern woman, yet she won't bob her hair. I still haven't made a decision on that. Every summer, I debate it. Annie got hers bobbed this afternoon. She looks so cute, and I imagine it's much cooler to have one's neck exposed. But I have the curly hair from Mama's side of the family, and it would be hard to make it lay smooth and straight.

Lillian ties a ribbon on the end of the braid when Annie finishes. "So what did you and Tommy do this evening?"

"We talked about how many children we want."

"What did you decide?" Annie picks up a movie magazine.

"I said three or four. Tommy said a baseball team."

Lillian gasps. "You aren't going to become a baby machine, are you?"

I laugh at her horror. "He was kidding."

Annie stares at us both, her nose wrinkling. "I don't want any. I'm not even sure I want to get married. All I want to do is act in movies." She buries her nose in the magazine again.

Lillian and I share a glance. Poor Annie. We're afraid her dreams have no chance of being fulfilled. There's nowhere for her to get any training in Sweetgum, and I don't know how to help her either. And at seventeen, she hasn't yet met a boy who captures her heart.

That makes me think of Hank. "Lillian, did you see the Detroit Tigers' scout at Sunday's game? I think he was watching both Tommy and Hank."

Lillian lays down her nail file and picks up a bottle of polish. "I sure did. If Hank gets a contract, I'll propose to *him*."

I gape at her. "You wouldn't!"

"Just watch me. I like Hank. He'd make a good husband, but I won't marry anyone who works in the mill. I want out of this town. So, if he gets a contract, you watch how fast I'll go with him."

"Even if you don't love him?"

She shrugs. "Our grandparents had arranged marriages. They learned to love each other."

Annie's attention leaves her magazine. "If you marry Hank, maybe you could go to California and take me along."

I lay my brush on the dressing table, then join Big Sis on the floor. Hugging my legs, I lay my cheek on my knees. "Lillian won't be going to California. Detroit is in Michigan. And the farm team is in Texas. That's where she'd go. Me, too, if they both get a contract."

Annie swipes a bottle of bright red nail polish from her nightstand and opens it. "Well, Texas is closer to California than Georgia. I'll take it. Then I can make my own way to Hollywood." She applies the paint to her toenails.

"Give me that." Lillian pulls a chair from the dressing table and sits, taking the bottle from her. "I'll do it. You're making a mess." Annie plops her foot in Lillian's lap.

I allow myself to daydream once more about joining Tommy in Texas. Try as I may, though, I can't seem to banish the small cloud that hovers over my dream. How will Mama, Daddy, and Sarah get along if we all leave?

Chapter 7

THE OLD DESK IN DADDY'S sparsely furnished office at the church is scarred with gouges from generations of pastors' children doodling while their daddies worked. Three unadorned, wooden chairs wobble when anyone sits in them. A sadly neglected pew rests against a side wall, its wood split in places for want of furniture oil. Tommy halts his pacing and joins Daddy at the window overlooking the cemetery. Ruthie's grave is now covered with newly sprouted grass, a few weeds, and a handful of fresh wildflowers.

I can't stand still, so I walk the floor while Tommy rests his hand on Daddy's shoulder. "In the past month alone since Ruthie's death, we've had three kids lose fingers, toes, and a whole foot."

Daddy nods and pulls his handkerchief from his back pocket, moping the perspiration off his face. "Representative Davis told Genessee and me that Sweetgum leads the state in accidents." He grimaces. "Not a record we want. We've got to do something—but what?" Now Daddy paces. "For too long, we've waited on the legislature. But politics is a slow-moving train. With this financial depression, it's even harder. Everyone claims they need more money—and so the children continue to work."

Still staring out the window, Tommy taps his foot. "I'm fixin' to take a couple days off and go to the Bibb Mill in Porterdale." He turns and leans against the sill, crossing his legs. "I know some of the guys from their team. Maybe we can set up a meeting of some kind."

Daddy slides the chair out and sits at the desk, a frown pulling his brows until they meet over his nose. "What kind of meeting?"

The old pew creaks in protest as Tommy lowers his weight onto it. He glances at me, then back at Daddy. "I think we may need to try a labor strike." He holds up his hand to stop any interruption from either of us. "I know it's risky, but these other accidents so close after Ruthie's death has people shook—shaken up."

Daddy looks unsure. "That's asking for a heap of trouble, Tommy."

I sit beside him, taking his hand. "Do you think it would really help?" I glance at Daddy. "Has anyone ever tried a labor strike here?"

My father lowers his chin and shakes his head. "Not here. It takes *everyone* being willing to risk everything. They could lose their jobs and be thrown out of their homes, or they can live with the way things are and maybe lose a child." He closes his eyes again and is silent. The dilemma is weighty.

Tommy stares at him, then quirks a brow at me. I hold up my hand, signaling him to wait. Daddy's seeking wisdom from God. After a moment, he nods and opens his eyes.

"First, we three commit to pray about this for seven days. *If* we all feel God is telling us to move forward, then we sound out some of the more influential men at the mill. Genessee, you'll talk with the women who have children involved in the accidents. I'll have your mama feel out Ruthie's mother. At the end of the week, I'll telephone Representative Davis and let him know what we decide. Just keep in mind, we're inviting trouble."

If Mr. Spencer gets wind that we're the instigators of this, we'll lose our jobs and our home.

As I have for the past three days, I get up a half hour early and drop to my knees beside my bed to pray. I haven't received even a flicker of an answer yet, but I can't rush God, no matter how much I'd like to. This morning, tears accompany my prayers as I relive Ruthie's death. I guess I'm not as immune as I told Mama. In the center of my being, I know God wants us to do something. I just don't know what that something is—yet.

Thank You, Lord, for the promise of answered prayer.

I hurry to the bathroom. Only Sarah and Mama are up before me, and they are already in the kitchen. The bathroom is mine alone.

Back in Annie's and my bedroom, I wake Little Sis. As usual, the threat of a cold bath spurs her to jump up. It amuses me that she doesn't catch on, but it works, so why change? If she ever cottons onto my methods, I've got another idea in my pocket. I'll tell her Clara Bow is at the front desk. That should get her moving.

After the lodgers have breakfast and leave for work, we sit around the kitchen table for an extra five minutes and enjoy another cup of coffee. Sarah made cinnamon rolls as a treat for the family. I'm reaching for one when the mill bell tolls loudly. Coffee sloshes out of my cup onto the plate of rolls.

"No!" I push back from the table.

Mama jumps up. "I'm going this time. You stay here."

Her words startle me as much as the bell clanging. "You're scaring me. Why shouldn't I go?"

She stares at me for a moment. "I don't know. I just feel I should be there. Come on, then. We'll go together."

We run out the front door. Lillian and Annie follow us as we run up the hill. Daddy is already there, waiting at the mill's giant door.

He sets his hands firmly on my shoulders, blocking my entry. "Don't go in. Nor you, Annie."

My stomach drops and my blood turns cold. "Not Tommy! Tell me it isn't Tommy!"

He shakes his head, his eyes red with unshed tears. "It's not Tommy. But sweetheart, it's his little sister. It's Vera."

Dear God, no! My chest feels like it's being squeezed in a vice. "How bad?"

Once again, Daddy shakes his head and closes his eyes. He pulls me into his arms. Normally, I feel safe in my father's arms. Not this time. They're a prison. I push back, but he holds me tight.

Tears flow down my face. "Please, she isn't ..."

This time, Daddy nods. A wail, primal in its intensity and loss, comes from within. But it's not mine that echoes in my ears. I know that voice. It's Mrs. Mack, Tommy's mama. I lift my head, searching

Daddy's eyes. His hands cup my face. "Genessee, it's the worst I've ever seen. You don't want to go in there."

"How can I not? It's Tommy's sister." I tug to get free.

"This is one time you can't help him. He has his hands full with his mother."

It's bad. Really bad. Daddy's never protected me from any other accident. Suddenly, I don't want to know. What I *do* want to know is why God has answered our prayers like this. Anger, hot and harsh, rises in me.

In an effort not to lose my breakfast on Daddy, I yank free and run from the mill. When the river is before me, I turn and race alongside it. Finally, I collapse on my hands and knees in the tall grass and empty my stomach.

When I'm done retching, I reach into the river and cup a handful of water to rinse my mouth. Then I lay down on my back. Thunderclouds gather overhead.

Where are you, God? Why did You let this happen?

The questions pound feverishly at my temples. My head tells me He knows the end from the beginning, but my heart wonders why He didn't stop it. Why hurt Tommy when he's trying to help the children?

Quick breathing and footsteps come my way, and Lillian drops onto the grass beside me. "Are you all right?"

"I don't know." My faith has been dealt a blow. I close my eyes.

My big sister pulls my head onto her lap. She strokes my brow, and with each pass of her fingers, the tension eases.

"You've asked me why I won't marry a man who works in the mill. This is why. I don't want to have my children die like that."

I open my eyes to look at her. "I'm worried about Tommy—what he'll do."

Her fingers stop. "Tommy's not a violent man. He won't go after Spencer, if that's what you mean."

"I know he won't attack Mr. Spencer physically. But he's talking about a labor—"

"Hush. Don't even say it, Gen. Not out loud. It isn't safe."

I sit up. "Spencer has everyone cowed. They're afraid to stand up to him, to demand some safety precautions."

Lillian's face darkens. Her eyes grow hard. "Unfortunately, he has no conscience. All he cares about are his profits. Do you realize he pays the lowest wages of all Georgia's textile mills?"

I didn't know that. "What do *you* think we should do?" I want some big sisterly advice. Lillian hasn't always been the most constant of advisors.

Her face softens, and she puts an arm around my shoulders. "Pray, like Daddy said. And remember, God's ways aren't ours." Her arm tightens around me. "I know what happened to Vera is really hard. I know you've been praying. But I also know God is sovereign and still sits on His throne." She twists to face me. "Gen, good *will* come from this. That's a promise, and God never breaks a promise."

She's right. And while I'm still not happy, I'm thankful for my sister. "I love you, Lillian."

She hauls me to my feet. "I love you too."

With my faith reinforced, we head home. Life goes on in Sweetgum. There are dinner bundles to fill, though the notion of taking them to the mill makes my stomach roil again.

And people to talk to about the coming trouble.

After a week, the sorrow over Vera's death still hangs thick and oppressive, clouding my world with a gray pallor. But what is clear is what must be done. Daddy, Tommy, and I all believe God's guidance is toward a strike, so the family lingers around the kitchen table after supper, trying to sort the details.

I stare at the saltshaker, turning it. Salt. We're to be salt. "Daddy, you preached a sermon a couple of years ago. You said, 'It falls to every generation to leave their world a better place for the next. If you aren't doing something to improve conditions, you are missing the purpose for which you are placed upon this earth.'"

He winks at Mama. "At least my children are listening."

Mama covers his hand with hers. "And she's got a good point, Frank. God gave you those words for a reason."

"And Tommy agrees with me."

My father nods. "I can't ignore the nudges I'm getting from Scripture either." He looks around the table at each of us. "All right. If we get people to come, where do we hold the meeting?"

Mama's smile makes her eyes crinkle. "In the church basement."

We all gape at her.

She shrugs. "Have people bring food and call it a church supper."

Annie stares at Mama as though she has loaves of bread rising out of her ears. "A secret meeting in the church?" Then her eyes grow large. Our actress sees drama in it.

But Lillian shakes her head. "That's lying. A lot of people won't like it. I don't like it, and I can't believe you suggested it, Mother."

Mother? Wow, what hornet took up residence in Lillian's chapeau?

Sarah pushes up from the table. She pulls a pitcher of sweet tea from the icebox, using her ample hip to push its door shut. "I seem to recall an Old Testament prophet disguising himself to *trap* King Ahab." She sets the pitcher on the table. "Isn't that right, Brother Frank?"

Daddy slaps his thigh and laughs. "Yes, by gum and by golly, it is. Sarah, you're brilliant. It's in First Kings, chapter twenty and verse thirty-eight." He picks up the pitcher and pours sweet tea in all our glasses. "And now we have Scripture to combat anyone who argues with us about the location."

Even Lillian grins. "I stand corrected. I apologize, Mama."

Daddy drains his glass. "So … we're all in agreement?"

Six heads nod, even Sarah's.

"All right, we'll start tonight. Report back here at nine o'clock."

While Mama leaves for the Ralstons' and I go to the Flynns' house, Annie and Lillian stay to help Sarah with tomorrow's meal preparations.

At the Flynns', Miss Eileen answers the door. While her dress, made from a feed sack, is washed and fairly new, she appears harried—older than her thirty-four years. Though they are members of our church, suddenly, my mouth turns dry, and I can't find words. *Lord, help me.*

She glances over her shoulder and slips out onto the porch. "Let's sit over here. It's a tad cooler." She moves to two rocking chairs where we settle ourselves. "Ruthie's funeral was heartbreaking, wasn't it?"

Thank you, Lord. My tongue loosens. "Yes, ma'am, it was. And that's why I'm here. We've got to have better safety precautions in the mill. You have two little ones working there." Her two are five and six years old.

Her hand trembles as she waves a funeral fan. "And every day when we go into work, I pray over them. But so did Nellie Ralston." Her lips flatten. "And we all know what happened." She glances into the alleyway, then back to me. "I wouldn't say this to anyone but you, Genessee. Somehow, I know you'll understand. I think God took Ruthie home for a reason—to save other children."

I blink, not sure I'm hearing right. Such wisdom and faith from a woman without schooling. "I believe you're right, Miss Eileen. And that's why I'm here." I quietly explain about the safety strike.

But her eyes narrow when I tell her where we plan to hold it. "I'm not sure the Lord will bless that."

"I understand your concern, but we've bathed this in prayer, and Daddy wouldn't have it there if God hadn't given us a precedent." I rise. "Look up First Kings, chapter twenty, verse thirty-eight. Then pray. If you feel God's favor on the meeting, let me know, then help spread the word."

My jaw firms as my determination hardens. I stare into her eyes, willing her to understand. "We need everyone or this won't work."

It takes a moment, but finally, she nods. And hope crackles to life in my heart. We're in for a fight, but maybe, together, we'll see this thing through. For Ruthie. And Vera. And countless others whose faces are yet a mystery, names yet unknown, who might be spared by our efforts—if we're successful.

Chapter 8

AFTER TWO MORE WEEKS OF whisperings in the village, we're gathering in the church basement. So many people are packed inside, there's barely a pint of air for each. The temperature remains in the eighties, even though the sun has set. I waft Ruthie's funeral fan in a futile effort to cool my face. Daddy and Tommy stand at the front of the room, waiting for the last few stragglers to squeeze inside. The remnants of supper remain on some of the tables.

My attention is drawn to the man next to Tommy. He's the one from Bibb Manufacturing in Porterdale. Dressed in dungarees that aren't worn out and a crisp, checkered shirt, he appears to be in his thirties. He's taller than the average ballplayer but athletic and muscular, like Tommy, who catches me watching and winks. Warmth rises in my cheeks.

When the fellow from Porterdale says something to Tommy, I let my gaze wander. By my hasty count, it appears at least thirty women are here, which pleases me. Some are widows, but a few stand by their husbands.

Finally, everyone seems to be in because Tommy nods, and the door is locked. He signals for everyone who can be to be seated. Those who can't find a place lean against the walls.

Tommy steps forward. "Thank you, Pastor Taylor, for allowing us to use the church basement. Obviously, the need for secrecy is vital. I want to introduce Daniel Kitchens from the Bibb Manufacturing Company in Porterdale. Dan works in the mill and is on their baseball team, The Blue Caps, which is how I know him."

Tommy surveys the room. I don't know what or who he's looking for, but he nods and continues. "I went to Porterdale a couple of weeks ago.

They have safeguard practices in place that prevent many of the accidents we have suffered. I've asked Dan to tell us about some of them."

After he speaks, explaining their rules and precautions, Tommy takes over again. "Dan told me about other mills that have had labor-safety strikes. I believe that is what we need to do. Spencer has got to bring in some of these precautions. Sweetgum Mill has the worst reputation in the state. Are we going to allow him to maim and kill more of our children?"

The room erupts with a resounding, "No!"

Tommy nods. "Then we need to agree on a date. I believe it should be early. We'll clock in, then walk out thirty minutes later. Each worker will make a sign bearing the words, *Safe Working Conditions*. Today is Friday. The element of surprise is crucial, so I think we should strike on Monday two weeks from now. Are we agreed?" Tommy raises his arm. All around the room, arms raise and heads nod solemnly.

"All right. And remember, nobody says a word."

It feels funny being at the ball field two days in a row. Late yesterday afternoon, everyone gathered here, bringing watermelons to share, sparklers, and a few firecrackers to set off for our Independence Day celebration. It's the safest place to avoid fires. Today's game will start in a few minutes.

Mary, Lillian, and I find a good spot on the bleachers. Annie stands with Fannie Spencer, but she isn't talking. Her eyes are huge, and it looks as though they're arguing. Or, at least, Fannie is. Her mouth moves so fast, spittle flies. Annie jumps back, spins around, and huffs away, arms swinging as she marches in our direction. My stomach churns as she climbs onto the bleachers, each stomp rattling my seat. Has her argument with Fannie ended their friendship? That girl has a reputation for being vindictive.

"Do you know what Fannie said? That Buster is a stupid pet!" Annie snorts as she sits next to me. "Shows what she knows. But she said if I don't say her stupid Percy is better, she won't be my friend. First of all, that's so childish. Secondly, what kind of friend is that? I tell you, I'm done with her."

That relieves me, but I glance sidelong at Mary, worrying that since her daddy is a supervisor, she might be softhearted toward Fannie. She doesn't show any signs of disapproval, though. Instead, she turns around and leans her elbow on the bench beside Annie.

"A good friend doesn't throw ultimatums at their pals. I think she's gotten in with a pretty fast crowd over at the riding club she belongs to. You're better off without her, Annie."

Lillian nudges me with her elbow and points to the other set of bleachers. "Isn't that the Lions' scout?"

I snap my gaze from Mary and Little Sis to where Lillian points. My heartbeat accelerates. "Yes, that's him." I grab my sister's hand and squeeze. "Now I'm really nervous."

Lillian winks at me. "No need to be. Our boys are terrific."

Our boys? I peer at her. "Have you gone out with Hank?"

She fingers her chignon. "I've been letting him walk me home from work every night."

"You sneaky thing." I prod her with my elbow. "Why didn't you tell me?"

Lillian shrugs one shoulder. "It's not a big deal right now. Not yet, anyway."

The boys run out onto the field. We stand for the Pledge of Allegiance and invocation. This week, it's the Catholic priest who prays.

Right after the *amen*, the umpire shouts, "Play ball!" and throws the ball to Tommy. The other team is up first. I switch my gaze to the scoreboard. I haven't paid any attention to who we're playing. It's the Porterdale Mill team. They're good. I sit on my crossed fingers, but I shoot up a prayer for our boys and for the coming strike. I don't know who chooses which teams our boys play against, but the significance isn't lost on me.

Tommy quickly strikes out the first two batters. The third makes a line drive and gains first base, but Tommy doesn't let the next one get a single hit.

"Okay, here's hoping for some runs." Lillian puts her hands together beneath her chin. Joe Ralston is the first batter for our team. He slams the second pitch, but it's a foul ball. He ends up striking out.

I lean toward Mary. "Looks like it's going to be a tough game."

"Poor Joe. He's usually good for a couple of bases."

Our next two batters strike out, then Tommy's back on the mound. He doesn't let the Porterdale team get anything more than a single base hit through several innings.

In the bottom of the sixth, Hank stands at the plate. Joe is on first and Tommy's on third. Hank takes a ball, then with the next pitch, he swings and slams that little leather sphere into far right field and over the fence. It's a three-run homer.

Tommy finishes up the game in a shutout. The Porterdale Blue Caps leave the field, shoulders slumped and heads hanging low.

"Gen, look!" Lillian points to the team bench. The scout huddles with Tommy and Hank in an intense conversation. My sister and I clutch hands.

"He's handing them envelopes." I stare at Lillian. "Do you think those are contracts?"

Big Sis doesn't take her eyes off the boys. "I'll give you my best beret if they aren't."

After a moment of pointing to things on the papers, the scout shakes Tommy's and Hank's hands. He's wearing a big grin as he tips his hat and leaves. Tommy and Hank shout and throw their caps in the air. The scout looks back and laughs, holding up his clasped hands in a "champs" gesture.

Tommy sprints over, grabs me up, and spins me around, lifting me off my feet. "Our dream has come true, Gen. Hank and I both have been contracted." He sets me on my feet and kisses me. "You still want to marry me?"

I'm breathless and giddy. "Oh, Tommy, you know I do!"

"Good, I'll come talk to your daddy in a little while. We'll make it official."

I look for Lillian, but she must have gone with Hank. I walk home alone, love putting wings on my feet.

I pace the hallway outside our private parlor. Tommy and Daddy have been in there for at least twenty minutes. What can be taking so long? This is just a formality, isn't it? Lillian walks down the hall on her way into her bedroom. She nods and mouths, "good luck." Do I need it? Has Daddy changed his mind? I pace again, certain I'll wear the polish off the floor before they finish and let me inside.

Finally, the door opens. I jump back, laughing. Daddy smiles and kisses my cheek, then goes to the kitchen. Tommy grabs my hand and pulls me into the parlor.

"Daddy said yes, didn't he?"

Tommy ends my question with a toe-curling kiss. When he pulls away, we sit on the settee.

"Your daddy said yes. We talked about me supporting you, and he gave me some good advice. Now, it's up to us to set a date. How about tomorrow?"

"What? Are you—"

He laughs. "I'm kidding. But we do need to speed things up. I have to report to training camp in six weeks."

"That doesn't give us much time, but I'm sure we can do it." I go to the writing desk and pull out a calendar. "Six weeks from Saturday is August ninth. So we could back up two weeks to July twenty-sixth. That gives me four weeks to get ready." I grab his hand, pulling him up. "Let's go ask Mama."

When we push open the kitchen door, she and Daddy are dancing to the radio in the kitchen. I stop at the threshold and watch them for a moment, then glance over my shoulder at Tommy.

He's intent on them. "I hope when we're their age, we're as much in love as they are," he whispers in my ear so as not to disturb them.

We wait until the music ends, then join them around the table. "Can we make some plans for the wedding?" I glance over my shoulder at Sarah, who's scooping coffee grounds into the percolator basket.

"Sarah, come join us. You're family … and you've got to make one of your spectacular cakes for us. Will you?"

She pulls out a chair and lowers into it. "You know I will, dearie."

Annie and Lillian join us, and I look around at the faces I love. And will miss when we leave. "So do you think we can pull a wedding together in a month?"

Mama nods. "As long as you don't want anything too elaborate."

"I don't. My one request is to wear your wedding dress." It's lovely, and the style is feminine and flattering.

Mama's eyes fill with tears. "I wasn't sure you'd want to."

I try to explain. "It carries the promise of deep, abiding love." I glance at Tommy. "The kind of love we want."

We finalize on having the wedding and reception at the church, since it will just be cake and punch. Mama and I talk about me carrying three of my favorite sunflowers tied with green and yellow ribbons. Giddy with excitement, I can hardly wait for the next month to be over. Tommy and I are finally getting married.

And I'll be leaving Sweetgum.

Chapter 9

TENSION IS HIGH, AND THE air in the dining room fairly vibrates. Since we chose today for the strike, the anticipation—held at bay for two weeks—has everyone jumpy. When I reenter the dining room with a fresh pot of coffee, Mrs. Grundy holds up her cup for more and, peering at me through slitty eyes, I don't know how, but she senses something's amiss. As I fill her cup, her attention leaves me and travels around the dining room. The lodgers who work in the mill are fidgety, and the usual morning chatter is subdued.

I glance at Annie, desperate for a diversion. She picks up a pitcher of water and winks. What is she about to do?

Little Sis crosses the dining room with aplomb, smiling at those she passes. When she reaches Mrs. Grundy's table, she picks up the half-full glass to refill. She tips the pitcher, but it slips in her hand, and in a full deluge, its content splash all over Mrs. Grundy.

The room hushes into silence.

"You stupid girl! Look what you've done." Mrs. Grundy jumps up and throws her napkin on the floor. "Now I've got to change. I'll be late for work, and if I'm docked any pay, you can bet it will come from my rent." She stomps out of the dining room.

A badly suppressed snicker sneaks from Irene Harp's nose. She claps her hands over her face and breaks into guffaws. Soft chuckles follow Irene's laughter, then all attempts to smother the mirth fail. Hilarity fills the room and surely follows Mrs. Grundy up the stairs.

Annie bangs a spoon on the pitcher. "Y'all better skedaddle. And don't forget your signs."

I release a pent-up breath and throw my arm around my sister. "You're the best, kiddo. Thank you." I shake my head. "That was worth a little lost income, if it comes to that, which I truly doubt it will."

Annie winks. "Glad I could contribute."

I glance at my watch. "It's six-ten. Twenty minutes until they clock in, so fifty minutes from now, the strike begins." My stomach pitches. "We need to get busy. Keep to our normal routine. I'll go collect the newspapers first, then meet you in the kitchen."

Annie's brows knit. "Did Lillian go to work already?"

"Not yet. Her shift starts at ten o'clock. She promised to bus tables before she goes." I can't help the grin that tugs my lips. "I think she wants to see what happens with the strike."

Our elder sister strolls into the kitchen. "Morning." She pours herself a cup of coffee and plucks a biscuit from the platter on the table. "How were the natives this morning?" She slathers her biscuit with butter and drizzles honey over it.

"Definitely restless. Mrs. Grundy knew something was up, but Annie sidetracked her by dumping an entire pitcher of water on her."

Lillian's jaw drops, revealing a mouthful of biscuit—quite a sight from our dignified Big Sis. I snicker. She snaps her jaw shut, then her lips turn upward. Pretty soon, she's laughing—behind a napkin, of course.

"Oh my, I wish I'd seen that. Annie, you're quick."

Little Sis shrugs one shoulder. "I do what I can for the cause."

We eat our breakfast, or what we can of it, considering our thoughts dwell with the mill workers.

At seven o'clock sharp, the bell clangs—Joe Ralston's suggestion to highlight the reason for the strike. I run out to the front porch. The door of the mill bursts open, and the workers pour out. Nearly everyone has a sign of simple paper or a piece of cardboard held aloft.

As prearranged, Joe moves to the front of the crowd and faces the mill doors, waiting for the supervisors to confront them. He volunteered for the job, saying, "Since I didn't get a contract from the Detroit Lions, I'll do it. Tommy and Hank can't jeopardize theirs."

I search the crowd for Tommy but can't find him. He made me

promise to stay on the porch in case tempers flare and things turn nasty.

It isn't long before the bell is silent and the doors slam open again. A dozen supervisors stream out and stand, arms akimbo, in front of the men. I can't tell if Mary's daddy is one of them, but I'm guessing he is. One of them, Manny Holland, the Yankee Mr. Spencer brought in last year, lifts up a megaphone.

"I don't know what you think you're doing, but all of you need to get back inside and start working. Now."

Joe steps forward, lifting his own megaphone. "Not until we have a meeting about the safety practices here. Sweetgum Mill has more accidents and deaths than any other mill in Georgia."

A new voice rises from the back of the crowd. "Who says?"

My gaze whips to behind the workers. It's one of Spencer's thugs. Intent on the mill and the supervisors, I didn't see them approach and doubt anyone else did. Spencer's strategy. They stand in three unified lines of—I count fourteen, billy clubs the size of baseball bats slapping against their palms. That's forty-two of Spencer's paid thugs against maybe a hundred of our men. I suck in a breath. Forty-two *armed* bullies against one hundred peaceful men ... and women.

The crowd turns as one. The bully-lines move as a single unit toward the workers. A few women skirt the supervisors and slip inside the mill. Others stand with the men. Joe's daddy puts an arm around his wife, his chest puffing out. Then he turns her toward the mill and pushes her gently until she nods and goes inside.

Then I see Tommy. He's in the front of the crowd, closest to Spencer's goons. "We're *peacefully* protesting unsafe practices. It's our right!" I thought Tommy wasn't going to be so prominent. My stomach pitches, and my heartbeat throbs in my throat. *Be careful, my love!*

"We'll show you scum your rights," shouts one of Spencer's torpedoes.

Joe steps forward. "Don't you care that children die in there?"

Taunts of "You can't bully us!" and "Murderer!" fly toward the approaching men. "We deserve a safer workplace!"

A brute in the center of the front line shouts, "You don't deserve nothin'."

A bottle flies, hitting him in the temple. My head snaps to the workers. Who threw it? The man grabs his head, blood seeping between his fingers. "Get 'em!" he shouts.

The hooligans scatter, swinging their clubs. Bile rises in my throat as I watch in horror. Clubs crack into skulls on the backswing and on the forehand. Blood spurts and several mill workers fall in the first thirty seconds. Rocks and bottles missile toward Spencer's mafia, but the workers are no match for the clubs.

Screams and cries for help rise above the shouting. It's pandemonium as the two factions merge into one throbbing, fighting mass. More and more of the workers fall. I lean so far over the porch railing, I'm in danger of tumbling into the flower bed. But I can't see Tommy.

It's all over in a matter of minutes. The only men left standing are Spencer's.

Sheriff Jackson arrives and arrests several men. He hesitates to handcuff some, but Spencer, who finally shows up after all the fighting is over, won't allow any leniency.

Though I search, I can't find Tommy. My feet want to fly up the street, but they're frozen in place, as though they remember my promise to him. An arm slides around my shoulder. It's Lillian.

"Tommy's in the kitchen. He needs stitches."

I stare at her. For what, I don't know. Maybe the reassurance he's okay? She gently turns me toward the front door and nudges me. That loosens my feet. I run and find Mama working over him, applying an ice pack to his head.

"Tommy!" I squat beside him and lift the edge of the ice pack to assess his injury. It's at least two inches long and runs from his eyebrow into his hairline. "I'll call Doc Adams. He won't be as busy as the hospital and can stitch as well as anyone. He won't talk either."

"I'll get him," Annie volunteers. "That way, the operator won't know."

"Good thinking." Lillian pushes her toward the back door. "Now hurry."

While we wait, Tommy rails against Spencer and his torpedoes. "Somehow, Spencer got wind of the strike. His mob was there too quickly and armed with clubs. A couple of them had knives, and one stabbed George Chambers. He's pretty bad off."

That's Dottie's daddy. "I hope they arrested the one who did the stabbing."

Tommy shakes his head, then winces. "Do you have some aspirin?"

I get him two along with a glass of water. "Do you have any idea who ratted?"

"I have my suspicions, and Elmer Dyer heads the list. He works in the baling room, keeps to himself." I stay by Tommy's side as he takes a long drink of water.

Mama and Sarah exchange glances. Sarah's expression turns to one of stealth. "We'll all have to be extra careful with what we say."

That goes without saying, so why did she? I glance between her and Mama. Those two are up to something. Before I can ask, Doc Adams arrives, setting his vet medical bag on the table.

As he pulls out some instruments, Sarah whispers to Mama. "Perhaps a well-placed red herring to flush out the varmint?"

I suck in my lips to keep from chuckling. Spencer's spies haven't dealt with anyone the likes of these two ladies.

Doc's all business but has a twinkle in his eye. "Tommy, let's take a look at this." He removes the ice pack. "Got yourself a pretty good whack, did you?"

He's probing Tommy's scalp beyond the wound. I peer closely. "What are you looking for?"

He leans his head near mine. "I want to make sure his skull is in one piece."

I gasp.

"Don't worry, Genessee. He appears to be hard-headed. No fractures."

"Can you be sure without an x-ray? Maybe he needs—"

Doc stops me with an intense stare. "I'm as sure as I can be without putting Tommy under Spencer's microscope. Now, Tommy, this might sting." He plunges a needle into Tommy's scalp.

When the area's numb, Doc puts eight stitches in him, then applies a bandage. "Don't get it wet for a few days. And come see me Saturday."

After Doc leaves, Tommy goes home to let his mama know he's all right and bring her and Willie back to eat with us. A few minutes later, Daddy arrives.

I run up to him. "Did you hear anything about the strike?"

He hugs me tight. "Scuttlebutt has it Spencer's looking for the organizers." He pulls back, putting both of his hands on my shoulders. "So far, Tommy's name isn't involved, but you'd better be ready if it is." He takes a deep breath. "Spencer's hot. His *sterling* reputation is at stake."

Mama unties her apron. "Did he talk to you, Frank?"

"So far, no, thankfully."

Before he can say anything more, Mrs. Mack, Tommy, and Tommy's seven-year-old brother, Willie, arrive. We all sit—Mrs. Mack between Tommy and me—and Daddy asks the blessing, adding a plea for mercy for the strikers. For Willie's sake, we keep the talk to our upcoming wedding.

Mrs. Mack lays her hand on mine. "I couldn't ask for a better wife for my Tommy. Welcome to our family, Genessee."

Tommy leans over and kisses his redheaded mama's right cheek.

I kiss her left one. "Thank you."

I've never figured out how Tommy missed out on his mama's red hair. Willie has dark auburn hair, but Tommy's brown is devoid of any red.

Daddy smiles at us, but his brow retains its furrow. There's something he's not saying. When Tommy, Willie, and Mrs. Mack— who says I'm to call her Mama Kara now—leave after dinner, Daddy pulls Tommy aside and whispers something to him. Tommy searches Daddy's eyes. Slowly, he nods.

Somehow, I know it's not good. Then again, nothing about this day has been. And I wonder...

Will anything in Sweetgum ever be the same?

Chapter 10

SOMETHING AWAKENS ME. I STARE into the darkness, listening. No crickets chirp. No owl hoots. Nothing. All is well.

So why the gooseflesh raising on my arms?

Unable to shake the eerie feeling, I slip from the covers and cross to my window overlooking the mill and woods. Nothing unusual. I turn—but stop and look again. This time, I wrap my fingers around the curtain, pull it back, and peer toward the village. A line of faint orange glows on the horizon behind the movie house. I glance at my wristwatch—only a little after midnight. That's no dawn breaking out there.

I suck in a breath and, with leaden feet, hurry down the hall to the lobby. One look out the front window confirms my fears.

Flames leap into the air above the mill village. Those houses are little more but clapboard and wood frame, fuel for a fire.

I tear back to the family quarters and throw open Mama and Daddy's door. "Fire in the village. Hurry!"

Dashing back to my room, I grab a robe and scream for my sisters. I haven't heard the bell of the fire truck clanging, so I snatch up the phone, tap the switch hook, and raise the operator. I don't give her a chance to speak. "Fire in the village!"

"Got it!" She hangs up.

Daddy runs into the lobby, his hair wild, shirt hanging out of his pants, and still fastening one suspender. "You girls need to stay here. Gather the other women for a bucket brigade. Annie, you get on the roof in case any sparks land there. The others can pass the buckets to you. Start soaking the roof." He races out the door with Mama on his heels.

Lillian rings the fire bell in the hotel, then marshals the few men to follow Daddy. We hustle the ladies to the barn for buckets from the supply we keep for this very reason. Lillian and I set the ladder against the side of the hotel, and Annie scampers up to the roof. Agnes Floyd mans the water pump.

"Get all the buckets filled and ready. Pass a few up to Annie now. Lillian and I are going door to door to wake people and get them out."

We race across Main and down Church Street until we're behind the supervisors' housing. The first two rows are fine, but just in case the wind changes, we help rouse them from their beds, then rush toward the buildings on fire. The firemen arrive, but flames are gobbling houses like a pack of starving wolves.

"Is everyone out?" I holler at Mrs. Barnett over the roar of the fire and shouts from the firemen. Thick smoke fills the air. Breathing is hard. Shouting difficult. A cough racks my chest.

"On this row, yes. Your mama came here first."

"Have you seen her and Daddy since?"

"No." She points toward the next row. "They went that way."

Lillian and I barrel ahead. Ash floats in the air, and acridity coats my tongue. Third Row has several houses burning, and on Fourth, at least six roofs have caught. On no! The fire has leaped to Fifth now.

Tommy lives on Seventh Row. I want to fly to his house, but the people here are in danger first. The heat is so intense from the flames, I have to turn my head away to draw a breath.

Lillian tugs my arm. "Come on, Gen. Get moving."

God, keep Tommy and his family safe!

Behind us, a house collapses in a roar. Sparks billow and fly. Another house catches. We race between two shanties on Fourth Row. On Fifth, I turn to the right, and Lillian heads left.

"Meet me in the middle." I can't believe people are still asleep, but then I realize only a short time has actually passed since I woke up.

I knock on the door, screaming, "Fire!" As soon as footsteps sound inside, I race to the next house. I pound and scream until I hear a response, then run to the next. On and on. My eyes sting so bad, I can hardly see.

When I meet Lillian, she grabs my hand and we hurry onward. More people join us to help roust others from their beds. When we reach the sixth row, I look back. The fire's not far behind.

And it's racing toward us.

"Lillian?" Blinking to clear my tears, I gaze around wildly. In the smoke, I've lost my sister. "Lillian, where are you?"

I can't see more than three or four feet. Everything's a blur and my throat burns. I sprint away from the fire.

But then a wall of fire rises up in front of me.

It's all around me.

The air sears. Houses disappear in flames like popsicles on a summer day. I don't know which way to turn. Another fire truck zooms up the alleyway between the sixth and seventh rows.

Thank you, Lord!

I follow it toward Tommy's house. Suddenly, someone grabs my arm and nearly jerks me off my feet, slapping my head.

It's Lillian. She is staring at me with fear in her eyes. "Your hair was on fire!"

I explore with my fingers, but my scalp is okay. "Thank you. Have you seen Mama and Daddy?"

She shakes her head, her brows puckering. "No, and no one else has either. At least not for a while."

"What should we do?"

"Keep helping where we're needed. Back at First Row."

For the next few hours, we work to keep people safe, deliver buckets of water to drink, and put salve on burns that aren't too bad. We comfort those whose homes are gone, offering clothing and food. If we need to, we could put cots in the barn temporarily. At least it would keep them out of the elements.

Soon, villagers whose houses didn't burn offer the victims a dress, a pair of shoes—whatever they have, they share. When it's all over, it's almost dawn. Fifty-eight houses are nothing but piles of ashes. Even more are damaged. That means fifty-eight families lost everything. Many more lost half their possessions. Four people have been taken to the hospital with burns, and the fire chief reports one death, but that person hasn't yet been identified.

My heart breaks.

In dawn's first light, men sift through piles of charred and smoking lumber, looking for hot spots and anything to salvage. They stack whatever isn't ash onto the street for owners to claim.

Our energy spent, and with eyes and lungs burning, Lillian and I trudge home. I'm anxious to find Tommy and my parents to hear what they may have learned about how the fire started.

I cross the street and run smack into Tommy. His arms slide around me. I cling to him and burst into tears. "I was so worried about you. Are you all right? Did your house burn? Your mama and Willie?" They can't take another loss.

"I kept looking for you. I knew you'd try to help people." His face is smudged with soot. Mine probably is too. His face is drawn, and he looks exhausted.

"You aren't thinking of going to work, are you?"

"No. I doubt even Spencer will expect anyone today. Maybe a few who live in the hotel and the tenements." He glances around, then pulls me close and whispers in my ear. "The fire spread too fast to be natural. A few of us went searching and found gas cans behind Joe's house. It's a miracle he and his family got out alive."

I blink. "Are you say—"

He puts his fingertips over my mouth and shakes his head. "Shh. Not a word. Just wait." He kisses me. "Go on home now." He disappears between two half-burned-out houses.

As Lillian and I approach the hotel, Annie runs toward us and flings herself into our arms, sobbing. "I've been so frightened. You didn't come, and neither have Mama or Daddy."

I rub her back in small circles. "Shh, we're here now, and they should be along any minute. Remember, they're helping people, consoling them."

Lillian wraps her arms around both of us. "It's what they do, sugar. It's what *we* do."

Annie sniffs and takes a stuttering breath. "I know you're right, but I was so scared. I watched from our rooftop, hoping to see you, but the fire was so huge, burning everything in its path."

I catch a whiff of my singed robe. "I stink of soot and smoke. I'm going to get a quick sponge bath, then wait for our parents. Holler if they get here sooner. Lillian, do you mind if I go first?"

She shakes her head. I hurry through washing, bathing my bloodshot eyes with cold water, then throw my pajamas and robe in the laundry pile. In a clean dress, I hurry outside, expecting to see Mama, at least. Only Lillian and Annie are on the porch.

Sarah slips out and joins us. "Girls, I need your help with breakfast. Fire or no fire, Mr. Spencer expects our lodgers to work today. And everyone is already late."

I nod. "You're right. Come on, Annie. We'll start getting gravy and biscuits ready while Big Sis bathes."

We go into the kitchen. In a few minutes, Lillian joins us. She lifts a large serving bowl filled with cheese grits. "We'll serve buffet-style today. I wonder what Mr. Spencer will do about the houses." She gives a covert glance around. Nobody is in the dining room yet. She whispers, "I don't know if you noticed, but the fire started at Joe Ralston's."

I pick up a platter of biscuits and a bowl of gravy. "Tommy told me."

She puts a finger to her lips and nods. I set the biscuits and gravy on the serving table as Mrs. Grundy and a few others enter the dining room.

Once all the lodgers are serving themselves, we take a few minutes to eat. Sarah pours coffee for us.

"You'll be needin' this today." She puts plates of eggs and grits in front of us.

The kitchen girls arrive, and I'm grateful for all five of them today. After I help Sarah get the pasties ready, the girls will wrap the dinner bundles and deliver them.

Sarah punches down the bread dough she's kneading. "Mrs. Mack stopped by while you were still bathin'. She said she'd come by to help with the cooking. She's a good woman, she is."

Lord bless my future mother-in-law. "That's wonderful. I feel like I'm about to drop." My eyes stray to the door, waiting for Mama and Daddy.

Lillian puts her arm around me. "Gen, I'm fixing to go to Norton's and let them know I can't come in today. Then I'll find Mama and Daddy. Okay?"

I breathe a sigh. "Thank you. I can't understand why they aren't home."

"I'm sure they're still helping people." She gives me a quick hug, then leaves the kitchen. I slide the last pan of pasties into the oven.

But only a moment later, Big Sis is back, her face pale. Annie's right behind her. Her sweet features are contorted, and her eyes are brimming. Sarah's hand flies to her cheek when she sees them. My stomach rolls.

I clutch my apron, afraid to ask but desperate to know. "What is it?"

"Mama's in the hospital. Daddy ... Daddy ..." Lillian breaks down, sobbing.

I grab her shoulders. "What about Daddy? Tell me!"

Annie throws herself at me, wailing, "He's gone."

Gone? What does that even mean?

I pull Annie away and stare at her. "Gone where?"

An ugly truth burns in her eyes, as god-awful as last night's inferno. Shaking starts in my legs and works its way up to my arms. "You don't mean—you *can't* mean he's—" My throat closes. I can't say it. It can't be! Not Daddy. Not *my* daddy. He's too strong. A rock. Our rock. I squeeze Annie's arms. "Stop it, Annie. Stop it right now!"

But her tears keep coming, and her lips keep quivering.

Lillian pries my hands off her. "The fire got him, Gen, when Daddy was helping people escape. That first house that collapsed near us? In there." My sister's voice is raw and far too thick with grief.

"Nooo!"

A wail rises to my ears. It takes a few long seconds for me to realize it's mine.

Sarah gathers us to her bosom. "My poor babies." Her tears join ours.

I can't imagine life without Daddy. *Mama!* She'll be lost without him. I struggle to stop sobbing.

"Lillian?"

She attempts to regain her composure, sniffing and mopping her face with her sleeve. "Wha ... what?"

"You said Mama was taken to the hospital. What happened? Will she be okay?"

Lillian glances at each one of us, then draws a shaky breath. "She was helping a family out and went back for a toddler. Just as she handed him to his mama, the wall collapsed on her. Someone pulled her out, but her right side is badly burned."

Lillian and I stand at the foot of Mama's bed, watching her chest rise and fall. The doctors have her heavily sedated. For the pain, they say. There's a cage over her keeping the covers from laying on her burns. One arm is swathed in white gauze, and blisters line her neck and jawline. My tears dot her bed covers.

The doctor—tall and imposing, with a hawk-like nose—makes a couple of notations on her chart. "Ladies, can we talk out in the hall?" He gestures for us to precede him. I glance at Lillian. She nods and nudges me forward.

Outside Mama's room, he leads us to a grouping of hard wooden chairs. "Your mother has severe burns on her right leg and arm, deep into the muscle. Those cause me grave concern. She will most likely lose the leg just above the knee. The arm will, at best, be severely crippled. The burns to her left side aren't anywhere near as bad."

My lungs empty in a whoosh.

Lillian gasps. "Can't you do anything to save her leg and arm?"

The doctor sighs. I guess he faces things like this all the time, especially in a mill village. "I'll watch the burns, but don't expect too much." He rises. "My condolences on your father."

I can't speak around the lump in my throat. Lillian nods as the doctor blurs before me. When he leaves, she links arms with me. "Let's get Annie and go home."

They wouldn't let Little Sis in to see Mama, saying she's too young. In the waiting room next to the front doors, Annie fidgets. Her head snaps up as we approach. She jumps to her feet.

"How is she?"

"Sedated, sugar. She wasn't awake and didn't even know we were there." I take her hand. "Let's go home." I'll wait until we're home and tell her the rest in private.

When we arrive, it appears half the church is in the hotel lobby. Tommy waits for me, and I fall into his arms, my tears wetting his shirt.

"Come out on the back porch." He leads me away from the crowd. "Everyone wants to help, but nobody quite knows where to start. Your parents always led any efforts like this."

I go to Buster's pen and pull him out. Tommy cleans the litter box and refills the ferret's water and food while I snuggle him. He doesn't seem any worse for the fire. The little fellow lifts onto his back feet, sniffing my tear-stained face.

As I pet Buster's silky fur, I peer up at Tommy. "There's something I've been meaning to ask you. The other night, before you left, Daddy whispered something to you. Can you tell me what he said?"

Tommy sighs and screws the lid on Buster's food pellet jar. "He warned me to be on the lookout for trouble." A frown creases his brow. "We all knew Spencer would do something. We just didn't know it would be so deadly." He sets the jar on the porch.

I close my eyes, staving off tears. "We've got to do something, Tommy. How can we fight him?"

"Gen, honey?" Tommy sits down on the porch step. "*We* can't. Sweetheart, I've got to go. Tonight. Now."

"Go where?" Buster squirms in my arms. I give him a goat kibble. "To Texas."

My brows knit. "I thought you didn't have to be there until after our wedding."

"That's not why." His gaze surveys the yard, and he glances behind us. "We're sure last night was retribution for the strike." He lowers his voice. "It could have been a lot worse."

"What do you mean?" How in the world could it possibly have been worse?

"Two more gas cans were found. One was empty, the other half empty. The only people with cars in Sweetgum are Doc Adams, Spencer, and a few of the supervisors. Your daddy has the use of one too."

"We know it wasn't Daddy, and it sure wouldn't have been Doc Adams. That only leaves—"

"Exactly." He reaches over and tickles Buster's tummy.

I frown. "But I don't understand what that has to do with why you have to leave."

"Spencer suspects I was involved in organizing the strike. Somehow, he found out Dan Kitchens came to speak with us. He connected him with Joe and Hank and me. We were all there. Joe's house burned and so did Hank's. It was only thanks to your daddy, ours didn't. But for Mama's and Willie's sake, I've got to go right away."

"But won't that prove you had something to do with the strike?"

"I don't know, but Spencer could have me arrested, and I'd miss training camp. I don't know if he could hold me for long, but he can make life miserable. And his goons could trump up phony evidence. I *have* to go." He takes my hands. "I want you to come with me. We can get married in Texas."

How could I possibly leave Mama? But how can I *not* go with Tommy?

Lord, why now? It's not fair!

My daddy's words fill my heart. *Life isn't fair, little girl. But what doesn't kill you makes you stronger.*

My heart splits in two. Duty and love. I open my mouth, but the words don't want to pass my lips. I have to force them out. "I ... can't. Mama ... with Daddy ..." I make a vague gesture behind me. "I can't leave now. They need me. Sarah ... Lillian. Annie."

His eyes brim. "I sorta knew that. But, baby, I can't stay."
He kisses me and holds me tight.

I didn't think I had any tears left inside, but here they are, raining hot down my cheeks. Buster squirms between us, struggling to break free. I sniff. "What about us?"

"Gen, I love you. That will never change. Maybe someday, when your mama is better ..." He leaves the rest unspoken.

I try to smile, but my attempt isn't very successful. "I guess maybe God is telling us to wait."

Tommy rises, pulling me up with him. "Genessee, I promise you, I'll find a way for us." He holds me close and kisses me once more. His lips taste like desperation and sorrow.

Behind us, a door clatters, and Sheriff Jackson's voice booms, echoing through the house.

"Where's Tommy Mack? I have a warrant for his arrest."

Chapter 11

Tommy disappears around the side of the hotel in a flash of his coattail, leaving me alone with Buster. I run inside and set him on the floor. "Do your best, little buddy." I stand back and observe.

Mrs. Mack, who has snuggled the ferret several times, winks at me and screeches, "Help! A varmint is loose."

The crowd scatters. Women scream. Men holler. Everyone's shouting at once.

The sheriff jumps, his hand jerking to his firearm. "Where is it? What is it?"

Deputy Limehouse clambers on top of the registration desk, gun drawn. "It went that-away." He swings his pistol toward the parlor.

"Holster that gun, you idiot," the sheriff hollers at Limehouse.

"No, it went that way." Lillian points to the dining room.

Freckle-faced, seven-year-old Willie runs in circles. "I'll get it!"

"Don't let it get into the kitchen!" Gladys Grundy clings to Deputy Limehouse on the registration desk. I don't know how she got up there, but Daddy would have laughed. The room blurs as my eyes fill with tears.

A streak of brown fur flies between ankles, speeding toward the back porch, leaving the women high-stepping and screeching. My little buddy knows where safety lies. I run after him and secure him inside his home. "Good job, Buster." For a reward, I hand him two raisins from his box of treats beside the pen.

Back in the lobby, a red-faced sheriff is under attack by Mrs. Mack. "Sheriff Jackson, shame on you." Her index finger pokes him in the chest, accentuating each word. He backs away with every jab. He should know a Southern lady takes no prisoners when angered. And a redheaded Southern lady? Hmm-hm! "This entire town is in mourning. We'd be a whole lot better served if you looked for the person those gas cans belong to."

Several folks gasp, and murmurs of "Gas cans?" circulate in the lobby.

Mrs. Mack huffs and crosses her arms, daring him to argue.

The sheriff squints, a nervous tic pinching his left eye. "What gas cans?"

Mr. Patterson steps forward, four cans clutched in his hands. "These, sheriff. Two were found last night behind Joe Ralston's house"—he raises his left hand—"where the fire started. These other two"—he raises his right hand—"were beside the Barnett house."

Deputy Limehouse jumps down from the registration desk, leaving Mrs. Grundy perched there alone. He swaggers over to Mr. Patterson. "How do you know one of them didn't start it?"

It only takes three strides for Doc Adams to square off nose-to-nose with the deputy. "Limehouse, that's about the dumbest statement I've ever heard. Why would they burn their own houses and put their families in danger? Besides, both men were rousted out of bed by Pastor Taylor."

The deputy's mouth contorts. Then it opens. It shuts again. Open and shut like a gasping fish. Finally, his lip curls. "Is that so?"

"Shut up, Limehouse." Sheriff Jackson flings out his hand at Mr. Patterson. "I'll take those." He tips his hat to my sisters and me. "Ladies, I'm sorry to have intruded on your time of sorrow."

Mr. Patterson helps Mrs. Grundy off the desk. After he, the sheriff, and a red-faced deputy depart, Mrs. Mack slips her arm through mine. "Brilliant diversion, Gen," she whispers. "He completely forgot his warrant."

The tightness in my chest won't loosen. I swallow the tears that beg release, barely able to nod.

"I won't ask if you're all right. I know you're not. Sugar, I'm so sorry things happened like this. Tommy loves you very much. Don't ever doubt that."

I lean my head on her shoulder. "Thank you. I love him, too, but right now, I can't see beyond today. Somehow, my sisters and I have to find the strength to pick up the reins of running this hotel by ourselves. Mama's going to be out of commission for a long time." *If she survives. Please, God, don't take her too.*

"You can count on my help. And that of several others."

Lillian weaves her way through the remains of the crowd with a notepad and pencil. Something is different in her manner.

"I've asked Elmer Dyer to move in with Leroy Allman." She leans close and lowers her voice. "Leroy will keep an eye on Mr. Dyer and feed him false information if need be." She straightens. "A couple of the other men have gone to the tenements and will room together there. That will free up the dormitory on the third floor. We can house at least four families in their place."

"How will they have any privacy, Lillian? Use your head. It's an open bunk room, for pity's sake."

"I already took care of that. Mr. Patterson said he and others will help put up some temporary privacy walls or curtains."

The enormity of loss sits like a huge boulder on my shoulders. I *know* it's not my responsibility, but … "That helps four families, but there are a lot of others." I appreciate my sister's foresight. In one way, I wish she didn't have her job at Norton's. Then she could help me more here. Then again, we won't make it without her wages.

A lock of hair drops over Lillian's forehead as she looks down at her list. She swipes it out of her eyes. "I overheard somebody say Mr. Spencer's bringing in some tents until the houses can be rebuilt. And he'd better rebuild. He needs the workers, and with this mess, he won't get anyone from outside Sweetgum."

After everyone leaves, Lillian, Annie, and I go to the kitchen to help get the dinner bundles ready. Beulah, Charity, Grace, and Glory already have the napkins laid out for us. No matter what happens, life goes on in Sweetgum. The workers will get peanut butter sandwiches today, but they'll understand.

Little Sis opens a large can of peanut butter while Lillian cuts open biscuits on the counter and lays them side by side. "Annie, don't spread it too thick. We're giving them two each."

I bend over and lift a heavy bucket of apples with both hands. Are we putting these in the dinner bundles? A memory of picking apples with Daddy floats through my mind, and the room blurs again. A layer of fog descends over my brain. I need to collect my thoughts, but they want to scatter like dandelion fluff on a windy day. How can life just "go on" with Daddy not here? We haven't even buried him. Tears wet my cheeks.

Beulah takes the bucket of apples from me. "I'll do this, Miss Genessee."

"Thank you."

My sisters gather close, both weeping. It's time I tell Annie that Mama might lose her leg and maybe her arm.

She cries bitterly but accepts it fairly well. "At least she's alive."

Sarah comforts her, then shoos us out of the kitchen. "Girls, you go into the parlor. Mrs. Mack and Mrs. Patterson have come to help. I'll telephone Mr. Pugh to come advise you."

I swipe my sleeve across my eyes. "I forgot about the deacons. Thank you, Sarah."

In the parlor, Lillian-the-list-maker pulls out a pad of paper and a pencil. "We need to write down everything we have to do. Number one." She licks the tip of the pencil. Why does she do that? "Arrange for Daddy's f-fu …" Her face crumples again. "I keep hearing that house collapse and knowing Daddy was in it …"

It's hard to breathe. I've got a lingering cough from last night's smoke. And my tears won't stop. Do we have a quota of tears within us? Is God keeping them in a bottle like I've heard? What will He do with them?

Annie grabs my hand and pulls me over to where Lillian sits on the davenport. As we huddle close, I feel a little strength in our togetherness seeps into my bones.

Little Sis draws a shuddering breath. "We have to think practical now. We can't fall apart. There's a hotel to run, and Mama to think of."

Lillian and I manage small smiles over her head. I squeeze her shoulder. "You're right. We need to collect ourselves. Lillian, the list?"

She nods. "Number one, call the funeral home." She stops and her eyes meet mine. "Oh, Gen. It just hit me. Tommy's gone too. Oh, honey—"

Like my lost dreams, my heart crumbles as if it were a cake of dry mud.

The morning dawns hot and sticky. Even the rooster's crow isn't as loud as usual. I open my eyes with the closing of the bedroom door. It's Annie and her hair's wet.

I sit up and push the covers to my waist. "I can't believe you're up before me."

A half smile pulls at one side of her lips, then fails. She shrugs. "I couldn't sleep. The bathroom's all yours."

"Is Lillian awake?"

"I don't know. Her door's still shut." Annie towel dries her hair as she stands before her closet.

I slip into my bathrobe. "What are you looking for?"

She turns, frowning. "My funeral dress. It's not here."

"Sarah took it last night, along with mine and Lillian's. She's ironing them."

Annie ties the belt to her robe. "I'll go get them while you bathe."

The normalcy of our conversation is weird. I sit on the edge of the bathtub as it fills with cold water. A bucket of hot water from the stove's reservoir stands beside the tub. Annie's thoughtfulness touches me. As I pour it into the tub, I see Mama doing this task for Big Sis and me when we were small. As I lower myself into the lukewarm water, I offer up a silent prayer for Mama's healing. It's going to be so hard to tell her about Daddy. *Help her fight any infection. And help us through today.*

Soon, we're all three dressed. In the kitchen, Sarah stands over us until we eat some grits. "I don't want any of you passing out during the service. You need some strength."

I try to smile and nod. My stomach can't decide whether it's upset because it needs food or because it doesn't want any. Either way, it's hard to force anything between my lips. Surprisingly, though, Sarah is right. After two bites, my stomach settles. I can't recall if I ate yesterday.

I glance up at my sisters. "Are you both thinking stupid normal thoughts?"

Annie sets her spoon in her bowl. "Yeah, and it feels really strange. Like I shouldn't. But then I do it again."

"My thoughts bounce all over." Lillian grimaces. "From Daddy, to the linen closet, to Mama, to the hotel account books. Which reminds me, who will do those?" She claps her hand over her mouth. "See?" Tears brim and spill over onto her cheeks.

Sarah stands behind her and puts her hands on Lillian's shoulders. "Girls, don't feel guilty for your thoughts. They're completely normal. I think it's God's way of not letting us sink into a grief so deep we can't escape."

After a moment, I nod, followed by Lillian and then Annie. Sarah's breath puffs from her round cheeks. "Good. Now, it's time to go."

The church service is beautiful. Daddy's casket is closed, but I bend over it and whisper, "I'll always remember what you've taught me, Daddy."

Bud Pugh, chairman of the deacons, speaks eloquently about all my father accomplished in the church and the community. Several people give testimony to his impact on their lives. I must have soaked a half-dozen hankies. I think Sarah filled her pocketbook with them.

Now, at the gravesite, a few folks tell funny stories about Daddy, making us all laugh. He would have loved that. Finally, at Mr. Bud's direction, we girls—his daughters—each take a handful of dirt and toss it onto the casket. Then, we whisper goodbye.

Lillian links arms with Annie and me. "It's not really goodbye. He lives on in our hearts, and we'll see him again. Remember that."

I lay my head on her shoulder. "I'm so glad you're my big sister. I love you."

Annie smiles through her tears. "Me too. I love both of you."

Sarah approaches us. "Let's go home. We need to see to the dinner, then your mama. Life doesn't stop for mourning in Sweetgum." Her words hold a bitter tinge.

"Mama? Are you awake?" I hover at her bedside and rest my hand gently on her uninjured arm. Her eyes remain closed, her lashes dark against her pale cheeks. It appears likely she'll keep her arm, but they amputated her leg yesterday. The bedcovers look strange, sinking to the mattress instead of in a raised formation over her lower leg. They're still keeping her sedated for the pain and for something the doctor calls "ghost pains."

Annie stands beside me, stroking Mama's shoulder. The doctor allowed her in when we promised she wouldn't make a scene. Lillian moves about the room, writing the names in a little notebook from the cards on the bouquets of flowers. Most are hand-picked from gardens or meadows, exquisite in their simplicity, conveying the sender's love. Each bears a scrap of lined paper, and a few have get-well cards. There is one display from Mr. Spencer, obviously from a florist, ordered by his secretary, Mrs. Grundy. There's no scent in its blossoms.

A sturdy nurse, who puts me in mind of a weightlifter, sweeps into the room. We step back from Mama's bed as the woman bustles around her, taking her pulse, reading her chart, checking her bandages, and making notes.

Annie sidles up to her as she replaces Mama's chart on its hook at the foot of the bed. "Has she woken up at all yet?"

Mrs. Harmon—her name tag reads—turns a practiced smile to us. "Not yet. It's best this way. She can heal and move beyond the worst pain while she sleeps." She strides to the door.

"Please." I put my hand out to stop her departure. "Will you call us if she asks for us or Daddy?"

Tender compassion shines in her eyes. "I'm not always here, but I'll leave word at the desk."

Lillian glances up from her note-taking. "If she wakes up and asks about Daddy, what will you tell her?"

Mrs. Harmon returns to our side. She takes Lillian's hand between hers. "Dear girl, we would not blurt out any news about your father. Nor about her leg. Not at this point in her recovery, especially. We leave that to the family or the doctor."

My "thank you" sounds weak in my ears.

"Why don't you girls wait a bit, and I'll see if the doctor can come speak with you."

I stroke Mama's forehead on the left side. There's a small area of blisters on the other. And her earlobe is blistered. Poor little ear. Annie leans on the foot of the bed and Lillian against the window ledge.

The doctor comes in a moment later. "Girls, what do you want to know?"

I glance at Lillian, then voice our question. "When do you think she'll be awake?"

"We will start weaning her off the medication in another few days when her healing is a little more advanced."

Lillian crosses the room and moves between him and Mama's bed. "Please make sure nobody tells her about our father. That's our job, and we can do it so she won't give up hope."

His eyebrows raise and he nods. "Excellent. I'll note it on her chart and tell the head nurse." He scribbles on the page. "However, if she asks me about her leg, I will tell her that. To put it off isn't smart. Your mama's an intelligent woman."

I stop Lillian from saying more. "That's fine, thank you, Doctor. One more question. Do you think she will be all right?"

"If her arm continues healing as it is so far, she will be able to keep it. But remember, there's muscle loss, and it won't be of much use. Her other burns are not life-threatening, and she's a strong woman. A fighter."

His words bolster my courage, but the main question, the one burning my tongue, still begs release. I move to stand between my sisters. "When can we take her home?"

"Not for another week or so. I want her stronger."

Anticipation swells ... but trepidation rides fast on its heels. How many special needs of Mama's might take us by surprise? Will we be able to care for her?

Chapter 12

OUT OF NECESSITY, THE DAYS and weeks have taken on more regimentation than ever before. Though weariness weights my limbs, I'm glad for that fact. It leaves me little time to succumb to my longing for the sight of Tommy's face or the sound of Daddy's laugh. Grief slaps me when I least expect it. Yesterday, as I kneaded bread dough, I burst into tears. That set off Sarah and Annie. Even the kitchen girls get teary-eyed the minute one of us does.

Annie and I are responsible for every aspect of the hotel except the food. Sarah has taken over planning all the meals. She orders the food, slaughters and prepares chickens, and inventories how much pork is left in the smokehouse.

However, Sarah mentioned she needed help with the chickens. Beulah can do the job quite neatly, but with just her and Sarah, it takes too much time. So Big Sis volunteered. Watching her wring a chicken's neck is possibly the funniest sight ever. She pulls a face and won't watch when she snaps her wrist, but she has a knack for it. One good twist and that bird is limp, on its way to cluck in glory.

"The last of the chickens are on the porch, ready to be plucked." Lillian washes her hands at the sink. "I'm leaving for work. See you at supper. I'm off tomorrow."

Oh dear. I hope— "You're not jeopardizing your job by taking the day off, are you?"

"Not hardly. Mr. Norton barely has enough—" Lillian sniffs.

Hmm ... what isn't she saying? "Enough what?"

"Nothing. Mama comes home tomorrow. I should be here." She turns and walks out the door.

Mama. Home. I can hardly wait. It's been a month since the fire.

When we told her about Daddy, she shocked us by saying she already knew.

Visibly upset, Lillian had thumped her hands on her hips. "Did a nurse tell you?"

Her wistful smile had tugged at my heart. "No, my darling. Your daddy came to me in a dream. He told me he's happy and waiting for me to join him someday. Then he disappeared." Her eyes welled momentarily.

That shut all our mouths. Mama says she's at peace with Daddy's passing, but sorrow has replaced the light that used to reside in her eyes. There is a subtle but definite change in her. It's as if without Daddy, she isn't whole.

Speaking of whole … when the doctor told Mama about her leg, he said she accepted it quite well. Whether she weeps at night, when she's alone, remains to be seen. She's never been one who wears her emotions openly for everybody to view.

The hospital ordered her a chair with wheels. How we'll pay for it, I don't know. We've lost Daddy's salary, pitiful as it was, from the church and the general store. The hotel houses and feeds us, but the money we earn is miserly, Mr. Spencer being the skinflint that he is. I hope at least he will pay for the wheeled chair.

"Annie, did you happen to hear what the nurse said about Mama's meals?" I plop a mound of bread dough into a greased bowl.

Little Sis pauses her chopping, her knife raised for the next carrot. "She can eat whatever she wants. And yesterday she said she wants chicken and dumplings and succotash. The hospital food is terrible. I know she's lost weight."

"I'm just glad finding out about Daddy wasn't a devastating shock to her." I cover the bowl with a towel and deposit it on the stove's warming shelf to rise. "Did she say anything more to you about the dream she had about Daddy?"

Annie's eyes glow. "Yes. He told her God called him home, and she'd be okay because Jesus would be with her. She said in the dream, she watched him approach heaven's gates, and when they swung wide for him, he disappeared."

Did Mama say that for Annie's benefit? She could have realized since nobody mentioned him, he was gone. Or maybe she saw the house collapse. We haven't spoken of it. Maybe one day, I'll ask her if the dream was real.

At least we still have her. *Thank you, God, for leaving her with us.*

I start another batch of dough. "Annie, when you get done there, would you go see what's in the salad garden? And if there are enough tomatoes, pick some green ones. Mama loves them fried."

"Okay. Oh!" She digs in her pocket and pulls out an envelope. "I'm sorry, I forgot to give you this." Her lips stretch into a wide smile. "It's from Tommy."

I brush the flour off my hands, sit at the table, and rip open the envelope.

My darling Genessee,

I long to hear your voice and hold your hand. How is your mama? I haven't gotten a letter from you yet, and I'm quite anxious for news. My mother wrote but it was mostly about Willie. It's strange, I was so worried about her grieving for Vera, but now with me leaving and your family's trouble, it's helped her forget, even if just a little. She feels needed. That's not saying we're glad for what happened to your daddy and mama, Gen. Not at all. But God has already brought some good from it, at least, if that's any consolation.

There's a smudge after *consolation.* He wrote something else but crossed it out and then tried to erase it. What could it have been?

Training camp is great. The fellas are nice, and the coach is terrific. He says I'm going to be a valued addition to the team. It's really something—to be appreciated as a ballplayer, I mean. They feed us really well.

I miss you, sweetheart. How I want you here with me! I know you can't leave right now, but maybe it won't be too much longer. Please write to me soon. I miss you.

All my love,
Tommy

I slide the letter back into its envelope. I'm glad Mrs. Mack feels needed again. Wait—I pull out the letter again, and my gaze flies over it once more. "He doesn't mention Spencer evicting his mama and Willie from the house."

Annie picks up a garden basket. "He probably hasn't heard yet. Do you know what Mrs. Mack is going to do?"

"I don't." I slip the letter into my pocket. "I have an idea, though. Go on and get the salad vegetables. I have some details to work out first."

The back porch is sitting height, so there are only two steps before the landing. Lillian and I carry the wheeled chair up with Mama in it. It's awkward, even though she's lost weight. Since her right arm is still heavily bandaged and in a sling, she can only cling to the chair's left arm. Her eyes are flooded with fear, but she won't give voice to it. But Lillian and I see it, and we're careful not to tip her. I realize, however, this couldn't be done with just one person. We lower the chair on the porch.

Lillian opens the back door. "Let's ask if Mr. Patterson would help build a ramp over the stairs here. You know, like the kind we have at Norton's for the delivery men to push their hand trucks up? That way, we can push Mama instead of carrying her and the chair."

"Now you're on the trolley, Lillian. It's a great idea." I push Mama into the kitchen, where Sarah, Annie, and the kitchen girls welcome her home. Steaming bowls filled with all of her favorites sit on the table.

Mama's smile is sweet but wistful. "My goodness, thank you for the warm welcome. It feels like a year instead of a month since I've been home." Her words are meant to be cheery, but her voice holds a quiver I've not heard before. Like an old granny's.

We roll her to the table. As we take our places, my eyes land on Daddy's empty chair. He should be here to ask the blessing. A lump lodges in my throat. When I pull my eyes away, Mama and my sisters are staring at his chair too. Then Lillian clears her throat and asks the blessing. Mama covertly raises her napkin to the corner of her eye. I reach out and squeeze her hand.

Lillian has Mama's food cut up for her, and with her first bite of chicken and dumplings, she closes her eyes and savors it. When she swallows, she smiles. "Oh, how I've missed home cooking. Those hospital cooks need some lessons, Sarah."

While she was still in the hospital, I approached the subject of bedrooms. Did she want to remain in her and Daddy's? Our conversation comes back to me.

"Of course I do. I'll feel closer to him there."

"It won't make you sad?"

"Maybe, but it's better than completely losing his presence."

I guess I'd feel the same.

We eat quietly, with only the sound of our forks against the dishes to break the silence. Too soon, Mama slides her half-empty plate to the side.

"Sarah, as much as I love this, I find I can't eat what I did before." She lays her napkin on the table. "We need to talk about some changes here. The doctor warned me it's going to be a long time before I regain my strength—if I do." There are dark circles beneath her eyes. "And then with this,"—she nods toward her crippled arm—"all I will be able to do is be the girls' mama. I can train y'all on my recipes, but I won't be much actual use in the kitchen. We're going to need extra help, someone to assist you."

Once Spencer knows the extent of her injuries, we'll lose her salary too. With the medical bills, I'm not sure how we're going to manage. Mill workers get treated for free at the clinic. We're not mill workers, though. Technically, Mama was hurt helping his employees, saving them, but Mr. Spencer is an unknown when it comes to compassion and duty—except to him.

While Mama and Sarah discuss possibilities for help, I push away from the table, taking our dishes to the sink. I turn around and lean against the counter. "Mrs. Mack and Willie have been told to vacate their house. Mr. Spencer says since they aren't a family of at least four any longer, they can't stay."

Mama sighs. "Poor Kara. Widowed with three children, then Vera dies, Tommy goes to Texas, and now this." Her eyes shine with unshed tears. "Did she tell you her plans?"

Mama and Kara Mack have been close friends since Mama came here as a new bride. I'm sure she'll like my idea.

"I haven't said anything to Mrs. Mack yet, but what do you think about her coming here? You know she's a good cook. All she needs to learn is our recipes and quantities. She and Willie quit the mill when Spencer tossed her out, so she needs a job. And Willie can go to school and help out after. What do you think?"

As usual, my mouth runs away with my tail in my excitement. But Mama's smile conveys gratitude.

"I think you're onto something, Gen. I wonder ..." She looks at each of us. "Lillian, would you want to share my room? Then we could let Kara and Willie have yours. Would you mind?"

Normally, Lillian, so much like Mama, wouldn't answer right away. She'd calculate the pros and cons. But not now. This time, she smiles immediately. "It's a swell idea." She reaches over and places a hand on Mama's shoulder. "And that way, I'm right there to help you during the night, should you need me."

Mama raises a warning finger at me. "Genessee, I want to talk to Kara about it first. It has to be approached the right way, or she'll think it's charity. Will you ask her to come over after supper? Right now,"— she puts her hand over her mouth to hide a yawn—"I need to rest."

Annie jumps up. "I'll take Mama to her room while all y'all do the dishes."

I smile at Annie's methods, but since Lillian and I brought her from the hospital, Little Sis needs some time alone with her mama.

"Be sure you let her have the rest she needs."

While Annie wheels Mama from the room, I bring the dishes to the sink. Charity puts the stopper in the bottom while Grace dips a bucket into the stove's reservoir. They'll wash the dishes while Beulah,

Glory, and Delilah help Sarah prepare supper for the lodgers.

I take Sarah's arm and pull her aside for a moment. "Sarah, now that Mama's home, do you suppose she'll want to take back over the ordering? I want her to feel she can do *something* to help out. Calling in orders is a small job but one she could do. I'll try to help with the baking more, but I also have to do all the various chores Daddy did." The amount of added work boggles my mind. How can I do it all?

"Let's tackle that when it comes, Genessee. Don't forget, we may have Mrs. Mack. She'll be a great help."

"I hope with it being Mama who proposes she live and work here, she'll accept."

"When does she have to be out?"

"Tomorrow."

Sarah grins. "The good Lord is right on time."

She really would be helping us. If she agrees. She and Tommy share a stubborn pride when it comes to what they perceive as charity. I cross my fingers and send up a prayer that she realizes how much she would help.

As I knead the last batch of bread, I pretend it's Mr. Spencer's neck and give it an extra squeeze. My hands pause. Will he disapprove of us hiring Mrs. Mack and Willie—not to mention having them live with us? And if he doesn't like it, what will he do?

The questions rattle inside my head, but, try as I might, no answers come to mind.

Chapter 13

I LEAN AGAINST THE KITCHEN COUNTER while Mama sits at the table with Mrs. Mack. Her face, so pinched with worry when she first walked in, registers a glimmer of hope at Mama's request.

"It's a genuine job offer, Kara." Mama gestures to her right arm and leg. "My days in the kitchen are over. Sarah needs someone who knows how to cook, which you do. My girls are fairly proficient, but not to the extent we need. Besides, they're busy overseeing the hotel operations."

I step closer. "She's right, Mrs. Mack. And besides cooking, Mama will need help bathing, dressing, and other things, I'm sure." *Please say yes.* I don a bright smile for encouragement. "It's the perfect solution. And Willie will be a great help with the animals."

Next to her, Willie's face lights up, and he jumps up and down. "Oh, Mama, can we? Pleeeease?" He hugs her arm for added emphasis. "I wanna help with the animals." His eyes are alive with happiness. That boy loves animals, especially our goats. He has since he was a toddler and Tommy brought him over to see the newborn kids. Rather than becoming fearful, he belly-laughed when the goats tried to eat his shirt.

Mrs. Mack mirrors my smile, the last vestige of concern wiped away. "All right. You've persuaded me." She ruffles Willie's hair. "Do you want to go to school?"

Bright-eyed Willie looks so much like a young Tommy that it tugs at my heart. "Yes, ma'am, I surely do. I wants to read *Huckleberry Finn.*"

I move next to Willie and put my arm around his small shoulders. "Then it's done. Lillian's ready to move her personal things to Mama's room. All we need to do is find another bed for Willie. We've got extra rollaways in the attic. After that, we'll go to your house and pick up your things."

Willie puffs out his chest. "I can help y'all with the bed, Miss Gen."

I shake his small hand. "Kippy! Let's shake a leg."

"Gen?" Mrs. Mack lays her hand on my arm.

"Yes, ma'am?"

"While I realize Tommy and you have had to put your plans on hold for now, I still want you to call me by my Christian name." She searches my eyes. "If you're uncomfortable with that, you can add *Miss* to it."

"Thank you. Miss Kara, it is. Come on, Willie, let's shake a leg."

While Annie takes Mama to get ready for the night, Willie and I find his bed in the attic and get it set up in the front bedroom—now his and Miss Kara's.

Willie is completely taken by its wheels. "I've never seen a bed that rolls before. I like it, Miss Gen." He gives the mattresses a pat. "And I can peek out the windah an' see who's a-comin' and a-goin' at the mill." He jumps down and crosses over to the chest of drawers. "An' my special box can go right here." He points to the floor next to the dresser.

"I suppose it can. What's in your special box?" I'm thinking of the toy chest we had as children. It was only a little smaller than a hope chest. Annie and I used to hide from Lillian inside it until she sat on it one day, and we couldn't get the lid open. I smile at the memory.

"My books and my toys." He looks up at me and his brow puckers. "Can we go get 'em? I'm a'feard Mr. Spencer will throw 'em out."

"Absolutely. We can go now, if your mama is ready."

Willie and I quickly make up his bed. I say good night to Mama, then Miss Kara and Annie join us as we go collect their belongings. We bring the luggage trolley with us to help carry everything.

I glance to the right and left as we walk, peering into the shadows. I'm anxious to get this over. I have no desire to have a run-in with Mr. Spencer. It would be just like him to have one of his thugs watch over the moving out—not that the houses have anything of value in them to start with.

We enter the door to Number Six, Seventh Row. An appallingly small pile awaits us. "What about your furniture, Miss Kara?"

She shakes her head. "It can stay for another family. The only thing I'd like to keep is the writing desk. It was my granny's. Did I ever tell you she was an author?"

"You didn't." I run my finger along the top of the desk. "How fascinating. I've often wondered how authors make up all those stories."

"It was always my dream to write a book, but I never had the opportunity."

Her shy smile pulls at my heart. "Well, perhaps now you will."

She shakes her head and lovingly runs her hand over the desk, as well. "No, I'll have too much to do to earn our keep."

I set down the clothing and clasp her shoulders. "Miss Kara, you're going to be my mother-in-law. You and Willie are family. *Of course,* you'll have time to write. Every evening and all Sunday afternoons after church."

I love how her eyes glow with delight. Just like Tommy's. "That sounds like heaven. A dream come true."

After all the sorrow she's gone through the last few years, she deserves to fulfill her dream.

Annie points to a pile of clothing. "Gen, put yours on top there, then let's lift the desk on the trolley." She turns to Willie. "Do you have your special box?"

"Yes, ma'am, Miss Annie." He lifts an eighteen-inch-long rectangular box. Over his head, Annie and I exchange a glance. It's pitifully small for a little boy's worldly possessions, even if it is only toys and books. I don't think I'd realized how little the Macks had to call their own. Of course, after losing Mr. Mack, I guess things got pretty tight for them. Tommy never let on, though, and I'm appalled that I never noticed.

We set Willie's box on top of the writing desk and then drape the clothing over those. I glance over my shoulder as we go out the door. "Is that everything?"

Miss Kara nods. "And good riddance to it." She winks at Willie. "We're going to be so much happier at the hotel with the Taylors, aren't we, son?"

Willie swaggers. "We'll surely be in high cotton."

We trudge past several lots of Fourth Row, where the burned-out houses have been leveled and the land cleared. A pitiful few have framed walls up, and tents sit on the others. But the village is quieter than it once was. People aren't outside like they used to be. Every evening before the fire, the villagers sat on their porches or walked and chatted with their neighbors. Children played in the dirt roads between the rows of houses.

It's like the fire stole their joy. Will it ever come back?

Miss Kara and Willie have been at the hotel for two weeks now, and it's like they've always been part of the family. In the morning, Willie helps Annie and me collect eggs. He thinks it's the best fun. He loves to feed the animals. He and I do that after breakfast before I walk him to school. But his favorite thing in the whole world—even more than the goats—is Buster. He figured out how to tie a little harness on the ferret and take him for a walk. And Buster loves exploring. It's the funniest sight in Sweetgum—Willie walking Buster down Main Street. The ferret loves to look inside the stores and see other children if there are any who aren't working in the mill.

That there are so few children still *not* working at the mill plagues me. They need to be in school. Willie's class is woefully small. I'll write to Mr. Davis and ask how the legislation is coming along.

Having Willie here makes me dream of the day when Tommy and I will have children. Right now, that's far in the future. Tommy's last letter was filled with his relief about his mama and Willie living with us.

Mama is not getting stronger, and I worry about her health. However, having her best friend living with us is good for her. Lillian tells me Mama still quietly weeps at night, though it isn't for terribly long. She has the same worries I do about Mama. She says Mama's become an observer of life instead of a participant.

Willie gulps down the last of his milk, clunks the glass on the kitchen table, and gives us a milk-rimmed grin. "I'm done, Miss Gen."

"Come on, then. It's time to go to school. Give your mama and Auntie Emma some sugar, and let's shake a leg." I demonstrate, making him giggle.

He kisses his mama and mine. It's so sweet how gentle he is around my mother. He's fascinated with her wheeled chair and likes to ride in it when she's on the davenport in the parlor.

The September morning air is still hot and sultry, and we work up a glow as we walk to the school. Willie looks up at me, a scowl wrinkling his nose. "Miss Genessee? You don't always have to walk me to school. I'm gonna be seven next week."

I look down at him in mock surprise. "Seven? Next week? *Tsk, tsk, tsk.* Here I thought you were thirty-four."

He giggles. "You're silly."

"I am?"

"Yeah."

"So say you. But tell me, what do you want for your birthday?"

He stops walking and stares up at me. "What do you mean?"

Is a present such a foreign idea to this little fellow? It's heartbreaking. "We always try our best to give something the birthday girl or boy really wants. Within reason, of course."

He nods as we start walking again. "I'll think on that while I'm in school."

I smooth his cowlick. "You do that, kiddo." I take him across the street, where he meets up with his new friends—a little, tow-headed boy and a gap-toothed, freckle-faced boy. The three immediately put their heads together—sharing secrets?—as they walk into the school.

On the way back, I stop by Sweetgum General Store to pick up a couple of items Sarah needs. When I step inside, a wave of grief crests over me. Daddy isn't here anymore. There's a new manager and a new layout. I can't find anything. Tears well in my eyes.

"May I help you?"

I jump at the voice. A man stares at me over crossed arms, near my elbow. Beneath dark, narrow eyebrows, his smile doesn't reach his eyes.

A mustache that's oiled and curls at the ends obscures his upper lip.

"Are you looking for something specific or just browsing?"

"I'm trying to … I need a bottle of vanilla extract. It's not where it used to be."

"We've made some changes in the store's layout. If you'll come with me, I'll get it for you."

I follow with reluctance. Daddy was fairly progressive in the way he laid out the merchandise. He believed if people could touch items, they bought them more readily and on impulse. This man has taken almost everything and put it behind the counter—more like old-fashioned general stores.

"May I ask why the changes?"

"When the inventory is out for people to pick up, things disappear—unpaid."

I take a step back. "Are you saying people are stealing from you?"

"No, because I don't give anyone the opportunity. The moment I arrived, I changed the displays. The former manager must have been daft or getting a kickback from theft." He plucks a bottle of vanilla extract from the shelf behind him. "That will be twenty-five cents."

I blink to keep sorrow at bay over these changes. Daddy would have been horrified. I lay a quarter on the counter and wait until he hands me the package. "You know, there has never been any theft in this store. And I'd appreciate you not saying things like that about the former manager."

He draws himself up and looks down his nose. "And what would you know about that?"

"He was also the preacher at the Baptist church." I take my leave but stop at the door, glancing over my shoulder. "And my father."

I walk slowly to calm myself before I go in the kitchen door. I won't tell Mama about that nasty man. She'll find out soon enough as it is. As sure as chickens have feathers, someone will say something to her.

In the kitchen, Charity and Grace are kneading bread dough. Beulah chops vegetables while Delilah irons napkins. The only one out of place is Sarah, who's at the table nursing a cup of tea, her back to the door. While she always takes a break for a meal, it's not dinner time. It's most unusual for her to sit like this. I put the bottle of vanilla on the counter and cross to her side.

"Are you all right, Sarah?" Her face is flushed. I put the back of my hand on her forehead. "Oh my. You've got a fever."

"Aye, I'm feeling poorly, that's for sure."

She pushes up from the table. Sweat pops out on her brow, and dread roils in my stomach. Daddy and I had read about a resurgence of polio. It's on all our minds.

"Go to bed. I'll bring you some chicken soup in a bit. What needs to be done for dinner?"

"Miss Kara has me recipe for vegetable loaves. A slice between bread is fine for the dinner bundles. I'll be takin' meself off to me bed, then. I just wanted to wait until you got back, darlin'. I should be better in the morning, I'm sure."

"Do you need any help?"

"No, dear, I'll be fine. It's just a cold, I'm sure. Oh, and your mama is in the bathtub. She'll need taking out soon." She lumbers out of the kitchen.

Miss Kara pushes through the swinging door from the dining room. Her crisp apron bearing the name *Sweetgum Hotel* looks so right on her. She embroidered that on all our aprons as soon as she and Willie moved in. "Where's Sarah? Did you get her to go to bed?"

"Aye—I mean yes. I'm worried about her. I've never known her to be sick. Do you think it's that polio?"

"Don't go borrowing trouble, Gen. We don't have a swimming pool in Sweetgum, and nobody here has polio. I'm sure she's just got a cold."

"Okay, what still needs to be done?" I look around to see if anything is out yet.

Miss Kara pulls a folded sheet of paper from her pocket. "Here's the recipe I got from Sarah." She opens it and reads, "Carrots diced. Navy beans mashed. We'd best start this now. Charity, please get"—she consults the recipe again—"twenty cups of navy beans cooking. Those should be in there." She points to the pantry.

"Yes, ma'am." Charity enters and comes back with a large bowl brimming with dry beans.

Miss Kara glances at the recipe. "Gen, are our eggs medium or large?"

"Mostly medium."

"Then I'll need two dozen. Do we have enough?"

"We sure do." I pull the bowl of eggs from the dairy icebox. "Delilah, please get the leftover bread from yesterday and tear it into small bits. Can you and Beulah do that? Annie, you work on slicing the bread for sandwiches. Grace and Glory, you two get the dinner bundles ready. Don't forget, we need forty-seven with the temporary residents."

Delilah nods and finds the bread. She and Beulah sit at the table and demolish it into crumbs.

Miss Kara checks the recipe again. "Gen, you and I will dice the carrots and onions."

"I'll do the onions." They hurt her eyes more than mine. "Oh, what about Mama?"

Miss Kara claps a hand to her cheek. "I forgot poor Emma. Girls, take over for me." She races out of the kitchen, her shoes clacking on the wood floors.

I chop the onions, dice the carrots, and put them in a large bowl. Then I go check the beans. They're nowhere near ready. How long does it take to cook beans? I can't remember what Sarah does.

"Annie, do you know how Sarah cooks the beans? Anytime we've had bean soup, they're already cooking when I get up."

Annie doesn't look up from chopping. "Nope."

Oh, well, we've got time. It's a little after eight-thirty. The loaves only have to bake for thirty-five minutes. I figure that with the time to cool, slice, and make sandwiches, the loaves have to go into the oven not a minute later than eleven o'clock. Sooner will be better. I cross my fingers and hope those beans soften quickly. If the lodgers aren't fed properly, they'll complain to Mr. Spencer.

And then not only will Mrs. Mack be on the street, but us along with her.

Chapter 14

Miss Kara returns to the kitchen, balancing an armload of clean napkins for the dinner bundles. "Your mama's in the parlor, embroidering. How are we doing here?"

I glance at the huge pot bubbling on the stove. "We're waiting on the beans. I just put the bread in to bake. We have time for a game of Dominos."

I love this new tradition Miss Kara brought to us, and for a half hour, Annie, Miss Kara, and I have a merry time playing with the kitchen girls. Well, as merry as it can be. The pall of Daddy's death still hangs over me like a dark cloud.

I check the beans again at ten o'clock. "What do you think, Miss Kara?" I hold out a spoon with my offering.

She blows on the bean for a moment, then bites. It crunches and she gives me an odd look. "Hmm, still not soft enough, but it's tasty, anyway."

"Then let's put it together and get the loaves in the oven." We drain the beans and mash them as best we can. Some are still not done, but I figure they'll soften when they bake. We follow the recipe, and by ten-fifty, we slide the pans into the oven. Miss Kara looks dubious, but there's no time to stew over it. I smile at my pun.

When the loaves are cooked, it's a race to get the dinner bundles ready. I send off the kitchen girls and Annie, each carrying two baskets.

When they return, Annie brings Mama into the kitchen for our dinner, a vegetable soup Sarah started yesterday. It's rich and hearty. Our lodgers will enjoy it for their supper. Hopefully, it will make up for any luncheon shortcomings.

∞

The front desk bell rings. And rings. And rings. I glance at my wristwatch. Five o'clock. Over the years, I've come to learn that means a lodger is in a rush or has a beef. Since we're not expecting anyone, I'm guessing it's a complaint. Hmm, what could it be about? I scurry to the lobby.

Mrs. Grundy stands at the counter, tapping her foot. Lovely. I plaster on a smile and step behind the desk. "Is there something you need, Mrs. Grundy?"

She slaps a partially eaten vegetable loaf sandwich on the desk. Uh-oh.

"Who made this mess? The beans are hard. Doesn't your cook know how to properly boil beans?"

Mrs. Grundy has been a resident here for at least seven years. She knows Sarah's name. I take a deep breath like Daddy taught me. "Sarah is sick, Mrs. Grundy. Mrs. Mack was helping care for Mama, so dinner was up to me and Annie."

She narrows one eye and stares at me as if she's trying to decide if there's truth in my statement. Then I remember one of Daddy's sermons about kindness heaping coals of fire on your enemy.

I bow my head contritely. "If you know how to properly cook them so they're soft, I'd surely be pleased to have you teach me."

Mrs. Grundy startles slightly. Her hand flutters to her neckline. "Oh. Well … my goodness, I suppose … "

Bingo! I pull out a sheet of paper from the desk, pick up the pen, and poise it over the paper, then look up at her hopefully.

Slowly, Mrs. Grundy's teeth appear. Heavens to Betsy! I've never seen this woman smile.

She proceeds to tell me how to presoak dry beans overnight. *Overnight?* Who knew? Well, I guess Sarah and Mama knew. But I sure didn't.

"That's apparently the only step you missed." She reaches up and pats my hand. "You'll know next time." She turns to leave, then glances over her shoulder. "Uh, what are we having for supper?"

I chuckle. "Not vegetable loaf. You can count on that. Sarah had a hearty soup ready before she got sick."

Mrs. Grundy smiles again. "Well, thank her, and tell her I'll pray for her recovery."

She disappears up the stairs. I shake my head. *Daddy, you sure had it right.*

I return to the kitchen, still chuckling. Annie and Miss Kara gawp at me when I relay the conversation. "When she smiled again before she went upstairs, I almost swallowed my tongue. Imagine that, Mrs. Grundy smiling twice in one day."

Miss Kara drops her chin and shakes her head. "Gen, I had no idea you didn't know to soak the beans. I thought the bowl Charity brought out had already been soaked. I'm so sorry I didn't question it."

Annie giggles. "It served a good purpose. Do you suppose Mrs. Grundy is truly changing her colors?" Little Sis pulls a pan of yeast rolls out of the oven and slides in two more.

I wonder about her statement as we get the lodgers' supper on the table. I hope all Mrs. Grundy needed was a little kindness. Maybe I can find other things to ask her opinion about.

I set the last basket of rolls on the serving table and ring the bell. As Mrs. Grundy fills her bowl, she keeps fluttering her left hand. I peer at it. A gold band resides on her finger. My gaze flies to meet hers.

"On my way upstairs after we spoke, a sparkle in the corner of one stair tread caught my eye, halfway beneath the carpet runner." Her smile is triumphant. "Upon investigation, it was my wedding ring."

An unseen hand nudges me, and I move to her. I put one arm around her shoulders and squeeze. "I'm tickled pink you found it."

She blinks several times as if a hug—albeit one-armed—is a foreign thing.

Supper is over and I'm about to drop. Even with Miss Kara here, the workload is large, probably because it's not second nature yet. Plus, worrying about Mama doesn't help. I carry a tray of sweet tea into the parlor, then settle Mama on the settee with a pillow under her thigh. The wound from the amputation is healing well, the doctor says. I only wish she'd regain some of her sparkle.

Willie lays on the floor, looking at all the toys in the Sears Catalog, while Annie shows Miss Kara an article in an old movie magazine. Lillian is missing, since she's at work, and Sarah has been in bed all day.

"Wait till I tell you what happened with Mrs. Grundy." I didn't share it during supper, thinking it would make a great tale for our parlor time. I relay her anger over the vegetable loaf sandwiches and the change in her after I asked for her help. "It makes me realize most people who are bad-natured are really hurting. I wish you could have seen her after I gave her that little hug. Her whole countenance changed. Then"—I pause for their undivided attention—"when she came down for supper, she'd found her wedding ring. The raccoon didn't steal it, after all. It slipped off her finger and caught under the stair runner."

Mama smiles. "Your daddy would be proud of you, Genessee. I'm proud of you. It's not easy to love someone who always lashes out in anger. Your father and I learned in ministering to so many over the years that hurting people hurt people. If you girls keep that in mind, you'll be able to look for ways to help them."

Annie turns the knobs on the radio until she finds the station she wants. "I finally learned all the steps for the Lindy Hop. Wanna learn 'em, Gen?"

Willie jumps up. "I do."

I motion to him with a smile. "Let Willie dance with you. I'm too tired."

Annie laughs and grabs his hands. "Come on, then." Nat Shilkret's *Lucky Lindy!* starts playing. Willie does his best to copy Annie's moves. He catches on quickly and makes a viable partner for her. Soon, both their faces flush with exertion from the lively dance.

Watching them makes my heart sore. I miss Tommy more than I've let on. This is the first time in nearly five years I haven't seen him every night.

Mama lays her head back and closes her eyes. I'm sure she's missing Daddy too. Most people didn't know their preacher loved to dance with Mama.

Miss Kara gets the wheeled chair and helps my mother into it. "Willie, come on now. It's your bedtime. You can push Auntie Emma to her room for me."

"Okay, Mama. 'Night, Miss Annie. Thanks for dancin' with me. That was fun. 'Night, Miss Gen."

It's Annie's turn to help Mama get ready for bed, and she follows them out, leaving me alone in the parlor. From my pocket, I pull out Tommy's latest letter, which I received yesterday. I've read it so many times, I've almost got it memorized.

My dearest Gen,

It sounds like my mama and Willie are settled in nicely. Thank you for giving them a job. That takes a weight off my mind. But are things getting any better? When do you think you'll be able to join me? I miss you and want you here beside me.

The letter blurs. I long to see him and hold the letter close to my heart, willing myself to feel his arms around me.

Our team is doing great. We play in small towns all over Texas and the Southwest. Some of them I think you'd really like. Maybe we'll buy a little bungalow and settle down in Texas. It's sure different from Sweetgum.

Has anything happened about the strike? Have any of our efforts had results? Have you talked or written to Representative Davis? I'm anxious for news, Gen. What—

The parlor door opens and Lillian enters. "Hey, Gen." She drops into a chair. "Another letter from Tommy?" She pulls a hankie from her pocket and blows her nose.

Her voice sounds flat. Lillian is usually more curious about Tommy's letters since Hank doesn't write much.

"It's yesterday's." I fold it and slide it back into my pocket. "You sound terribly blue, sis. What's got you down?"

She shakes her head. "Everything. The accidents, Daddy, your

Tommy leaving, and we can always toss in the economic state of the country. It's getting worse, not better." She crosses her legs. "Yesterday down by the river, I saw two tents pitched about thirty yards back into the woods."

My eyebrows fly up. "Who do you think it is?"

Lillian shrugs. "Who knows? Off hand, I'd guess a new shantytown is starting there. Spencer isn't getting the houses replaced as fast as he should."

That can't be all of it. There's something more, I know it. I lean forward and touch her knee. "Sis, are you pining for Hank?"

One side of her lips rises. "No, not really. I liked Hank a lot, but I wasn't in love with him." She picks up a magazine Annie left beside the chair.

Okay, that's not what has her in a blue funk. "Annie and I had to make the dinner bundles today. We made vegetable loaf. Have you ever cooked dried beans?"

An unenthusiastic "hmm" is my only answer. I probe further. "How do you do them?"

"You boil them."

"Ah, so you don't know either. I wonder how the three of us never learned you have to soak them overnight first?"

"Probably because Sarah does that part after we go to bed at night." She leans her head back and closes her eyes, the picture of relaxation— but her foot is bouncing, so she isn't sleeping.

"Lillian?"

She blows out a huge sigh. "I lost my job at Norton's."

My stomach drops to my toes. Lillian's job at Norton's was our last source of cash money. "Why? What happened?"

"The stock market crash is filtering down to us. Spencer hasn't given anyone a raise in over two years. Mr. Norton was apologetic about it, but he had to let two of us go. He said nobody's buying anything," She twists the hankie, then wads it in her lap. "I'm so sorry. I don't know what to do." A lone tear makes its way down her cheek.

I launch out of my seat, cross to her, and sit on the arm of her chair.

I slide my arm around her shoulders. "We'll manage. We always do."

She shakes her head. "We've never been in a situation like this." She jumps up and paces. "Think about it. We've lost Daddy's salary, Spencer has taken what Mama earned away from us, and now this." She stops and spins around. "I don't have a head to know what needs to be done or keep things organized like you do, but maybe I can take over what Mama did in the kitchen. Do you think Mr. Spencer would pay me?"

Would he? "Or you can do some of that and take on what Daddy did. Can you fix a sticking door?"

She fists her hands and plants them on her hips. "I can learn anything."

"I believe you can." I hug her. "See? We'll be all right." I yawn. "Are you going to bed soon? Mama's tucked in and I'm beat."

"You go on. I'll wait until Mama's in a deep sleep so I don't wake her. I don't want to have to tell her about losing my job tonight."

"Don't be too hard on yourself. It's not like you did something wrong to lose your job. It's beyond your control."

She taps her head. "I know that up here. But here?" She points to her heart. "Not so much."

The kitchen bustles with activity the next morning. Lillian normally helps, so her presence doesn't cause a stir, but we agreed last night not to tell everyone until the time is right. We don't want to add any stress to Mama or have Miss Kara feel like she should leave. Besides, unless she went to Texas and stayed with Tommy, there's nowhere else for her to go.

Lillian slides another two pans of biscuits into the oven. I grab tongs and put the first batch on the cooling racks. Annie stirs gravy under Miss Kara's direction. They are frying a little sausage to add to the gravy. We don't have much left and will have to butcher the hogs as soon as the weather cools enough. *Oh, Daddy, I miss you.* How am I going to direct a butchering I know nothing about?

At least we're managing breakfast, but I'll be glad when Sarah's feeling better. I glance at the clock as I apply the biscuit cutter to the dough. "We've got one more batch of biscuits to bake, then we'll be ready."

I send my gaze to the table next to the dining room door where we plate the food. Only Beulah, Charity, and Delilah are standing at the ready to serve.

"Where are Grace and Glory?" The girls' eyes shift to one another but not to me. "Beulah?" She's been with us the longest. If anyone knows, she will.

Her gaze flits to Annie, then back to me while she twists her apron strings. "They're working at the Spencers' house."

Chapter 15

BACON FOR COUNTRY GREEN BEANS sizzles and pops, splattering. Flames leap from beneath the pan, gobbling up the grease, then die back to await another splash. "Grace and Glory? Working at the Spencer's?" That makes no sense. They work here. For us. "What do you mean, Beulah?"

She takes a step back, her forehead puckers, and her voice drops to a whisper. "Miss Fannie offered them a dollar a week more if they'd start today."

Annie's spoon falls from her hand and into the pot, splashing gravy down her front. "That dirty rat. I ought to—"

"Don't do anything, Annie, except mop the mess on your apron. Glory and Grace can work wherever they want." I turn back to the biscuits with a sigh.

I don't blame them, really. If Fannie offered me an extra dollar a week, I'd be tempted to work for her too. I pick up a basket and move fresh biscuits from the baking pan until the basket is mounded high.

Annie grabs a washcloth from the sink and jerks it down her front. "Well, it sure seems unfair." She cuts her hand through the air. "You *know* she did it on purpose. She could have hired anyone." Annie continues muttering.

Lillian slides the last biscuit pan into the oven. "Twelve minutes and we dish up breakfast. Delilah, will you ring the meal bell in twelve minutes?"

"Yes, ma'am, Miss Lillian."

Miss Kara lays her hand on my arm. "Gen, if you have everything under control here, I'll go get your mama up and dressed, then see how Sarah is today."

"Thank you. We're fine, I think, but I'm sure glad you're here. We'd be in a real pickle without you."

Even with her help, we're just getting by. None of us has a spare minute anymore. And to think I told Miss Kara she'd have time to write. Ha! We're lucky to be able to sit in the parlor for thirty minutes before we go to bed. Some nights, I go straight from the kitchen to the barn to my bed. Still, I should thank the good Lord for what we do have—a roof over our heads and food on the table. But before, we had Daddy's salary. And Lillian's. Now, we're totally beholden to Mr. Spencer's good graces, and from what I've seen, the man hasn't any. Now with Fannie—

"Miss Genessee?" Beulah breaks into my pondering.

"Yes?"

"Delilah just rang the meal bell. Let's get the food on the tables."

"Of course. Thank you."

And thank you, Lord, for Beulah.

While Miss Kara and Lillian dish up the food, Annie, Beulah, Delilah, Charity, and I carry the plates into the dining room. We set the last plate on the table as the lodgers enter.

Mrs. Grundy lifts her hand for my attention. I hurry over.

"Yes, ma'am?"

She leans close and whispers, "Now, I don't want to bring you any trouble, dear, but I saw the sorriest sight yesterday evening on my constitutional down by the river." She covertly glances around. "It was a raccoon, younger than the one you had here before. It was caught in a trap. I know there is a new shantytown down there. Do you suppose someone is going to eat it?"

"No, I doubt it. They usually want the pelt for a hat."

Mrs. Grundy's face reflects her abhorrence. "That's terrible."

"Was the one you saw dead?"

She sits and takes a sip of coffee. "Yes. The trap was around its neck. Poor thing." She blinks and glances up. "You don't suppose it had babies, do you?"

"If it's a female, it's possible, even if it was young. I'll go search the woods and see if I find any kits."

"I'd feel better if you did. And Genessee?" Her hand on my arm stops me from leaving. "I want to thank you for bringing me out of my ... self-pity. You made me feel needed again. With my William's passing, I'd allowed myself to sink into a blue funk. I forgot to lean on the Lord."

My burdens lighten. "I'm so glad. I'm only sorry it took me so long to recognize you were hurting." I squeeze her hand and leave her enjoying her biscuits and sawmill gravy.

In the kitchen, I take Annie and Lillian aside and relay what Mrs. Grundy said. "It's a good lesson for us all."

Annie wrinkles her nose. "Except for people like Fannie. She's not hurting. She's just plain mean."

"She could be, but think about this. If you are a Spencer, do you suppose you'd have many friends? And what about the ones you do have? You'd always wonder if they were true friends or trying to make an impression with your father."

Annie and Lillian stare at me like I've got feathers sprouting out of my ears. Finally, Lillian shakes her head. "You're sounding like Daddy."

A good aspiration to have.

Miss Kara bustles back into the kitchen. "I left your mama in the dining room playing hostess to the lodgers. She reminded me that we need to strip the beds and do the laundry."

I clap my hand over my mouth. "Oh, my goodness, I forgot. Beulah?" I turn a furrowed brow of supplication to her. "You don't have any more sisters hiding somewhere, do you? We need help."

"I don't, but we'll manage. You'll see. Miss Lillian's here, and she's a lot smarter than either Glory or Grace."

A snide chuckle gurgles in Lillian's throat. "I don't know what smarts laundry takes, but I've got two hands."

She's always worked at the Five & Dime—or has for the past eight years—and didn't have to do the hotel laundry. I chuckle. She has no idea what's ahead of her. My mirth fades. We also have to slaughter hogs, butcher them, and smoke the meat. Other than scraping a scalded hog of its hair, I've never done any of it. Where in the next two months can I learn?

Overwhelmed, I stare at Lillian and Annie. "We've got to divide the labor. We have dinner bundles to prepare. Miss Kara, we have a load of cold potatoes. What if we make Jenny Lind potato pasties with a little chicken in them?"

Tommy's mama nods with confidence. "I can do that. Sarah is feeling better and should be in the kitchen tomorrow. If I can have Beulah and Charity, I think we can manage. I hope."

I hope so too. "All right, my sisters and I will take Delilah with us. We will divide and conquer. Onward, ladies."

The six of us go upstairs and strip all the beds. We'll start the laundry, then I'll send Beulah, Charity, and Delilah to get clean sheets from the linen closet. With the extra folks staying here, I hope there are enough. If not, some beds will have to wait until after supper when the sheets are dry.

Out behind the barn, we pump water into buckets and fill the first cast iron tub Daddy rigged up for the laundry. When the water is hot, we add lye soap, dump in a half-dozen sheets, and start moving the paddles around to wash them. Soon, all four of us are wet. It's not bad on a hot September day, but in another month or so, we won't enjoy it so much. But for today, I throw off my troubles and laugh with my sisters. Annie lifts a load of bubbles on her paddle and flings them at me.

When the first batch is clean, we drop them in the rinse tub and swish them around, then Delilah runs them through the wringer.

While Annie and I wash the second batch of sheets, Lillian takes the clean ones and hangs them on a clothesline. Six sheets clean, six in the tub, and twenty-four to go. My arms already ache.

"Genessee?" Mama's voice drifts into the dining room from the front desk a few hours later. "There's a telephone call for you."

Who would be calling me? It couldn't be Tommy. Could it? I set down the flatware tub and hurry to her. "Do you know who it is?"

She shakes her head. "I know it's not Tommy. I'm sorry."

I take the earpiece and pick up the stick phone. "Hello?"

"Genessee, this is Representative Davis. I wanted you to be the first to know. All the work you and your father have done has paid off. The Georgia legislature passed an amendment to strengthen its child labor law today. It removes some of the loopholes and keeps the younger ones in school, at least until they're eight years of age. It's not everything we wanted, but it's a start. You should be proud. I only wish your father had seen this day."

The lobby blurs as tears fill my eyes. "Thank you, Representative Davis. I truly hope it helps the little ones." I hang the earpiece on its hook, set the phone on the desk, then slowly turn to Mama.

She speaks before I can. "The child labor law?"

I nod.

Mama's hands come together in front of her lips. Her eyes close and she gives God praise. While I'm grateful for the passage, I worry it isn't enough. What's wrong with me? I should be thrilled. Maybe I'm only sorry Daddy can't see this day, but I'm not jumping with glee. My concern is how Spencer will enforce it—or if he will.

"Gen? It's a start, sugar. Your daddy always said, 'Don't try to get everything at once. Be happy with each slice of bread until you have gained the whole loaf.'"

A tiny smile tugs my lips. "I remember him saying that. Thank you, Mama." I move the phone to the back counter. "Are you finding enough to keep you busy?"

"Yes. I'm going through the registry and the accounting books. I can't do what I did before, but I can take that task off your hands."

My hands worry my pockets. "I hope everything is in order."

"It is. You've done a good job with them."

I breathe a sigh of relief. I don't need any more trouble, please, Lord. "Then, if you're all right, I'll go see if the laundry is dry. And after the beds are made up, I need to see about supper."

Mama's eyes fill with sorrow, and her brows dip. "I don't like to see you and your sisters working so hard and not have any time for fun. It's not normal."

I lay my hand on her shoulder. "We no longer live in normal times, Mama. We're better off than so many."

I go out back and check the laundry. The sheets are dry. Before I go inside to get everyone to come fold them, I stop and check on Buster. The little rascal is racing around his cage beneath the old rug we put on the cage floor for him. As soon as he hears the lock rattle, he pops his head out to see me. I snuggle with him for a few minutes, then reluctantly latch the lid.

"I'll bring you a treat later, Buster." With Willie in school, the poor little fellow could do with a playmate.

I gather my sisters and Beulah and Charity. Lillian works alone, while we work in teams of two, pulling the sheets off the clothesline and folding them. Lillian is fast at folding by herself and does almost as many as we do.

We lay the folded sheets in the laundry cart Daddy built. He framed chicken wire, put it on wooden legs, and attached toy wagon wheels. We can push the whole load of folded sheets inside the back door to the linen closet.

It took us a little longer than I'd hoped, and now we hurry into the kitchen to see how Miss Kara and Delilah are coming along with supper.

Annie sidles up to Tommy's mama. "What do you need us to do?"

She swipes her forehead with the back of her wrist. "Make bread and rolls. I've got split pea soup simmering. I pulled the last ham out of the icehouse, Gen. With the extra villagers staying here, we've gone through it all."

Lillian pulls out a scoop of flour from the bin. "I'll ask Mr. Spencer if we can get a few supplies from the general store."

"Thanks, Big Sis. I don't know if I could be very cordial to him right now." The Lord knows I try to forgive him, but every time I think I do, something reminds me of Vera, Ruthie, Billy—Daddy—and I get angry all over again. "I'm working on it, but ..."

I glance at the clock. We only have ninety minutes before suppertime. We're barely going to make it. And that's Fannie Spencer's fault. I frown. My attitude stinks. I never used to be a fault-finder. *Lord, help me.*

"Gen?" Miss Kara interrupts my prayer.

"Yes?"

"Tell me the history of y'all's icehouse. I've never seen one beneath a barn. Seems mighty strange to my way of thinking."

That icehouse makes everyone scratch their head. I smile and recite the words exactly as Daddy told them to me.

"The hotel was built in 1853, not long after the mill. There was originally an icehouse behind the barn, but when the war broke out, the mill owner didn't trust a Yankee as far as he could throw one. So he dug out a large area beneath the barn, put in timbers to support it, and nailed wood to them. He moved in ice and the meat, then camouflaged the entrance with bushes. Turned out to be a better place. Besides hiding the food from the Yankees, the ice lasts longer."

"Southern ingenuity." She gives the soup another stir, then seats the lid.

We prepare the dough for rolls and loaves, and when they're rising, I drop into a chair at the table with a glass of sweet tea. I take a sip and lean my head on the back of the chair, closing my eyes for a moment.

Delilah edges over to me. "Miss Genessee?"

I open one eye. "Yes?"

She slides off her apron and holds it out to me. Uh-oh. This can't be good.

"This is my last day. I've been hired by Miss Spencer."

My heart drops to my belly. We were barely getting by, but now what are we supposed to do?

Chapter 16

I FORCE ONE FOOT IN FRONT of the other, but try as I might, my legs just don't want to carry me to the mill. Twice I turn back, but I can't allow myself to give up. It's up to me to see that everyone is fed. That's what the hotel manager does—makes sure everything runs like a well-oiled weaving machine. While there was never a formal role change, that duty has fallen to me. Lillian was never involved in the day-to-day management, and Annie's too young. I was the child who tagged along after Daddy or Mama, learning it all. And now I'm bound by it.

We're fortunate we can grow our vegetables and keep animals for food, but I still have to buy flour, sugar, and other staples from the general store. In all my born days, the new manager there is the most uncaring man I've ever met. I don't know what wages he thinks we make, but it's not enough to pay his prices. And while he raises prices, the Rome newspaper reports food costs are down. Where's the equity?

I stare at the gold letters glittering on the mill's front door—chicanery of what's inside. Finally, I then pull it open and turn to the left. I half hope Mr. Spencer isn't in his office. Mrs. Grundy stops typing when I open the door and smiles.

"Genessee, how nice. Do you need to see me or Mr. Spencer?"

I still can't get used to her smile. Does Mr. Spencer see the change in her? Maybe, just maybe, that will help me. "Mr. Spencer, please. If he's in."

She nods. "He is. Have a seat, dear." Her knuckles rap softly on a door with his name painted on the glass. She waits, then opens it and disappears inside.

My stomach is all aquiver. I can't do this. I want to flee.

"Genessee? He'll see you." Mrs. Grundy stands on the threshold to his office. When I don't rise, she tilts her head. "Now?"

"Oh, yes, thank you." I take a deep breath and step past her into the lion's den. The room—far from a cave—is richly appointed, even nicer than the county seat office in Rome with polished dark wood, thick carpet, velvet drapery, leather chairs, and the largest desk I've ever seen.

Mr. Spencer glances up from his paperwork and waves his hand toward a chair. His dark, thick eyebrows draw together, making a strange contrast to the thinning gray hair atop his head. "Have a seat. I'll be with you in a moment. I'm reviewing the hotel's accounts."

How does he have a copy? Have we always sent him one? I sit on the edge of the chair, knees knocking. It takes every bit of strength and discipline not to wring my hands or fiddle with my skirt. Finally, after what feels like a week, he lays the papers down.

"The accounts are in order."

Of course, they are. What did he think he'd find?

His brows knit slightly, causing two vertical creases above his nose, one longer than the other. "Why are you here?"

I clear my throat. "Things are pretty tight." His attention moves to the papers again. I hasten to explain. "We have more lodgers since the fire—"

His gaze snaps to mine, eyes narrowing.

I swallow. This isn't going well, so I suck in a breath and plod ahead, anxious to get it over with. "We need to buy more sheets since we have more guests. There are several other things that need to be replaced, plus the extra food, and well—I need a budget increase." There, I said it.

He leans back and folds his arms over his chest. "Food prices have dropped in the past few months. That should make up the difference."

"Not at the general store. The manager has raised the prices." Mr. Spencer smiles at that. I grit my teeth. "Don't forget, we are feeding those who lost their homes in the fire."

"Get creative. Cut back on meat."

What would he know about getting creative? I'll bet there's never been a meal in his house without meat.

I clutch my skirt in my hands. "One other point. Since my father died, I've had to take on his responsibilities plus my own. In my way of thinking, that deserves a raise. After all, you don't have two salaries to pay, just one. And while I'm on that subject, you cut off my mother's wages, but she's doing the books—something my father used to do."

"You've chosen of your own free will to give her that job. I'm already paying for the books to be done."

"No, you're not. Daddy did those. You stopped paying his salary."

Mr. Spencer stares at me through beady eyes. "Count yourself lucky I don't bring in a new manager to watch over all of you." He nods once as if satisfied with his remark. "No, there's no reason for me to pay twice, is there?" A smirk plays across his face.

He has no idea, sitting in his ivory tower. I stare at him, trying to take his measure. He blinks and looks away, but in that second, I see it. Greed. Naked and ugly. And secrecy. What secret does he harbor?

He swivels his chair so he's facing away from me. "I don't think we have anything more to talk about."

I rise and step toward the door.

"Miss Taylor?"

I glance back. "Yes?"

"I assume you like your job?"

What is he saying? That he's going to fire me? Bring in that new manager? I pretend confusion. "I'm sorry?"

"Your job. Hotel manager. I assume you like it?"

I'm not about to let this man put me under his thumb. "I'd prefer my father was still alive and working."

He blanches. I allow a tiny smile to lift one side of my lips. I want him to realize I'm not a pushover. And that I blame him for my daddy's death. He gives a single sharp nod of his head.

We understand each other.

But if he ever finds out I'm quaking like a six-point-five earthquake inside, I'm done for.

∞

Save for Tommy and Daddy, the people I love most in this world sit around the kitchen table—Mama, Sarah, Miss Kara, and my sisters—waiting for me to tell them about my meeting with Mr. Spencer. Only little Willie is missing. He's getting some extra tutoring from Mrs. Grundy in the parlor. Those two have taken to each other like ducklings to water.

Lillian scoops up a spoonful of the blackberries she and Annie picked along the river. "What did Mr. Spencer say?" She slides the fruit into her mouth.

Annie's blackberry-filled cheeks already bulge like a squirrel's with acorns.

"He told me to get creative. What he means is, he's not giving us any more money. He tried to intimidate me, suggesting he'd take my salary away and hire a new manager to watch over us."

Mama pales and Lillian gasps. A blackberry falls from Annie's gaping mouth, and Sarah's face scrunches into a mask I wouldn't want to encounter on a dark night. Miss Kara shakes her head. Boy, do I love my family.

"Don't worry. I fixed his wagon. I told him I'd rather my father were still alive and holding the job. I think he nearly swallowed his tongue. He definitely knows I hold him responsible for Daddy's death. And somehow, someway, I'll prove it."

Mama lays a hand over my clenched fists. "Guard your heart, Genessee. Don't let it harden with unforgiveness."

I smile, hoping to reassure her. "Until that moment, I hadn't realized I blamed him. But it served a purpose. I have a feeling he'll leave us alone." I lean over and kiss her cheek. "However, we have to address the budget. We get a slight increase for food for the new lodgers, but he hasn't increased the linens budget. Those are a bit of a problem." I push my empty berry dish aside. "How are we going to get new sheets?"

Miss Kara brightens. "Flour sacks."

Annie does a double take. "Flour sacks?"

"Yes. They're strong and soft. You know that. We all wear them. Why not make the sheets we need out of those?"

Sarah's eyes roll upward as she calculates. "With all the flour and sugar we go through, there should be a treasure trove in the storage room."

Lillian jumps up and quickly disappears. A moment later, her muffled voice calls out from the linen storage closet. "We've got a huge stack of them in here." She comes back with a sampling. "We can stitch these together like a quilt. With the old sheet stitched to the back, nobody lays on the seams. Then it's a two-ply sheet. What a great advertising slogan." She laughs, taking an Annie-center-stage-stance. "'The Sweetgum Hotel, managed by the Taylor family, has the prettiest sheets in all of Georgia.' We'll start a new fad. Printed bedsheets!"

She flings her arms out for a dramatic end, then takes a bow. Annie claps her hands, nudging me to do the same. Applauding and chuckling, we revel in our cleverness.

"Take that, Mr. Spencer." I draw a line on my notepad through bedsheets. "One item checked off the list. Here's another. How are we going to manage slaughtering and butchering the hogs? And how many do we need?"

"Hogs or men?" Annie quips.

I start to roll my eyes—then realize she's right. We need men too. "Both, actually." Except for Willie, we're a household of women. Granted, several of the lodgers are men, but I don't want to ask them to help.

Again, Tommy's mama has the answer. She waves her hand over her shoulder, gesturing to the mill. "There are men working there who used to be farmers. The promise of meat for their families for a weekend of labor is a powerful persuader."

Sarah pushes up and crosses the kitchen to one of the iceboxes. She pulls a booklet from its top and thumbs through its pages. "Here it is. A hog weighing two-hundred-fifty pounds yields about one-hundred-twenty pounds of meat. With using the bones for soup and other parts to add flavor to dishes, we can get away with eight hogs. A ninth will be needed to give away meat." She closes the book and sets it back on top of the icebox. "In summary, you need six men, and they each take home twenty pounds of meat, plus soup bones and fat. That's good pay."

I mentally scan the pigpen. "We only have four ready to butcher. Two are still nursing litters. Where do we get the others, and how much do they cost?"

Sarah returns to her seat at the table. "Anywhere from four to twelve dollars."

Four dollars is doable. Twelve makes my heart beat fast. "What does the price depend on?" I hope it's how pretty they are because I don't care if they're pit-ugly if that means cheaper.

Sarah shrugs. "I have no idea. I just remember your daddy mentioning the cost."

I rest my forearms on the table. I direct a glance toward Big Sis. "Where or who do we get them from?"

"That will be in the invoice records," Mama says. "Annie, if you'll push me into the office, I'll find last year's bill."

We still don't know *how* to butcher them. "Lillian, you've been in our library more than I have in the last couple of years. Do you suppose they have a book on how to butcher a hog?"

She frowns as she thinks. She needs to stop that, or she'll get a permanent line between her brows. "I can't recall one."

A sigh escapes me. "How can I learn? I can't just depend on some men. What if they can't do it?"

Lillian's face brightens. "Hey, remember that columnist I told all y'all about? She has that helpful hints column in the newspaper. I first read one when I was in Lawrenceville. I went there with Mrs. Norton on a buying trip. Anyway, the column was so good I wanted our paper to carry it. I brought a copy back and gave it to Ralph Flournoy. He added her column to *The Sweetgum News*."

Sometimes, Lillian forgets where she's going with a conversation. I angle my head at her. "And?"

She blinks, a blank expression in her eyes. "And what?"

"Is there a reason you bring up this column?"

She laughs. "Oh yeah. She wrote about a good method to get blood out of an apron. She said they butchered several hogs for her grocery store. She sounds quite knowledgeable. We should see if she'd give us some pointers or something."

Sarah and Miss Kara exchange glances, and Sarah raises one scraggly, gray eyebrow. "An' would you be having her name?"

Lillian's posture straightens. "I certainly would. It's Maggie Parker. And she's in Rivers End, Georgia. We can write her a letter."

Another sigh rips out of me. It's not much, but at least it's something to go on. The question is, will this Maggie Parker agree to help us?

Chapter 17

EACH DAY, WHEN I HELP my sisters, Charity, and Beulah carry dinner bundles into the mill—which I'm doing because Delilah went to the Spencers'—I expect to see *him* beckoning me into his office. I have nightmares about that ogre firing us and casting us out into the street. In my dreams, we end up in the shantytown down by the river. I wake up shivering and in tears, thinking of Mama wasting to skin and bones and my sisters in rags.

It's been three weeks since I talked with Mr. Spencer. I'm not sure why, but he hasn't done anything. And Fannie hasn't tried to hire Beulah or Charity. I'm certain he knows of our involvement in the labor strike. I can only hope his realization that I hold him responsible for Daddy's death is the reason he's backed off—for now. That's what bothers me the most—the waiting for the other shoe to drop.

I wind my way to the baling room, where I hand the last bundle to Elmer Dyer. As he empties out his dinner, he gives me an odd look, as though he's calculating its cost. From the backwoods of Kentucky, his appearance is that of a moonshiner, tall and imposing. When he first arrived, he had a long, unkempt beard, but he's since cut it short so it won't get caught in any machinery.

I stiffen and square my shoulders. "Is something wrong, Mr. Dyer?"

"No, nothing's wrong. I'm just wonderin' 'bout somethin'." He holds out the cloth from his dinner.

Suspicious that he's our leak, I don't ask what. I take the napkin. "Well, enjoy your dinner."

Anxious to get away, I turn and go to the door. As I reach for the doorknob, I peek over my shoulder. He hasn't moved. He's still in the same spot, staring at me. I quickly step through the door and close it behind me with a shudder. That man gives me the creeps.

At home, Annie meets me in the lobby. "You have a letter from that lady from the newspaper column." She holds out her hand with two envelopes in it. "And one from Tommy."

Taking both, I go to the parlor and settle into Daddy's favorite overstuffed chair. I open Tommy's letter first and hold it to my nose, breathing in, hoping for a little of his scent to remain on the paper.

My Darling Gen,

Thank you for your last letter. From what you write, Sweetgum sounds the same despite the changes in the labor laws. Something isn't right there, but for the life of me, I can't think what it is. Watch yourself and your sisters. You and I both know you-know-who isn't trustworthy. Or honest.

The team is doing well. I hit a grand slam last weekend to win the game. I got a nice bonus, and I'll send a check to Mama to help out.

I've made some good friends on the team. Ernie, my roommate, is a swell guy. He's from South Carolina. He arrived the same day I did. Hank is rooming with a fellow from Virginia, called Bubba. He's a bit of a goof-off but a great hitter.

I miss you so much, Gen. I want you here with me. When can you come? I find my mind is on you and home instead of on baseball. Hurry to me, my love. I need you.

All my love forever,

Tommy

His pleas split my heart straight down the middle. How can I leave? Lillian may be the eldest of us girls, but she has no idea how to run the hotel. It's up to me. And I don't want it to be.

Oh, Daddy, how I wish I could turn back time. I'd have gone with you and Mama and watched out for you. Then you'd be here and I'd be with Tommy.

Now, I don't know when I'll be able to go to him. If ever.

A tear drops onto his letter, blurring the ink. I pull a hankie from my belt and wipe my cheeks. After a moment or two, I open the other letter. It's from Mrs. Parker. I unfold two pages with slanted, loopy handwriting. My eyes fly over the lines. I can't believe what I'm reading, so I start over. Yes, I read it right. She's coming here. Soon.

I run to the kitchen.

At the stove, Miss Kara stirs a pot while Sarah kneads a large batch of bread dough. Annie chops peaches—I hope for a cobbler—and Lillian puts up plates and flatware in the storage room, with the help of Beulah. Charity has table-cleaning duty, so she's in the dining room. Mama looks up from an invoice.

"I've got the name of the stockyard, Genessee."

"That's good because we're going to have fantastic help. Maggie Parker is coming here and—" I glance at the letter again. "Her friend Sadie Moreland is too. They're going to direct the slaughter and butchering."

Lillian gapes. "How can that be?"

I wave the letter and dance a little jig. "It's all here. She says she'll be in Lawrenceville right after the New Year to see an editor at some newspaper. It should be cold enough to butcher by then, she says. The timing coincides with her trip, which, I might add, is being paid for by the newspaper."

Mama's face shines. "I think God has His hand in this, my dears."

"I know He does, Mama, because I'd offered to pay her something for her trouble and consultation. She won't take anything, though— says she doesn't need it, and helping other women in this time of trouble is near and dear to her heart."

Using her wrist, Sarah pushes a wayward strand of hair out of her face. "It was quite timely, our Lillian reading that column."

I throw an arm around my sister. "It sure was. And now we'll learn how to do this so we can manage it ourselves next year."

I write a letter back to Mrs. Parker, telling her how grateful we are to her and Miss Moreland for their help and that we will look for her right after the New Year. I seal the letter, wanting to get it off to her today. I check the box where our lodgers place their letters to go to the post office. Two envelopes wait to go out. I pluck them up and poke my head back into the kitchen.

"Do any of y'all have a letter to go out? I'm going over to the post office to mail a reply to Mrs. Parker."

Sarah wipes her hands on her apron and pulls a letter from her pocket. "Thank you, dear. I was going to put it in the box but haven't had time yet. And here's the money for the postage." She hands me her mail and two nickels.

The cool, mid-October air is such a relief from the stifling summer heat. A few people stroll along Main Street, mostly wives of shop owners, and I wave to them as I cross the street.

The post office is almost a straight shot from our front door. Once inside, I get in line. The woman in front of me glances over her shoulder. It's Fannie Spencer. The instant her gaze meets mine, she looks away.

Should I say something to her? Then again, what would be appropriate? Anything other than *good afternoon* might release a torrent. Since I don't really know what transpired between her and Annie, I keep my mouth shut. She buys her stamps, and as she leaves, our eyes meet. My smile and nod receive a frosty dip of her chin.

Behind the desk, the postmistress frowns. "My word, someone needs to teach that girl some manners." Her salt-and-pepper curls bounce when she shakes her head.

I answer with a smile. "Good afternoon, Miss Wilma. I'm trying to understand her."

Miss Wilma sniffs. "A whistling woman and a crowing hen never come to a very good end."

I glance over my shoulder, then lean close to Miss Wilma's window. "Well, I'm not sure Fannie has any idea who she really is." I set my letters on the ledge in front of her.

The wrinkles in Miss Wilma's cheeks raise to new heights as her face pinches. "I'm not surprised, judging by the crowd she runs around with. I haven't seen her with your Annie in a coon's age."

I don't want to go any deeper, but with Miss Wilma, one has to give her something, or she won't leave it alone. "No, they had a falling out.

I need some stamps, please."

She puts the postage on the letters for me, cancels them with a rubber stamp, and drops them into a canvas bag. "They'll go out this afternoon. I see Sarah is writing to her Irish relatives. I hope she didn't invite them to come here."

"I have no idea." I smile again and bid her good day. Wilma Teague only allows for those born and bred in Georgia. Anyone else is an outsider who needs to stay away. I shake my head. Attitudes like hers make me weary.

I close the hotel's front door behind me. Mama is by the desk on the phone, and she holds up a hand for me to wait. It's her right arm. This is the first time I've seen her raise it. It isn't far, but at least it's something. I hoist myself up to sit on the counter while she finishes her phone call.

"Thank you. I'll be in touch." She hangs up the earpiece. "That was the stockyard. We can get the hogs for five dollars. If we bought six, we'd get them at four dollars. We don't need to spend five dollars to save four. That doesn't make sense."

No, it doesn't. "Did you order them?"

Mama clips an earring back onto her ear. No matter what, my mother always wears earrings simply because her mother taught her to. I can hear my granny say, "You're not dressed until your earrings are in place." Today, Mama's earrings are little painted daisies.

"No, but I told him we'd be back in touch soon. He said it only takes a couple of weeks to get them delivered. We'll order when Mrs. Parker gives us a firm date."

"Okay." I get behind her to wheel her chair through the door of our family quarters when the front door opens. I glance over my shoulder, thinking it's Annie or Lillian come back from an errand.

A tall fellow in deliverymen's overalls closes the door. His gaze flicks from me to Mama and settles on her. "Mrs. Taylor? I'm here to collect for the kerosene."

"Certainly. My daughter will handle it. Give us a moment, please."

I wheel Mama into the kitchen, then return to the lobby.

While he takes the new kerosene barrel to the barn, I look into the cash box in the family parlor safe. Annie must have put her egg money in this morning, bless her heart. I'll turn this in to Mr. Spencer and see if he'll reimburse it. He should since it's a hotel expense, not a personal one.

I remove the money and close the box. Other than the few coins in the bottom, it's now empty. We've got to find a way to replenish it. I need to ask Sarah. As usual, she's in the kitchen.

She looks up when I enter and smiles. "Now, there's a face as glum as a turtle with no shell if I ever saw one. What's wrong, sugar?"

"Can we stretch the eggs so I can sell more to the general store?"

She turns a quizzical eye on me. "Aye. I could add some water or milk to the eggs that wouldn't be noticed. You could get an extra dozen that way."

I do some quick mathematics. We get a barrel of kerosene every other month. If we save fifteen cents a day, we've got it. "Sarah, if you'll do that, the extra dozen each day will more than cover the cost of the kerosene."

Should Mr. Spencer agree to pay for the kerosene, then we can keep the extra money. It will purchase other items he refuses to take responsibility for.

"I just don't understand Mr. Spencer." Sarah punches down the dough as if it's the man's head. "These things are for his workers. The better off they are, the better they work. Doesn't he see that?"

I raise one shoulder in defeat. "Not when he's blinded by greed." I push up from the table. "I'll go find Annie to help me fill the lamps."

I'm a little worried about the kerosene. We're going through it pretty fast with the extra lodgers. Some burn their lamps late into the night. But does that really account for it all? Or is someone siphoning some extra and stashing it away? And if so, for what?

Lord knows this town couldn't survive another fire.

Chapter 18

ANNIE AND I GATHER THE lamps from the third floor and take them to the barn using the luggage cart. While Lillian scoops kerosene and pours it through a funnel, filling each lamp, we go for another load. By the time we return to the barn, she's ready for us. Little Sis hands her an empty lamp, and I load full ones onto the wagon. Now comes the tricky part—replacing the lamps in the rooms without spilling anything.

On our way across the yard, one wheel hits a rut and bounces the wagon. I grab the handle on the closest lamp, kerosene sloshing inside. "Watch out!"

"Sorry." Annie pulls the cart again, avoiding any problem areas on the path from the barn to the house.

Mr. Spencer should connect the hotel—the town, for that matter—to the hydro electrics. That would eliminate so much of the ever-present danger of fires. Even gas lights would be preferable to kerosene.

Annie and I carefully wipe each lamp before replacing them in the rooms. We repeat the entire process until all the hotel's lamps are filled and back where they belong.

In the kitchen, Miss Kara, Sarah, Beulah, and Charity have supper preparations underway.

I wash my hands in the sink to rid them of the smell of kerosene. "If we aren't needed here, we'll get the rooms cleaned."

Mama sits with a bowl of beans in her lap, snapping off the ends as best she can and wearing a smile of satisfaction. "You girls, go ahead. You've got just enough time before everyone gets home."

Thankfully, we don't have to change the beds today, just clean the rooms. We start on the third floor, where the displaced families are.

The makeshift walls give them a little privacy, but they will be happier once the new houses are completed. Still, those who are with us have it better than the ones in tents by the river.

When we get to Leroy and Mr. Dyer's room, I have to discipline myself not to snoop into Elmer's dresser. Leroy promised to let us know if Elmer's a mole for Spencer. My snooping won't help the situation.

By the time we complete the cleaning and getting supper on the tables for the lodgers, I'm so tired I can hardly eat. And we're not done yet. Beulah and Charity work hard, but we need at least five kitchen girls to make everything work smoothly. If I could have my druthers, I'd prefer six. Lillian, Annie, and I have to put off our own chores to do what the defectors did. At least Willie helps feed the animals, but it's a continuous struggle to get everything done.

By quarter to nine, all the dishes are put away and the breakfast tables set. I need to get ready for bed. Four-thirty comes way too fast. I drag my feet to my room.

Brushing my hair, I think again about having it bobbed. Then I could skip braiding it each night and simply fall into bed even sooner. I lay my brush on the dressing table. It's almost too much work to cross the room to crawl under the covers.

In the distance, I hear the sound of glass breaking.

"Help! Fire!"

Fear is an instant energizer. I leap to my feet, grab my robe, and run into the hallway. More screams of "Help! Fire!" come from upstairs. I'm unable to distinguish which floor they're coming from. All I can think of is the last fire and losing Daddy.

Lillian is already in the hallway when I reach it. "Mama! Kara! Fire! Get out."

Willie and his mama open their door.

I tug her sleeve. "Get Mama and take her out front."

Miss Kara runs to Mama's room. Willie sticks close to her. My feet feel as though they're glued to the floor.

Lillian shakes me. "Gen, Mama's safe. We need to get the second floor clear. I think the fire's in the dormitory."

We race up the stairs. My slipper falls off on one of the treads, but I don't stop to get it. Lives are at stake. On the second floor, everyone is milling in the hallway.

I shoo them down the stairs. "It's on the third floor. Get a bucket brigade started and call the fire truck!" My heart pounds in my throat as flames crackle above.

Leroy and Albert grab buckets from beneath the stairway, where we keep several filled with sand for this very reason. Buckets in hand, they fly up the stairs.

Agnes and Irene—two of the stronger women—race with Lillian and me downstairs. Sarah is in the lobby calling the fire department as we sail through.

I don't stop but keep running, shouting over my shoulder, "Come on!"

In the barn, we grab buckets. Miss Kara finds us there.

"Your mama and Willie are safe out front on the sidewalk." She and I grab the ladder and slap it up against the side of the hotel.

One window explodes from the heat. As I pull back from the falling glass, roaring flames leap out. "Hurry! And be careful of broken shards on the ground."

Leroy opens a window farther down and leans out. "Use this one."

We set the ladder where he indicates, and while Annie scrambles up with a few women behind her, Miss Kara and I hold it steady. Buckets are sent up as fast as they can fill them. Water sloshes out as they pass each one upward, so there's not much left in them by the time Leroy grabs them.

"More! We need more water!"

The empty buckets fly out the window and land on the ground. In the distance, a bell clangs. It's the fire truck, but we can't stop. Flames lick the side of the hotel.

Leroy sticks his hand out for another bucket. His face is black with soot. I hope he isn't burned.

I crane my neck and shout over the fire's angry roar, "Is everyone out of there?"

"Yes, it's just me and Albert. But we're not gaining on it. Keep the ladder there. Al and I are gonna have to get out." He takes a bucket from Annie and disappears inside. A moment later, he reappears. "The firemen are here."

The ladies back down the ladder, with Annie, Leroy, and Albert following them.

We run around the front, where the rest of the lodgers gather on the sidewalk. Mama is crying. I know she's reliving what happened in the last fire. Standing near her is Minnie Scott. Her nightdress is half burned, and a doctor attends her.

Beside her, her husband, George, weeps. "We're so sorry, Mrs. Taylor. Minnie was showing me her new shawl, and when she spun around, it knocked the lamp off the table."

Mama reaches for his hand. "George, it was an accident."

So that's how it started. I move alongside them. "More important, is Minnie all right?"

The doctor glances up. "She will be. Thanks to her husband, her burns are no worse than second degree." He applies a salve and wraps her arm.

As George drapes his robe around her, Minnie looks into her young husband's eyes with adoration. "He grabbed me and rolled me in a blanket. He saved my life."

The unabashed love between them brings tears to my eyes. I turn away as deep longing for Tommy fills my chest until I can scarcely breathe.

When the fire is out, the third floor is a total loss, and several second-floor rooms have damage where the fire burned the ceilings or water leaked through.

My sisters and I move among the lodgers, comforting those who bear another loss. And where is Mr. Spencer? My gaze scans the crowd gathered on the street. Nowhere to be seen, although Mr. Patterson is there. His gaze captures mine, then he closes his eyes, slowly shaking his head. Will he press our cause with Mr. Spencer?

When the firemen are sure there are no more hot spots, they pick up their equipment and leave. By now, it's well past midnight. Sarah has taken Mama inside, and I encourage everyone to go home.

Lillian gathers our lodgers. "Let's all go inside. We'll set you up in the parlor for tonight."

Fortunately, it isn't too cold out, so we can keep the windows open to help get rid of the odor of charred lumber.

Mrs. Grundy turns to Irene Harp and slips her arm through hers. "Come along, dear. You'll double up with me in my room. Everything will be fine. You'll see."

Following her example, other women whose rooms are inhabitable offer to have ladies double and triple up with them too.

I reach out and touch Mrs. Grundy's shoulder. "Thank you." She smiles and leads Irene inside.

Once again, fire interrupts all our lives. I'd like to go pound on Mr. Spencer's front door and demand he do something right now. But tomorrow will have to do. I follow the last of our residents inside.

Early the next morning, I count the ways I'm grateful for Mr. Patterson as he treads with care through the dormitory, inspecting the damage. Right after the lodgers left for work, he showed up with Mr. Spencer in tow, saving me from having to go to his office begging once again.

While Mr. Patterson assesses the damage, Spencer remains in the doorway. "Whose carelessness caused this?" His face a contorted mask, he glowers over his shoulder at me as if I were to blame.

Mary's daddy picks up a chunk of broken glass. "It was an accident, not carelessness. If the hotel had electricity and guests didn't have to use kerosene, we wouldn't be here examining any damage. However, that's a moot point. We need to get this fixed as quickly as possible. Our workers shouldn't be in tents in the woods."

Mr. Spencer stares at him. Finally, he nods once. "Oversee it." He turns, nearly toppling me, and leaves.

Mr. Patterson heaves a sigh. Then he puts his arm around my shoulders. "All right. Let's get this repaired, shall we?" He pulls out a small notebook and pen. "We'll need a new roof and a complete new floor. The front wall is okay, but the others will need replacing." He makes some notes. "Let's go down to the second floor. I want to make sure no other rooms but those you showed me sustained any damage."

"Thank you. You have no idea how much—" My words are cut off by the lump in my throat.

His eyes reflect fatherly care, and he hugs me. "Genessee, your daddy was my closest friend."

He says no more, but I understand. He's still a supervisor, and his job and family depend on Mr. Spencer. We just don't speak of what we both know about the man.

Mr. Patterson takes his time going over all the second-floor rooms. He found three other rooms with some water damage on the ceilings. "We'll need new ceilings in all these rooms. Let's go find your mama."

In the kitchen, Sarah pours a cup of coffee for him and Mama. I get busy helping with the lodgers' dinner bundles. After a moment, their voices stop. I glance over my shoulder at Mr. Patterson sitting at the table with Mama. He's frowning.

"Where are your other helpers?"

Before any of us can say anything, Charity says, "Fannie Spencer offered them more money." Her tone hints of discontent. I tense at the idea she might be thinking of leaving too.

Mr. Patterson raises one eyebrow. "I'll see if I can do anything about that." He turns back to Mama. "How are you doing, Emma?"

Her good hand flutters to her collar. "As well as can be expected. My right arm won't bear any weight, although my fingers work enough to snap beans. I'm more of a burden than useful anymore."

Yesterday, Lillian said Mama still weeps sometimes late at night. I pause my rolling pin and turn. "Mama, don't say that. You keep our spirits up."

"You're right, sugar. I gave into a moment of self-pity." She smiles at Mr. Patterson. "Irving, thank you for your help."

He pushes his chair back. "I see more than you realize, Emma. I'm not sure what to do about it, but I'm working on it. Now, I need to use your telephone to make some calls. We've got to cover your roof until the repairs can be made."

While he makes the calls, we take the dinner bundles to the mill. He's gone when we get back. After we eat our dinner, Mary—dressed in overalls—and her mama arrive. I blink. Mrs. Patterson's dress is made from a flour sack. The buttons on its front are stretched to their limits. Mary grins at me and winks.

Mrs. Patterson pats Mama's shoulder. "Irving told us about the kitchen girls leaving, Emma. We're here to help. No arguments. You know full well you'd do it for me, were the tables turned."

Mama's eyes bear a sheen of gratefulness. "Thank you, my friend."

While Mrs. Patterson works in the kitchen, Mary helps us clean. We sprinkle all the rugs with bicarbonate of soda. That should get the smell of smoke out. Then we roll them and load them on the utility cart to take to the clotheslines. We'll hang them to air, then we'll beat each rug to get the powder out. It takes a few loads, but they're finally all on the clotheslines.

In the yard, Annie holds out a handful of carpet beaters. "Grab one and let's whale on these."

Lillian, with her hair tied up in a scarf-turban, uses a two-handed approach.

Mary laughs at her. "Hey, batter, batter, hey."

Lillian snickers and whacks the rug in front of her. "And it's a line drive!"

It takes us three hours to finish beating the rugs, but we have a little fun while we work.

I glance at the clear sky. Not a sign of rain. "We'll leave them out here to air until tomorrow."

While we head back to the house, Mr. Patterson arrives with some men and large, oiled canvas tarps. He waves but doesn't stop to talk. I stay and watch as the men set up tall ladders—taller than any we have—and carry the tarps onto the roof. After they're laid over the fire-damaged section, the men tie ropes to the grommets and secure them to the eaves.

I walk toward the house. Mr. Patterson is such a good man. His oversight of our repairs will mean they are done the right way. I only hope it doesn't come back to bite him—or us.

Chapter 19

Two days later, pots bubble merrily on the stove, sending up a savory steam. I take a peek in one, sniffing appreciatively. Chicken and rice soup, a new recipe Miss Kara found. If the aroma is any indication, it should be delectable. I set the lid back on the pot.

Once the lodgers' breakfast is on the tables, we can have ours and relax for a few minutes before the next wave of chores. My stomach growls in anticipation of the egg and cheese pie Sarah made special for us this morning. I take my place at the table, and after the blessing, dive in. The added red pepper flakes give it an eye-opening zing.

"Sarah, this is amazing."

She blushes. "Thank you. I thought you'd like it." She cuts off a large bite with her fork. We eat in silence for a few minutes, thoroughly enjoying the treat.

Annie collects every last crumb from her plate. "I sure hope they can get the roof done before we have any rain. I hate to see our people out of their rooms. I mean,"—tears glisten in her eyes—"those rooms are their homes."

Mama smiles indulgently at her youngest. "Your tender heart serves you well, daughter. I'm sure Mr. Patterson will hurry them along. We need to remember to thank the good Lord for having a friend on the management team at the mill."

She's right. It's providential. "Mama, do you suppose God knew we'd need help from a friend on the inside?"

"Of course, He did." She sets down her fork and picks up her coffee cup. "From the foundation of the world, He knew this day would be upon us and what we'd need."

"I know it in my head, but my heart always finds it hard to believe that God takes notice of the mundane details of our lives, not that the fire was mundane. But still—" I shake my head, mostly in amazement.

Lillian grimaces. "It's a good thing I'm not God. I'd slap some sense into Mr. Spencer instead of letting him cause all this trouble."

I swat her shoulder, but deep down, I couldn't agree more.

As we enjoy our coffee, talk turns to the quilts Miss Kara and Mama are making for those in shantytown. When we realized their plight, their need outweighed hotel sheets.

"We have to find some more feed sacks. Our own supply is nearly gone." Lillian reaches for the sugar bowl.

I push it closer to her. "How many quilts are you making?"

"Four of our lodgers are there, and another half-dozen families are waiting for houses."

I do a mental calculation but give up. "Goodness, that could be a lot of quilts."

She shakes her head. "Not as many as you think. Most families make do with two beds. The kids sleep together for warmth."

"That's so sad." Annie's tears look close to spilling.

A truck pulls into the yard. She jumps up and peers through the window. "Oh good, Mr. Patterson isn't wasting any time getting our repairs underway."

Lillian's brow lowers into a scowl. "I'll bet Mr. Spencer is having a cow over it too. He wouldn't concern himself if all his workers lived in shantytown."

I don't understand him. He lacks all decency. I slam down my cup, coffee sloshing over the sides and Mama frowning at me. "Does anyone know why he's that way?"

Mama and Miss Kara share a private glance.

"There was a time ..." Tommy's mama spoons a little sugar into her coffee. There's a story coming for sure. She smiles. "Way back before I met my husband, Ben Spencer courted me. Yes, pick up your jaw, Genessee. The minute I met Tommy's daddy, I forgot any other boys existed."

I simply cannot picture her with Mr. Spencer. I lean forward.

She waves her hand. "But I'm going down a rabbit trail. Ben's family didn't own the mill back then. They owned the general store. He worked there with his daddy. Ben wasn't always overly ambitious or so driven. That happened when he went off to Harvard when he was seventeen." She stops to take a sip of coffee. "Ben came home four years later with a very rich wife in tow."

I knew the family had money but always wondered where it came from. "So how did he come to own the mill?"

"With his new business degree and his wife's money, they moved to Buckhead, and he began investing in businesses around Atlanta. About ten years later, the owner of Sweetgum Mill died in a huge train wreck. Ben decided to buy it."

I rise and peek out the window. Several men unload and stack lumber in the yard. Turning, I lean against the sill. "Did he think the mill would make him richer?"

"Who knows?" Miss Kara shrugs. "When his first wife died giving birth, he had her money, and for some reason, he decided to come home. He married Fannie's mama a couple years later."

Annie twirls a knife on the table. "Why do you suppose he's such a tightwad if he's got plenty of money?"

Mama stops the knife with a gentle smile at Annie, who puts her hands in her lap. "One can never be sure when or how greed gets a man in its clutches."

Coming back to the table, I ponder for a moment. "Do you suppose once he had a taste of money, he wanted more? Or maybe that when his first wife died, it broke his heart, and he became bitter?"

"The only thing I know for sure is somewhere along the line," Miss Kara continues, "he stopped caring for people and became a miser. When he had to make any major investments in the mill, he skimped."

Investments. *Mr. Forsythe.* My eyes narrow. Is he aware of how Spencer operates? He doesn't seem like that kind of man.

"Mama, did Daddy ever mention anything about Mr. Forsythe to you? He's the man who inspected the hotel a few months ago and is Mr. Spencer's business partner." I don't want to influence her impression of him, so I don't say any more.

"He didn't say much, only that he looked around and gave us a clean report. Why?"

"I'm curious, that's all. Somehow, I don't think he's cut from the same cloth as Mr. Spencer is."

Annie frowns. "What does that mean?"

Mama smiles at Little Sis. "It means they aren't the same kind of man."

I tap the side of my nose, something Granny Taylor used to do when things were at odds. "They're strange partners for sure. But I don't *really know* Mr. Forsythe."

Does he *really know* his business partner?

There's a knock on the back door, and Mr. Patterson steps inside.

"We're fixing to set up scaffolding on the side of the hotel so the men can get into the upper floors with as little interference as possible to y'all and your lodgers. We'll make a doorway up there, then replace it with a window when we're done."

I need to let the lodgers know. "When do you think you'll be finished?"

"The contractor says three to four weeks. He pulled this team from replacing houses. There are still several left to do, so he's anxious to get back to those."

Mama smiles at him. "Thank you, Irving."

When he leaves, I sit back down to finish my coffee and glance at Lillian. "Spencer can't even have houses built in a timely manner. Why doesn't he hire a separate crew, even if he has to find one in another town?"

Miss Kara shakes her head. "It breaks my heart thinking of friends living in those tents by the river. The nights are getting pretty cold."

She's right. The fire affected so many of us—nearly the whole town. Everyone except the Spencers. Once again, I exchange glances with Lillian. Lately, she's become my confidant and advisor.

I nudge her shoulder. "Speaking of timely matters, I wonder how the sheriff's investigation is going. There aren't any rumors floating around town."

Her eyes widen. "You're right. It's been nearly three months."

Mama watches me closely. "What are you thinking of doing, Genessee?"

I shrug and confess my thoughts. "I'm not sure. But I know one thing. We should have had an arrest long before this. Do you suppose the sheriff has been bought by one of Spencer's men?"

Miss Kara shakes her head vehemently. "I can't believe that. I've known Roy Jackson since I was six years old. Remember, he wasn't appointed to the office, Gen. He was duly elected by the town's people."

"I know." A sigh huffs out of me. "But I don't understand why nothing has happened. I think I'm going to go ask him what he's learned."

Mama stares at me for a moment, then finally nods. "Be careful. And choose your words wisely."

When we were little and wanted an extra cookie, Lillian and I always sent Annie to get them. She has a way of disarming people without saying a word. That's why I asked her to accompany me to see Sheriff Jackson after dinner. She and I push open the door to his office.

The sheriff sits at a desk, turning the pages of a newspaper. There's no sign of Deputy Limehouse. Sheriff Jackson looks up as we enter.

This is the first time I've ever been to the jailhouse. Made of cinderblocks, it must be an absolute oven during the summer. A quick glance takes in the tiny front area used for logging in prisoners. The furnishings are sparse and utilitarian. Besides the wooden desk and the sheriff's chair, there's a file cabinet and a rickety table at one end of the small room with a coffee mug and newspapers on top. A second chair is pushed beneath the table. Doors with iron bars connect the two cells to the "office."

The sheriff lays the newspaper down and folds his hands over it. "Genessee. Annie. What can I do for you girls?" He doesn't offer us a seat. A sinking feeling takes up residence in my stomach.

"Sheriff, may I ask how the investigation is coming?"

"What investigation?" The deputy's voice comes from behind us. The sheriff sighs.

"I believe the Taylor girls are asking about the fire, Limehouse." His eyes never leave us. If he's trying to intimidate me, he's doing a good job.

I wipe my palms against my skirt and plunge ahead. "Did you find out who started the fire? Because whoever it was killed our father."

The deputy hitches up one hip and plops onto the corner of the sheriff's desk. "That's privileged police information."

If he thinks I'll roll over and go home, he's in for a surprise. I take a breath and spear him with my gaze. "As family of the murdered man—and make no mistake, he *was* murdered—we have the right to know."

The sheriff's gaze bounces between the deputy and me. Finally, he picks up a half-empty mug, looks inside, then hands it to the deputy. "Go get me some fresh coffee at the cafe." He waits for the door to close, then pins us with his gaze. "Look, girls, it's not as easy as you may think. We managed to get a single fingerprint, and that was only a partial. The kerosene dripping down the can obliterated most of them."

Annie snorts. "So what are you actually doing?"

Her question catches him off guard. "I ... uh ... I'm doing what I can. I sent the print off to Washington."

Little Sis leans forward. "To run for Congress?"

He snorts. "I sent it to the FBI to search for a match."

Annie frowns. "I don't understand. Why would the FBI have copies of someone from Sweetgum's fingerprints?"

Sheriff Jackson quirks his mouth to the side and scratches his nose with his index finger. "All fingerprints are sent to Washington. If any of our townspeople were ever fingerprinted, they'd be there."

I put my hands on his desk and lean forward. "But if they weren't—I mean, if the person who did this never was fingerprinted, then we won't get any answers."

He stares at my hands, then lifts his chin. "Now you know the problem."

"Do you have any people you suspect?"

He studies me for a long moment. I hold his gaze without blinking. Finally, he nods. "I do."

Hooray! "You do? Then why haven't you taken their fingerprints?"

He shakes his head. "I can't do that. There's no concrete evidence."

Annie jumps up. "My daddy's dead. That's your evidence."

The sheriff grunts and rises. "All right, girls. That's the end of this inquisition. Go home. Let me do my job."

So much for Annie winning him without any words. I take her hand. "Come on." I pull her away from the sheriff's desk. At the door, I look over my shoulder. "I understand more than you think I do, Sheriff."

He cocks his head as if a different perspective on my words will help him understand their meaning.

I close the door. Instead of crossing the street to home, I take Annie's hand, and we turn toward the village. I want to remind myself what this is all about. It's more than just our father.

Annie drops my hand and shoves hers into her coat pockets to protect them from the bite of the cold wind blowing between the houses. "Do you think the sheriff's hiding something?"

I sure do. "Not in the way you mean. I think he's up against some people who are hiding evidence. He's an honest man. I'm sure of it."

While we walk, my thoughts go 'round and 'round about who the sheriff suspects. The mill has eight supervisors. Of that number, I rule out three. Mary's daddy tops that list.

I glance at First Row and the supervisors' homes. "Annie, I remember that two other men besides Mr. Patterson—Dougie Anderson and Lonnie Culpepper—didn't retaliate against the strikers. Instead, they slipped inside the mill as soon as Spencer's goons attacked. That leaves five supervisors who have cars."

Little Sis glances sidelong. "What does owning a car have to do with anything?"

"Because they're the ones with—" I stop dead. Annie's right! We may have been on the wrong track. I throw my arms around her. "We're all looking for someone with a car and reason to have gasoline. What better way to throw off suspicion from the real perpetrator?"

Her face scrunches in thought. "Hey, what about those goons who beat up our men?"

I'd forgotten about them. "It could easily have been one of them, especially if Spencer paid them. But the sheriff knows all this, Annie. He's working on it the best he can."

She kicks a stone and starts walking again. "I wish there was something we could do."

I grab her arm, stopping her. "Wait. There is. I forgot."

"Forgot what?"

"Tommy told me Lonnie Culpepper and Dougie Anderson lost their jobs right after the strike."

She twirls a lock of her hair. "Do you think it was because they didn't fight our guys?"

"I'd bet you my favorite neckerchief it was. I wonder if the sheriff ever questioned them."

Little Sis steps off the curb. "Maybe we should."

My mouth turns down. "There's one problem."

"Oh? What's that?"

"They don't live in Sweetgum anymore. They moved away when they lost their jobs."

But I cast away that concern as soon as the words leave my mouth. Even if I have to trot to the end of the world, I'll find out some way to question those men.

Chapter 20

BITS OF HAY FLOAT ON beams of light as Annie, Willie, and I search the loft for the Christmas ornaments. I find it hard to believe the holidays are already upon us. Strands of garland swag across Main Street, and each streetlamp is festooned with greenery and giant wooden candy canes. The privately owned stores display pots of bright red poinsettias beside their doors and fill their windows with Christmasy scenes and affordable gift ideas.

I wish I could dredge up some holiday enthusiasm. While the hotel normally thrums with anticipation and laughter during November and December, this year, there's a layer of grief subduing our festivities. Lillian, Annie, and I strive to add a little extra cheer for Willie's sake. Oh, to be that young again, when sorrow doesn't cling like ivy to a tree trunk.

We made it through Thanksgiving without too many tears. Mr. Patterson organized a wild turkey hunt and bagged three for our lodgers' dinner. We roasted a chicken for our little family. Turkey without Daddy's stuffing would have brought on more grief for Mama. Since most of the work was done the day before, we let Beulah and Charity have the day off with their family.

Now, there's just a week left before Christmas, and we need to get the tree for the guest parlor and ours. We already decorated the lobby and the staircase. Our lodgers and guests expect and deserve it, especially those who live with us year-round. We put the garlands and bows up the day after Thanksgiving to celebrate the return of our guests to their rooms.

"See the box with the green bow on it, Willie?" I point to the far end of the hayloft, where we store the Christmas ornaments, stockings, and mantel decor.

"Yes, Miss Gen, I see it."

"Bring it to me, please. And be careful, it's got the tree ornaments inside." I peer around for Little Sis. "Annie? Have you found the other boxes?"

Her head pops up from between two hay bales at the far end of the loft. "Yes. There's only four. I'm stacking them by the ladder. We can hand them down to Lillian and Miss Kara."

I check one other box. I don't want to miss anything. I need to mark all the family ones with a bow like the ornament box. It will make it easier to distinguish those from the hotel decorations next year for—the air whooshes out of my lungs.

It's me for whom it will be easier. I won't be anywhere but here, certainly not in Texas with Tommy.

His letters of late have continuous pleading with me to come, but I can't leave. I've got too much responsibility here. Lillian gave up the possibility of a life with Hank to care for Mama. It's my duty to manage the hotel. After a week of heartbreak and tears, I finally wrote to him, releasing him from our engagement. I've repeated the words so often to myself, they are branded on my heart ...

Dearest Tommy,

This is the hardest thing I've ever had to do, but I can't keep you tied to me.

You need to move on with your life. Find a girl in Texas who can give you her whole heart. I only have half of one to give. The other half must face my responsibility to Mama and my sisters. They cannot manage alone.

And so, my dearest, I release you from our engagement. Please know I've always loved you, and I want the best for you. Keep your mind on baseball and achieve your dreams.

Forever yours,

Genessee

After I mailed it, I told Miss Kara and together, we wept. She says she'll always think of me as her daughter, and she isn't giving up. She's praying for God to provide a way for me to be Tommy's wife.

While I appreciate her heart and her prayers, in this case, they're futile. I'm bound by duty to my family, and Tommy is tethered to his dream. I can't—I *won't* take it from him.

"Here's the last box." Willie stands beside me proudly holding the box with the green bow. His eyes widen and he giggles. "You've got hay in your hair, Miss Gen."

I feel my head. "You're right." I pull out the ones I find. "Now, then, my boy, let's get these down to the parlor. This afternoon, we go cut ourselves a Christmas tree."

It's a merry bunch that climbs into the old hay wagon. Mr. Patterson borrowed two horses from a neighboring farm just outside of Sweetgum. Mary and her parents join us as we prepare to head into the forest.

Mrs. Grundy takes a seat next to—Clarence Nesbitt? How have I missed this? She smiles up at him as he settles a lap robe over her legs. Years seem to have fallen off her. I blink. Am I really seeing what my eyes show me?

"Lillian," I whisper so only my sister hears, "do you see that?"

A giggle bursts from her lips. "I do. Isn't it a hoot? A couple of old coots finding love."

I slap her hand. "Stop. It's sweet. And I'm happy for her. It's been over seven years since her husband passed away. And they're not that old—mid-fifties is my guess."

Lillian leans over and kisses my cheek.

I draw back to peer at her. "What was that for?"

"Because if you hadn't been so nice to her that day, she'd still be mired in bitterness. And we wouldn't be the recipients of her joy. Do you know she helped me in the garden last Saturday? She pulled weeds, turned soil, and mulched."

"I think we're our lodgers' family in a way. At least, those who allow us to be." The wagon lurches forward, and I grab her hand.

Mary, who's sitting on my other side, grabs my other one and laughs. Soon the wheels move smoothly, carrying us out of town, and she releases her grasp. "What do you hear from Tommy? I was surprised he didn't come home for Thanksgiving."

I haven't told Mary yet, and this isn't the place. Not in a wagon full of people. "I suppose there wasn't time for him to come home between games."

She frowns. "Surely—"

She looks past me and doesn't go on. I don't know who or what stopped her, but I'm grateful. Though my lips tremble, I force them to pull up in a smile.

Tucking my lap robe tighter around my legs, I ask no one in particular, "What kind of tree are you looking for this year?"

Thankfully, that starts a discussion on the merits of a tall tree compared to a shorter-but-fuller one. Our lodgers are allowed small trees in their rooms, so long as no one uses candles. After the fire, I don't have to worry about that. Opinions fly back and forth along with plenty of laughter, which allows me to withdraw into myself. Next to me, Lillian squeezes my hand. Love for and from my sister helps soothe my sore heart.

Once in the woods, it doesn't take us long to find the trees we want. Mrs. Grundy is drawn to a short, fat tree. The Pattersons choose an eight-footer. Lillian selects one that is the same height and very full. It will go in the lobby. Then we find a seven-foot tree for the lodgers' parlor.

Willie is still looking for "the right tree" for our parlor. I'd just as soon forego it this year, but that wouldn't be fair to him.

"Over here! I found it." Willie's voice travels over a hill and through the woods.

"I see him." Annie points in his general direction. "Follow me."

Down in a hollow, Willie stands beside his perfect tree. And for him, it is. It's close to five feet tall with full, fluffy branches. It's just right.

When we get home, the men nail two pieces of crossed wood to the bottom of all the trees. Clarence and Leroy take the hotel's tree into the parlor for the lodgers to decorate. Sarah delivers bowls of popcorn and cranberries for them to string together.

Willie and Annie have the most fun adorning our tree. Mama watches them with rapt attention. The only glimmer of grief is when Annie lifts Willie up to place the star on top of the tree. Mama's eyes hold the sheen of tears. Soon, though, she's laughing as Willie sets up his toy trains around the base of the tree, pine needles sticking in his hair as he plays.

Annie goes to collect our mail and returns, waving a letter in her hands. My heart flutters. I couldn't bear one from Tommy. It's easier if I don't hear from him again. "It's from Maggie Parker."

Thank you.

I tear open the envelope and read the short note, relating the contents. "She'll be here in the late afternoon on January second. That's perfect since it's a Friday. We'll work all day Saturday and Sunday after church. She said that will be enough time if we have enough people." I lay the letter on the side table. "I'll order the hogs to be delivered on Friday." And I need to make sure the old spare pen is in good repair. We don't need any escapees.

With most of the lodgers in the parlor decorating their tree, I have a bit of privacy to make the call to the hog supplier. Someone answers on the second ring, and I give them my instructions.

"Yes, deliver them on January second. Send the bill to the Sweetgum Mill. Yes. Benjamin Spencer. Thank you." I hang the earpiece back on its hook and cross my fingers on both hands, at the same time shooting up a prayer for him to pay the bill without any arguments.

The injustice of Mr. Spencer's greed gnaws at me. Has it always been this way? I find Mama is in the kitchen with Sarah.

"What do I need to do?" Lillian, Annie, Beulah, and Charity have most of the meal on the tables in the dining room.

"Ring the bell and take out the last of the bread." Sarah hands me the cloth-covered bowl.

The lodgers descend on the dining room, their chatter full of Christmas cheer.

"Mama?" I scoot my chair up to the table. "Has Mr. Spencer always expected y'all to provide the lodgers' food from your salaries? I can't comprehend Daddy standing for it."

She shakes her head. "No, the food allowance is part of the rent he takes from their wages. That's always been my understanding."

Sarah's brows dip as she sips her soup. "I remember Brother Frank commenting on Mr. Spencer's greed. I believe he started cutting back on the budget we were given a little over a year ago." She blots her mouth with her napkin. "Yes, it was just before Thanksgiving last year."

Ah-ha! That sheds a little clarity. "Right after the stock market crashed. Do you think he lost a lot of money?"

Annie looks up through her lashes as she scoops a spoonful of soup, a chunk of carrot balancing precariously on its edge. "I never heard Fannie say much about the stock market. She used to brag about her daddy's money." The carrot falls from Annie's spoon, plopping into her bowl and splashing soup on her blouse. She wrinkles her nose and dabs at the stain with her napkin. "Fannie did say something about investments, but I didn't pay any attention. I'm not interested in that."

I'm interested, but only in Mr. Spencer *investing* in his workers' meals. "Knowing the past won't help us. The point is, he now expects us to pay for their food out of our salaries, which are less than ever before, while he still collects the same money from our lodgers." He's taking advantage of Daddy being gone. I narrow my eyes. The dirty rat.

"Genessee." Mama waits until I meet her gaze. "Don't let bitterness take root, daughter."

"I'm not bitter. I'm mad—angry at his greed and his lack of compassion. If we don't spend *our* money,"—I sweep my arm in a wide arc toward the dining room—"*they* don't eat decently. And in good conscience, I can't let them pay the price for that man's greed."

"Sister's heart's good, Mama." Lillian's hand hovers over the roll platter. "You don't need to worry about that. We just have to find a way to change this. Make it equitable." She sends a conspiratorial wink in my direction, then selects the bun she wants and butters it.

Clearly, she has something in mind, something she's not ready to share with everyone … but what?

Chapter 21

THOUGH IT'S NEARLY CHRISTMAS, THE kitchen is hot with both ovens going, even with the door and the window open. I wipe my forehead with the back of my wrist, then muscle a lump of pastry dough onto the counter. There's lots of Christmas specialties being made. I push the rolling pin, first one way, then turn the pastry and roll again. The bell in the lobby rings.

Sarah moves next to me and takes my rolling pin. "You see to whoever it is. I'll do this."

Hoping I don't have flour on my face, I hurry to the lobby. A man with a long, white beard—looking for all the world like Santa Claus except for the overalls—leans against the front desk. My first instinct is to call for Willie; however, not knowing this fellow, I squelch it.

"Good afternoon. May I help you?"

He holds out a crumpled paper. "Miss Taylor? Lee Campbell at your service." He doffs his cap and dips a little bow. "I've gotcher five hogs. I parked my rig at the side of the building."

Are all hog farmers so courtly?

He grins, staring at my forehead.

Automatically, my hand wipes at the flour I suspect is there. His grin widens, and he jerks his head to the left. I wipe that side. Then he winks.

Laughing, I thank him. "We're in the middle of pie making. Follow me, and I'll show you to the hog pen."

Reaching his truck, I leap up on the running board, hold onto the mirror, and direct him to the rear of the property, where we have the barn and hog pens. After he pulls his truck inside our fence, I jump down and close the gate behind him. One of the big hogs eyes me through the truck's wooden slats.

I smile at Mr. Campbell. "If you'll help me get these boys in there, I'll give you some pie and coffee for your trouble." Hopefully, Willie will still be in the kitchen so he can meet our unlikely St. Nick.

His eyes brighten. "I'd be obliged." Again, he winks just like Santa. "But I would have put 'em in without the pie." He lifts the lock-arm on the back of the truck. "You stand back, now."

I hold the pen gate open, remaining safely behind it. Hogs can be mean if they don't know you. The animals lumber down the ramp and go straight into the pen without any trouble. Mr. Campbell secures the gate for me.

I smile up at him again, attempting to sound nonchalant. "Has the bill been sent to the Sweetgum Mill?"

"Yes, ma'am. This"—he holds out the paper—"is just the bill of lading."

I take the receipt, praying the actual invoice doesn't find me. *Please let Mr. Spencer pay it.*

Watching Mr. Campbell close up the truck brings to mind the visit I made to Santa when I was Willie's age. That Christmas remains vivid in my memory. I had no idea the Santa was Mr. Patterson dressed up. And Mr. Campbell's whiskers are real. After all that's happened this year, Willie needs a special Christmas treat.

"May I request a favor? I know it's asking a lot, but we've got a little boy living here, and you look so much like Santa—"

"Claus, I know." He waves his hand. "I play Santa for the kids in our church. Usually, I have my suit with me, but the wife is cleaning it. Still, if you don't mind overalls, I'll be glad to."

Once he's sure the hogs are settled in and happily rooting, he turns the rig around, then parks it beside the kitchen entrance. Together, we go in. Willie's helping his mama snap beans.

Mr. Campbell spies our little guy, and I nod.

"Ho, ho, ho."

Wow, he sounds exactly right. Willie jumps and spins at the first "ho," his eyes huge and his jaw gaping.

"Do I see a young master Willie helping in the kitchen? This adds extra marks next to your name on my *nice* list."

"Santa?"

He sweeps the cap from his head and bows. "At your service."

"Wow! Where's your red suit?"

"Ah, well, a little boy, who is now on the naughty list because he didn't obey his mama and ate too much candy, threw up on my suit. Mrs. Claus is washing it."

Willie creeps closer to him. Miss Kara covers her mouth with her hand. Sarah's shoulders shake, and Mama stares at her lap while Annie stares at me. I know she's wondering how I managed this. I waggle my eyebrows.

Santa sits at the table and gestures for Willie, who hops onto his lap. While we were still outside, I gave Santa Willie's requests, so he's ready.

"So, young Willie, do you still want Santa to bring you a toy truck and a six-shooter like the Old Ranger on *Death Valley Days?*"

Willie's jaw drops as though it unhinges. I didn't think his eyes could grow any wider, but they have. Then he comes alive. "I sure do, Santa!"

Miss Kara already has those hidden in Mama's room.

"Well, now, you keep on being a good boy, and I'll see those get slipped into my bag."

Willie throws his arms around Mr. Campbell's neck. "Thank you."

I cut a slice of warm pie. "Willie, would you like to give this to Santa? Since we don't have cookies on hand." I offer him a wink.

Willie reverently hands the plate to him and sits at the table, watching him eat. I set the promised coffee in front of Mr. Campbell. We chat and tell Willie that Santa's elves have the North Pole well in hand, so he came to help deliver our hogs.

"After all, that's what I asked for, remember?"

Willie's awe is worth the fictional tales.

After Mr. Campbell departs, I check on the next delivery of ice. So far, Mr. Spencer continues to pay for that. The delivery for the icehouse is tomorrow. It will be ready for all the fresh meat once it's smoked.

"Are we all set, Gen?" Lillian stands at my shoulder.

I nod. "The icehouse will be refilled tomorrow, then replenished as needed. We're all ready, thanks to you. When—"

An old touring car pulls up and parks out front. Lillian and I share a grin and hurry out to meet Maggie Parker and her friend Sadie Moreland.

Maggie is exactly like the mental picture I have—slender and of average height, although a little shorter than me. Her brown hair, poking out beneath her cloche, shines with golden highlights in the afternoon sun. Her eyes are light brown, almost the color of nutmeg. Her smile is wide and open.

Her friend surprises me. Sadie Moreland is more than I expected. In her first letter, Maggie told me her friend is half Yamasee Indian and quite the character, and she's right. Miss Sadie puts me in mind of our Sarah. Oh, not in looks, but there's something about her that invites confidence. I love a woman who wears trousers. I've thought about getting some. They're so practical.

I step forward. "Ladies, I'm Genessee Taylor, and this is my sister Lillian." I thrust out my hand. "You'll meet our younger sister shortly. Miss Sadie, I'm honored to make your acquaintance. And yours, Miss Maggie. Thank you for coming."

Lillian greets them, then we pick up their bags and usher them inside.

"I'm not that much older than either of you, so please drop the 'Miss' and just call me Maggie." There's a shade of humor in her words. "Sadie can make her own choice."

Her companion snorts. "I'm plain Sadie, except to children." She pulls a tin box from her pocket, opens it, and slips something into her mouth. I'm pretty sure it's not snuff—at least, I hope not. Maggie doesn't pay any attention to the movement, so I'm guessing it isn't. Lillian glances at me and shrugs, then grins. We follow them into the lobby.

I set down Sadie's bag. "I've already registered you. It's a formality in this case. But would y'all prefer separate rooms? We have twin beds in every room, but you're welcome to—"

Maggie waves away my chatter. "One room is fine. We're country folk, Genessee, and the best of friends."

"If y'all would like to freshen up first, we could—"

Maggie smiles. "We're fine, and I'm anxious to look around. Do you know this is the first time I've ever stayed in a hotel?"

That puts me at ease. "If we didn't manage this one, we would say the same. We'd be delighted to give you the grand tour, then we'll go into the kitchen so you can meet the rest of the family."

I laugh so hard, tears run down my cheeks, and I'm in danger of choking. If Maggie and Sadie do nothing more than sit around our kitchen table telling stories, the weekend will be wonderful. None of us have rocked with laughter like this since Annie was eight years old and tried to baptize a barn cat.

Sadie grins and pops another clove in her mouth—I finally figured out that's what they were when she laughed close enough for me to smell her breath. "If you could have seen that pack of polecats turn and abandon Cal, leaving him all alone with his jaw wagging and spittin' out excuses for his behavior, while Wade's shotgun was aimed at his back and mine at his nether regions, you'd have cheered."

I sure would have. I could use some of Sadie and Maggie's moxie. "I don't know how you did it. I'd have been frightened to death."

"Oh, I was," Maggie admits. "But Sadie kept telling me not to let it show. I tightened every muscle so I wouldn't tremble. And I hurt all over the next day."

Hero-worship shines in Annie's eyes. Apparently, Maggie notices it because she looks directly at her. "All I ever wanted to do was take care of my son and keep the grocery as his legacy. It's all I had to give him."

Miss Kara's brows draw together. "But you write those helpful columns—I've read them in the newspaper, and Willie loves your bedtime stories." She glances at me, then back to Maggie. "I ... I dabble with writing." Heat rises to Miss Kara's cheeks.

I nudge her. "Maybe, if Maggie doesn't mind, you could show her one of yours."

Tommy's mother shakes her head, the curls surrounding her face jiggling. "Oh, I couldn't."

Maggie grins. "Sure you can. I'd love to see one. I've never known a single author who burst from the womb a brilliant writer. We all need varying degrees of mentoring. Please allow me to read something. I promise I'll be kind but honest."

Hesitating, Miss Kara rises slowly. "Then I'll go get a short story."

I reach out and stop her. "The one about Vera. Make it that one."

Her eyes question. Then she nods and leaves the kitchen. I turn back to Maggie.

"Thank you. I've been trying to encourage her, but she lacks confidence and just thinks that my opinion is because she's—" How do I explain without opening the floodgates again?

Annie's mouth overrides her tail. "She was going to be Genessee's mother-in-law."

"Annie!" I hiss, mortified.

Sadie winks at me and rises. "Sounds like a story for another time. Right now, I'm going to bed. Good night, ladies."

Maggie waves her off. "I'll be up as soon as Kara brings me her story." She yawns behind her hand.

I breathe a sigh of relief and give Annie the stink-eye for her runaway tongue. Miss Kara returns and shyly hands the papers to Maggie.

"I can't thank you enough. You can be honest. If nothing ever comes from this, writing my daughter's story has been cathartic."

When I go to turn down the lamp wicks, I pause in the lobby. Maggie stands as still as a statue halfway up the staircase. She's reading the papers in her hands—Miss Kara's story. A satisfying smile pulls my lips. I'll come back for the stairwell lantern in a few minutes.

A rifle shot startles me from slumber. It's quickly followed by two more. It's still dark. Fear, sharp and encompassing, rattles me until I remember today's the slaughter. But who——?

I hurry and dress in overalls and a flannel shirt, then run downstairs. Sarah is in the kitchen starting breakfast.

"Slow down, Gen. That's Sadie. She wanted to get the hogs put down before anyone else messed with them. She's a crack shot, I understand."

I let out the breath I've been holding. "That's good to know. I'm sure everyone else will be awake by now." I chuckle. "I'll admit she's a good alarm clock." I grab a coffee mug and pour myself a cup. "Did Sadie get any coffee?" More rapid gunshots make me jump. Hot liquid sloshes on my hand. "Ow!"

"Be careful, lass. And no, she didn't."

I blot my hand, pour Sadie a cup, and take them to the pen behind the barn. Sadie is directing five men from the village. They dispatch the last few hogs quickly and humanely with a single shot each.

I hand Sadie her cup and welcome the men. "Sarah will bring us more coffee soon. I didn't know all y'all were here already. Thank you so much for helping."

While Sadie drinks, she shows me something that looks like a tent frame. "The hogs will hang there. There's a lot to do before we actually butcher them. They have to be bled, scalded, scraped, and shaved. Tomorrow, we'll do the actual butchering." She nods in answer to a question by one of the men. "The hogs will hang out here overnight. That's why you have to wait for cold weather."

There's a lot to take in if we're going to do this on our own next year. It's a good thing we put all the animals in the barn. Stationed between the garden and the pig's pen, there are four large kettles.

"Those are for rendering the fat," Sadie tells me. Wood for the fires are laid beneath each one. They'll be started right after church tomorrow.

Once again, I thank God for Maggie and Sadie. And my sister Lillian. She corresponded more with Maggie than I did about what was needed. She got all this ready. And here I thought she didn't have any idea how to manage anything but ribbons and merchandise at

Norton's. I need to apologize to her.

Everyone is busy. By nine-thirty, the hogs are scalded, then we pick up the scrapers and get to work. Maggie and I are on opposite sides of the same hog.

I peek over and clear my throat. "Tell me more about Sadie. She fascinates me."

Maggie peers at me, then nods. Last night, I noticed how she watched everyone's reaction to Sadie. She's protective of her friend.

"I imagine she's faced a lot of prejudice in her life," I add.

Maggie smiles. "She sure has. And though she's spent most of her life in Rivers End, some folks still turn their noses up." She grimaces. "Sadie became my first friend when I arrived in town, a new bride." She glances over at Sadie, who is laughing with Mrs. Grundy.

I nod toward them. "Now there's an oxymoron." I tell her about Mrs. Grundy's metamorphosis. "I'm glad she's making a new friend."

Maggie grins, running a razor over the pig's skin to remove the hair. "Sadie will befriend everyone if they let her." She goes on to tell me how she nursed her friend through the Spanish flu and about Sadie's years on her own as a small child, making me gape.

"I can't imagine it. I never would have made it." I take a moment's rest and let my gaze find my sisters. Would they have? Sadie rises even higher in my esteem. But my favorite story Maggie tells is of Sadie getting back at some woman who threw a tomato at her. She hit the woman in the head with her suffragette sign and knocked her out cold. That makes me laugh out loud, which draws Annie over to find out why.

Sharing with Maggie makes the morning's work fly by, although my arms are aching from using different muscles. We stop for dinner at noon. Everyone sits at two old wooden tables in the yard. Once we all are eating fried chicken, Maggie's eyes twinkle with mirth.

"I should tell y'all about our hog slaughter and my sister, Duchess, cooking fried chicken."

I can tell Maggie is a writer because she's a fantastic storyteller. She makes us see her sister and her culinary mishaps. Soon, we're all chuckling over the escapades and cheering her success.

Annie sighs. "Rivers End sure sounds like a fun place."

Maggie's smile is indulgent. "Annie, the fun is with people you love. Rivers End is actually smaller than Sweetgum." She waves her hand toward the street beyond the hotel. "It's only one short block long, with stores on one side of the street. The train station is on the other side. We make our own fun, as I'm sure you and your sisters do."

Annie thinks on that for a moment, then her bright smile appears. "I get what you mean. My sisters *are* a lot of fun, especially when we play charades." She snickers. "They're pretty silly."

Lillian crosses her eyes, making Annie giggle. The work continues after dinner and up until nearly suppertime. When we call it quits for the day, Sadie surveys where we are in the process.

"Y'all have done well." She spits a chewed clove into the dirt. "We'll be able to finish the butchering after church and be done before suppertime."

I have mixed emotions about that. I'll be glad for the meat, but I'll hate to see Maggie and Sadie go. I've made two new friends I may never see again.

Chapter 22

BY LATE AFTERNOON SUNDAY, SMOKE curls from the full smokehouse, sending tantalizing ribbons into the cold evening air. The icehouse contains all the fresh pork we will need in the coming months. Tomorrow, Sarah will make sausage, and once it's in the casings, the links will join the other meat for smoking. The men who helped us were grateful for the pork and rendered fat they took home.

At noon, Maggie told Miss Kara she had a gift. "You made me cry and laugh while reading your story. It's unforgettable. You must keep writing. I wish we were closer so I could offer more help, but you'll do fine. You're a natural-born storyteller."

"Thank you." Miss Kara's cheeks glowed with Maggie's encouragement.

"I suggest you show your stories to your local newspaper editor. If you send me some, I'll show them to mine at the *Lawrenceville News Standard.*"

"Thank you so much, Maggie." Miss Kara's eyes glimmered with moisture. "Your opinion means the world to me."

Sadie and Maggie need to depart before supper, so we prepare to send them on their way with their meal in a basket to eat on the road. They're going back to Lawrenceville and then to Rivers End in the morning.

"Maggie?" I lay my hand on her arm as she climbs into the passenger seat of their car. "I can't thank you enough. If I can ever be of help to you, please don't hesitate to call. You have our number now. I hope we can exchange letters too." I like this woman and want to remain friends.

She flashes a bright smile. "I'd like that, Genessee."

Lillian links arms with me after we wave goodbye from the porch. "They were such fun. Sadie is wise, and I really admire Maggie. I'd love to meet her sister, Duchess, someday. She sounds like someone I'd like."

I touch my head to Lillian's shoulder. "I love you. You know, when Maggie told me about her sister and how she changed after moving in with her, I thought of you."

She looks at me, blinking. "Me? Why?"

"Because *you've* changed. You never had much time for anything but working at Norton's and planning to escape Sweetgum. But you quickly gave up that dream for us when Daddy died. You're the one who made this weekend work, Lillian. I never even thought about all the details you arranged. Thank you."

She doesn't say a word, but her smile does as we go back into the lobby. My big sister is deeper than I ever realized. I have yet to plumb her depths, but I'm looking forward to it. She's an amazing woman and the one person who has an inkling of how sore my heart remains over Tommy.

Will Lillian ever marry and leave us? Unless things change dramatically at the mill, I doubt it. I know I never will. There isn't another man like Tommy. Not for me, anyway. He's the right to my left. The bottom to my top. The front to my back.

And I miss him with all my heart. Will I ever be able to stop?

Normally, Annie sorts the mail, but this afternoon, she's learning the fine art of bread making, so I'm doing her chore. It's mindless. Read a name, slide the envelope in the right slot. We don't get a lot of mail, and neither do our lodgers, although a few of the ladies subscribe to magazines. Those are always interesting to see. Annie thumbs through them first, something I have to remind her not to do. I roll a magazine and slip it into its owner's mail cubby after reading its cover.

"Afternoon, ma'am."

I glance up and my jaw unhinges. Before me stands the most handsome man I've ever seen. Surrounded by dark lashes, startling blue eyes meet mine. A lock of dark blond hair curls onto his brow. His suit appears to be custom tailored—it fits him too well to be off the rack or from a Sears Catalog. Who is he?

He sets his bag on the floor and leans on the counter. "Archie Quigg's the name. I'm in need of a room."

I snap my jaw shut. His accent is definitely not Southern. I can't tell if it's Yankee or Midwestern. Could he be a businessman? Or a partner with Spencer and Forsythe? No, he's too young to be an investor. Then again, how old does a man need to be to invest money? Old enough to have some, I guess.

I set down the mail and push the registry book toward him. "Yes, sir. Are you here on business?"

"You could say that."

Is that a yes? "How long do you plan to stay?"

He completes filling in his information, signs with a flourish, and turns the book back to me with a grin. "Depends. How much is the room?"

Surely, money can't be the determining factor. He's too well-dressed. "Since we're a full-service hotel, that depends on whether you plan to take your meals here or at the Evans Diner."

"What time do you serve them?"

"Breakfast is at five-thirty, dinner at noon, and supper is at six-thirty."

He grimaces at the early morning time. "Probably at the diner, then. I never know how long my appointments will take."

"In that case, it's a dollar-fifty per night."

He reaches in his pocket and pulls out a large roll of money, licks his thumb, and peels off three five-dollar bills. "Let's start with ten nights, then. I'll see how business is going."

Reeling from the size of the wad of money in his hand, I turn to the key rack. Since he's an extended stay, I remove the key for room two-twelve. "I'll show you to your room."

He holds out his empty hand. "I'm sure I can find it if you'll point me in the right direction." The three five-dollar bills lay on the counter, and his bankroll is no longer in sight.

I give him the key and point. "Up that stairway, second door to your left."

He smiles, picks up his suitcase, and disappears up the stairs. Oh, my … wait until Annie sees him. *Annie.* Could he be—no, there's no reason for a movie star to be in Sweetgum. But he's definitely got the looks. Opening the registry again, I glance over Mr. Quigg's information.

Full name: Archibald Louis Quigg

Address: 9 Spearmint Avenue, Kansas City, Kansas

So he's not a Yankee, but aren't all men from the Midwest cowboys? I cross to the window. There's not a horse out front—no car either. So how did he get here? I look back over my shoulder and grin. I've got to tell my sisters.

They should be in the dining room. "Annie? Lillian? Let's get the rooms cleaned." With the slaughter over the weekend, we barely got the sheets changed. We still need to clean the rooms today. And do laundry. Ugh. My arms ache at the thought of the washtubs.

As soon as I see my sisters setting the tables, I beckon them to hurry. Beulah and Charity can finish that chore without them. "Keep your eyes alert and the room doors open while you clean. You might get to see our newest lodger. And you've got to see him to believe me when I say I've never seen a more handsome man. Ever." I waggle my eyebrows.

Annie turns her head and eyes me sidelong. "Movie-star handsome?"

She has conditions for that label.

I nod and turn for the guest rooms. "You better believe it. He's so fine looking, I got tongue-tied."

Annie's eyes widen.

Lillian's more practical. "Who is he?"

"Name's Archie Quigg. He's some kind of businessman."

She frowns. "You didn't find out any more?"

Juggling a broom and dustpan, I open the door to room two-ten. "What could I do? All we require is a name, address, and cash." I hold a warning finger to my lips to hush them, nodding to room two-twelve. I repeat his full name. "He's from Kansas City. That's all I know. He seems very nice." I don't mention the one thing that still bothers me. It's strange for a businessman not to have a car. He *could* have arrived on the train, but how will he visit his customers?

While Annie runs a carpet sweeper across the rug, I whisk the broom over the wood floor. Lillian dusts, and we're done in ten minutes. Big Sis and I turn to leave only to discover Annie with a glass up against the wall, listening.

"He's whistling."

Lillian pulls her away. "Not kosher, little girl."

We continue down the hall through all the rooms on the second floor, then do the third floor, where we have four private rooms and the dormitory. We finish them all in an hour. We're on our way downstairs when Archie's door opens, and he steps out.

At the same time, Lillian's and Annie's jaws drop. They quickly recover and close their mouths simultaneously, making me smile.

He tips his hat. "Ah, the lovely Miss Taylor. And who are these beautiful ladies?"

Lillian's smile is flirtatious, and Annie sighs. Oh dear. Annie's reaction I expect, but Lillian's? There's a surprise.

"These are my sisters, Mr. Quigg. This is Lillian." I nod toward her. "And this is Annie."

"Charmed, ladies." He pulls out a watch from his vest pocket and opens it. "Since it's nearly dinnertime, can you point me to that diner you mentioned?"

"Dinner? It's su—" I step on Annie's toe to shut her up. I can't have her embarrass our guest over our Southern culture.

Lillian inches closer. "Evans is out the front door, turn to your left, and it's the second establishment from the corner."

He doffs his hat and bows. "Thank you, Miss Taylor."

The three of us stand, frozen in place, as he disappears down the stairs.

"So do you believe—"

"Who do you sup—"

"He's the most—"

I throw up my hand, laughing. "Stop! Let's not become a huddle of starry-eyed-thirteen-year-olds."

Annie leans over the banister, trying to get a final glimpse. "You sure were right about him, Gen. He's as handsome as any movie star I've ever seen."

Lillian smooths her hair. "I know Mama always says, 'handsome is as handsome does,' and I'm just positive he's going to prove her right." She starts down the steps.

I grab her apron strings, stopping her. "Where are you going?"

"I suddenly have a yen for Josie Evans' cherry pie." Lillian yanks the apron off, leaving it dangling from my fingers.

Annie runs after her. "Me too!"

This is ridiculous. I follow them. "Cherry pie in January?"

"Ever hear of canning, Genessee?" Annie tosses over her shoulder.

"Get back here! We have lodgers to feed." They reluctantly halt at the front door and turn back. I wag my finger at both of them. "Be glad I stopped you. Y'all are so obvious, it's embarrassing. Not to mention unbecoming."

Annie sticks out her tongue. "You're just jealous." She tosses her head, pushes through the door to our quarters, and flounces to the kitchen.

After supper is over and the dishes done, Annie and Lillian find all sorts of reasons to stake out the lobby, waiting for Mr. Quigg to return. I must say it's odd that he's still gone. In truth, it's none of my business, but I'm afraid I forgot to tell him we lock the front door at nine o'clock.

Miss Kara pushes Mama into the lobby. From her chair, Mama studies us. "What has you girls all a'flap and a'flutter?"

I grimace. "Our newest guest. I forgot to tell him what time we lock the doors."

Annie clasps her hands beneath her chin. "Mama, you should see him. He's absolutely the bee's knees."

Miss Kara's gaze snaps to me. I give her a wry grimace. "She's right.

The man is beyond good looking. And my *sisters* are smitten."

Mama opens her mouth, then closes it. Her eyes find mine, and she worries her necklace. Whatever she wants to say, she isn't forthcoming with it.

I bend down. "Don't worry. I'll keep an eye on them."

At nine o'clock, I enter the lobby and lock the front door with reluctance. Mr. Quigg has not yet returned. I gnaw at my lip. What should I do? I can't leave it open. There are so many hobos around, anyone could wander inside.

I reopen the door and step out on the front porch. The night air is cold, close to freezing. I shiver and rub my arms while I peer down the block, first toward the diner and then toward the mill. The town is silent and dark. There's no sign of Mr. Quigg.

Back inside, I turn the lock and go to my room. My alarm will ring at four-thirty no matter what time I go to sleep.

Annie is sitting up in bed, reading a movie magazine. She drops it to her lap when I come in.

"Did Archie get back?"

"That's Mr. Quigg, Annie. And no, he didn't."

She heaves a sigh. "Fine. But I hope you didn't latch the door. Did you?"

I catch her gaze in the mirror as I brush my hair. "What was I to do? We can't leave it open."

She folds her arms and pouts. "But you can't just lock out a guest. Besides, it's your fault for not telling him."

"I know ... and I feel bad."

She throws back the covers and grabs her robe. "Well, I'm going downstairs. I'll wait for him in the parlor."

"Annie, you cannot meet him in your bathrobe."

She huffs and yanks off her robe and nightie. "Fine." She pulls a dress over her head and slides her feet into slippers. "There. Is that all right?"

I nod, but I'm not happy with her attitude. Mr. Quigg is causing trouble, and he isn't even aware of it.

Or is he?

Chapter 23

A LOUD RINGING JARS ME AWAKE. Yawning, I slap the off-switch on my alarm clock. I shove the covers back and glance at Annie's bed. It's empty. She's never been up *before* me. What could've—oh, of course. Mr. Quigg. I throw on a robe and hurry downstairs and into the parlor, where I find her sound asleep on the settee. I shake her shoulder.

"Annie? Wake up, sugar. It's time to collect eggs."

She stretches and starts to turn over, then pops up. "Where's Arch—Mr. Quigg?"

"I don't know. Didn't you let him in?"

"No. He never came to the door."

We stare at each other in disbelief. I recover first. "There's nothing to be done, and we have chores. Come on."

I shoo Annie into our family quarters when Archie's voice startles me.

"Good morning, Miss Taylor."

I pull my robe tighter around me and turn. He's either up very early, or he's just coming in. But I haven't unlocked the door yet. I need to know, but how do I ask? Casually is probably best. "Good morning. How was your night?"

"Wonderful, thank you. That's a very comfortable bed." He tips his hat and goes out the front door—the *unlocked* front door.

Who unlocked it? And where is he going at four-thirty in the morning?

And did he really sleep in his bed, or is he just being nice and not telling me he was locked out? I run upstairs. I have to know. After glancing over my shoulder, I use my key and open his room. The bed has definitely been slept in. I back out of the room and lock his door.

Downstairs, Annie's in the kitchen picking up the egg baskets.

"Are you positive you don't remember letting Mr. Quigg in last night?" I keep my voice low so nobody but my sister hears.

"I told you I didn't. Why?" She hands me one of the baskets.

I take it and pull her out the back door. "He slept in his room."

Annie frowns. "How could that be? Did he slip past us somehow?"

"That's what I'm trying to find out." I shiver in the cold morning air. "And the front door was unlocked when he left just now."

"Well, did you ask him?"

I shake my head. "No. I didn't know how without sounding like a snoop."

Annie pauses for a moment, her hand on the henhouse door. "You don't suppose he's got magical powers, do you?"

"Don't be silly." I can't help my eyes rolling.

She opens the door and steps inside. "Then you explain it."

"I can't. But I'll sure be keeping an eye on him to find out."

"I'll be glad to help you do that." A cheeky grin pops on Annie's face.

I reach beneath the first hen, take her egg, and move on. "What I can't figure out is what business he has in Sweetgum unless it's with Mr. Spencer."

"Who cares?" Annie snickers. "He's the first bit of fun to land here in years."

My hand finds nothing in the third nest. That's not totally out of the norm. Chickens don't always lay every day. The next nest is also empty. When the fifth is bare as well, I know we have a problem. "Are you finding any empty nests?"

"Uh-huh. Several of them."

"I've counted five so far. Multiple hens in a row not laying spells trouble." Not to mention, lost money. If they're sick, I need to find out how bad and maybe isolate those hens. "Mark the nests that were empty."

Annie doesn't move, worry playing across her brow. "I didn't pay much attention at first. Not until you said something." The sheen of welling tears shines in her eyes. The poor kid is beginning to realize how shaky our financial state is.

"It's all right, sugar. Just pay attention to the rest. Mark any nests." Then I realize we have nothing to mark them with. I blow out a sigh. "Let's just get finished. I'll call Doc Adams."

We complete the egg gathering, and I estimate a quarter of our flock is affected with—whatever it is. We don't have any eggs to sell to the general store today.

Doc Adams sets the chicken back on the ground. With a squawk over the rude examination, she flaps and scuttles away. "Fowl pox."

"Chicken pox?"

Doc smiles but shakes his head. "People get chicken pox. Chickens get fowl pox." He lifts up another hen. Gently, he spreads apart her feathers. "See these white spots on the skin? And the scabby sores on the combs? Those are a couple of the symptoms. There are others, but you'll notice these first. Since some have stopped laying, we know they're developing fowl pox."

"Is there a remedy? What should I do?" The idea of losing the whole flock is devastating. I'd throw up if I had anything in my stomach.

Doc soothes the hen in his arms. "Don't give up yet. You can feed them soft food and give them a warm, dry place to try to recover. With adequate care, there is a good chance your birds can survive this illness."

"Do you think all of our chickens have it?" *Mercy, Lord, please?*

"You'll have to wait and see. Do you have another coop?"

"No. We can make one, but where?"

"The barn should be fine. It's dry. Remove the hens that didn't lay and isolate them in the new coop. I'll give you a recipe for a mash for them to eat. Each day you find one not laying, move her over."

He packs up his bag, scribbles the recipe for me, hands me his bill, and leaves. On top of everything else, I've got to build a coop for our chickens to recoup. I snort at the rhyme. Then tomorrow, we'll have to note which hens need moving and then take those to the new coop. All while gathering eggs. And pay Doc Adams.

Feeling overwhelmed, I sigh, flex my fisted hands, and open the kitchen door. Everyone is at the table, waiting for me. Should I tell them about the chickens? Then I realize it's dinnertime. "Thank you for picking up my slack." I wash my hands, wishing I didn't have to tell them the news. I finally pull out my chair and join them.

No one says anything for a moment. Then everyone starts at once.

"What did Doc say?"

"Are the chickens gonna die, Miss Gen?"

"What do we do about this?"

One side of my lips pull up in a mock smirk. "One at a time, please. Willie, we're hoping none of them die. They have fowl pox. We have to build a new coop in the barn to isolate the sick birds."

Lillian frowns over her coffee cup. "Do we know how to do that?"

I shake my head. "I'll have to ask around or try to find a book in the school library. But we need to do it quickly."

"I'll go to the school for you right after we eat." Lillian flaps her napkin and lays it in her lap. "I think we might have some leftover lumber in the barn from the fire repairs. And there's a roll of chicken wire in the hayloft."

Thank you, Lord. I sit up hopefully. "Do you think there's enough?"

Lillian shrugs. "I haven't the slightest idea. But we'll find out soon enough." She picks up her fork and spears a bite of chicken. Then stops. She peers at the meat. "Uh, do we think this is okay?"

"Yes. Doc said we can't get it."

But she lays her fork down. "I think I'll go see if I can find that book now." She jumps up and leaves before any of us can react. She's always had a sensitive stomach.

Mine's swirling from Doc's diagnosis. If we lose the chickens, we not only lose the money from the eggs we sell, we'll have to buy eggs from the general store to feed the lodgers—at a high price. And chicken. We'll have to buy that, too, for a while. My heart sinks to my toes. For Mama's and Willie's sake, I smile. Beneath the table, Miss

Kara squeezes my hand.

Faith. I need to exercise faith. I smile at her. "What are the plans for supper?"

Sarah chuckles. "Soup, and it's already simmering. We've got the bread rising, so you can concern yourself with the chick—"

The back door bangs open, and Lillian rushes in with Archie Quigg in tow. "Guess who knows about fowl pox and how to build a chicken coop?"

I'm still processing having a guest in the kitchen and can only hope my smile looks genuine. I introduce Mr. Quigg to Mama, Miss Kara, a disapproving Sarah, and Willie.

I understand Sarah's feelings. Lodging guests do *not* belong in the kitchen. Little Willie stares with interest at the stranger. I hope I don't have a case of hero-worship on my hands. My sisters are enough to worry about.

When the pleasantries are over, I ask, "Is building chicken coops part of your business?"

Mr. Quigg's laugh is contagious, and I find myself grinning. "No. I was raised on a farm. We had chickens and they got fowl pox. We were able to save most of the flock. But we have to move quickly. Miss Lillian mentioned you have some extra lumber in the barn. May I see it and your flock?"

Annie jumps up first. "Come on, I'll show you." She grabs his arm, and they disappear through the back door with Lillian on their heels.

Mama shakes her head and shares a chuckle with Miss Kara. "These modern girls. In our day, we wouldn't have been so forward."

I sigh and stand up. "I'd better go make sure this is about a coop and not a battle between sisters." Mama's laughter rings in my ears as I go out the back door. What does she find funny?

When I open the door to the henhouse, Willie runs into my back. "I wanna see, Miss Gen."

"Okay, sugar." He loves those chickens and is good with them. "Maybe you can help us."

Archie turns at our entry. "You've got quite a large flock here, Miss

Taylor." He removes his hat and hangs it on a nail.

Willie takes off his cap and hangs it on another peg beneath Mr. Quigg's.

"Well, we feed at least fifty people three meals a day. Eggs and chickens are a large part of that."

"I'm impressed. The first thing that needs to be done is removing the chicks from the coop."

"I've got just the place for them." I pick up one of the chicks and hand it to Willie. "Buster's pen. We'll take him into the house."

Mr. Quigg glances from me to Annie to Lillian and back. "Buster?"

Willie strokes the chick with one finger. "He's Miss Genessee's pet ferret."

"He probably wouldn't hurt the chicks." Annie flutters her eyelashes. "He hasn't been in the wild since he was a baby and doesn't know how to hunt."

She's right, but … "Let's not test that theory right now. Y'all get the chicks, and I'll take care of moving Buster."

Lillian's hand stops me. "What if one of the lodgers finds out?"

"I think anyone would agree, the eggs are a priority." I hurry out to move Buster into the house.

Soon, the chicks are in the ferret's pen under the porch. I leave Willie to make sure they settle in and go see if the temporary coop is underway.

In the barn, Mr. Quigg finishes counting the boards. "You've got enough lumber here. Let's get started."

I select the best spot to put the coop. Annie measures the boards, Lillian saws, and Mr. Quigg nails them together with swift precision.

I step in to help him. "You're quite good at this."

He glances sidelong at me, then back at the nail he's holding. "You sound surprised." His hammer falls true once, twice, thrice, and the nail is flush with the wood.

"I'll admit, I am. Building chicken coops isn't normally a skill required of businessmen."

He chuckles and picks up another board. I hold it steady for him to nail to the one below it, then try a different tactic.

"You said you grew up on a farm. What was it like?"

Annie and Lillian stop their work and move closer.

He glances at me, then returns his gaze to his work. "Just like this, only larger."

"Like this?" Annie laughs. "We aren't a farm."

"Sure, you are. You raise animals and grow crops."

Huh, he's got her there. But he's not giving up any information either. I find it strange, but then, maybe he just doesn't like to talk about himself.

Lillian steps to his side. "Was your farm in your family for generations?"

Is she curious or flirting?

"My grandparents homesteaded the land in 1863."

I hand him another board. "Didn't you like farming?"

A one-shoulder shrug is my only answer. He pounds the nails in swift and straight.

"I must say, your carpentry skills are quite impressive. Even Daddy bent a few nails when he built things."

This time, all I receive is a grin. I give up. But did something bad happen between him and his family? I kind of feel sorry for him.

We finish the coop and situate the sick chickens in it. I have the soft mash ready to feed them, which Sarah made for us. I put it into a few bowls.

Mr. Quigg leaves us with a tip of his hat and without looking back. My sisters stand beside me, watching him disappear around the side of the hotel, but I'm pretty sure their reasons are different from mine.

I'd give up my Sunday shoes to know his story. For some reason, he makes me uneasy.

Chapter 24

"Gen, telephone," Annie calls from the hallway.

I drop the sheets on Mrs. Grundy's bed and run downstairs. Picking up the earpiece, I jerk my head toward the second floor and mouth "sheets." My sister nods and leaves to complete the chore.

"Hello?"

"Miss Taylor, this is Lee Campbell. I delivered your hogs."

A mental picture of his face flashes through my mind. "Yes, I remember. You also played Santa for a very excited little boy."

A chuckle rumbles through the crackly telephone line. "I was glad to do it. But right now, we have a little problem. Mr. Spencer refuses to pay the bill for the hogs."

"What?" This is the last thing I need on top of fowl pox. I take a deep breath, hoping it calms the trembling in my voice. "Can you give me a day so I can have a talk with him? I promise I'll call you back right away."

"Yes. Thanks, I appreciate that." I rest the earpiece on its hook.

Lillian passes through the lobby with an armload of sheets stacked to her hairline. She peers around them. "Give me a hand?"

"Sure." I take half the stack and we head upstairs.

She eyes me sidelong, worry lines creasing her forehead. "You look down. What's wrong? More chickens sick?"

I shake my head. "Mr. Spencer refused to pay for the hogs."

Lillian trips and drops the sheets. Two tumble down a few steps. "What? How can he do that?"

"Quite easily, it seems, according to Mr. Campbell." I set down my stack, and we both bend to retrieve hers. "Mr. Campbell called. I've got to confront Mr. Spencer, but it sure won't be pleasant."

Lillian bumps shoulders with me. "I'll tag along if you want."

"Thanks." I'll be glad for her support. When she wants to, Lillian can be intimidating.

We complete changing the beds and cleaning the rooms—all but Mr. Quigg's. Lillian knocks on his door, as we always do, just in case someone isn't working. He opens it.

His shirt is untucked and he's barefoot. "Ah, the Miss Taylors." He eyes the sheets in Lillian's arms. "Let me have those. I'll save you the trouble. I'll just leave the dirty ones right here in the hall. Thank you." He takes the sheets from her and shuts the door.

My sister and I stare at one another in bewilderment.

"I don't believe that." Lillian raises her hand to knock, but I quickly stop her, pulling her toward the next room.

"If he wants to make up his own bed, we can't stop him," I whisper.

One of her shoulders lifts. "I know, but I wanted a chance to chat with him."

"You're besotted." I shake my head. "And we don't know anything about him."

Her grin is cheeky. "Sure we do. He's from Kansas and grew up on a farm."

I follow her down the stairs. "Do you hear yourself? You sound like Annie."

"Piffle. Annie's too young for him. But you have to admit, he's the best-looking man we've seen in Sweetgum for many a moon, or anywhere else, for that matter. I'll go toe-to-toe with her for him." She tosses her head and goes into her room, closing the door.

Miss Kara pokes her head into the hall. "Did I hear Lillian say something about going toe-to-toe with Annie?"

I sigh and follow her into the kitchen. "Yes. They're both infatuated with Mr. Quigg. I'm a little worried about them."

Sarah stirs batter for a cake. "A little worry, like a little leavening, keeps you on your toes."

I do a double take, then laugh. "That doesn't make sense."

Sarah chuckles. "I know. Me mother used to say it all the time. But what she meant was it goes a long way to keeping you watchful—on your toes."

I measure out flour for a triple batch of bread dough. "My concern is, he's very close-mouthed and not forthcoming with information about himself." I measure and add yeast, sugar, and salt to the flour.

Miss Kara peels potatoes at the counter next to me. "What do you mean?"

"I've asked him several questions, and somehow, he avoids the actual answer." Making a well in the flour mixture, I pour in the water and eggs in its center, then mix it in with my hands. "I think he had a falling out with his family, and that's why he left their farm."

"It would have to be a pretty bad falling out to make him leave hearth and home, methinks." Sarah dips a spoon into the stew and tastes it. She nods and lays the spoon in the sink for washing.

"Would it? I don't know. Men are more competitive. Maybe a brother inherited the lion's share of the farm." I'm grasping at dandelion fluff, but Mr. Quigg is hiding something. I'm sure of it.

"Well, he seems to have made a successful life for himself," Miss Kara says. "That's the important part."

"I guess." After kneading the dough, I plop it in a large, greased bowl, cover it with a cloth, and set it on the warming shelf to rise. Immediately, I start another batch. Making bread is a never-ending job.

As I mix the dough, I rehearse what I'll say to Mr. Spencer. What will I do if he refuses? I can't send the hogs back. He'll have to pay for them, or he needs to give us the money the lodgers pay for food.

But what if he doesn't? Then what? A chill settles over my shoulders.

Last time I sat in Mr. Spencer's office, I was so nervous, I paid little attention to how incongruous the space is with the mill building. The main mill is weathered brick and raw wood. This room boasts polished mahogany and heavy velvet draperies. Even the richly upholstered furniture screams money. That absurdity testifies to greed.

Beside me, Lillian's struggling to keep from showing disgust. She clenches and unclenches her fists in her lap.

Mr. Spencer leans back in his chair and folds his arms over his chest. His eyes narrow, and his lips turn downward. "I don't 'got' to do anything, Miss Taylor. You receive a generous salary."

Generous? The man's delusional.

"You can order the hotel's food from the general store," Mr. Spencer continues. "Put it on account. If it's to feed the lodgers, I'll take it from what they pay me for meals. But if it's for your family, you'll pay for it out of your salary."

"We save you money by butchering hogs and chickens ourselves."

He shrugs. "That's *your* choice."

The door opens. "Daddy, can you—ohh." Fannie Spencer stands at the entrance, looking like she stepped in a pile of goose droppings when she sees us. Mr. Spencer's eyes light up at the appearance of his daughter. Her soft pink suit has a fur collar, and I'm guessing it isn't fake.

"Come in, my darling. The Taylors are just leaving."

I rise. "And that's your last word?"

"It is."

Lillian squares off with him. "You're a hard man, Benjamin Spencer. We already butchered those animals to feed *your* workers."

One eyebrow flicks upward momentarily. "Your choice. You never asked."

My stomach churns as we leave. As soon as the door to the office closes, Lillian grabs my arm, nearly dragging me off my feet. My skirt flies out behind me. Outside, the blinding sunlight makes me blink, and I trip on the threshold. I jerk my arm free of Lillian's grasp so I don't miss a step going down the stairs.

"There's one thing left for us, Gen."

"What? And slow down, for pity's sake." Only then does she notice my plight as our feet gobble up the sidewalk.

"Oh, sorry." She reduces her pace. "Write a letter to Mr. Forsythe. I'm pretty sure he doesn't know what Spencer is like."

"I think you're right. I still can't believe he's so bullheaded. His greed has no end. He *owes* us the money for the food. It's over and above their room rent." My nails dig into my palms.

"No need to tell me that. Our lodgers would complain pretty fast if we cut back on the meat too much." Lillian shakes her head. "I don't want to do that, but we may have to." She sighs loudly and glances over her shoulder at the mill. "I'd like to—"

I catch her hand. "No. Remember what Daddy always said. Revenge and bitterness are brothers." A new thought hits me like a load of bricks. I stop. "What if Mr. Forsythe *does* know and is okay with what Mr. Spencer's doing?"

"Then it would be time to reconsider what *we're* doing." She faces me. "How long can we go on without losing all we have?"

We don't have much. But if we left, where would we go? The country is in a depression. Some are calling it the Great Depression.

My stomach sinks. There aren't many jobs out there, and all we know is how to run this hotel.

∞

After supper, I go straight to the parlor, where Willie is already sitting on the floor in front of the radio, waiting for his favorite show, *Mystery House,* to start. I need to write this letter, so I sit at the desk and pull out a sheet of stationery.

Words refuse to flow. I chew the end of the pen and stare at the blank sheet. What was it Sadie Moreland said the other night? Oh yeah, Southern women have iron in their veins. I like that. I gather up some steely determination and dip my pen in the inkwell.

Dear Mr. Forsythe,

My hand pauses. How do I best put this? Your partner is a crook?

Miss Kara pushes Mama into the room, with Lillian trailing them.

I look up from my letter as they enter. Mama asks Miss Kara to wheel her to the writing desk.

"What are you working on, sugar?" Mama tucks the lap robe close around her leg.

"I'm drafting a letter to Mr. Forsythe, telling him what is going on with his business partner."

"Be wise in your word choices, Genessee. They can accuse or make aware."

"That's my dilemma, finding the right words."

Mama pats my knee. "I'll pray for you."

"Thank you." I lean over and kiss her cheek.

Lillian pushes Mama close to Miss Kara and Willie by the radio, then comes back to stand at my shoulder.

"Do you want any help?"

"Let me get it written, then I'd like you to look it over." I frown, glancing around the room. "Where is Annie?"

Lillian raises one corner of her upper lip. "She escorted Mr. Quigg to the general store. It seems he wanted a book to read."

I start to rise. "Oh no!"

Mama peers over her shoulder. "I gave my permission, Gen. Don't worry about it."

I glance at Lillian. It's one thing to have *her* infatuated with the man, but Annie has not the years or the wisdom of Big Sis.

Finally, she grimaces. "We'll just have to watch things. The store is closed now, so they should be back any minute." She joins Mama on the davenport.

I pick up my pen.

Dear Mr. Forsythe,

I hope this finds you well. I'm writing out of concern—

I stop and lay the pen down, then raise my eyes. *I need wisdom, Lord.*

After my short prayer, I pick up my pen again, but nothing comes. No words. Only the odd feeling I should wait. I scratch the back of my neck. Mama glances up and meets my gaze. She tilts her head and raises her eyebrows in question.

I cross to her and, bending down, whisper, "Can we talk?"

She nods, so I push her out into the hallway, closing the parlor door behind us. Across the hall, Miss Kara's bedroom door is cracked open.

"Mama, I know you were praying for wisdom for me, and I asked too. But all I keep feeling is to wait. But there isn't time. I don't want to worry you, but Mr. Spencer has refused to pay for the hogs."

Her nostrils flare, but she doesn't say anything.

"At least next year, we won't have to buy any more. We've got eight piglets in the pen."

She smiles at that. "God is still in control, Genessee. And I got the same answer that you did. Wait." She reaches over her shoulder and squeezes my hand. "He'll tell us when it's time."

"Well, I hope it's soon. Sarah is stretching the eggs, but with the chickens sick, we're falling short even more. I doubt I'll have any eggs to sell to the general store."

My heart squeezes, and a feeling of dread wells up from my belly. Without eggs, how will I pay Mr. Campbell for the hogs? And if we can't pay ...

I don't finish the thought. I know what will happen if we can't pay. We'll be tossed out on the street. Worse, our name will be ruined. And that, I can never allow. No matter what it costs.

Chapter 25

LILLIAN BURSTS THROUGH THE FRONT door into the lobby, startling me so badly, I drop the mail. "Slow down. You scared me out of my wits."

Breathless, she grabs my wrist. "You're just the one I'm looking for. Guess what?"

"You and Mr. Quigg got married?" I'm only joking ... sort of.

She waves me off. "Don't be silly. I'm only having fun with Annie over him. The man is too good looking for my taste. He'd probably hog the mirror all the time."

Relief washes over me and I laugh. I gather up the mail from the floor and lay it on the front desk.

"But you didn't guess." Lillian raises an eyebrow. "I just came from the sheriff's office."

"What did he have to say? Anything about the investigation?"

"He wasn't there. But good ole Deputy Limehouse was." She grins and dips her head like a coquette, placing one hand at the back of her head. "I practiced a few skills I've learned in the art of flirting."

I gasp. Dignified Lillian? "What have you done?"

She chortles and dances a little jig. "After I ruffled his stalwart-deputy personae, he let it slip that they've tabled the investigation." Her elation fades. "They ran into a wall of silence." She strolls in a circle, gesturing with a wave of her hands. "Nobody knows anything, saw anything, or heard anything. As far as they're concerned, it was some kind of explosion." She frowns, arms akimbo, then blows out a large sigh. "Deputy Limehouse told me never to let the sheriff know he said anything. I assured him I wouldn't."

I couldn't care less about the deputy. "Where does that leave us?"

She crosses her arms. Her self-satisfied grin—she's having fun baiting me! That means ... I narrow my eyes. "What else did the infatuated deputy tell you?"

"He also let it slip where Dougie Anderson and Lonnie Culpepper can be found. And you'll never guess where."

Why my big sister wants to turn everything into a guessing game, I'll never know, but this time, I've got her. "Porterdale."

Her mouth turns down and she frowns. "How'd you guess?"

I can't help snickering. "Three reasons. Number one." I hold up my index finger. "Bibb Mill is the largest in the state." I hold up two fingers. "Two, Porterdale is the closest location. Three, they're always looking for good people. So did they get supervisor jobs?"

She picks up the mail and flips through it, handing them to me one by one. "I don't know. Three-o-one."

I take the envelope from her and stuff it into the correct mail cubby.

She reads the next envelope. "Two-o-seven. But let's see if we can borrow a car and go down there. Three-oh-four."

"Doc Adams has a car, but if he gets an emergency call, he'd need it, so his is out." I pull my ear, thinking.

Lillian hands me a magazine. "For Mrs. Grundy. Hey, what about Mr. Patterson? Do you suppose he'd let us borrow his wife's? You wouldn't *have* to tell him why."

"There's no reason not to be honest with him. He's as suspicious as I am. Mary told me he's thought about quitting but decided to stay to try to influence Mr. Spencer to do the right thing."

"Like that will work." She hands me the last envelope. "Two-oh-eight. There are too many unscrupulous supervisors, not to mention some of Spencer's hatchet-men work there. Actually, I'm surprised Mr. Patterson hasn't been fired just for being our friend."

My brain feels downright waterlogged, trying to figure all this out. "There are some strange things happening. First, Spencer eases off the pressure on us and lets the building crew repair the hotel. Now, he steps up the heat again by not paying for the hogs. Either he's up to something, or he's forgotten what we know."

"What we suspect." Lillian raises a warning finger.

I huff. "Okay, fine, suspect. But come on, anyone with an ounce of common sense can see the truth. What's that Scripture where the disembodied hand writes on the wall?"

"Daniel chapter five, verse five." Mama rolls out from the doorway to our private quarters. She chuckles as Miss Kara pushes her into the lobby. "God uses some startling ways to get our attention. He sure got King Nebuchadnezzar's."

I grin at Lillian. "That's right! The previous king had taken the gold and silver cups from the Jewish temple. Nebuchadnezzar wanted to drink from them and had them brought to him, but before he could defile them, God intervened."

A wicked gleam enters my sister's eye. "I wonder what God will do to get Mr. Spencer's attention. He's doing evil to God's children right here in Sweetgum."

The supervisors' houses are larger than the regular workers'. The Pattersons have three bedrooms. Their facilities are on the back porch, not out in the common yard between the rows of houses. Instead of raw wood, the walls are covered and painted. Mrs. Patterson has beautiful curtains on all the windows, like Mama has in the hotel, although the hotel ones are not as colorful or made from such luxurious material.

Afternoon sun streams through the Venetian blinds, making sunlit stripes on the hardwood floors as I wait in their parlor while Mary gets her daddy. When he enters the room, I jump to my feet.

"Genessee, what can I do for you, my dear? And sit down. No formalities in this house."

Other supervisors expect everyone to kowtow to them, but not Mr. Patterson. I sink onto the settee with a grateful sigh. "Thank you. I need a huge favor and don't quite know how to ask it of you."

Mary sits next to me, lending her support, while her daddy sits in a beautifully upholstered blue wingback chair adjacent to the settee. He reaches over and pats my arm. "I've always found the easiest way is to simply say it."

I take a breath. "I need to go to Porterdale and have no way to get there."

He smiles and raises one eyebrow. "That's not a problem. We can lend you a car, but can you tell me why you need to go there?"

My stomach churns. I didn't expect him to ask. I know I can trust him, but there's that tiny seed of worry. Daddy always used to take care with what he said around Mr. Patterson, too, for Mr. Patterson's sake, so he wouldn't say something inadvertently at the mill and get us all in trouble.

I choose my words with that same care. "I need to talk to a couple of people who work at the Porterdale Bibb Mill. Mr. Spencer has refused to pay for the hogs we butchered. I want to know how they do things there."

When I mention the hogs, his smile fades and his lips flatten. "You'll take Mrs. Patterson's car. She doesn't need it tomorrow, if that suits you. I'm not happy about the way Benjamin Spencer is treating your family. I'll see if I can do anything to help ease the situation."

"Thank you so much, Mr. Patterson. You know how much I appreciate you." I don't need to tell him to be careful, but I send up a silent prayer for God to watch over him.

He rises and gives me a hug. "Mary, get your mother's keys for Genessee." He nods goodbye and then exits the parlor.

Mary retrieves the keys, then walks me to the door. "I'd sure love to go with you, but tomorrow is Mother's and my day to do the altar flowers at church, then call on the sick."

I hold back a sigh of relief. "And I would have loved to have you. But it's boring business and not a fun trip, anyway."

Since I plan to leave early in the morning, I drive Mrs. Patterson's car home and park it behind the hotel. Annie and Mr. Quigg are sitting on the back porch. He's holding a baby chick in his hands.

"Is that chick all right?" I stop on the step beside Annie.

Mr. Quigg's head bobs. "I think they're all okay. We got them out in time. But you've lost five hens. Annie and I just buried them."

My heart sinks.

Annie's brow creases. "I showed him where, Gen. Poor things. Maybe we should get Doc Adams to come back."

With one finger, I rub the chick's downy fluff. "We're doing what he told us to, Annie. I think we'll just need to wait and see." I don't want to say we can't afford a doctor's visit in front of Mr. Quigg, or anyone, for that matter, but it's true. I know it. And deep down, I know it's only a matter of time before everyone else does as well.

I shiver as I crank the engine of Mrs. Patterson's old Ford Sedan. Lillian and I dressed as warmly as we could and brought quilts to wrap around us, but my toes are still cold, even with two pairs of socks inside my lined boots. It will get a little warmer once the sun comes up, but the trip is one-hundred-twenty-seven miles and will take us about three hours, each way.

"Here we go." I ease off the clutch. "Do you have the directions?"

Lillian holds up a piece of paper. "Right here."

For a little while, I watch the road and familiarize myself with driving again. It's been a while. Fortunately, we don't encounter any other cars, at least not yet. Once we're closer to Atlanta, we will.

"I hated not telling Mr. Patterson the real reason we're going."

Lillian hugs her quilt close around her neck. "You didn't lie. You simply allowed him to connect two points of information. It's in his best interest not to know details." Her breath fogs in the car. "Wouldn't it be nice if this thing had a heater?"

"It would, but Mrs. Patterson doesn't drive far enough to justify the expense—at least, that's what Mary told me."

Lillian shivers and burrows deeper into the blanket. "So what do you hope to get from these two men today?"

"Something to pin the fire on Mr. Spencer. But"—I glance sidelong at her—"I'm not even sure they'll talk to us. They don't know we're coming."

Lillian's quilt slips. "You mean this could be a wild goose chase?" She pulls the blanket back in place.

"What could I do? I don't have a telephone number. I don't have their addresses. All you found out is where they work."

She grimaces. "What will we do if they don't talk?"

"I think they will. We've known both of them since we were kids. They were church members and friends of Daddy's. I'm pretty sure they'll talk to us." I hope. "Anyway," I continue, "I think we'll get there close to dinnertime. I'm hoping to catch them when they come out of the mill. If we don't, we'll go to the office and ask to see them. Tell the superintendent we're old family friends."

"Okay. So let's say we find them and they talk to us. Then what?"

"I'll write that letter to Mr. Forsythe."

"I know I suggested it, but we're pinning a lot on him being a good guy. How do we know he's not okay with what Mr. Spencer's doing?"

I take a quick glance at her. "Do you have any other suggestions?"

"No. I just think we should have some sort of backup plan." She leans her head against the seat and stares out the window.

I turn onto the main highway. "Let's think about that after we see if we find Dougie and Lonnie."

Porterdale is a big town compared to Sweetgum. The mill is huge and has more than one building. And the houses—the mill workers have much better housing than Sweetgum workers do. We park the car and walk toward the mill. As my sister and I stare wide-eyed at our surroundings, a whistle blows, and a moment later, the mill doors fly open and workers pour out.

Lillian grabs my elbow. "There's Dougie Anderson." She points to the steps and waves. "Mr. Anderson!"

He turns in our direction. When his gaze lands on us, his face lights up in recognition. "Lillian and Genessee. How are you?" His smile disappears and compassion replaces it. "How's your mother?"

Lillian lifts her collar to ward off a cold wind. "She's getting stronger but is limited in what she can do."

"Terrible business. Just terrible." He shakes his head, a lock of blond hair dropping onto his forehead. "What brings you to Porterdale?"

I step closer to him. "We came to see you and Lonnie Culpepper. Is there somewhere we can talk?"

He peers at me intently, then nods. "Sure, come with me. I'll take you to dinner. I know where Lonnie likes to eat." He chuckles but it sounds forced.

Still, I share a victorious glance with Lillian, and we walk with Dougie to a cafeteria-style diner. Lonnie is third in the line.

Dougie leads us to join him. Nobody seems bothered that we cut in front of them.

"Lonnie, look who I found."

He greets us warmly. "Good to see you, ladies. They've got terrific pimento cheese sandwiches here if you're interested."

"That sounds wonderful," Lillian replies for us.

Soon, the four of us are seated at a table.

I take a bite, then after I swallow, I ask, "How are you liking your work here? Compared to Sweetgum, I mean."

They share a puzzled glance. "It's great," Lonnie says.

That didn't tell us anything. So after a few more pleasantries, I jump in.

"I think we all know that fire was intentionally set. Mr. Patterson found the gas cans. Our father was killed, and we want justice."

Again, the two exchange a secretive glance, then with his voice low, Lonnie asks, "What about Sheriff Jackson? He's investigating, isn't he?"

Lillian sets her sandwich on its plate. "He's tried, but nobody saw or heard anything. Apparently, the entire town came down with a case of deaf and blind." She wipes her hands.

"You realize, if our names come out ..." Lonnie pauses, searching for the right words, maybe? "Our lives would be in danger."

Spencer is a creep, but would he go so far as to condone murder? "Mr. Spencer has a business partner. We met him when he inspected the hotel and stayed with us. He's an upright man, honest. I don't think he really knows how Mr. Spencer runs the mill. I plan to put it in a letter."

Lillian nods and blots her mouth with a napkin. "But what my sister hasn't told you is that Mr. Spencer has stopped giving us the meal allowance money for the hotel lodgers. He expects us to feed them out of our own wages. The man's greed is growing. What if we keep your names out of it? Just tell the partner what an insider knows?"

My sister calmly takes a small bite of her sandwich. I'm too nervous to eat. Lonnie takes a bite of his sandwich also, slowly chews, then swallows. I've got my fingers crossed beneath the table.

Finally, he wipes his mouth. "What is Irving Patterson doing?"

"The best he can to try to influence Mr. Spencer to do right, but he's not making any headway."

Dougie shares yet another meaningful glance with Lonnie. What concerns me is the fear in their eyes.

"I've got a lot of respect for Irving for staying. My kids are young, and I needed to get them away." Dougie's gaze scans the room. "Things are good at this mill, but I don't know everyone. How do I know Benjamin Spencer doesn't have people working here?"

I glance at the various tables and their occupants. "Have you seen anyone you recognize?"

Dougie wraps the rest of his sandwich. He pushes back his chair, shaking his head. "No, but I can't risk it."

I watch his back disappear out the door before turning to the man still perching on his chair across from us. "Mr. Lonnie, we need your help. Please?"

Lillian's eyes narrow. "Sir, aren't you and Mr. Dougie giving too much credence to a small town bully?"

He locks his gaze on my sister. "Maybe. But I can't take the chance either. I'm sorry."

He walks away and, with him, the evidence we so desperately need.

Chapter 26

THE PARLOR IS EMPTY. EVERYONE is either finishing their chores or relaxing before supper. Taking advantage of being alone, I attempt to compose the letter to Mr. Forsythe, but once again, the blank page taunts me. Why can't I find the words? I went to Porterdale yesterday expecting to have two men tell me what they know, but instead, fear of Spencer's goons silences them.

I can't allow fear to gag me. I send up a prayer for help, then dig for the iron Maggie and Sadie say we have flowing through our veins and pick up the pen. My hand hovers above the page. I take a deep breath. When I blow it out, determination replaces the air. *Iron.*

My pen sweeps across the page, detailing Mr. Spencer's noncompliance with the newly amended child labor laws. There are still children under the age of eight working in the mill. Soon, I'm tightly gripping the pen as it flies, pouring out what has happened and the facts I have, including how Mr. Spencer refuses to pay for the hogs we butchered.

When I finish and sign my name, I flex my fingers and massage my hand. I slide the missive into its envelope. Now, before I lose my nerve, I'll walk it to the post office.

"Genessee?" Sarah's voice stops me at the front door. "Can you help me, dear?"

I drop the letter in the box for the hotel's outgoing mail. I'll retrieve it later and take it to be posted. "Sure. What do you need?" My gaze sweeps the kitchen. "Where's Miss Kara?"

"At the school, visiting Willie's teacher. My large cake pan is on that top shelf." She points above her. "Can you get it down for me, please? Bloomin' arthritis is givin' me fits today. It must be fixing to rain."

Sarah's quirky mixture of Irish and Southern tickles me. I slide the kitchen step stool in place and climb up, retrieving her pan. "What are you making?"

"A sheet cake. Tonight's supper is a tasty but meatless peanut loaf. A nice cake should make everyone forget it's all vegetables and legumes."

"That's a good idea. Do you need me for anything else right now? I forgot to check on the hens earlier."

"You go ahead, but I think Annie's out there now."

I stop on the way and look at the chicks in Buster's pen. They all appear to be healthy, pecking and scratching. And growing nicely. Inside the barn, Annie shoves a dead chicken into a bag.

"How many are there?"

She glances up at me. "Only two. I don't see symptoms on any others. I think all the rest have recuperated."

"That's swell. I wish I could have Doc Adams come check them, just in case, but ..." I trail into silence.

"Why not have Archie look at them? He knows chickens."

The familiarity in her voice concerns me. "Aren't you a little forward calling him by his first name?"

"He told me to." Her chin lifts as she aims a bold stare my way.

"Annie, he's sophisticated and much older than you. He's used to women who are closer to his own age."

She huffs and drops the bag. "You don't want me to have any fun just because you and Tommy broke up."

Though I've never been like that, I ignore her accusation. "You realize when his business here is finished, he'll be leaving. I don't want you hurt."

"You can't know what he'll do. Maybe he'll decide to stay."

"Why? The only jobs are in the mill. Can you see Archie Quigg working in a mill?"

Her mouth opens, but no words come forth. After a moment, she pulls a face. "Oh, horsefeathers." She picks up the bag. "I'm going out to bury these. Are you coming to help?"

"Sure." Her odd response doesn't stop me from following her out behind the smokehouse. With her mercurial emotions, by the time the chickens are buried, she's in a good mood again.

I'll have to ask Lillian and Mama what they think about her and Mr. Quigg. Right now, I'm having second thoughts about that letter I wrote. If my judgment is wrong about Mr. Forsythe—if he isn't all I think he is—we could be out on our ears without jobs or a home.

When I reach the lobby, a stack of mail rests on the front desk, and the outgoing box is empty.

∞

"Genessee?" Mrs. Grundy approaches the front desk. It's almost time to leave for church. I hope she doesn't want me to look up something for her or buy a stamp right now. I raise my eyes and blink to be sure I'm really seeing what's before me.

She's not wearing her usual mourning black.

Mrs. Grundy has put on a pale gray skirt and a light blue shirtwaist. A broach with painted blue and pink flowers is pinned at the neckline. Her cheeks are rosy, and Mr. Nesbitt stands by her side.

"My, you look lovely today, Mrs. Grundy. How may I help you?"

She glances up at Mr. Nesbitt and blushes. "We want you to be the first to know. Mr. Nesbitt and I are getting married next week—next Sunday." Her face grows deeper red, and she drops her chin. "He will move into my room with me afterwards."

Well, shut my mouth. "Congratulations!" I come out from behind the desk and hug her, then shake Mr. Nesbitt's hand. "I'm delighted for you both."

"Oh, I almost forgot." She glances up at Mr. Nesbitt again. "Last night, we went walking by the river. We saw a strange car in the woods. It had branches over it as though it's supposed to be hidden. We saw it last week, but I didn't think to mention it to you. Anyway, there was a bear cub nosing around it. We scurried away, but if its mama is gone, you and Dr. Adams should look into it."

"Thank you. I'll let Doc know." More importantly, whose car could it be? And why would they want to hide it?

Mr. Nesbitt gazes fondly at Mrs. Grundy. "We'll see you at church." He escorts her out the door.

It seems as though they just started seeing each other, but I guess that was a couple of months ago. I suppose at their age, time is of the essence. I hurry to the kitchen to tell everyone about Mrs. Grundy. Sarah is there alone.

"Is our picnic basket ready? It's time to leave for church."

She sets her hat atop her head, sticking a hatpin through it. "Aye, it's by the back door. Miss Kara and your mama already left."

"What about Lillian and Annie?"

Lillian enters the kitchen. "What about us?" Little Sis follows on her heels.

"Let's go, and I'll tell you my news on the way. You'll never guess who is getting married."

Annie's attention piques. "Who?"

I pick up the picnic basket and walk out the door, tossing over my shoulder, "Mrs. Grundy and Mr. Nesbitt."

Lillian catches up to me first. "Really? When?"

"Next week."

We cross the street and enter the church. I leave the basket on the narthex table with all the others. We'll retrieve it when we leave. While we search for where Mama, Miss Kara, and Willie are seated, I look for the Pattersons. I hope to get a few minutes to talk with Mr. Patterson and tell him what happened in Porterdale. And about my letter to Mr. Forsythe. My stomach pitches. *Please let Mr. Forsythe believe me.*

At the end of the service, Mr. Bud announces the wedding of Gladys Grundy and Clarence Nesbitt will take place next week, right after the service. Everyone is invited.

"And I hear that Sarah Wilkes is making the wedding cake. Nobody will want to miss that." He grins and licks his lips, then he consults his notes. "Now we have one more bit of news. The pulpit committee has made a recommendation." He pauses and glances at us.

My stomach suddenly feels as though I've swallowed a boulder. I peek at Mama, but her smile is beautiful, peaceful. I try to copy her, but my lips won't obey. I hadn't thought about the church getting a new pastor. Oh, I knew it had to happen, eventually. But I wasn't expecting it now. I catch Mr. Bud's gaze on me. Compassion fills his eyes. I blink against the sudden tears.

"It was an incredibly hard task finding someone to fill Brother Frank's shoes. We looked long and hard and finally believe we have the right man. The pastor-in-consideration will preach next week. All y'all will have plenty of time to talk to him, get to know him some, and then the following Sunday, we'll call for a vote."

He prays, then gives a benediction and dismisses us. As soon as he steps down from the pulpit, he walks over to us. "I'm sorry I sprang it on you like that. I was handed the note just before the announcements."

Mama reaches for his hand. "It's a necessary move forward, Bud. I've been expecting it. You do a marvelous job preaching, but the congregation needs its shepherd. And now, I would like my dinner. Will you join us?" He accepts and takes over pushing Mama's wheeled chair to the yard.

Mary waits for me by the table where I left our dinner basket. She has it in her hands along with her family's. "How was your trip to Porterdale?" I shoot a glance at her, but of course, she has no idea why we went.

"It was unproductive, actually. Are your mama and daddy here?"

"They're at the table with your mama and Mr. Bud. I told them we'd get the baskets."

We hurry to join the picnickers.

As I lay napkins on the table, I casually ask Mr. Patterson, "Are you going to the game this afternoon?"

"Wouldn't miss it." Mary's mama drops a scoop of macaroni salad onto his plate, and he immediately partakes since it's a favorite of his.

I button my sweater against a chilly breeze and sit between Lillian and Mary. Down by the river, the cherry trees are in riotous bloom, along with the Bradford pears. March is fickle in North Georgia.

Annie is seated at the end of the table with Archie Quigg, where he's entertaining everyone with stories. Little Sis hangs on his every word. I glance at Mama to see if she notices. Her brow pinches, her only outward sign of concern. Catching her eye, I cast my gaze their direction, then back. Her only reaction is a barely perceivable shake of her head.

Mr. Bud laughs at something Willie says and ruffles his hair. Conversations punctuated with laugher float over the grounds. With the problems facing us and the sorrow we endure, through it all, we have our friends. And for that, I'm grateful.

Mary nudges me with her elbow. "Guess who I went to the movies with last night?" She swirls chunks of ice in a glass of sweet tea.

I've been able to hide my grief over Tommy well enough that everyone *thinks* I'm fine. But Mary's news rips off the Band-aid I'd applied to my heart. Tears well in my eyes. I don't want to spoil her news, so I cough, covering my face with my napkin, quickly blotting away the tears.

"Let me see. The name *Allman* comes to mind."

Her grin is contagious, and I'm able to muster joy for my friend. She's had a crush on Leroy for at least six months, maybe longer. "What did you see?" I wave a tenacious fly away from my chicken leg.

"*The Bachelor Father.*" She sighs, making me laugh.

"Do you remember anything about the movie?"

She swats my arm. "Yes. It stars Marion Davis."

"Okay, so did Leroy hold your hand?"

Her shy nod is sweet, her red cheeks sweeter. "I think I'm falling in love."

I swallow the lump in my throat and squeeze her hand. "I'm so happy for you."

I know my friends are going to fall in love. Get married. Have babies. After all, life goes on in Sweetgum. But does it have to be so hard?

All around us, people are cleaning up the remains of their picnic dinner. Mary and I jump in to help. While my sisters take the trash to the bin, I help Sarah stuff the leftovers—not that there's much—in our basket. She's going back to the hotel before the game starts and will meet us there.

Mr. Bud pushes Mama, and Miss Kara walks beside them. The Pattersons follow behind, while my sisters and I bring up the rear. Willie has run on ahead of everyone. When we enter the bleachers, I choose a seat next to Mr. Patterson. Annie and Mr. Quigg sit two rows in front of us, and Mary's daddy frowns and glances at me.

He leans close. "What is your sister doing with him?" His voice is low so only I hear.

I follow suit. "She's slightly infatuated. While he's nice and hasn't done anything out of line, I'll be glad when he finishes his business and moves on."

Patterson loosens his tie. "What is his business?"

I shrug. "We have no idea."

"I've seen him before, but I can't think of where."

I need to tell him why I borrowed Mrs. Patterson's car. "I went to Porterdale to the Bibb Mill. I talked with Lonnie Culpepper and Dougie Anderson."

His gaze snaps from Archie and Annie to me. "What did they say? Did they give you any information that can help us?"

I shake my head. "They know something, but they're afraid to say it. Mr. Lonnie believes Mr. Spencer has spies working there."

Mr. Patterson turns his eyes back to the field as the teams take position. "Spencer is shady, but I doubt he has a net that wide. However, it's hard to convince a man who's fearful for his family." He glances sidelong at me. "So … now what?"

"I wrote to Mr. Forsythe. I told him about Mr. Spencer still employing little children and cutting off the money for the lodgers' food. I also gave the details about the safety strike, the fire and gas cans, and about my suspicions."

"Good. I believe he's an honest man."

I hope he's right. Our future depends on it.

Chapter 27

WITH MY CHORES COMPLETE UNTIL it's time to serve supper, I walk to Doc Adams' vet clinic. Two days ago, we rescued the bear cub Mrs. Grundy told us about, but we didn't see the car she mentioned. When she left for the mill this morning, she said she and Mr. Nesbitt saw *another* bear cub last night. And the car. Whose is it, and why do they keep apparently moving it, then hiding it again? Maybe it belongs to one of the people living in Hooverville. But why would they camouflage it?

As I walk, my thoughts move from bear cubs to Mr. Archie Quigg, who is, I believe, up to something. I've seen no evidence of his business, nor have I heard anyone talk about their dealings with him. Lately, he avoids me—and even Lillian—keeping his attention to Annie, who, for all her interest in movies, is naïve. I worry about her. She went to the flicks with him again last night. What if he asks her to leave with him? I don't believe his interest in her is healthy. Scenes with her stranded on a highway in the middle of nowhere or abandoned in a one-horse town play out in my mind. And for some reason, I feel like the bear cubs are somehow tied to Mr. Quigg. I suppose I'm just being paranoid.

I step inside Adams Feed Store and go to the clinic in the back. Katie looks up from her desk.

"Afternoon, Genessee. Paul's in the back."

"Thanks. How's the cub?"

"We moved her to a place where they rehabilitate wildlife. Once she's old enough, they'll release her into the woods far from here."

"That's good because I've heard of another one that may be a littermate."

"Go get Paul. His afternoon is open."

I find the vet in his office, tap on the door frame, and fill him on what Mrs. Grundy saw. "Should we go see about it?"

Nodding, he quickly grabs his bag, a gun, and an animal baby bottle filled with milk. We head out to the river and the area Mrs. Grundy described.

"How are your hens now? Any new cases?" he asks as we walk.

I pick my way over a fallen log. "No. They're doing nicely. We took them all back to the coop once we thoroughly cleaned it like you showed us."

He nods approvingly. "Is Buster glad to have his pen back?"

"You should have seen him." I laugh. "He ran around and around, rolled in the wood shavings, and had himself a grand time. I hope we can find him a friend one of these days."

Doc holds his finger up to his lips. "Listen," he whispers.

I stop and concentrate. There. A bleating, almost like a lamb. I look at Doc. "The bear cub?"

"I think so." We walk toward the sound, then I see it—the car covered in branches. And a bear cub inside it.

"The poor baby. It sounds weak, Doc."

"It probably doesn't have any idea how to get out."

We approach the car, watching carefully for any signs of the mother bear. There aren't any. We pull a good portion of the branches away to get inside.

While Doc feeds the cub, I examine the car. There's something—some kind of box or case—wedged beneath the front seat. The hairs on the back of my neck twitch. I pull away.

"Doc, if you don't need my help, I'm going to get the sheriff. There's something off about this car."

"I'm fine. This little fellow is too weak to put up a fight."

"Will it be okay?"

"In a couple of days, yes, it will be fine. Then I'll deliver it to the same place I took its littermate."

"Thank you. See you later." I make note of where I am so I can show Sheriff Jackson.

He's at his desk when I open the jailhouse door. "Genessee. What do you need?"

"Mrs. Grundy told me about a bear cub and a car hidden in the woods." I repeat what we found the first time. "This morning, she told me she saw another cub. Doc and I were just there, and this time the car was too. Doc's got the cub, but there's something strange about the car. And there's a briefcase or something wedged under the driver's seat." I finally breathe.

Sheriff Jackson frowns but rises. "Take me to it."

"Okay." I walk beside him. "Have there been any reports of stolen cars?"

"There have not."

When he doesn't elaborate, I don't push it. Our sheriff is a man of few words. When we reach the woods, I lead the way. After a couple of minutes, I stop.

"There it is." I point to the car. "Doc and I removed most of the branches. We might have missed it except the bear cub had gotten inside and we heard it crying."

"You did good, Genessee." He kneels down and peers under the driver's seat. After a couple of grunts, he comes up with a briefcase. Balancing it on the car's fender, he opens it.

Inside, neat stacks of fifty-dollar bills fill half the case.

While we prepare supper, I share the afternoon's events with the family. "I have no idea how much money was in there, but I'll bet it was thousands of dollars."

Willie's eyes are wide, and he doesn't blink. "Did the sheriff dust for fingerprints?"

I ruffle his hair. "I don't know. He made me leave."

"Did some bad guys come?" His eyes never stray from mine.

"No, but I think the sheriff was worried they might and didn't want me there."

Lillian shivers. "I think I'd have been frightened to death, finding that. You're brave, Gen."

"I don't know about that. Just being there gave me the creeps."

"This is the stuff they make movies about." While Annie's eyes are bright, her attention is not on my story. What occupies her mind that she doesn't find this exciting?

With her hands on her hips, Sarah peers over her readers. "Right now, the lodgers will be fixing to come down to supper. Let's get a whistle on."

I chuckle at her attempt at modern slang. "It's wiggle."

"Wiggle, waggle, whistle. Let's move." She grins and turns back to the two large soup pots. I help her lift and move them to the cart.

"That smells delicious. Bean and ham?"

She nods while Lillian loads bowls of bread rolls onto the cart, then wheels it into the dining room. Annie rings the bell, and shortly afterward, footsteps clatter on the stairway. Lodgers file in and grab bowls from the stack at the end of the serving counter.

Little Sis lingers near the line. I try to catch her eye, but her attention is on the lodgers. Her fingers pluck her belt, pulling it away from her waist as her gaze darts to the dining room's entryway.

Most of the lodgers are in line or at their tables when Archie Quigg finally arrives. Last night, he changed his mind about eating here, saying the food smells really good.

Annie's eyes light on him, and she smooths her skirt. I know my sister, and her smile is manufactured. Everything about her is off. Her movements are mechanical, her attention is sporadic. Her gaze flits from one place to another. What has Quigg done to her?

Lillian moves next to me. "Annie's in a state, isn't she?"

Without taking my eyes off Little Sis, I nod. "Do you have any idea why?"

"I sure do, and he's about to serve himself a bowl of soup."

Archie sidles up to Annie, and she turns a bright smile to him. Too bright. What is going on?

Lillian's eyes grow round. "You don't suppose he's—"

When she stops, my stomach drops to my toes. She couldn't think he'd taken advantage of Annie. "No. I'm sure of it."

"Are you? Look how she keeps pulling her belt like it's too tight."

Oh no! My gaze snaps to Lillian. "But when?"

An undignified snort flares her nostrils. "You sleep like the dead. She could have slipped out of your room and into his. She's been so besotted by the man."

"I'll kill him." I take a step, but Lillian grabs my arm.

"Not here, you dope. Not in front of all the lodgers. What if we're wrong? Annie would be mortified. We'll wait, then waylay him before he goes back to his room. We'll confront him and—"

Sheriff Jackson and Deputy Limehouse, along with two other officers, enter the dining room. The sheriff has his hand on his holstered gun. "Ladies and gentlemen, I'm sorry to disrupt your supper, but I need to evacuate the room for a bit. Please go out front."

Oh dear! What is going on? Chairs scrape as the lodgers obey him, even as they grumble about missing their supper. Lillian and I start to follow them. Archie Quigg heads toward the kitchen.

"Not you, Quigg. Stop where you are."

In response, Archie grabs Annie. A gun appears in his hand. He aims it at her head.

"Nooo!" rips from my lips. This can't be happening.

Quigg yells, "Shut up. Sheriff, drop your gun and get your men out of here, or she gets it."

Why is he hurting Annie? None of this makes sense.

The sheriff slowly sets his gun on a table. "Easy, Quigg. Let the girl go. Don't add assault to armed robbery."

Robbery? The money! Quigg's a robber? *God, help us!*

Archie laughs. "I'll let her go when I'm good and ready." He pushes Annie toward the kitchen. "Move, little girl."

Annie shows no fear and strides ahead with confidence. They disappear through the kitchen door. The sheriff grabs his gun and follows them. Lillian and I start to follow when we hear banging and clattering.

A shot rings out. I scream.

Forgetting everything but my baby sister, I burst through the kitchen door. Lillian is right on my heels. Annie squats behind the baking counter. She sees us and grabs our hands, pulling us down with her.

At that moment, a maelstrom of gunfire drowns out all other sound.

Screams rend the air in front of the hotel. In the kitchen, Lillian faints while Annie and I try to protect her and each other. Then, with the suddenness of an earthquake, all is silent.

The back door opens. Annie peeks over the top of the baking counter and slowly rises to her feet. "Is it over?"

"Yes. You can come on out." The sheriff's voice reassures me, so I stand on shaky legs, glancing down at Lillian.

"Is Quigg dead?"

Sheriff Jackson shakes his head. "Nope. He'll be able to stand trial just fine. He threw down his gun like a little girl after he didn't have Annie to hide behind." He grins at Little Sis. "Annie, thank you. You've done a great service to Georgia."

Annie?

Her grin is wide, and she rocks on her feet.

My gaze bounces between the two. "What did Annie do, Sheriff?"

"She came to me a couple of weeks ago with some suspicions about Quigg." He turns and heads for the back door. "She can tell you about it, but she's a regular heroine."

I turn to her. "So you're not pregnant?"

Annie gasps. The sheriff gapes at me, then a huge grin spreads across his face. He roars with laughter as he closes the back door behind him.

Annie gives me the evil eye. "You thought I'd let that man do that to me?"

A groan comes from behind the baking counter. I bite my lip. "Let's help Lillian first."

I grab a damp towel and put it on her forehead. She startles. "Where's Annie?"

"Calm down. She's right here. Apparently, you and I were really on the wrong track."

Lillian sits up, frowning. "What do you mean?"

"I'm not in the family way, as you two thought." Her disgust in us is apparent in her tone.

I help Lillian up, then go to Annie's side. "Sugar, you have to admit, you acted so besotted with Archie, what were we to think? Then in the dining room, you kept pulling at your belt like it was too tight. That's what made us think maybe ..."

Sarah pokes her head into the kitchen. "The sheriff sent everyone back inside. You might want to go explain to them and your mama what just happened."

Annie grins. "My pleasure." She walks away from Lillian and me, but we're right behind her.

In the dining room, Annie waits for everyone to settle. She leans her back against the serving counter. "Thank you, everyone, for cooperating. Here's what happened. A few weeks ago,"—Annie smiles and nods at Mrs. Grundy—"Miss Gladys saw me going into the woods and told me about a strange car covered in branches. All y'all know me and my curiosity. I went to see it. Inside the glove box, I found a card with Archie Quigg's name on it." She hoists herself up onto an empty table. "Anyway, I got suspicious. Gen had told me about the large wad of bills Archie used to pay his rent. So I told the sheriff my suspicion. He went to see the car, but it was gone. Then, he thought I'd made it up, but it turned out, Archie was driving it that day. After that, the sheriff made some calls and found out about a bank robbery where an employee was shot."

She slides off the table. "He asked if I thought I could get more information from Archie, so I pretended to have a crush on him." She shrugs one shoulder. "It worked. He told me a few things that by themselves wouldn't be noteworthy. But with what I already thought and what the sheriff knew, they led us to believe he was the bank robber. We lacked evidence to arrest him until today. Gen found the car and the missing money." She grins.

All eyes turn to rest on me. Warmth floods my cheeks. "I ... I was just looking for an orphaned bear cub."

How nicely the mystery of Mr. Quigg is wrapped up. Now, if only I could find some hard evidence to find out who set that fire and killed my daddy.

Chapter 28

MISS GLADYS WAITS IN FRONT of the standing mirror in her room as I lower the veil on her hat so it covers her eyes. Her lavender dress sets off the rosiness of her cheeks. She's a vision of loveliness—even at her age. As I stick a final pin into her hat, melancholy tries to drop its shroud over me. I refuse it, though, for her sake. She's asked me to stand up with her.

"Miss Gladys, when he sees you, Mr. Nesbitt isn't going to be able to string words together in a coherent sentence. You're breathtaking."

She turns and clasps my hands between hers. "I owe so much to you. You brought me out of my self-pity, allowing me to enjoy life again. My William didn't want me to grieve forever." She pats my hand and releases me, then turns back to the mirror. After a final tweak to her eye-length veil, she nods.

The wedding will be at the end of church service this morning, with Mr. Bud performing the ceremony. He's an old friend of both the bride and groom. She told him she prefers him to any potential new pastor.

In the hotel lobby, her entourage awaits, including her groom. At her entrance, Mr. Nesbitt proves me right. He swallows, his Adam's apple bobbing. "You ... you're ... beautiful." He steps forward, his elbow crooked, to escort her.

But before she can take his arm, Willie steps between them. "No, sir." He lifts his chin until he's looking up at Mr. Nesbitt. "Miss Gladys asked me to give her away, so I'll escort her to the church."

She hides a smile behind her fingers. "He's right, Clarence, but I'm sure you can walk with us, right, Willie?"

Willie eyes the tall man. "Yeah, I guess so."

With everyone dressed for the occasion in their best bib and tucker—as Daddy used to say—we follow them across the street and into the church. I walk beside Mama, who glows with peace as Miss Kara pushes her. We lost Daddy a mere eight months ago, and I know she misses him terribly. Like I miss Tommy. Grief engulfs my heart, and the sidewalk blurs. Could it be that her peace is because Daddy is in heaven? Is my sorrow because Tommy's here on earth, but I can't be with him?

Lillian and Annie come alongside me and take my hands, lending me their strength. I send up a prayer of thanks for sisters who understand.

Inside the church, two pews have been reserved for the wedding party. The pastor-in-consideration sits on the platform beside Mr. Bud. He's a mountain of a man with hair the color of sand, well over six feet tall—maybe six-foot-five—and as muscular as a lumberjack. His suit strains to contain him.

He's also younger than I'd imagined. Piercing brown eyes gaze back at us. Beside me, Lillian's foot catches the edge of the pew, making her stumble slightly. Her hand tightens around mine. I peer at her, but her gaze is on the platform—or more correctly, the pastor.

And his gaze is locked on our Lillian—for a long moment. Then he blinks and whispers to Mr. Bud.

The spell broken, we take our seats. After the first hymn, Mr. Bud stands at the pulpit. The pastor's eyes continue to stray to my sister. Her cheeks are flushed.

"Good morning, y'all. And a fine mornin' it is. I'm pleased as punch to introduce the pulpit committee's recommendation, Pastor Kaden O'Neal. Now, I know some of y'all are a-lookin' at this man and wondering how a whippersnapper like him can pastor a church. Mighty well, I assure you."

Mr. Bud continues to enlighten us on Pastor O'Neal's present church and how the folks there don't want him to leave. "I'm going to let him tell you in his own words what God said to him." He sits in his chair behind the pulpit.

Pastor O'Neal rises, but instead of stepping behind the pulpit, he stands beside it, dwarfing it. He lets his gaze take in the congregation.

His smile draws interest from all the single ladies, judging by the titters from around the sanctuary. Beside me, Lillian's smile is most interesting. This is different than her interest in Archie Quigg. Quite different.

"Good morning."

Lillian and I stare at each other in surprise. His baritone voice is soft and melodic. Soothing. Perfect for a pastor but startling from a man so big.

He grins and scratches the back of his head. "This feels strange, facing a new congregation in view of a call. I was quite content in my old church. I grew up there, got the call to preach there, and was ordained there." He walks across the platform. "But God doesn't like us to get too comfortable. Or complacent." He moves down one step on the platform. "Close to nine months ago, God nudged me to get ready for a change."

That's about a month *before* Daddy died. I know God knew what was coming, but the fact that He set this in motion even before the fire changed our lives awes me. I hang on the pastor's every word.

He chuckles. "Nine months to prepare for a change? I didn't want any changes. I liked my life as it was. But during those months, the Lord rearranged the desires of my heart."

He continues by delivering a sermon on God's sovereignty that makes me examine my own heart. At its end, he says, "And if this is where the Lord wants me, then this is where I want to be."

His gaze lands on Lillian once more, and he smiles, then he nods to Mr. Bud and takes his seat.

Our deacon chairman rises. "Pastor O'Neal will be staying at the hotel all week, so all y'all will have plenty of time to go talk with him. Next Sunday, we'll vote. Now turn to page …" He gives the hymn number, and we stand to sing.

Lillian sticks her elbow in my ribs. "Did you know he's staying at the hotel?"

"No, Mr. Bud probably arranged it with Mama."

Lillian's face is a study. First awe, then uncertainty, then another rosy blush.

At the end of the hymn, Miss Gladys taps my shoulder. I join her in the aisle and then precede her to the platform, where Mr. Nesbitt awaits. Willie proudly takes her arm and escorts her down the aisle, his feet moving in time to the wedding march.

The ceremony is sweet and over quickly. Mr. Nesbitt delights the congregation when he dips Miss Gladys backward for their kiss, taking her completely by surprise. Her hand flies to her hat, but she doesn't struggle, making everyone chuckle.

Outside, a table for the wedding party sits in the midst of all the others on the picnic grounds. The cake Sarah made draws several little fingers to the chocolate icing, but she's quick with a wooden spoon to warn them away. A stray cherry blossom petal carried by the breeze lands on the cake.

Mr. Bud takes a seat with my family, motioning for Pastor O'Neal to join them. I'd sure like to hear the conversation, but I'm at the bridal table. I study this man conversing with my family. His demeanor is open, inviting both questions and confidence at the same time.

Mama chats freely with him, then she laughs at something he says and lays her hand on his arm. He rests his over hers, and his expression is one of respect.

Mr. Bud claps the pastor on the shoulder and rises. He beckons the bride and groom to come cut the cake. While they do, he takes a seat next to me.

"I think I made the right recommendation to the pulpit committee." He nods his head toward Lillian, who's blushing.

Laughter bubbles up. "I think you definitely did. I like him."

As the family and residents spill into the hotel foyer, I lay my hand on my sister's arm and pull her aside. "Lillian, why don't you show Pastor O'Neal around the hotel and grounds? Willie, Annie, and I have chores. Animals have to be fed even on Sundays, and I have to help Mr. Nesbitt move into Miss Gladys' room."

As Big Sis leads the pastor outside to see the grounds, Annie snickers. "What a day. A wedding and a new infatuation appears to be blooming."

Willie's face scrunches, and he tilts his head, looking at Annie like she has toads peeking out her ears. "What's fat shuns?" He swivels his head, looking all around. "I don't see none blooming."

She puts her hands on his shoulders and directs him toward the back door. "Never mind. Let's go feed the animals." She gets no argument from him. It's his favorite thing to do.

Upstairs, Mr. Nesbitt is ready to move his belongings. I help him carry them down to his wife's room, then I give his old room a thorough cleaning and change the bed. Miss Gladys will put the vacancy on the worker's bulletin board tomorrow.

In the parlor, Mama is in Daddy's old overstuffed armchair, reading out loud while Miss Kara darns one of Willie's socks.

I close the door behind me, then join Miss Kara on the settee. "What did you two think of Pastor O'Neal?"

They share a smile. Mama's eyes twinkle. "I like him. And apparently, so does your sister."

I raise my hands, palms up. "I know. I was so surprised when I saw their reaction to each other. It was like they were gobsmacked." I chuckle and lower my hands to my lap. "What did you think of his comment about God leading him here? Do you think it's because of Lillian?"

Mama's eyes remain on me, and Miss Kara watches me closely. Their concern is touching. How can I explain that while my heart is broken, I don't begrudge my sisters finding love?

Instead, I smile. "I, for one, hope it is. How exciting to know for certain he's the man God has for her. I think our Lillian would make a wonderful pastor's wife."

Mama's shoulders relax. "I just hope Annie doesn't try to flirt."

"She won't, Mama. Her heart is set on acting in Hollywood, and I don't think she'll let a man come between her and that dream. Look at Archie Quigg. Here we were all worried about her, and she was playing a part. Most convincingly too."

Mama pulls off the afghan covering her lap. She folds it and lays it over the arm of the chair. "I have to confess, Annie told me about it. But it was important none of you knew."

"I still can't believe he chose Sweetgum to hide in." I glance at the clock. We have an hour left before supper has to be served. "What do you suppose drew him here?"

Miss Kara peers over her mending. "I've thought about that. There's nothing to recommend Sweetgum. There's no lake or resort—not that anyone has money for vacations. We're certainly not a tourist attraction. I think he was on his way somewhere else when he drove through here. He took one look around and decided unremarkable Sweetgum is a good place to hide." She laughs. "But he didn't reckon on our Annie."

Lillian opens the door, and Pastor O'Neal follows her into the parlor.

Mama smiles and points to the settee next to Miss Kara. "Sit and relax. You've got about an hour before people start to grill you." She chuckles. "Was this morning stressful for you? My husband often found times like this to be tense."

He leans back and crosses his long legs, his right ankle resting atop his left knee. "I expected it, but there wasn't any tension in the room. Faces were open and interested." He turns to Mama. "I attribute that to you, Mrs. Taylor. We'll see what happens next." His gaze flickers to Lillian, then back in an instant.

My sister runs her fingers down her skirt, pinching its pleats. I've never seen her so fidgety. Her dignity went out the door when the pastor came in. "Did you explain mealtimes to Pastor O'Neal?"

"Please call me Kade."

Lillian draws one leg up beneath her. "Didn't they call you *Pastor* at your old church?"

His laugh is the kind that's contagious. I find myself smiling.

"They've known me since I was a baby. They call me Kade. A few of the children called me *Pastor*, but anyone near my age or older calls me by my Christian name."

"Was that hard?" Miss Kara lays a darned sock back in her mending basket. "Becoming pastor to your fellow church members, I mean."

"Surprisingly, it wasn't. When I felt God calling me, I talked to the deacons about attending Bible college. After I graduated, they asked me to be associate pastor. It was a natural transition when our pastor retired."

I rise. "I hope it goes as well here. I, for one, think you're the right man. Now, if you'll excuse me, I'll see to supper."

Lillian jumps up. "Me too. When the bell rings, go to the dining room. Miss Gladys said for you to join her and Mr. Nesbitt at their table."

I laugh. "That's perfect. She can keep anyone from getting too cantankerous with their questions."

Once we're in the kitchen, I turn to Lillian. "You like him, don't you?"

She takes my hands and looks me in the eye. "I think I do. My heart quickened the moment I laid eyes on him, and I felt at peace deep down in my soul. I believe he's the man God has planned for me."

I breathe a quick prayer for my sister. I don't want to see her hopes soar for her only to be left with a broken heart.

Like me.

Chapter 29

"JUST HOW OLD ARE YOU, Pastor? You still look kinda wet behind the ears." Snickering, Elmer Dyer looks around the dining room for support, but not one face wears a smile.

I frown. What's he doing here, anyway? He moved out of the hotel and into a tenement last month. He better not try to get any supper.

Kade rises. "I'm twenty-seven, Mr.—?"

Elmer's gaze follows the pastor's height upward until the man towers over him. His grin disappears. "Dyer."

"Mr. Dyer. I am young, although I've pastored a church for five years."

Elmer backs away a step and tries again. "Kicked ya out, did they?"

I roll my eyes. He just can't leave it alone.

Kade's right eye twitches, but he doesn't react. "I guess you weren't in church this morning, Mr. Dyer. Brother Pugh here"—he tips his head toward Mr. Bud—"explained to the congregation that my old church doesn't want me to leave."

Oh, he's good. I would have told Elmer what he could do with his question. Lillian looks as if she'd like to do the same. I edge a little closer, not wanting to miss any of this battle.

"Dyer in church? Ha!" Leroy Allman slaps his thigh, laughing. "The ceiling would fall in. Sit down, Elmer. You don't even belong to the Baptist church."

After Elmer grumbles and leaves the dining room—most likely, headed to the bar where he's been spotted spending most of his evenings—several members of our church stop by the table, greeting Kade and asking his opinion on theological matters.

I can't find fault with any of his answers, and apparently, neither can Mr. Bud. He's quick to put anyone straight if their comments don't line up with the Bible. He beams at Kade like a proud papa.

Nellie shyly approaches the table with Joe beside her. They're back in their new house. I guess they came by this evening just to talk with Kade.

"I'm Nellie Ralston, and this is my son, Joe. I know we haven't voted yet, but we'd still like to welcome you, Pastor. Since God has called you here, I'm looking forward to what he's going to do with you and us. God bless you."

Kade's smile is tender, and his gaze never leaves her face.

Earlier, Lillian said she told him about the mill accidents and whose children had died because she wanted him to know who might need special attention or prayer.

Nellie's soft welcome and benediction make an impression on him. He takes her extended hand between his large ones. "Thank you, Mrs. Ralston. Your support means a lot to me. I'll be looking to you for help in the future should the congregation vote me in." He releases her hand and shakes Joe's. "Did I hear you play on the mill's baseball team?"

I share a smile with Lillian. Kade is going to make a wonderful pastor. He's a lot like Daddy was. He really listened to all Big Sis told him. And Joe will be a good ally for him and maybe become a friend. After all, even pastors need friends.

Joe's lips twitch. "Yeah. Do you play?"

"Love baseball. I've been on a team or two."

The line to talk with Kade has dwindled, so the two men continue to chat. A couple of Joe's teammates join the conversation.

I wander into the kitchen, taking a load of dishes to be washed.

I miss Tommy so much, my heart squeezes as though it's wringing out tears, even when my eyes are able to keep them at bay. I know Miss Kara still prays for God to make a way, but I'm seeing nothing more than a future without my life's partner.

Kade's sermon stirs our hearts. I feel like God spoke through him directly to me. Now, as Mr. Bud prays, the sanctuary is silent except for the occasional "amen" and "yes, Lord." Kade waits outside the church until he's called back in. Lillian keeps him company while the congregation votes.

"Amen." Mr. Bud raises his head and leans one elbow on the podium. "Now, the pulpit committee has charged me to request a vote to call Kaden O'Neal to pastor this church. Their decision is the nomination. Do I have a second?"

Mama raises her hand. "I second it."

Bud's smile grows warm and wide, making his mustache dance. "Then, all in favor, raise your hand." He waits until two of the deacons tally the hands. At their nods, Mr. Bud says, "All opposed?" A single hand raises in the back.

Mr. Bud squints. "Elmer, you ain't a member here, so you cain't vote. Therefore, it's unanimous." He nods to Joe Ralston, who mans the door. He steps outside and brings Kade back in, with Lillian following. She takes her seat next to me.

Mr. Bud waits until Kade reaches the platform. "The congregation has unanimously voted to call you to be our pastor. Do you accept?"

Lillian sucks in a breath.

A wide grin stretches Kade's face. He locks his gaze on my big sister as he says, "I sure do."

Nobody stands on ceremony now. Everyone exits their pews, swarming around Kade, welcoming him, and every deacon slaps him on the back. It's a typical Sweetgum celebration.

After a few minutes, Kade breaks free of the crowd and goes to Mama. He bends down and quietly speaks to her alone, causing her to smile. She nods, stretches upward, and kisses his cheek.

Mr. Bud steps back on the platform. He claps his hands to gain attention. "Let's continue this howdy-do on the grounds. I'm hungry!"

He gets the result he wants—laughter and a move outdoors. On the grounds, even people from the other churches stop by to welcome Kade to Sweetgum. Finally, Mr. Bud leads him to sit at our table. After he asks the blessing, food passes in all directions.

Mr. Bud waits until plates are filled and everyone starts to eat. "Kade, the deacons have discussed housing options for you. We can keep you at the hotel or build a small home. There aren't any vacant mill houses." He glances at Mama. "If he chooses to remain at the hotel, the church would pay the room rent to the mill. However, we will pay you directly for his meals, Emma, since he's not an employee of the mill. Is that good for everyone?"

I silently bless the deacons.

Kade nods and swallows a mouthful of potato salad. "If it's all right with Mrs. Taylor, I'd prefer not to have to eat at the diner, and I'm a lousy cook." He grins and spears a bite of ham.

I picture the available three rooms, imagining he'll want a quiet spot. "Mr. Nesbitt's room is empty, and being at the far end of the hotel, it's not as noisy as those closer to the stairs. We can move you to that room."

Kade shakes his head. "Don't bother, Genessee. I like the room I'm in, and noise doesn't bother me. Besides, if I'm ever needed during the night, I'll be able to leave without disturbing your other lodgers."

Mr. Bud pulls out a small notepad. "We'll pay for a telephone to be wired in your room, Kade." He makes a note to call the Southern Bell in the morning. "That way, members can get you directly and not disturb the Taylors."

With those issues solved, we finish dinner, then Sarah and I start cleanup. "Lillian, you take Kade to the ball field. You can fill him in on the teams. I'm going to help Sarah take this home first. See you later." I shoo them off.

Sarah eyes me as we put the dirty plates into the picnic basket. "Your poor heart never gets a chance to heal, does it, me darlin'?"

I grimace and shake my head. "I try hard not to show it."

"I've known you since you were in nappies. I know when y'all hurt, just like your mama does." She reaches across the picnic basket and touches my cheek. "We both pray for you every night."

I hold back the tears threatening to fall and nod. Some days, I can go a few hours without thinking of Tommy, but then I see something that reminds me of him, and the pain rips open. I can't imagine how he feels about me. How he hurt, reading my letter. He probably hates me.

I look around the tables. "Is that it?"

Sarah nods, and we carry the baskets back to the hotel kitchen.

"I'll wash, you dry." She tosses me a dish towel, then plunges her hands into the water. After a moment, she passes me the first wet plate. "Did I ever tell you about me Bobby?"

I take the dripping dish. "No. Was he your son?"

A sly smile pulls her lips upward. "No. Bobby was me husband before Angus."

I gape. "I never knew you had another husband."

She hands me another plate. "Well, not at the same time, lass." She chuckles. "No, I was seventeen, and Bobby was me childhood sweetheart. We married in the spring, but that winter, he died in a fishing accident."

My heart grows heavy for the brokenhearted young bride she once was. "You must have been devastated."

She nods and passes a serving dish to dry. "I railed at God for months. Then after a while, the pain didn't cut so deep a trough in my heart. Finally, one day, I found I could treasure the sweet memories." She glances at me. "The day I met Angus, me heart stopped hurting." She dries her hands and takes mine, looking deep into my soul. "The good Lord will heal yours, too, lass."

Maybe. When I'm old and gray, an auntie to my sisters' children?

I slide a magazine in the mail slot, smiling at the name, *Mrs. Clarence Nesbitt*. She and her new husband have settled in nicely in the week since their wedding. Two letters for Leroy Allman go into his cubby. One is from his sister. Hopefully, this letter announces that he's an uncle. I chuckle, remembering Leroy's joke about not knowing the baby's sex yet, so he didn't know if he was going to be an aunt or an uncle. Silly man. He'll lead Mary Patterson on a merry chase.

The next envelope is another bill for the hotel. This one is from

Mr. Campbell, which means it's not for Mr. Spencer but for us. Mr. Campbell is graciously allowing us to send what we can each month to get the hogs paid off. *Lord, bless that man and multiply his finances.* We've stretched everything the best we can to spare the money. At least the chickens are finally well and laying again. That gives us four or five dozen eggs to sell to the general store and send that money to dear Mr. Campbell.

The front door opens and a boy wearing a Western Union uniform steps inside. In his hand is a yellow envelope.

A telegram!

My heart slams against my ribs, and the mail remaining in my hands falls to the floor. The only time anyone ever got a telegram in Sweetgum was when Tommy's daddy was killed in a train wreck.

The boy peers at me. "You Miss Genessee Taylor?"

I can scarcely breathe. "Yes." The word comes out in a squeaky whisper.

He hands me the envelope. I stare at it. How can such a small piece of paper carry potentially life-altering news?

The boy stands there, not moving. I blink. Is he waiting for a reply? Oh, of course not. He wants a tip. I dig in a box beneath the desk and find a nickel. He takes it and, apparently satisfied, smiles, touches his cap, and leaves.

When he's gone, I carry the envelope into the kitchen, dropping into my chair. I lay the yellow rectangle on the table. I have no idea how much time passes before I sense Lillian behind me.

"Gen?" Her hand rests softly on my shoulder. "Who is it from?"

"I don't know. I'm afraid to open it."

"Do you want me to?"

I raise my eyes to her gaze. "Will you?"

She sits beside me and picks it up. "Of course." Sliding her finger beneath the flap, she pulls out the telegram. Her eyes move back and forth, then widen. She lifts her head, her gaze meeting mine. She whispers, "It's from Tommy."

My heart pounds harder. "Is he all right?"

Her smile is wide. She hands the wire to me. "He's coming home." I grab it and read.

"Dearest Genessee STOP I'm coming home STOP Arriving Tuesday STOP Meet me by the sweet gum STOP Seven o'clock STOP Tommy STOP"

I don't know what it means. I search Lillian's eyes. "What do you think he wants?"

She stares at me as though I've got bread dough rising on my head. "You, of course."

"How can he? I sent him that letter, breaking our engagement. I know it hurt him. I told him not to write to me, and he hasn't."

"Until now." Lillian takes the telegram from me and lays it on the table. "You can do one of two things." She rises, pulls two glasses from the cupboard, and pours sweet tea. I wait while she drops ice chips in both. She's like Mama and won't rush something important. She wants to be sure I listen carefully. She hands me a glass and sits. "You can meet him and see what he has to say, or you can stay away and never know. But I warn you, if you choose the latter, it will eat at you all your life."

Lillian's grown so much since Daddy died. Love for my sister warms me. "You're right. I'll meet him."

With those words, my heart begins to pound so fast, I'm in danger of becoming lightheaded. What will he have to say? Will he be angry? He's arriving tomorrow. Then a new thought snakes its way into my head.

What if he did as I asked? What if he's bringing home a new wife?

Chapter 30

I LAY IN BED, LISTENING TO the clock tick ... tick ... ticking away the minutes and hours all through the night. Each time I close my eyes, they pop open again, imagining what Tommy might say. Guilt claws at me for hurting him. The knowledge I did what I had to makes no difference. In my mind, I see Tommy waiting for me by the sweet gum tree. He stands and raises his hand to stop me. Then he turns his back and walks away.

Like I did from him.

My eyes fly open, and I realize it was a dream. Tears dampen my face. Around four o'clock, I must have fallen asleep. I glance at Annie's bed, but it's empty. The clock hands sit on four-forty-five, and I'm late. Dragging my body out of bed, I throw on some clothes and head to the chicken coop. Annie and Willie are more than halfway through.

"Thanks for letting me get a little sleep. I was awake most of the night." I pick up Willie's basket and follow him.

Annie slides her hand beneath a hen and withdraws an egg. "I know. I heard you tossing and turning."

"I'm sorry."

Willie hands me a large brown egg to put into the basket.

"Don't be. I understand. You're nervous." We finish both sides of the henhouse. "The girls are back to laying well. We should have five dozen to sell today. And soon, several of those chicks will be old enough to start laying, adding more."

Willie heads for school while we put the eggs in the icebox. Annie takes the extras to the general store to sell, and I start making pastry for the dinner pasties. "Sarah, what's the filling today?"

"Pork, carrots, potatoes, and peas."

"Is there plenty?"

Sarah nods as she chops the carrots. "Let's make seven-inch rounds today. Give them a treat. There may not be plenty tomorrow."

While the pastry rests, it's time for our breakfast. Kade joins us. I find it amusing that Sarah doesn't mind his presence in the kitchen, even though he's technically a lodger.

He asks the blessing, and we share a merry time over coffee, grits, biscuits, and eggs scrambled with bits of ham. We made sure there was enough for our new pastor. He can eat up a storm, although there isn't an ounce of fat on the man. Thankfully, the church is paying us accordingly.

After breakfast and two more cups of coffee, the morning chores keep me awake and moving. The fog is gone from my brain, replaced with a desperate need to keep busy. The morning flies by. I don't know whether to be thankful for that or fretful. I'm as nervous as a long-tailed cat in a room full of rocking chairs.

Annie, Beulah, Charity, and Willie—during his school dinner break—take the baskets of dinner bundles to the mill. I start on bread for supper and tomorrow morning. I've got two batches rising when they return.

During our dinner, Kade volunteers to help with chores around the hotel. Since we can always use an extra hand with the animals, we agree gratefully.

"Thank you, Kade." Lillian picks up her coffee cup. "When Willie gets home from school, we'll have him show you what to do. He'll enjoy that."

Annie, Lillian, and I run upstairs to clean the rooms. I can't stop thinking about this evening. What if Tommy says I ruined his life? My broom stops moving as I return to my middle-of-the-night fear. What if he's at the sweet gum tree but not alone? What if he's there with a wife?

I resume sweeping in a frenzy, doing nothing but stirring up the dust. Annie grabs my wrist and gently takes the broom from me, patting my fingers.

"Gen, easy. I know you're nervous, but you're making more mess than you're cleaning up. Now I'll have to dust again."

I drop my chin to my chest. "I'm sorry."

She rests her arm atop the broom handle. "You want my advice?"

I'll take anyone's right now. "Sure."

"Do what I do. Take deep breaths, then think of the worst thing that could happen. Then ask yourself if you can survive it." She rests the broom against the wall and dusts the dresser again. "Why don't you go lie down for an hour? You look like you can use it."

"I think I will. Thanks, sis."

In my room, I lay on the bed, but my eyes won't close. My dresser drawers have been wanting a good organizing, so I pull open the top one and refold my already folded underwear. Annie said to think about the worst that could happen. That's easy. Tommy bringing a new wife home—a wife other than me.

Even though that's what I told him to do, my heart would break. But … it's already broken. I guess I could survive, at least the physical part of me. But what about my soul? It would shrivel up.

The Bible tells me the Lord is my joy. I know that's true. I can be filled with joy without being happy. God never promises happiness, only joy, and there is a difference. I blow out a breath. I need to give my happiness to the Lord.

Likewise, if another wife is best for Tommy, don't I want that for him? Like I did when I wrote the letter, I firm my resolve and prepare myself. And I give it to God.

The bedroom door opens, and Lillian pokes her head in. "So you aren't sleeping." She closes the door and sits on the bed with me. "You, who never has messy drawers, are cleaning them? What's up, sis?"

I pull some joy from my heart and smile. "I've strengthened my resolve to what Tommy might have to say. I'll survive … whatever it is."

Lillian pulls me into her arms and hugs me. My resolve wavers and my eyes fill.

∞

After school, Willie is excited to show Kade the barn. "I'll teach you how to do everything!"

"Thanks, little buddy." Kade accepts Willie's hand as he pulls him out the kitchen door.

Lillian and I share a chuckle. She peeks through the window. "This should be interesting. I'd love to sneak out there and watch, but"—she turns around—"it's time to bake supper rolls."

We keep busy baking, cooling, and setting rolls in large bowls. Sarah has a pot of split pea soup bubbling on the stove, filling the kitchen with a delicious aroma. I cut dough for another tray of rolls to bake, grateful my hands aren't shaking like they were. Joy. *Thank you, Lord.*

In my heart, I hear, *Lean on me.*

At supper, Kade eats with the lodgers. Around our table, we're getting the "barn report" from Willie.

"Pastor Kade learned a lot about mucking out stalls. He's pretty good now, but I had to show him where to step." His gaze takes us all in with a dramatic flair. "So he doesn't slip again."

Lillian raises one eyebrow. "Again?"

"Yeah." Willie snickers. "He slipped and sat in a cow patty." His giggles become gales of laughter.

"We only have two milk cows." Lillian wags her finger at the little boy. "They don't make that many patties. How did he manage to find one to slip on?" She dissolves into giggles.

Willie's mama and mine gasp. Miss Kara holds her hands up. "Where are those pants?"

Willie grins, obviously proud of himself. "I made him take them off outside. I gave him a sheet to wrap them in."

Mama blinks and chuckles. "Thank you for that."

"They'll get washed on Saturday." Miss Kara passes the rolls. "Oh, unless you think he needs them before that."

"As long as he doesn't find any more of those patties, he said he's fine." Willie plunges his spoon into his soup.

My gaze catches the clock. It's six-thirty. I glance at Mama as my stomach pitches. I try to pull up joy again, but nerves are blocking its entry.

I run out back to the privy where I lose my supper. I've never been this nervous in my entire life. I go back inside but through the front door and run to the bathroom. After I rinse my mouth and brush my teeth, it's close enough to the time I'm supposed to meet Tommy. I don't dare linger to look at my reflection. I'm too afraid of what I might see.

With my heart hammering in my throat, I slip out the front door and walk to the town circle. The sweet gum tree is blooming. Its berry-like green flowers contrast with the leaves, and the spiky gum balls hang from its branches.

I approach the tree and stop. He's not here. Has he changed his mind? My heart sinks.

Then, from around the other side of the sweet gum, Tommy steps out.

Alone!

My pulse pounds in my ears as he slowly walks toward me. I move to meet him, glancing as I do to see if one of Mr. Spencer's men is spying on us. The street is clear, and my gaze snaps back to Tommy.

His eyes search mine. From my heart, all the love I've ever felt for him swells, and I smile.

His gaze is hopeful, and he reaches out his hand. I hold out mine. And he pulls me into his arms.

I'm home. Where I belong.

After a long moment of just being together, his fingers find my chin, and he raises it. His kiss is tender and filled with longing. How I've missed the taste of his lips. When the kiss ends, he holds me a moment longer.

Finally, he leads me to the bench. We sit sideways, facing each other.

"I've missed you so much." He releases a long breath. "I have a lot to tell you, but first, I have to know for sure. Do you still love me?"

Though we're sitting, I throw my arms around his neck. "I never stopped loving you." This time, I kiss him. I'll never get enough of his kisses.

He runs a thumb over our clasped hands. "When I first read your last letter, I couldn't believe it, and yet I knew you were right. I couldn't ask you to abandon your family." His gaze won't release mine. "But my heart wouldn't let you go." He shakes his head. "It's hard to explain, but after a little while, I knew I had to come back. Gen, nothing is good without you."

"But what about your dream of playing professional baseball?"

Tommy leans forward until his forehead touches mine. "Baseball is only *part* of my dream." His lips kiss one corner of my mouth, then the other, and then he leans back.

"I began to closely observe the other players. Those who are married and had their wives with them did better than the ones whose wives or sweethearts were back home. They were focused. Content. And watching them made me realize that without you, baseball didn't hold me like I thought it would. The tether snapped." He puts his arm around my shoulder and draws me close. "I found myself comparing everything to you or Sweetgum. That's when I realized *you* are the best part of any dream."

My heart thrills. "And you're sure you won't miss baseball?"

"I don't need it. I came home because I *wanted* to. I want us to get married right away. Mama wrote me about the new preacher, and if he can marry us tonight, then I'm for it. I figure I can take over what your daddy did for the hotel."

Tears—happy ones—blur my vision as he kisses me once more. *Thank you, Lord.*

"Let's plan to have the wedding this weekend. We can get married Saturday."

With a shouted, "Whoop," he rises and pulls me into his arms. "Let's go home and tell everyone."

Hand in hand, Tommy and I burst into the lobby and stop. Apparently, they've all been at the window watching us. I'm sure it doesn't hurt that our faces have our story written all over them because they surround us, laughing and all talking at once. Willie hops from one foot to the other in his excitement, while Miss Kara hugs her son long and hard.

Mama sits in her chair, a wide smile of joy glowing on her face, which is wet with happy tears. I slip out of the circle and squat next to her.

"We want to get married on Saturday. Will that be all right with you?"

Her eyes light up. "Kara and I have prayed for this day for so long. Yes, it's more than all right." Her smile turns bittersweet, and her eyes show her sorrow. "I only wish your daddy was here to see it. He loved Tommy so much."

Tommy joins us. "Who loved me?"

"Gen's daddy. Even before you two started dating, Frank told me you were the boy he hoped she would marry. He was so pleased when you asked his permission. I'm glad he was here for that, at least."

"I loved him, too, Miss Emma. My dad died at a crucial time in my life, but Mr. Frank stepped into his place as my mentor."

We migrate into the kitchen for pie and milk, along with making plans.

"I saw a cake in a magazine that had several layers, each smaller than the one below it. I saved the photo." Sarah digs in a drawer for the page. "Here it is." She shows it to me. "I'd like to try this, in a smaller version, for your wedding, Gen."

"I love it."

"And I would love to help with it." Lillian reaches for the magazine page, then peers closely at it. "This one has the layers held up by some tiny columns. But I'll wager my best beret we can do it by laying them right on the layer below." Her eyes sparkle with delight. "Can you imagine what that will look like when it's cut? Especially if we use some color in each layer."

Sarah catches Lillian's enthusiasm. "We could add strawberries to one layer. I put some up last summer, and we can use those. Maybe blueberries for the next layer."

"And if we do one plain vanilla, it will be a red, white, and blue cake."

I couldn't care less what kind of cake they make. I'm too happy—and yes, joy-filled, too—to chime in on their plans. Lillian refills all our coffee cups. Like a love-sick puppy, Kade smiles up at her as she pours his. If they keep on like this, we'll be planning another wedding in the not-too-distant future. I glance at Tommy to see if he notices. He's noticing all right—like a big brother. I hide a smile behind my napkin, pretending to wipe my mouth.

After she puts the pot back on the stove, Lillian returns to her seat next to Kade. "Come on, let's plan this wedding."

Mama claps her hand to silence all the chatter. "We can do that in the morning. Right now, we need to hear all about Tommy's experiences in Texas."

With breakfast consumed and the dishes cleared, Mama gives her chair a little push with her good arm, rolling it back a few inches from the table. "Kara and I pulled out my wedding dress for you to try on this morning, Gen."

"I'll do that right after we get the dinner bundles off to the mill. Kade, will you marry us Saturday evening?"

His brows raise. "I'd be honored, but are you sure you don't want Mr. Bud to?"

Tommy glances at me, then answers for us. "We talked and would like you to do it."

"And I'm asking Mr. Bud to give me away." I don't want Kade to feel like he's usurping our favorite deacon.

"Then, yes. But I'd like to talk privately with you both. We can meet in the parlor or at my office in the church."

"Sure, but"—I glance at my sisters—"it will have to wait until this afternoon."

Sarah turns around and wags a finger at me. "You leave the kitchen to us, Genessee Taylor. We have the menu planned to be simple for today and tomorrow. We can manage without you."

I jump up and kiss her cheek. "Thanks." Pulling out the list I made last night, I glance over it. "What about flowers? Lillian, Annie, and I need a posy to carry."

Willie leaps from his seat. "I can do that, Miss Gen. I'll pick wildflowers. There's lots starting to bloom."

Tommy twiddles his little brother's ear, making him giggle. "Thanks, buddy. That will be a big help." He pushes back his chair. "Mama, will you look over my suit?"

Miss Kara nods. "It's fine. When you first asked Brother Frank for Genessee's hand, I checked it—and mended the pocket."

Tommy folds his napkin and lays it on his plate. "Thank you. I'd forgotten it was torn." He turns to Kade. "Would now be a good time for us to talk?"

"Sure. Genessee?" Kade pushes back his chair.

The three of us go to the parlor. Kade takes Daddy's old chair. Tommy and I sit on the settee, holding hands. I'm tickled the two men are so at ease with each other. They were still in the parlor talking when I went to bed last night.

Kade rests his hands on the arms of Daddy's chair. "You two have a long history with each other, but you don't know one another as well as you soon will. Marriage is about four Cs—Christ, Commitment, Communication, and Compromise. It's putting the Lord first and at the center of your marriage. It's about putting your spouse's desires above your own and loving one another as Christ loves the church." He crosses his legs, one ankle resting on the opposite knee. "You'll need to work hard to always communicate with each other. Genessee, Tommy won't know how he hurt your feelings if you don't tell him, and vice-versa. Another important factor is giving up your right to be right. Are you both ready to commit to each other like that?"

Tommy nods. "I believe I can say we are." He caresses my hand.

Kade directs his gaze to me. "Genessee? Is he right?"

"Absolutely."

"And you both realize there will be little things that annoy you. The way Tommy squeezes a toothpaste tube might be different than the way you do. And the way Genessee puts the toilet paper on the roller might not be the way you prefer it, Tommy. You have to decide if it bothers you enough to communicate it."

I can't imagine anything Tommy does could ever bother me. But I guess Kade's right. "So you're saying I will have to decide which is more important, Tommy, or the way I hang the toilet paper." I grin at my fiancé. "That's easy. Toilet paper." Tommy and I both laugh at Kade's shock. "I'm teasing."

Our pastor grins. "Glad to know that." Then his face sobers. "What about raising children? Have you talked about if you want children and how many? And how you plan to raise them?"

He's really getting into the details of marriage. Tommy explains we've already discussed it—after all, we've been in love since we were young teenagers. I just hope Kade doesn't want to talk about the marriage bed. I feel my cheeks warming.

Relief washes over me when he pushes up from the chair. "I think you two have a firm foundation for this marriage." He chuckles. "But it sure will be fun to revisit this conversation again in twenty-five years."

Tommy's hearty laugh fills the room. "Gen's daddy talked about that when I asked for his blessing to marry her." Tommy helps me rise and keeps my hand in his. "He and Miss Emma have been a wonderful example of married love. My own father had died by the time I fell in love with Gen. Before that, I never paid much attention to his and Mama's relationship, so the Taylors became my example."

Kade shakes Tommy's hand. "I wish I'd known Pastor Taylor."

I reach out and touch Kade's sleeve. "You would have liked him, and I know he would have liked you. I've seen a lot of similarities in you."

And so has Lillian.

Only one small worry worms its way into my happiness. The warrant for Tommy's arrest. Now that he's back, will Mr. Spencer insist the sheriff enforce it?

Chapter 31

It's my wedding day! Joy swells my heart, and with it, more gratitude than I can contain. *Thank you, Lord. Help me be a good wife to Tommy, and bless our marriage.*

Unable to sleep any longer, I bounce out of bed. It's only four o'clock, but I won't wake Annie. I can manage alone.

Tommy and Willie enter the henhouse shortly after I start collecting eggs.

"We heard you. Willie made me get up and come help." Tommy tousles his little brother's hair.

"Grab a basket and help me, then we can get an early cup of coffee. I smelled cinnamon in the kitchen when I came through, so Sarah has something delicious in the oven."

After a quick kiss, with Willie hiding his eyes and us laughing, we get to work. Tommy makes the first chicken squawk and gets pecked, then his little brother shows him how to do it the "right way."

Annie arrives when we're nearly finished and aims a scowl in Tommy's direction. "Well, if I'd known you were going to help, I'd have slept in."

I touch her arm. "I'm sorry, Little Sis. I couldn't sleep and didn't know Tommy was coming. But we're done, so join us and have whatever it is Sarah's baking."

A few minutes later, the sugary taste of Sarah's celebration cinnamon rolls coats our tongues. Our lodgers will love these.

As the aroma of bread baking fills the kitchen, I take a final gulp of coffee, place my cup and plate in the sink, then toss Tommy a teasing grin. "How was sleeping with your mama and brother last night?"

He sets down his empty coffee cup and returns my grin. "Fine. Not a lot different than in the old house."

I lean against the counter. "We'll have to figure out which room we'll have after the wedding. We need to stay in the hotel, and since you can't go back to work in the mill, you might as well take on what Daddy used to do."

I don't voice my concern about whether Mr. Spencer will pay him for that work. I take a quick glance at the clock. "Beulah, will you get me the grits? They should be soaking in the pantry in a pot of water."

When she brings them, Tommy stands behind me, watching me work over my shoulder. "What kind?"

"Cheese—your favorite."

He kisses the back of my neck, sending chills down my spine.

Sarah laughs, then harrumphs. "You keep that up, and you'll be getting burned grits."

Tommy's laugh sends happiness all the way to my toes. He grins at Sarah and sits at the table. "That better?"

"A mite," she says with a sniff that turns into a chuckle.

I drain the grits and pump fresh water into the pot. "Are we sure nobody will let it slip that you're home?" Now that I have him back, fear takes up residence in my belly over the possibility of losing him again.

Lillian stands next to me, adds goat cheese, and grates a little Parmesan as well. "Since Mr. Dyer moved into the tenements, we don't have any of Spencer's moles living here. When we serve breakfast, I'll remind everyone. After all, they love Tommy too."

The rest of the day flies by in the flurry of activities, which include our chores. Life goes on in Sweetgum, even if it's my wedding day.

Finally, the appointed hour arrives, and I gaze at my reflection in the standing mirror in Mama and Lillian's room.

Mama's Victorian wedding gown—mine now and maybe someday, my own daughter's—has an ivory lace flounce that flows from the high collar to just below my shoulders. The waist nips in with a wide satin belt before the skirt drapes softly to end in three rows of tiny ruffles at the bottom.

Lillian sighs. "Tommy won't be able to think straight when he sees you."

I'm glad neither of my sisters favor the style of Mama's gown. Lillian is built more like Grandmother Taylor, tall and long-waisted. Annie's tastes run modern. But this suits me perfectly. I smooth the skirt, then turn so Tommy's mama can place the coronet of flowers and veil on my head. Annie hands me my posey.

My sisters, wearing their best dresses—Annie's pink and Lillian's a pale green—pick up their posies, and we're ready to go. I've asked Mary Patterson to be in charge of the guest book at the reception.

I bend and kiss Mama. "I love you. How I wish Daddy were with us." I dab my eye so the mascara I allowed Annie to put on me won't smear.

Mama taps my chest. "He's here, my love, and watching."

As we go to the lobby, my heartbeat thrums in my ears. My wedding day—it almost feels like a dream.

Mr. Bud steps inside the front door. He's wearing his best suit—the one from the last century—and has slicked his hair back with pomade.

"I've got a car out front."

I blink. "We need a car? The church is all of two-hundred feet from here."

He laughs. "Girlie, you're a-goin' in style. I had me a talk with your daddy last night, and I told him I'd do this. And so I am."

A talk with Daddy? Well, if Mr. Bud says he did, then he did. He's always been eccentric, but we all adore him. "Then let's go."

Mr. Nesbitt and Miss Gladys push Mama in her chair to the church. It would take longer to maneuver her into the car and out again. They arrive before us because it takes Mr. Bud four tries to crank the engine. Three minutes later, we pull up to the front of the church. Everyone must already be inside because Sweetgum's streets are empty. Mr. Bud opens the car door for us, and we pile out.

We're barely in the door when the music begins. The Nesbitts escort Mama and Miss Kara down to their seats in the first pew, then they sit behind them.

I take a deep breath. My stomach must have a thousand monarchs flying to and fro. "Willie, do you have the rings?" Mama gave me my granddaddy's wedding band for Tommy. His grandmother's wedding ring will become mine.

"They're tied onto this little pillow, Miss Gen." He lifts it up for me to see. The rings dangle from satin ribbons.

Then we're ready. Am I?

Oh yes!

Annie gives Willie the signal for him to start walking down the aisle. Then she kisses my cheek and follows him. Lillian steps before me.

"Genessee, I—" Her eyes fill with tears. I have to blink to stop mine. She licks her lips and smiles. "We're growing up, sister-mine. Things will be different from now on. But I'm so proud of you." She turns and follows Annie.

The music swells into Lohengrin's wedding march. Mr. Bud grins broadly and pulls my hand through the crook of his arm.

"Are you ready, girlie?"

I share a loving smile and repeat what my daddy taught me. "I was born ready."

The congregation rises, and Mr. Bud and I step through the doorway. Though our church isn't large, the aisle looms long before me, and at its end waits my groom. My Tommy. The right to my left. The bottom to my top. The front to my back. My completion.

His eyes widen when he sees me. His smile stretches. Beside him, Joe Ralston nudges him and whispers, his eyebrows rising.

When we reach the platform, Tommy steps forward. Mr. Bud kisses my cheek and places my hand in Tommy's. He takes a seat with Mama and Miss Kara.

Tommy gazes into my eyes. His expression offers his heart to me. I hope mine tells him the same thing. He bends as if to kiss me. I lift my lips.

"Ahem." Kade clears his throat.

We chuckle and my cheeks grow warm. Annie giggles. Kade crooks his finger for us to join him on the platform and face the altar. We step up, and my sisters join us, along with Joe. Lillian straightens the hem of my gown, then takes my posey.

"Dearly beloved ..."

I can't believe I'm here, marrying Tommy. I'd given up hope. I sneak a sideways glance at him. His expression is solemn, but his heart is in his eyes. Even when I sent the letter, he continued to love me.

Daddy, do you see us? I hope so.

"Who gives this woman to wed this man?"

I glance over my shoulder. Mr. Bud's chest puffs out and he stands.

"Her mother, her father, and I do." He swipes a knuckle beneath his eye as he sits back down beside Mama ... as Daddy's stand-in. He sees me watching him and winks. A memory floats into my mind of Daddy and Mr. Bud teaching me to fish down at the river. My hook caught in a tree branch. Mr. Bud climbed the tree, while Daddy—

"Genessee—"

What? I snap my attention to Kade.

Tommy softly repeats Kade's question, "Genessee, do you take me to be your wedded husband from this day forward?"

"Yes." I think that's what I'm supposed to say now. Or is it, "I do."

Kade smiles, then addresses Tommy. "Do you, Thomas James Mack, take Genessee Louise Taylor ..."

Tommy gazes into my eyes and says, "I do."

Finally, Kade pronounces us husband and wife.

I'm a wife!

"You may kiss the bride."

My husband raises my chin and kisses me. This time, his kiss tastes of promise and joy, and my insides quiver. The congregation laughs as our kiss lengthens. We break with a grin, then, turning, we race back up the aisle.

The flashbulb on the photographer's camera blinds me, and the parlor momentarily disappears. First, he had us stand, then sit with Tommy standing at my shoulder, then—

I gaze with longing toward the door. "Are we almost done, Mr. Ralph? I want to join our guests."

Ralph Flournoy, who owns the newspaper and has known us both since we were babies, sets his camera down. "Yes, that will do. I'll get these developed and back to you by next week." He shakes Tommy's hand and kisses my cheek. "You two go have fun."

We escape to the dining room, where all our friends have gathered. Mary still has a line waiting to sign our guest book.

Sarah, Beulah, and Charity have moved the tables against the walls. The center of the floor is free except for one large table with our wedding cake in the center.

When Tommy and I make the first cut, the heavenly aroma of hummingbird cake rises to tease my nose and make my mouth water. Sarah's got a grin as wide as the Etowah River. And here she had me thinking blueberries and strawberries. The sneaky thing. It's been a secret, her gift to us. And each layer has a different color! Tommy and I feed each other a bite of the cake, then Beulah and Charity finish serving our guests.

After we enjoy a whole slice of cake and a glass of punch, my groom and I circulate, hand in hand, among our lifelong friends and family.

Finally, somebody turns on the Victrola. The cake table is pushed back, and now it's time for dancing. Daddy was not against dancing if proper distances were kept, and apparently, Kade isn't either. Pretty soon, all the young people dance the Balboa while the older generations look on. All except Miss Gladys and Mr. Nesbitt—they're dancing with us. Miss Gladys can sure cut a rug. Mr. Nesbitt's no slouch either. There is so much joy in the hotel tonight.

Then the music slows to a waltz, and Tommy pulls me a little closer, gazing into my eyes. "I'm so happy."

I grin at him. "Me too." He lowers his head to kiss me.

The front door bangs open. Feet pound into the dining room. Eyes wide, I turn as Sheriff Jackson and Deputy Limehouse rush up to Tommy. Women scream and scatter. Limehouse pushes me aside.

The sheriff wrenches Tommy's arms behind his back, his baritone voice booming. "Tommy Mack, you're under arrest for arson and accomplice to murder."

Chapter 32

THE SHERIFF SLAPS HANDCUFFS ON Tommy. "You won't get away this time."

"Tommy didn't start the fire!" I struggle to pull his hands away from Tommy, but the sheriff doesn't budge. The expression he levels at me is one of sorrow yet stalwart determination to do what he must drives him. "Stand aside, Genessee."

He and the deputy are on either side of Tommy, half dragging him to the lobby.

I stretch out my arms for my husband. He looks over his shoulder. "It'll be okay, Gen."

Okay? How will it be okay?

The sheriff stops at the door. "I hope you've got a lawyer, Mack." He glances back at me. "You'd better call someone."

A lawyer? The only one I know is Mr. Spencer's, and he's a snake. I'm not about to call that man.

Fear registers on the faces of our friends as Tommy—my brand-new husband—is taken away by the police and put in jail. Fear instilled by Benjamin Spencer. I burst into tears.

Immediately, Lillian is at my side. "Call Mr. Forsythe."

I take the hankie she offers. "How do we know he's really on our side? What if Mr. Spencer got to him with his lies? Because they are lies. I *know* my Tommy. He did *not* start any fire."

"Gen?" Mama Kara tugs on my arm. "What are we going to do?"

The raw grief on my new mother-in-law's face breaks my heart. She's lost so much in her life already. I pull her into my arms and nod at Lillian. "I'm going to call Mr. Forsythe."

A voice resounds in the lobby entrance. "You won't reach him at his office number."

With all our friends surrounding me, I have no idea who it is, but I turn, searching for the speaker in the crowd. "Why not?"

"Because I'm here."

Our guests part like the Red Sea.

My jaw drops. Before me stands the one man who can help us. With a head of thick, silver hair and an expensive gray suit, he appears like an avenging angel. "Mr. Forsythe! What are you doing here?"

His smile is wide. "Do you think I'd let the sweetest hotel manager in all of Georgia get married without me congratulating her?" He steps forward and clasps my hand, drawing me near, and whispers, "Annie let me know about your wedding, and I saw what just happened. We'll get Tommy out of this jam. I've been investigating our *friend*, Benjamin Spencer, for a while—even before I got your letter." He leans back and surveys me at arms' length. "You look lovely. I don't know what Tommy was thinking, leaving you right now."

A few gape at his joking, but I laugh, and even my mother-in-law smiles. Relief at seeing him and knowing he's on our side makes me giddy. We're still in a jam, but Mr. Forsythe believes us. And that sparks a ray of hope within me. He places a kiss on my cheek, then slips an envelope into my hand. "Open it later." Then Mr. Forsythe leaves me to go chat with the two mamas. From the look on Mama Kara's face, he's giving her hope too.

Our guests decide the party's over since the groom is no longer here. I thank them and bid them good night as each offers their heartfelt support and displeasure with the sheriff.

Annie comes alongside me and takes my hand. "I doubt Roy Jackson will be able to win another election as sheriff or anything else in this town. People are pretty mad at him." She steps in front of me and looks me in the eye. "Everyone knows Tommy had nothing to do with that fire, Gen. *Everyone.*"

While I appreciate her words, there are a couple of people who don't agree—or at least want to make others think he did it—Mr. Spencer and the men who started that fire.

"What's this?" Annie tugs on the envelope I'm holding.

"I don't know. Mr. Forsythe gave it to me." I open it and gasp. It's two fifty-dollar bills.

Annie whistles. "That's one swell wedding present."

I look sidelong at her. "Thank you for inviting Mr. Forsythe, but how did you know he was safe to invite?"

His and the mamas' voices filter from the dining room, where he's enjoying a slice of my wedding cake. Annie puts a finger over her lips. "Wait." She walks into the kitchen.

I join Mr. Forsythe and my two mamas. Tommy and I should be … my eyes well.

"Genessee, no tears." Mr. Forsythe gently admonishes me. "They won't help Tommy." He pats the chair next to him. "Come sit and let me tell you what I've uncovered."

While Sarah brings coffee, I thank this generous man for the wedding present. "This will allow us to pay the last of the bill for the hogs and start a savings account."

"You're welcome." His smile is enigmatic. "But have your sisters come join us. This includes them as well."

"Beulah, please send my sisters back in here."

When they arrive, Mama Kara starts to get up, but Mr. Forsythe stops her. "Stay, please. What I have to say involves you all." His warm eyes land on me. "First, Genessee, I owe you a tremendous debt. You have saved me thousands of dollars."

Me? I frown. "What did I do?"

He chuckles. "You braved a letter that could have backfired on you. However, I have long had suspicions about Benjamin, even before the ferret complaint. When I inspected the hotel, I was under the impression there were several problems, but I found none. I purposely didn't tell Benjamin I was making that visit nor inspecting the hotel. I wanted to see it for my own eyes."

"I don't understand. Why would he tell you there were problems with us or the hotel?"

Mr. Forsythe lays down his fork. "Excellent cake, Sarah." He wipes his mouth with his napkin. "Money. Benjamin was always asking me to invest more money. This time, the reasons didn't ring true. Before I left Sweetgum, I gave him some of what he asked for, reminding him I needed an accounting of where the investment is spent for my tax accountant. He agreed." He pauses and takes a sip of coffee. "What he sent me was exactly the opposite of Genessee's letter. He listed the payment for the hogs, extra money coming to the hotel for food, and—this one really got me—salaries for both Mr. and Mrs. Taylor after the fire, along with those of the very kitchen girls whom his daughter hired away from the hotel."

I gasp. "That dirty, no account dog."

Mr. Forsythe laughs. "His greed has gotten way out of hand, but that sealed his fate with me. From there, I had my accountant and attorney dig deeper." His gaze falls on each one of us. "I owe all of you, except Annie and Miss Emma, an apology for an elaborate con job."

Annie's grin is conspiratorial. What is going on?

Mr. Forsythe chuckles. "Annie, you want to tell them?"

"Abso-tootin-lutely!" She wiggles in delight. "Archie Quigg is Mr. Forsythe's attorney."

"What?" The word explodes from my mouth.

Lillian startles so bad, she spills coffee on the tablecloth.

Mama laughs. *She* knew? I give her the evil eye while Little Sis is loving the spotlight. Mr. Forsythe leans back and motions for her to go on.

Annie naturally takes a bow before she begins, making the others chuckle and me want to throttle her.

"The morning after Mr. Forsythe inspected the hotel, he encountered me in the guest parlor, acting out a scene. We chatted for a few minutes about my aspirations to become an actress. Then he left. A couple of months later, I got a short letter from him asking me to call him when I could have a private conversation."

My eyes pop open so wide, they burn. Then I glower at Annie. "And you didn't tell anyone?"

Annie giggles. "Mama knew."

Mama smiles, nodding. "Mr. Forsythe called me first."

"But why wasn't I included in all this?"

Annie shrugs. "Because you're not an actress. Your emotions play out on your face for all the world to see."

I wrinkle my nose at her, but she's right. "Okay, go on with this story, please. What about Mr. Quigg?"

"Mr. Forsythe told me about what he and his attorney suspected Mr. Spencer of doing. They needed someone to help them flimflam him. That's where I came in. Mr. Forsythe didn't want us to call the sheriff on Archie until they were ready. He needed to have all the evidence first."

I shake my head, hoping to rattle my impressions of this into clarity. It doesn't work. "I'm still confused. So Archie is your attorney and not a bank robber?"

Mr. Forsythe grins broadly and nudges Annie. "See? Your sister's a smart cookie."

"I'm not so smart. I bought the whole thing. But why the elaborate hustle?"

Mr. Forsythe's entire demeanor changes. He's all business now. "My dealings with Benjamin Spencer were always a tad off in my mind, but I couldn't put my finger on what it was. Archie and I suspected he was using the money that another partner and I invested for purposes other than the mill. Through Archie pretending to be a bank robber hiding out, he made a connection through friends of Spencer's daughter, Fannie. That girl runs with a dangerous crowd." He sits back in his chair and crosses his legs. "Archie gave them money to purchase narcotics. He managed to trace the marked bills. When you found the briefcase in Archie's car, Genessee, half the money was gone. Anyway, we traced it to a narcotics dealer in South America. Now, we're bringing in the FBI."

I press him. "But I don't get why this had to be so secretive from all of us, except Annie and Mama."

His smile reminds me of Daddy's. "Because the fewer people who knew, the less chance of whispers and a leak. There are millions of dollars in narcotics, making it an extremely dangerous business.

Benjamin Spencer was trying to move into the big leagues."

"But why didn't y'all let the sheriff in on it?"

Annie snorts. "We aren't absolutely sure how honest the sheriff is. I know Miss Kara says he is, but he's been known to do Spencer's bidding. Archie said we couldn't take that chance."

Annie sounds like a gun moll—some longtime mobster's girl—but my admiration for her acting ability grows. She had me convinced of her crush on Archie. "Hey, what about when Archie ran outside? We heard gunfire. How could y'all be sure he didn't get killed?"

"I gave him some acting lessons when we were on our 'dates.'" Annie laughs. "When he ran outside, he shot his gun in the air, then threw it on the ground and gave himself up."

"Okay, that answers that part, but how does Tommy—not to mention the safety strike—come into all this? Why is Spencer so bent on framing Tommy? What has he ever done to that man?"

Mr. Forsythe's demeanor is confident. "Tommy is merely a convenient distraction, taking everyone's focus away from Benjamin. Once the Feds get here, and we can get all this out in the open, everything will become clear."

I certainly hope so. Then a new thought makes my heart stop.

If Mr. Spencer is arrested and convicted, what will happen to the Sweetgum Hotel?

Chapter 33

"ALL RISE." THE BAILIFF'S VOICE resounds off the Rome, Georgia, courtroom's gleaming floors and filters to every burled nook and cranny of the ceiling high above.

Mr. Forsythe touches my elbow, and I stand, following his lead. I've never been in court before since all trials are held in the county seat. I don't know the protocol. But this room inspires awe with its polished wood walls and railings.

The judge enters, a long, black robe flowing down to his ankles. With salt-and-pepper hair, he appears to be in his fifties. Is he wise like Daddy was? He moves to a raised platform, reminding me of a large pulpit, except he sits behind it. Mr. Forsythe says it's called a bench, but it doesn't look like any bench I've ever seen.

The judge surveys the courtroom. When his gaze lands on Mama in her wheeled chair, his brows knit. Archie told us to have her stay in the chair since she'll be able to be moved quicker when she's called to be a witness for Tommy.

Sitting at the end of the row next to her, I reach over and lay my hand on Mama's, stopping her hankie-twisting. I understand it, though. Like hers, my nerves are stretched to their limit. If the judge is trying to intimidate us, he's doing a good job of it.

Tommy sits at a table with his lawyer. It's still strange to see Archie Quigg in that light, but we're grateful Mr. Forsythe hired him for us. Tommy leans toward Archie and whispers.

When Tommy first entered the courtroom, his haggard appearance, after ten days in jail, made me want to run to him. I had to be content with biting my knuckle.

How I wish Lillian and Annie were here to lend me their support, but they're doing everything for us at home. And I know they're praying. I can feel it.

Even so, I start to twist my hankie. I'm as bad as Mama.

"Courage, Genessee," Mr. Forsythe leans close, whispering. "Archie is one of the best orators I know. His father is a renowned trial lawyer, and Archie has spent the past few days working with him on Tommy's case."

I pull my lips into a smile, but a quiver keeps it from stretching wide. My stomach spins like a sink full of draining water.

The prosecuting attorney—a tall, imposing man with slicked-back, pomaded hair, named Mr. Van ... something—rises and begins his opening argument. Though Mr. Forsythe told me last night what the prosecutor might say about Tommy, I didn't expect this.

"We are prepared to show that Thomas James Mack was an accomplice to arson in that he willfully led Mr. Spencer's loyal workers in a labor strike which contributed to the fire. We also have a witness who puts Mr. Mack at the scene and in possession of a gas can."

The slanderous statements are spoken as if they are gospel truth. I almost leap out of my seat. "That's not true!" I whisper, staring aghast at Mr. Forsythe.

He places a finger to his lips. "Shh. Watch."

He may be confident, but I don't like this—not one bit. That Mr. VanWhosits doesn't even know Tommy.

"I'd like to call Stanley Kirkland to the stand."

I twist my neck, searching for the witness. A man in an ill-fitting suit swaggers to the witness box. His longshoreman build seems familiar. My eyes bulge in recognition. One of Spencer's thugs. The bailiff swears him in.

"Mr. Kirkland, please state your full name and place of employment."

His eyes shift from Mr. VanWhosits to Tommy and back. "Elvis Stanley Kirkland, Silver Creek Auto Repair."

The prosecutor frowns and looks at his notepad. "Do you not work for Mr. Benjamin Spencer?"

"On occasion." His tone is edgy.

"I see." The lawyer leans one elbow on the railing surrounding the witness chair. "When was the last time you worked for Mr. Spencer?"

"When he needed muscle to break up a labor strike."

This guy acts like he's bored. I'd bet Buster's new harness it would be a different matter if he were the one on trial.

"And how did he learn of the strike?"

"We have our ways." Kirkland curls his hand and examines his fingernails.

Mr. VanWhosits raises one eyebrow. "Please enlighten the court."

"Uh, I don't exactly know. Mr. Spencer has people who tell him stuff. Then he tells us."

"All right, let's move to the night of the fire. You told me you saw someone at the corner of the Ralston house with a gas can. Is that correct?"

Now, Kirkland is all attention and bluster. "Yes, sir."

"Can you point him out to the court?"

He raises his arm—the arm that wielded a billy club which cracked open the heads of my friends—and points at Tommy. "That's him."

Gasps whoosh around the room. "That's a lie!" murmurs a deep voice.

The judge bangs his gavel. "Quiet the courtroom!"

I lean toward Mr. Forsythe and whisper, "Is it always like this?"

He nods. "Remember what I told you last night? Judge Kramer keeps strict control of his courtroom. All the lawyers know his reputation. They have to mind their Ps and Qs, no matter who they are."

Mr. VanWhosits turns a slimy smile to Archie. "Your witness."

Archie shakes his head. "No questions at this time, your honor, although I reserve the right to recall Mr. Kirkland." Tommy stares at Archie, but the lawyer whispers to him, and he relaxes.

I wish I knew what Archie said so I could relax.

The prosecutor calls one of the mill's unscrupulous supervisors, who says Tommy was a troublemaker. Again, Archie postpones questioning. I sure hope he knows what he's doing. Right now, it isn't looking good for Tommy.

A door closes at the rear of the courtroom. Mr. Forsythe glances over his shoulder and quickly turns back. "Don't look, but Benjamin Spencer just came in. He's sitting in the rear corner near a side door." He grins at me. "Today, he's going to see the handwriting on the wall."

I startle at the reference and stare at him, but his attention is on VanWhosits.

Finally, after nearly two hours of questioning, the prosecutor says he rests his case.

Archie rises. "Your honor, I'd like to call Mrs. Emma Taylor to the stand."

Mr. Forsythe steps past me and wheels Mama to the witness stand, then lifts her into that chair, leaving the wheeled chair at the front of the courtroom. He returns to his seat.

I can't help but wonder what Mr. Spencer thinks about his business partner helping us. I bend down, and as I do, I take a peek at the rear of the room. I can't see Mr. Spencer, but four men in dark suits stand against the wall.

I look sidelong at Mr. Forsythe, mouthing, "FBI?"

A slight dip of his chin confirms it.

Archie approaches Mama and smiles. "Mrs. Taylor, please state your full name and occupation for the court."

"Emma Louise Taylor—" I can hardly hear her.

"Mrs. Taylor," the judge interrupts gently. "Please speak up."

Mama clears her throat. "Emma Louise Taylor." This time her voice is loud and clear but contains the old-lady-quiver I noticed before. "I was a former cook at the Sweetgum Hotel. Now I'm unable to work."

"Can you tell us in your own words what happened on the night of July fourteenth?"

"All of it?"

"Please."

Her thin shoulders straighten, and she clutches her handbag in her lap. "I guess it was a little after midnight when our middle daughter, Genessee, woke my husband and me, shouting there was a fire in the mill village. My husband and I raced to wake people. The mill houses are little more than kindling for a fire."

"I object." The prosecutor's voice rings out from the other side of the courtroom. "This witness is not an expert on home building. Or on fire kindling."

"Sustained."

Mama turns a puzzled look to Archie, but he directs her. "Where specifically did you go?"

"My husband and I started on Third Row. When I realized we'd need more young men to help rouse people, I went straight to the Macks' home and rousted Tommy and his mama and brother from their beds. Tommy hurried back toward Fourth Row to help."

"So within a short time of the fire starting, you found Tommy Mack in his home and in bed?"

"Well, he was in his pajamas and sleepy-eyed when he opened the door. It was obvious he just woke up."

"Objection."

"Sustained."

They can object all they want, but the words are said, just like the bad ones about Tommy have been. I glance at the jury. I sure hope they remember what Mama says.

"Mrs. Taylor, how are you related to Tommy?"

Van Whosits jumps up, his hair as oily as his personality. "Objection. That has no bearing on this case."

Archie turns to the judge. "Your Honor, I am trying to establish the substantive effects of this fire—effects Mr. Mack would have clearly understood as a mill worker and longtime resident of this town. This is crucial to proving the improbability of motive, among other things."

The judge considers a moment and then nods somberly. "I will allow it."

The prosecutor frowns but takes his seat. Archie holds out his hand for Mama to continue.

Her lips curve into a soft smile. "He's my son-in-law." Her pride in him is evident.

"Was he your son-in-law on July fourteenth?"

"No, he was still my daughter's fiancé then."

"And is it your opinion that he would put all his friends, their families, and that of his fiancée at risk by starting a fire?"

"Absolutely not. He risked his own life helping fight the fire and getting people out of burning houses."

"Mrs. Taylor, one more question. What happened to you?"

Mama glances down. Through the railing surrounding the witness chair, everyone can see a single leg—not two. "I helped a woman flee her burning house, but her baby was inside. I went back in, found the toddler, and as I handed her to her mother, the wall collapsed. I was trapped beneath it and burned. Subsequently, I lost my leg and the use of my right arm."

The prosecutor's arm shoots up. "Objection. That has no bearing on this case."

"Sustained."

"Thank you, Mrs. Taylor. Your witness."

VanWhoseits strides to the witness stand. He leans on the railing, close to Mama. She eyes him and tries to scoot back but is unable to.

"Emma—may I call you Emma?"

"No, you may not. You may call me Mrs. Taylor." Even the judge snickers.

VanWhosits glowers and faces the jury. "Mrs. Taylor, then. You weren't at the Ralston house when the fire started, so there's no way you could know whether Tommy Mack started it or not. Could you?" He doesn't allow her time to answer but swings around to Mama and peppers her with questions. "In fact, Mr. Mack could easily have been pretending to have been abed, isn't that right? And since you mentioned nothing of his feet, am I to assume you didn't bother to look to see if he was wearing shoes?"

"Shoes?"

"Shoes that could have been worn outside of the house but which he had no time to remove upon his return!"

"I object. Badgering the witness," Archie says.

"Sustained. Watch your tone, Mr. VanGorder."

Ah, that's his name. My hankie lies in a knot.

"Yes, Your Honor." He leans against the railing again. "Mrs. Taylor, be honest, do you think you used good judgment when you allowed your daughter to marry the accused?"

Uh-oh. His condescending tone is something Mama can't abide.

She stares forward and into the man's eyes. "I don't believe my judgment is on trial here." She turns to the judge. "Is it?"

"No, it isn't. Mr. VanGorder, be careful. You're treading on thin ice."

"I withdraw the question." He walks away from Mama, crossing in front of Tommy and Mr. Quigg, squinting as though taking their measure. Then he whirls around, and a sneer pulls up one side of his lip. "Mrs. Taylor, did your son-in-law's attorney tell you to make a big deal of your injuries? Because I propose, they aren't as bad as you make them out to be. I believe this is to sway the jury with a disgusting bleeding-heart display. In fact, I don't believe your injuries are from the fire."

Whoa, he really made a bad mistake this time. He's put Mama's honor in question. A huge grin pulls my lips, and it's my turn to whisper to Mr. Forsythe, "Watch this."

Mama rears back and stretches as tall as she can while sitting. "Mr. VanGorder, is that how your mother taught you to address your elders? To malign their integrity?"

The judge snorts. VanGorder turns several shades of red. "No more questions."

Mama sniffs. "I should think not."

Tittles and muffled giggles break out in the courtroom. The judge taps his gavel once but doesn't say anything.

Archie nods to Mr. Forsythe, who comes forward, lifts Mama back into her chair, and rolls her to where we sit. Archie now approaches the jury box. "Does anyone honestly think a man would jeopardize his friends and his fiancée's family by starting the fire, then running home and jumping back in bed?"

"Objection!"

"Sustained." The judge levels his gavel at Archie with a scowl. "Be careful, Mr. Quigg. You are very near contempt. I will not warn you again."

Archie's face is most contrite. "Yes, Your Honor. I'd like to call Anthony Jessop to the stand."

My eyes widen as another of Spencer's thugs comes forward, although this one doesn't swagger like that Kirkland man. This man shuffles, his shoulders stooped. The bailiff swears him in.

A side door opens, and three more men in dark suits enter and join the others standing against the wall. I glance at Mr. Forsythe, whose attention is on them.

"Mr. Jessop, state your full name and occupation for the court, please."

Mr. Forsythe turns to watch the witness. I follow suit.

"Tony—uh, Anthony Roland Jessop. I work at the Silver Creek Auto Repair."

"I see, so you work with Mr. Kirkland?"

"Yeah."

Right, works at breaking heads.

Archie smiles at the jury while he addresses the man. "Mr. Jessop, will you please tell the court what you told me?"

"Mr. Spencer pays me and Kirkland and some others to do things for him. Things he doesn't want known—"

Kirkland jumps to his feet. "Shut up, Jessop!" He rushes forward, but the bailiff and another policeman scramble to stop him, holding him by his arms. The bailiff claps handcuffs on him.

Again, the side door opens, and a man slips out, his coattail almost getting caught in the door. Who could he have been? A reporter? What Jessop just said would make a great headline. *Mill owner pays thugs.*

The judge pounds his gavel. "Remove Mr. Kirkland from the courtroom. The prosecution had better keep his witnesses under control."

Two of the feds follow the bailiff out with Mr. Kirkland.

Archie nods at Mr. Jessop. "Continue, please."

"Well, Mr. Spencer pays us to do his dirty work. In July, after we stopped the labor strike, he paid the two of us to start the fire that night." He turns his face to the judge. "If I didn't, I knew it could happen to my own family." He fidgets in his seat. "Then last week, Spencer—he tells me he wants me to start another one—another fire—in the barn at the hotel."

I gasp and turn to Mr. Forsythe. "Why?"

He pats my clasped hands and shakes his head. "Who knows how Spencer thinks?" He nods toward Archie. "Pay close attention now."

Mr. Jessop clasps the railing. "I told him no. I wasn't going to do no more for him. I ain't above a little mischief, but I'd had enough of Spencer's threats. I wanted out. He told me if I didn't do it, he'd finger me. That's blackmail, so I goes to Mr. Forsythe—he's Spencer's partner."

Things are moving fast, but I'm starting to see a little light.

Archie stands to one side of Mr. Jessop, facing the jury. "Let me get this straight. Mr. Spencer paid you and Kirkland to start the fire on the night of July fourteenth?"

"Yes, sir."

"And was Tommy Mack involved in any way?"

"No. The only thing he ever did was help organize a labor strike for a safer workplace. That's what riled Spencer and made him target Mack. But the kid didn't have anything to do with starting the fire. Kirkland was paid by Spencer to say he did."

The courtroom erupts. The judge bangs his gavel. It takes a few minutes for everyone to finally quiet down.

As soon as it does, as though he were a jack-in-the-box, Mr. VanGorder leaps to his feet once again. "Your Honor, this is Jessop's word against Kirkland's."

Archie steps to his table and pulls out something from his briefcase. "May I approach the bench, Your Honor?"

The judge leans forward, his gaze intent on Archie. "You may."

He hands two pieces of paper to the judge. "You hold the note, written by Benjamin Spencer, ordering Jessop and Kirkland to start the fire. The other is a copy of the bank draft from Mr. Spencer's account to Jessop's. It is larger than anything Spencer would pay the auto shop for car repairs and much more than Jessop would make working there."

The judge raises his gavel again. He looks right at Tommy and Archie. "In light of this new information, Mr. Jessop's testimony, and the lack of any credible evidence against Mr. Mack, I declare this case dismissed." He bangs the gavel once more.

This time, the courtroom erupts with cheers. Mr. Forsythe's grin is toothy. He nudges me, tilting his head toward Tommy. I run to my husband, who lifts me off my feet as he hugs me.

Mr. Forsythe passes us and approaches the bench. He and the judge whisper, then the judge nods, rises, and leaves the courtroom.

All I care about is Tommy. He's free. "Tommy, your mama! She's waiting to hear. We have to call the hotel and tell them you're free."

"Already done." Mr. Forsythe shakes Tommy's hand. "I've asked the judge to call her himself."

He must have a lot of pull with people like the judge.

Archie claps Tommy on the back, his grin triumphant. "How are you holding up?"

Tommy wipes the sheen from his brow with his sleeve. "Okay, but I was pretty nervous after Kirkland testified."

"I'm sorry I didn't tell you about Jessop, but Darrell and I didn't want anyone other than the prosecutor to know until he spoke at the trial. He made a plea bargain for turning state's evidence. And Benjamin Spencer is being arrested as we speak. Those men who entered earlier were the FBI. When Spencer snuck out, they followed him and have him in custody."

Mr. Forsythe throws an arm around Tommy and me. "Let's take this celebration back to the hotel."

Tommy puts his arm around me while Mr. Forsythe pushes Mama's wheeled chair to the parking lot, chatting with Archie as we walk.

There are so many questions I still have, but right now, I'm just happy to have my husband beside me.

Once we're in the car, Mr. Forsythe climbs in. "When we get back to Sweetgum, I've got a proposition for you."

Chapter 34

THE HOTEL'S FRONT DOOR BURSTS open, and the entire family rushes out to greet us as we climb out of Mr. Forsythe's car. Mama Kara weeps out her happiness in her son's arms. Little Willie clings to his big brother's leg.

"I thought I was going lose you again, son." Mama Kara dabs her eyes. "I was so afraid. When that judge called us, I swear I heard angels singing *Happy Days Are Here Again*."

Willie giggles. "Mama, that weren't no angels. It was Miss Annie and Miss Lillian an' me."

Joy makes me giddy, and I laugh at the image of him and my sisters singing. I'm thankful our lodgers are still at work. There's time to gather in the parlor and fill everyone in on the trial. Mr. Forsythe and Archie go up to their rooms, saying they will join us in a few minutes.

Tommy keeps hold of my hand as we sit on the settee. The ten days he was in jail were the longest of my life—even longer than when he was in Texas. Then he lets go of my hand and slides his arm around me, squeezing my shoulders. Leaning close, he kisses my temple. His sigh is long and content. I can't begin to imagine what he's been through, but I know he'll tell me later when we're alone.

The parlor door opens, and Sarah joins us, bringing scones and coffee with her. Mr. Forsythe and Archie aren't far behind, along with Kade and Irving Patterson.

Mr. Patterson is a surprise. Who called him and why?

Kade stands behind Lillian's chair, his hands on its back. They inch downward toward her shoulders, then slide back up.

I nudge Tommy and shift my eyes toward Kade. If ever a man matches the old saying about wearing one's heart on his sleeve, it's our preacher. And Big Sis keeps looking up at him with a secret smile. It may be a secret to others but not to me or to Annie, who winks. Tommy dips his chin once to tell me he notices.

"Kade's talked to me about her," he whispers.

I frown. "When?"

"Two days ago." He chuckles at my confusion. "Being my pastor, he had jail privileges."

His answer placates me some. "What did he say?"

Tommy shakes his head and points to Archie, who has a folder in his hands with a lot of papers in it. He sits in Daddy's old chair, pulls out a few of the sheets, then sets the folder on the side table.

After enjoying a scone and coffee, Archie brushes crumbs from the corners of his mouth. "A few moments ago, I used Kade's telephone to place a call. Benjamin Spencer has been arrested and charged with racketeering, arson, and murder. He's being held without bail." He nods his head toward Mr. Forsythe. "Darrell has asked me to handle the paperwork for what he's about to tell all of you."

Mr. Forsythe's smile is like a barn cat's that lapped the cream. My heart is soft toward this man, who first frightened me with his inspection, then became a friend and ally. He winks at Tommy and me. Then he turns his attention to Mary's daddy.

"Irving, I've signed the papers dissolving my partnership with Benjamin Spencer."

What's going to happen to the mill? To Sweetgum? I glance at Tommy, but he doesn't look worried.

Mr. Forsythe continues. "I now own Sweetgum Mill outright, and I'd like to hire you as the superintendent, overseeing all operations. You may keep the supervisors you prefer and fire those who don't meet your standards. You've proved yourself, and you have my complete confidence and backing. The Spencers' house is owned by the mill. By next week, you'll be able to move your family into it."

Mary's daddy will make a wonderful superintendent. I glance at Annie, feeling a little sorry for her former friend, Fannie, but as our granny used to say, "If you lie down with dogs, you'll get up with fleas."

Mr. Patterson swallows and rises, holding out his hand to Mr. Forsythe. "I accept and thank you. The first thing I'd like to do, if it's all right with you, is implement the new safety practices, and all children under the age of fourteen will go to school."

Mr. Forsythe shakes his hand heartily. "Good decision. I will give a pay increase bringing Sweetgum Mill up to the standards of the other mills in Georgia and help make up the loss of the children's wages."

Mr. Patterson congratulates Tommy and me, then takes his leave, anxious, I'm sure, to go home and tell Mary and her mama the news.

After he departs, Mr. Forsythe turns his attention to Tommy and me. "Now for you two."

Whatever he's about to say, he's pleased with himself. He reminds me of Daddy when he gave out rewards to Lillian, Annie, and me for something good we'd done.

"Tommy, I'd like you to join Genessee in the duties of hotel manager. But I have an offer for you both. First, the reason I'm doing this is because without Genessee's warning about what Benjamin was up to, I might have lost everything. I had suspicions, but she handed me proof." He nods toward Archie. "The papers Archie has drawn up are for the sale of the hotel to you and Tommy." He holds up his hand to forestall our objections.

"I know you don't have the money. Archie, explain it, please." He sits back, looking again like Daddy might have. My eyes grow misty.

Archie picks up the papers and reads, "All rents and meal payments will go directly into the hotel's bank account. An additional amount of two thousand dollars per year will be deposited into the hotel's account for repairs and upkeep until such time as the hotel is self-supporting. It is anticipated to reach that status within three years. Payments to Mr. Forsythe for the purchase of the hotel will begin at that time, with said payments of an amount not to put a strain on the management and buyers. Until such a time as the hotel is completely self-sustaining, the Taylors, the Macks, and all others working in the hotel will have their salaries paid by the mill.'"

He raises his gaze from the papers and meets ours. Tommy grins and I gape. I'm not sure I understand everything I heard. I blink. All I can think of is, we're staying in our home. And it's really *ours*.

Tears of joy overflow my eyes. Mama can remain in the home where she and Daddy raised us. Tommy has a job as manager. My sisters have jobs. Mama Kara has a job.

Tommy and I scramble to our feet and meet Mr. Forsythe in the middle of the parlor. The men shake hands, but I weave my arms around Mr. Forsythe's waist and hug him. "Thank you." That's all I can manage.

Tommy is better with his sentiments. "We accept, and I appreciate your confidence, Mr. Forsythe. We will work hard to make the hotel self-supporting."

"I know you will, son."

The front door opens, and the lodgers pour inside, home from work. Somebody knocks on the door to our private quarters, and we go into the lobby. As soon as they see Tommy and Mr. Forsythe, congratulations ring loud.

Apparently, Mr. Patterson went directly to the mill from here and told the workers about Spencer and the new owner, Mr. Forsythe.

Sweetgum is blooming again.

And once again, it's time to get supper on the table. No matter that my husband was on trial, life goes on in Sweetgum.

Supper is over, and I go out on the front porch to take a few minutes and write in my journal.

It's been three months since Tommy's case was dismissed, and so many changes have taken place in Sweetgum, I want to record them here. The one that blesses me most is seeing the streets alive with neighbors greeting friends and children playing games outside once more. Joy has replaced sorrow and the somber aftereffects of the fire. Sweetgum is happier than ever, and so am I, being married to Tommy, although I wish we still had Daddy with us. I know he's content walking the halls of heaven, so I guess I wouldn't wish him away from there.

"Gen? You out there?" Lillian's voice floats through the open window.

"I am. Come join me." I scoot over so she can sit on the porch swing beside me. There's another hour or two of daylight left yet. The temperature is still comfortable, and the sky promises a beautiful sunset.

She carries two glasses of sweet tea and hands me one as she lowers herself onto the swing. "Where's Tommy?"

"Willie's showing him again how to clean the pig house without stepping in anything."

We chuckle, remembering when Kade first helped Willie.

Lillian glances at my journal. "Joy has replaced sorrow." Smiling, she sighs. "It really has."

On Main Street, several people window shop, greeting passersby. One stops and waves at us. Lillian lifts her arm and waves back at Catherine Owens, the new social worker Mr. Forsythe hired to organize events for the town.

My sister pushes against the porch floor with her foot, setting the swing in motion. "Mr. Spencer's trial was an eye-opener, wasn't it?"

"Even I was surprised at some of the stories people told. The man is pure evil." I drain my tea, then set the glass by my feet. "What boggles my mind is why everyone kept silent about it."

She gapes. "You're kidding? He kept them under his thumb with fear. It didn't take a whole lot more than a few whispered rumors of men showing up at night and dragging the dissenter into the woods to keep everyone in line. All but Daddy, you, and Tommy." She nudges me with her elbow. "I'm so proud of you."

Annie slips out the door. "Can I join you two?"

We both slide over to make room for her in the middle. I pat the vacant seat. "Always. Are the bills paid?"

She nods. "The envelopes are addressed and stamped. I left them sitting in the out-box for morning."

Lillian and I watch her, waiting for her to go on. With an expression similar to Lewis Carroll's Cheshire cat, she has something she's dying to share.

I break first. "Okay, spill it."

Annie laughs with delight. "Catherine Owens, the new social worker Mr. Forsythe hired, Mary Patterson, and I are renting one of the mill houses and moving in together. And ... I've been asked by Catherine to teach classes in acting. We're going to start a little theater! We'll use the school's auditorium for performances."

No wonder she's bursting with excitement. "Oh, Annie, you're finally getting to use your talent." I frown. "But wait ... what about your dreams of going to Hollywood and being in movies?"

She grins and shrugs. "That doesn't seem so important anymore." She stares out over Main Street. "Sweetgum has changed. I find I don't want to leave. And now, I don't have to since I'll be able to do what I love right here."

I pull my baby sister close. "It will seem strange without you living here."

A giggle slips from her lips. "You'll see me all the time. After all, I pay the bills for you."

She's right. But it won't be quite the same. Cattycorner across the street, Kade closes the front door of the church. He turns, locks it, and walks our way. When he raises his head from the steps, his face lights up, he waves, and Lillian glows.

Annie's gaze moves from Kade to her. "You're hooked, Big Sis."

"I know." She grins. "I can't help that it's fast. In my heart, I know that he's the one God has prepared for me. And he says the same thing. We're just trying to wait long enough so people don't talk."

I snort a soft chuckle. "Let 'em talk, and when you're celebrating your fiftieth wedding anniversary, you can thumb your nose at all the naysayers." I think of what almost happened to Tommy and me, and a sudden urgency grips me. "Don't wait for anyone, Lillian. We aren't promised tomorrow. Grab what happiness you can now."

"You sound exactly like Mama."

"That's because we're right."

Kade climbs the steps to the porch, and I smile at him. "Evening, Kade."

"Evening, Mrs. Mack. Annie."

He's called me *Mrs. Mack* since he married Tommy and me. I never tire of hearing it. "Join us?" I slide over as far as I can.

He eyes the full swing, looking doubtful. "Actually, I was hoping I could talk Lillian into taking a little walk with me."

Oh, I hope he's going to propose to her.

Annie waves them off. "You two go ahead. We're going to sit here a little longer."

Kade reaches for Lillian's hand, and they head toward the river.

Annie sets the swing in motion once more. "Remember when you were worried about me having a crush on Archie?"

My attention snaps back to her. Sisterly intuition tells me she's about to make another important announcement. "I remember."

She turns sideways, folds one leg beneath her, and faces me.

"What would you think of a lawyer for my suitor?"

"A lot more than a bank robber."

Annie smacks my knee with the back of her hand. "He asked Mama if he could court me. Isn't that romantic?"

"It is. I've got high regards for Archie. Now."

"Did you hear he's building a house in Sweetgum?"

"No, but I suppose it's natural since he's the mill's attorney now too. When Mr. Forsythe moved his family here, I thought that was a little funny. But he told me he's grown to love our little village."

Annie leans back in the swing. "I'm glad they're both here." She glances at me. "To be honest, it wasn't so hard to pretend I had a crush on him when I first met him."

"He's a bit older than you."

"Only by seven years. It's not that much. Not really."

My little sister has grown up in the past few months. "You're right. Daddy was nearly seven years older than Mama. I forget that. Speaking of Mama, what does she think?"

"That all her chicks have chosen well. She's very pleased."

I take Annie's hand and pull her up. "Our life is changing as much as Sweetgum, and I'm happy for you. One part of me is reluctant to move forward, but then I think of Tommy and our life together, and I can't wish you any less." I hug her. "I love you, Little Sis."

Annie kisses my cheek, then crosses the street to the general store.

I add one more paragraph in my journal about another little change coming. I smile as I write. I wonder if Daddy knows. Then again, I'm sure he does.

When I'm done, I date the entry, then close the journal, leaving it on the swing for now. I head to the barn to see what Tommy and Willie are doing.

I want to hold my secret close to my heart a little longer. Later tonight, when we're alone, I'll tell Tommy.

The End

Vinegar Pie

Pie serves 8.

Ingredients:
   1 pie shell, prebaked
   3 eggs
   3 TBSP butter, at room temperature
   2 TBSP vinegar
   1 ½ C hot water
   ¾ C sugar
   ½ C flour
   1 pinch salt
   ¾ C chopped, roasted walnuts or pecans

Directions:
   Combine sugar, flour, and salt in a medium bowl.
   Beat eggs until very light, then add butter, vinegar, and hot water.
   Add dry ingredients and blend well.
   Cook over double boiler, stirring constantly until thick.
   Add ½ C nuts.
   Pour into pie shell and sprinkle with remaining nuts. Cool and serve.

VEGETABLE LOAF

One 8 x 4 loaf serves 4–6 people.

Ingredients:
2 C cooked carrots, diced
2 ½ C cooked lima or navy beans, mashed
2 large eggs or 3 small eggs
1 tsp salt
¼ tsp pepper
A dash Cayenne pepper
¼ tsp Worcestershire sauce
½ C milk
3 C breadcrumbs, not too stale
½ onion, chopped fine
4 TBSP melted fat
2 TBSP chopped parsley

Directions:
Combine carrots and mashed beans.
Beat eggs slightly. Add seasonings and milk.
Combine bread crumbs, onion, fat, and parsley; add to vegetables and mix thoroughly.
Turn into a well-greased loaf pan.
Bake at 375° for 35 to 40 minutes.
Turn out onto platter and serve with tomato gravy or catsup.

Notes:
Leftover vegetables, such as cooked celery, corn, beets, etc., may replace the cooked carrots.
Mashed parsnips, turnips, or potatoes, etc., may wholly or partially replace the mashed beans.

Pork Shepherd's Pie

Pork Layer:
> 1 lb ground pork
> 1 small onion, chopped
> 2 garlic cloves, minced
> 1 C cooked rice
> ½ C pork gravy or ¼ C chicken broth
> ½ tsp salt
> ½ tsp dried thyme

Cabbage Layer:
> 1 medium carrot, diced
> 1 small onion, chopped
> 2 TBSP butter or margarine
> 6 C cabbage, chopped
> 1 C chicken broth
> ½ tsp salt
> ¼ tsp pepper

Potato Layer:
> 2 C mashed potatoes
> ¼ C shredded cheddar cheese

Brown pork over medium heat until no longer pink.
Add onion and garlic. Cook until tender; drain.
Stir in rice, gravy, salt, and thyme.
Spoon into a greased 11x7 baking dish.

In the same pan the meat cooked in, sauté carrots and onion in butter over medium heat for 5 minutes.
Stir in cabbage; cook for 1 minute longer.
Add broth, salt, and pepper; cover and cook for 10 minutes.

Spoon over pork layer.

Spread mashed potatoes on top; sprinkle with cheese.

Bake, uncovered, at 350° for 45 minutes or until browned.

JENNY LIND POTATOES

Serves 4–6.

Ingredients:
    4 large, cold, boiled potatoes, peeled and sliced
    2 TBSP butter
    1 pint hot milk
    2 TBSP flour
    Salt
    Pepper
    Parsley, chopped

Directions:
    Melt butter and add hot milk and flour. When thick, add salt, pepper, and parsley to taste.

    Put a layer of the flour and milk mixture in the bottom of a greased baking dish. Add a layer of sliced potatoes, continuing to alternate layers, with a layer of milk/flour last.

    Top with cracker crumbs and bake for 15 minutes.

    (The Taylors made enough to serve 50 people. To make potato pasties, they laid a scoop of cooked Jenny Lind potatoes in a pastry round, folding and sealing it over potatoes. Then they baked the pasties until the pastry was golden brown.)

Author's Note

ALTHOUGH THE TOWN OF SWEETGUM lives only in my mind, it's patterned after numerous mill villages in Georgia. Most of those were a good place to live and work. But not all, and for *By the Sweet Gum*, I needed to have one that wasn't one of the best. My research took me to the village of Porterdale (see the acknowledgments), one of the best mill villages in Georgia. It's referenced in the book.

I was surprised to learn that most of Georgia, with the exception of the large cities like Atlanta, did not get electricity into homes until the 1950s. I hadn't realized that. Since I placed Sweetgum in Northwest Georgia, near the county seat of Rome, the town, including the hotel, does not have electricity. The mill has its own hydroelectric plant, but the owner did not allow the village to tap into it.

The flour sack dresses, shirts, and sheets were common in the 1920s and '30s. Georgia was still struggling to rebound from the Civil War, and the rural areas were quite poor. When the manufacturers of flour, sugar, and animal feed discovered women were using the cotton sacks to make clothing and bedding, they began to print designs on them. The nicer the design, the better their product sold. Some even printed dress patterns on the inside of the sacks.

I hope you enjoy *By the Sweet Gum*. If you do, I hope you'll consider leaving a short review on Amazon, Goodreads, or BookBub. Reviews are an author's lifeblood. And follow me on social media:

Facebook: https://www.facebook.com/anemulligansouthernfriedfiction

Amazon Author page: amazon.com/author/anemulligan

Goodreads: https://www.goodreads.com/author/show/8061216.Ane_
Mulligan

BookBub: https://www.bookbub.com/authors/ane-mulligan

The Write Conversation: https://thewriteconversation.blogspot.com/

Twitter: http://twitter.com/anemulligan

Instagram: https://www.instagram.com/anemulligan/

Pinterest: http://www.pinterest.com/anemulligan/